The Shadow Cabinet

W. T. TYLER

The Shadow Cabinet

A NOVEL

1817

HARPER & ROW, PUBLISHERS, New York

Cambridge, Philadelphia, San Francisco, London,

Mexico City, São Paulo, Sydney

Grateful acknowledgment is made for permission to reprint: lines from "The Tower" and "The Ballad of the Foxhunter" from *Collected Poems of William Butler Yeats* (New York: Macmillan, 1956). "The Tower" copyright 1928 by Macmillan Publishing Co., Inc., renewed 1956 by Georgie Yeats. Reprinted by permission of Macmillan Publishing Co., Inc. and A. P. Watt Ltd. Line from "The Auroras of Autumn" from *The Collected Poetry of Wallace Stevens* by Wallace Stevens. Copyright 1948 by Wallace Stevens. Reprinted by permission of Alfred A. Knopf, Inc.

FIRST EDITION

Designed by Ruth Bornschlegel

Library of Congress Cataloging in Publication Data

Tyler, W. T.
  The shadow cabinet.

  I. Title.
PS3570.Y53S5   1984   813'.54   82-48839
ISBN 0-06-015169-2

---

84 85 86 87 10 9 8 7 6 5 4 3 2 1

With today's mass civilization it isn't absurd
to suggest that in some rich, advanced and neutral
country, power might one day be seized, for
example, by a coalition of athletic clubs. In
that case, we might have a sportsman in shorts or a
beauty queen in a bathing suit at the
helm of state. But even then, public affairs
would not become crystal clear.

—IGNAZIO SILONE
The School for Dictators

Part One

It had been a gray Monday in Washington, a day too chilly to be autumn and too wet to be winter, a day when the trees seemed as bare as January, naked against a sodden sky, but a day when some leaves still fell out across the Virginia and Maryland hills. Darkness had fallen as Haven Wilson reached Farragut Square in his old Chevrolet station wagon. The commuter exodus had been snarled by a brief deluge that drowned visibility and crippled a few stoplights. Some intersections were blocked. By the time he found a parking garage, he was fifteen minutes late.

The address Charles Larabee had given him over the telephone that afternoon led him to a rain-darkened old structure that more resembled a private residence than a businessmen's club. No lights showed; the interior shutters were drawn. In the dimming subversive light beyond the reach of the streetlamps, the empty sidewalks pocked by a light steady drizzle, he thought he'd made a mistake. The massive door at the top of the narrow steps under the broken pediment was painted a greenish black and decorated by a polished brass knocker in the shape of a mermaid. A small brass plate, recently polished, held the name Larabee had given him—*The Six Hundred Club*.

Wilson, a tall, gently bred Virginian who'd spent twenty years in Washington as a government lawyer, first with the Department of Justice and then with two Senate committees, had never heard of it. The foyer inside was softly lit, upholstered in red plush and illuminated by brass fixtures with art deco milk-glass shades, something like a New Orleans bawdy house. A hostess in a black velvet jacket, velvet shorts, and black fishnet hose took his name and led him to the steamboat room at the rear where Larabee was waiting, hunched over a small table, a margarita in front of him.

Wilson had had only the dimmest recollection of Larabee when he'd called that afternoon, and now he remembered him no better. Larabee was in his late fifties. His coarse face was darkened below the wiry reddish hair by what may have been a golf course suntan, and he was heavy in the neck and shoulders. The dark-blue jacket seemed too small, like the starched collar, which had squeezed a beading of water from the tan flesh above the sandy brows. His rough voice had a cardiac wheeze, a faintly aspirate echo from too much tobacco, too much alcohol, and too little exercise. In the lapel of his dark jacket was a small flag of the Republic of China.

"It's a backstreet place, this club," Larabee informed him as he lit another cigarette. "Gives you a little privacy, something you can't buy in this town. The foreigners go for it, especially the A-rabs and the Latinos, so we do a little business here. They go for the skin show." He lifted his pale-green eyes toward a bare-shouldered waitress who was approaching. "What are you drinking?"

Wilson asked for a martini on the rocks. The waitress couldn't have been more than eighteen. Her pitted face was heavily rouged, her penciled eyebrows not her own, but she had a nice smile that showed her small milk teeth. She wore black hose and a pink-and-black boudoir corset, laced tightly in the back, squeezing unnatural cleavage from a youthful figure remarkable in its own right. Around her neck above the bare shoulders was a black velvet band, like a dog collar, to which was pinned a cameo inscribed with the club logo. Wilson felt sorry for her.

"Bring me another margarita, would you, dolly?" Larabee asked, his drink still half full in front of him. His eyes followed her back across the room. "Like I said, it's a fun place. You go to the Army-Navy Club, you see too many people you don't want to see, you know what I mean? Keep it confidential, like you used to do, right? How long since you left the Senate Intelligence Committee?"

"About eight months."

"You got tired of it, we heard, fed up. Resigned, was that it? Someone said you broke your pick with a few senators, is that right?"

"No, I just left. No hard feelings. They understood."

"That's the way to play it—don't burn your bridges, right? Ten years hacking away with those Senate committees is long enough, believe me. A bunch of prima donnas. They squeeze you all the time, those assholes, and then election time rolls around and they play with your balls like a pussycat. I thought you might be interested—that's why I called you up. Some pals of mine are looking for a guy with your kind of experience."

Larabee had claimed he had a small interest in a management and consultant firm handling U.S. military sales, PL-480 shipments, communications contracts, and special projects for several foreign clients. Wilson's recollection of Larabee was as dim as ever. He recalled that Larabee had had a desk in a Senate office building, part of a Pentagon liaison team putting special briefings, Quantico quail shoots, Air Force planes, and European commissaries at congressional disposal, but he couldn't recall which service.

"What's your role with this consultant firm?" Wilson asked.

"I'm a contact man, you might say."

"You've done pretty well, then." Wilson let his eyes drop to the Republic of China flag in the buttonhole.

"Oh, shit, yeah," Larabee said, looking down at the flag too. "They're giving a small reception tonight, which is why I've got to cut out early, quarter to seven at the latest. A purchasing mission in from Taiwan."

The waitress brought the drinks. Larabee drained his first glass, then hunched forward over the table to toy with his second.

"Shifting vocational gears, yeah, I know your problem," he resumed as he watched the waitress's saucy promenade across the room. "Someone said you were selling real estate now. Lemme tell you something. The bucks aren't there these days, you know what I mean? Not for a lawyer like you. You've got something to sell, right? Ten years on the Hill, ten years over at Justice, sure. That's worth a bundle in this town, believe me."

"That's what my wife says," Wilson replied without irony, wondering where Larabee had got his information. He wasn't selling real estate. He was handling the legal work for a small brokerage in Virginia in which he had a small interest, while he considered his options.

"She's right. The little woman's right, Haven. It's Haven, isn't it? I'm Chuck. So listen, Haven, you've got something to sell but you've gotta pick your spots, the way I did. Two years ago, these pals of mine were just getting off the ground, but the Carter types made them look bad. Now they've got more than they can handle. They're putting together a couple of military packages for the Persian Gulf, a couple of emirates out there. A few C-130s, some commo equipment, maybe a few Hueys. Saudi financing, some of it. It'll run—what?—maybe seventy, eighty million."

The pale eyes lingered on Wilson's face, searching for a reaction. Wilson said nothing. "That's a lotta bucks for a guy that was just hanging around CINCPAC five years ago, waiting for another stripe."

"So you were Navy, then," Wilson said.

"Navy, sure. Two tours in 'Nam, two in Taiwan, one in Seoul. I had a Special Forces hookup, real tough, and I didn't shit in my britches in 'Nam like a lot of them did. I lost my cherry up near Pleiku, Cambodian border." He drank from the margarita and pulled another cigarette from the package of filter tips on the table. "Real estate won't cut it, Haven. Maybe you're doing something else too, right? Maybe you've got your own sideshow going in addition to this real estate. Some sort of special consultancy? You look like you're keeping in shape. Me, I try to work out twice, three times a week. Keep down to a hundred and ninety, hundred and ninety-five. Gym work. How much do you weigh?"

"A hundred and ninety."

"That's what I figured. So maybe you've got something cooking, some kind of project your old pals over at Justice cut you in on." He seemed to smile as he lit the cigarette, both thick hands brought to his face to shield the flame, the way an old Navy line officer would.

"No, just some real estate legal work while I make up my mind," Wilson said, watching the ribald face through the curtain of smoke. Larabee, he decided, was trying to hustle him.

"Waiting for an offer from some blue-chip law firm?"

"No, nothing like that."

"So what is it, a guy with your contacts?" Larabee leaned forward to again toy with his drink. "You've got a lot of contacts around this town. Justice. Up on the Hill. Senate committee on intelligence, special investigations staff. Some big opportunity came along, your pals wouldn't just hang you out to dry—not with all those years you put in. What is it—something they cut you in on?"

"I'm on my own now, still looking around," Wilson said.

"There's a lot going on these days—not domestic stuff, either. You don't wanna limit yourself, you know what I mean? Take Honduras. A couple of my friends got some big projects down there—real tough, real quiet too. I'm helping them out—their contact man, you might say. Training packages, a little ordnance. I did a job down there in Nicaragua a couple of years back—consultant on some Navy ordnance. Somoza's brother-in-law was a buddy of mine." Cigarette held in his mouth, Larabee took his wallet, opened it, and passed a faded business card across the table. It was in Spanish. Larabee's name was in the corner, an agent for an import firm. He passed another card proclaiming him a member of the Managua Chamber of Commerce.

The waitress returned with another margarita and a second martini. "Thanks, doll," Larabee said. "I've got a whole lot of drinking ahead of me tonight, but you get used to it. It's out at Ben's place. Spring Valley. Real classy." His voice dropped. "These pals of mine I was telling you about, they've got a few old Agency types on board. They've got people know the Middle East as good as anyone. Persian Gulf too. Charley Finch, you know him? Station chief in some stinkhole out there. Now they've got him aboard. George Rawson's another, an old Agency type, retired two years ago. You remember George?"

Wilson met the pale lifted eyes, remembering Rawson's name. He'd been retired in 1978 under dubious circumstances. "I don't think so."

"Speaks Arab like a raghead," Larabee continued. "So they've got people know the Middle East and have the contacts out there, same as Latin America, where they're in solid. It's the legislative side they're trying to build up, not the senators so much—the salad boys in the back room, oiling up the cabbage. And it's big cabbage, too, Haven, lemme tell you— big bucks. You worked with the Foreign Relations Committee, didn't you? You say the word and I could get you together with these friends of mine."

"That was a few years ago. I don't think it interests me much these days."

Larabee wasn't daunted. "You got the experience, the nuts and bolts. Take El Salvador. They had a piece of the El Salvador package, maybe five, six million, but the fuckers turn the water off. It's still in the pipeline. So you got Latin America heating up, the administration's gonna open things up down there, like this Honduras operation I was telling you about, closing off this Cuban-Nicaraguan arms corridor to El Salvador, but Congress has to get its shit together. You've got the right contacts for that. . . ."

Wilson didn't reply. Larabee rambled on:

"Some of those Senate and House staffers still act like it's the goddamn Carter administration, you know what I mean? They're still in a reactive mode. You take the defense budget. It's a big-ticket operation—that's what the White House wants, what the public wants. So you gotta keep Congress honest. I had one guy over on the Hill say to me last week, 'Look, Chuck, we gotta think about political answers before we talk about beefing up military sales, right?' Well, that's bullshit, lemme tell you."

"How many Latin American countries do your friends handle?" Wilson asked with only polite interest. The nearby tables were beginning to fill as more members entered from the rainy street. The din from the bar in front had grown louder.

"Three, I think it is," Larabee said, his eyes restlessly prowling the room. He looked at his watch. "So Latin America's heating up, this administration's blowing the lid off down there. That's why my friends need to beef up their legislative staff, make sure those guys on the Hill get the right message about what the Sandinistas and Cubanos are doing to our friends down there. You say the word, I'll put you in touch." He leaned down to bring his briefcase from beneath the table and removed a large manila envelope. "Basically, when it comes to national defense, I'm a PR purist, Haven, no schlock. That's how they made up this brochure—it tells it like it is. It tells you how this firm is set up, who their clients are, where you'd fit in if you want to come aboard. Take a look at it. If you're interested, give me a call and I'll get you together with them."

"I'll do that," Wilson said, hoping to bring the conversation to an end.

"Like I said, these are fast-moving times," Larabee said, signaling for the waitress. "Historically, over the last couple of years they've been moving like Gangbusters, but you factor in Reagan and that's what you'd expect, right? A cloud-buster, right out the fucking roof. Now's the time to go for it, Wilson." Larabee paid the check.

Outside, the rain had stopped momentarily. A taxi was waiting for Larabee at the curb.

"Thanks for the drink," Wilson said. "Glad to hear you're doing so well."

"Anytime. It's Chuck, remember. Sorry I have to run." He crossed the pavement, but turned back at the door of the taxi. "You're ready to roll, right? Nothing you're working on except this real estate deal. I can tell my pals that, right?"

Wilson watched the cab drive away and turned back toward Farragut Square. Traffic was lighter. With the rain gone, a fine mist hovered in the air. At the parking garage two blocks away, he stood under the overhang, waiting for his car. He was still puzzled. If Larabee had been trying to hustle him, he was very confused about something. Confused or uncertain, perhaps both. He'd been trolling for information.

A pair of young businessmen in beige car coats and Irish hats waited nearby. "The world's greatest grandma and they franchised her," he heard one say. "She didn't think much of the idea at first, but it went over like Rubik's cube."

Wilson lifted his eyes, depressed.

"What, the franchise?" asked the other. Both looked to Wilson like advertising or public relations executives. Their Italian shoes and calfskin briefcases were identical, like their Irish hats.

"Yeah, the Pacific Northwest," said his companion. "She drove a forklift for Boeing, I think it was. Sixty-eight years old, with a red bandanna around her neck and one of those blue-and-white engineer's hats. 'World's Greatest Grandma,' that's what she had stenciled on her forklift. When the snack bar vending machines were pulled out by the concessionaire, she started bringing in homemade cookies to sell to the day shift. They caught on big; just a cottage industry, you know, but she kept at it, still driving her forklift. She didn't think about going public, but her kids franchised her. 'The World's Greatest Grandma.' Just like that. Now they've got vending concessions all over. It's a great success story—a four-million-dollar account for our L.A. office."

A gray Ford LTD moved up the ramp, stopped, and the two men climbed in. Stupidly, still holding Larabee's envelope, Wilson watched them drive off.

"This yours?" a black youth called from across the ramp, leaving the front door of the old Chevrolet station wagon. On the rear window was a

Georgetown University logo and on the bumper below, a tattered *I Don't Brake for Republicans* sticker. The vehicle had belonged to Haven Wilson's younger son during his final two years at Georgetown but was too old and too undependable to take him across country to Oregon, where he'd taken a job with a newspaper after graduation. Wilson had bought it from him for the price of a plane ticket to Portland.

"Yeah, it's mine." He tore up Larabee's envelope and dropped it into the trash barrel on the ticket booth island. Thunder boomed across the rooftops.

"Say what?" the black youth asked. A wooden African comb was stuck in the back of his woolly hair.

"Washington," Wilson said, digging fifty cents from his pocket. "The world's greatest grandpa and they're franchising him."

2.

At the rear of a McLean shopping mall and only a few miles from Washington in the Virginia suburbs, The Players still drew a regular luncheon crowd from the nearby beltway consulting firms, from assorted federal agencies, and from CIA headquarters at Langley, but the evening trade in the back room had moved elsewhere after the tavern was bought by an enterprising Vietnamese who'd changed the menu and the decor. Bamboo and tropical plants had replaced the gin-and-bitters English pub atmosphere. The dark oak, the sporting prints, and the polished brass were gone; so were the obscure photographs, the foreign maps, and the tattered red-and-blue Vietcong flag that had once hung, under glass, next to the WC—all packed away by the former owner for a new nautical fish and steak house in Boca Raton. One more casualty of the post-Iran withdrawal syndrome, some said, taking their memories elsewhere.

On Monday nights in autumn and winter, a few diehards from the old days still gathered in the back room to drink, grouse, and watch Monday night football. With the decline of the Redskins, the economy, and the dignity of federal service, now challenged by that spirit of feckless amateurism that had overrun Washington with the Reagan victory, the back room gatherings were often as churlish as a last poker game in a condemned firehouse.

Haven Wilson was an occasional member of the back room chin and chowder society. It was a morose group he found assembled there this Monday night, watching a public television documentary on the Moral Majority. Senator Bob Combs was on the tube, his performance videotaped during a recent Senate hearing.

"Someone ought to burn his ass," he heard Buster Foreman say. "Burn him big, bigger than Nixon." Foreman was a large man, an ex-CIA rowdy with a large man's bullying contempt, his voice burdened by twenty years of bureaucratic grievances.

Someone had turned down the sound on his way to the bar in front, wearied of Combs's courtly South Carolina drawl as he chastised a trio of regulatory bureaucrats. Now they sat looking at the pink pubescent face. Without the sound, the cherubic head ballooned larger than life, the bubble-gum kiss on the Moral Majority valentine PBS was blowing the nation's capital on a rainy night following another Redskins loss.

"He's an airhead," said Cyril Crofton, a thin, dyspeptic CIA analyst.

"Pure celluloid," Buster Foreman said, "a Baptist shyster—Genesis, grits, and shit. Ask Murphy when you see him, ask him about Senator Combs. He was at the embassy in Athens when Combs came through. Ask him what kind of shyster Combs is."

"Where is Murphy these days?" asked Nick Straus, his gray head still damp from the rain. Haven Wilson was surprised to see him there. He'd come wandering in a few minutes before Wilson, like a stray cat, arriving on foot from his house a few miles away. Small, fiftyish, with mouse-gray hair and mild brown eyes, he'd worked twenty-five years at the Agency as a Soviet analyst and arms control technician, but had been retired during the housekeeping sweep of the late seventies. He'd hired on with a beltway defense firm, lost his job, been treated for acute depression, but six months earlier had been hired by the Defense Intelligence Agency at the Pentagon.

Improbably, thought Wilson, who couldn't explain it. The Nick Straus who sat next to him now was only the ghost of the man he'd known for fifteen years. He'd attended his retirement luncheon at Langley, when Straus had received the career intelligence medal. Wilson thought he'd deserved better. He remembered the luncheon now, looking at Nick's shoes. His socks didn't match, the shoes were shapeless black oxfords with worn ripple soles, and the feet didn't look like Nick Straus's feet at all.

"Murphy's selling commo systems out of a place out in Rockville," Buster Foreman said. Fuzzy Larson came back from the bar in front. "A letch," Foreman continued, still watching Senator Combs. "He doesn't sweat much, either, you notice that? It must be a hundred and five under those lights and he's not cooking, not even sweating."

"The guy's a jerk," Fuzzy Larson said loudly. He was short and blond, the dome of his head covered with a fine feathery down, like an Easter chick. A former FBI and CIA technician, he'd left Langley a year earlier to open a forensics crime lab with Buster Foreman and a retired FBI lab man.

"Look at that mouth, how wet it is. Always working too, you notice that. All juiced up."

"Tell them the story about Combs in Athens," Buster suggested, "the story Murphy told us."

"Oh, yeah," Larson recalled. "It was one of Combs's staff aides. I forgot all about it. Do you know who I'm talking about, Combs's number one aide, what's his name?" He appealed to Haven Wilson, who knew the name but only shook his head. "Anyway, Combs comes through Athens with this staff aide, who gets some Greek broad in the rack and tries some funny business with her, the way he thinks the Greeks do. So she yelled her head off and someone had to shut her up quick. This aide is drunk, the control room crowd at the hotel in Athens is running around like crazy, doing the funky chicken, and so the station did it, deuces wild. Three o'clock in the morning and they get the goddamned station chief out of bed to buy off a ten-dollar hooker. Combs was sleeping right there in the next room, so you know he's gotta know what kind of meatball his staff aide is. What do you think of that?"

"They're all meatballs," Buster Foreman said, his eyes still lifted to the television screen. "Look at that idiot. I'll bet he diddled his way through Bible school down in South Carolina or wherever it was. I'll bet he's still diddling."

"So what did Murphy have to do with it?" Cyril Crofton asked.

"He had to come up with the dollars to buy her off," Fuzzy said. "The next day this jerkwater staff aide says he doesn't remember anything about any Greek girl, the station chief was out of pocket, and so Murph paid him back out of some operational account. Then a week later in Rome, super-dick gets into the same kind of jam again, and the station had to pull his pants back on there too."

"Which proves what I said," Buster Foreman drawled. "Which proves it right there. The guy's a hypocrite. Look at that goddamned prissy little mouth."

"It's the holier-than-thou crud that gets me," Cyril Crofton said. Cyril knew Congress only at a distance, Haven Wilson remembered, unlike Buster Foreman, who'd spent some time in secret testimony on the Hill after the Angolan debacle. "How the hell do they get away with it?"

"Money," Buster said. "Big dollars. He talks like that, roasting those bureaucrats, and the bucks come rolling in. Look at his face. He's blowing every right-winger in town with that spiel, blowing 'em big, right on the tube. What do you think, Haven? Are these guys for real or not?"

"I'd say so," Wilson replied. It was time to go but he didn't move, curious as to what Combs might be saying. "But there are plenty of screwballs around these days, not just Bob Combs. A lot of other people think they've got a piece of this administration." He was thinking of Chuck Larabee. Their conversation still made no sense to him.

"Like who?" Cyril Crofton asked, turning.

"The big chili-and-taco crowd from Texas, the funny-money millionaires from the West Coast, the tightwad burial insurance tycoons in between. Who've I left out?" he asked Nick Straus, smiling.

"The committee for the coming deluge," Straus said.

"You think he's kidding?" Buster Foreman broke in. "See what he's saying now."

"The same old crap." Fuzzy Larson got up to adjust the volume.

". . . an' what you burr-o-crats have to unnerstan' is that the good folks o' this country who're paying for all these reg-u-lations have had enough. Y'all think you can jes' set there, set here in Wash'n'ton the way you been a-doing since the Great Society giveaway an' mandate social mor-*ees* by reg-u-lation an' *fee*-at. Well, lemme tell y'all—it's not a-gonna happen anymore. Those good folks out yonder have had enough. They've given us a man-date. . . ."

"What kind of mandate is that clown talking about?" Buster Foreman broke in irascibly.

"The one the White House keeps telling you about," said Haven Wilson. "A Republican landslide."

"A bullshit landslide," Buster said. "It didn't happen."

"Hell, no, it didn't happen," Larson joined in. He turned the dial to the Monday night football game and they watched a Dallas Cowboy cornerback strip the ball from an opposing tight end. The Dallas free safety scooped up the ball on a lucky bounce and carried it out of bounds to stop the clock, hands lifted to take a few high fives from his teammates as he joined them on the sidelines.

"The receiver was down, for Christ's sake!" Fuzzy shouted. "Did you see that! He was down! Where the hell was the whistle!"

"Dallas has already got them by four touchdowns," Buster Foreman complained. "What the hell are they stopping the clock for?"

"The killer instinct," Haven Wilson offered. "What the Redskins don't have. Democrats either."

"We don't wanna see Dallas score another touch," said Buster, "not those crybabies. Always trying to rub it in. Turn it, why don't you?"

"No one's blowing the whistle," Fuzzy said. "That's the whole goddamned problem." He turned back to the public television special on the Moral Majority. The screen, dissolving into shades of Easter egg pastel as a late jet from National Airport passed over, wobbled briefly toward a psychedelic smear, then Senator Bob Combs's face came throbbing back.

". . . an' I can tell you the way we're gonna go," he was saying. "I can tell you right now. We're gonna create an America where private initiative is the dominant social force—you unnerstan' what I'm a-saying. . . ."

Larson turned down the volume. Foreman sat slumped in his chair, gazing vindictively at the irradiated pink face. "Look at that face," Cyril Crofton muttered. "The man's an airball, a bubble-gum airball."

"It's about time this country woke up," Fuzzy declared.

Haven Wilson laughed. "What do you think's happened? Where have you been, anyway? They did wake up. Why do you think we've got that TV cowboy in the White House?"

"He didn't win it," Fuzzy insisted. "That goddamned Carter blew it."

"That's right," Wilson said. "Like the Redskins blew it yesterday, like the Cowboys aren't winning it tonight—just the other team blowing it."

"I still think someone ought to bounce that meatball around," Buster Foreman suggested, eyes narrowed on Senator Bob Combs's simpering face. "Just the way he's dumping on those bureaucrats. What do you think, Haven?"

"Sure, dump on him big," Wilson replied, searching for his most authentic Players' voice, the same one he had sometimes employed with his two sons, sitting wet and cold in a Maryland duck blind, listening to their complaints about undergraduate inconstancy and the ubiquitous grunginess of the world, most of it centered in suburban shopping malls on a Saturday afternoon. "Another Abscam. Break out the sheets and the dark glasses, get yourself a Halloween beard and a rubber nose. Only that kind of freak show won't play twice in this town, not with a Sunday school teacher like Bob Combs."

"The guy's a phony," Fuzzy insisted.

"So are a lot of politicians."

They sat in silence, listening to the rain come down.

"The rage of Caliban at seeing his own face in the glass," Nick Straus offered mildly. "Someone once said that explained our contempt for politicians. I think he was right."

"Combs is special," Buster said.

"How special?" Haven Wilson was looking beyond Buster toward the door to the bar, where someone stood shaking the rain from a mackintosh, face hidden beneath his hat brim. "You'd better keep your voices down," he suggested.

"Who the hell's that?" asked Fuzzy.

It was only Herschel Kinkaid, a deputy division chief from Langley on his way home after a long evening at his desk. "What's happened to this place?" he asked as he approached the table, pulling off his coat. "What is it—Saigon east?"

"The old soldiers' home," Buster said.

"What happened to the old sign out front?"

"It was sold last summer," Fuzzy explained. "The new guy's going to change the name, but he hasn't decided yet. Get yourself a chair. We don't get waitress service back here anymore."

Kinkaid brought a chair from one of the empty tables. "Still the same old wrecking crew. These guys recruited you, Haven? You, Nick? What's happening? How come you're watching Senator Combs?"

"Ask the Klan here," Wilson said. "They're cooking up a tar and feather job."

"Fuzzy wants to do a number on him," Cyril said. "Fuzzy and Buster both—a big number."

"How come?"

"Because he's a meatball," said Buster. "It's no joke about the Klan, either. Sometime I'll tell you what I've heard about Bob Combs. Anyway, he's a goddamned hypocrite. You know how much those outfits of his have grossed this year? Citizens Washington, Moral Minutemen, the New Congress Coalition. You know how much dough they've raked in?"

"I know it's a lot."

"Seven million," Buster announced. "Megabucks. They had to file with the Federal Election Commission, and I read it in the *Post*. The Democrats are flat busted, which is maybe what they deserve, and these turkeys raise seven million just pinching open envelopes, nickel and dime stuff, old widows' carfare. It keeps rolling in."

"That's too big a goddamned slush fund," said Cyril.

"Hell, yes," Fuzzy agreed. "All the more reason someone ought to bust him. It wouldn't be hard, either. Maybe Murph remembers the dates Combs and this staff aide were in Athens. Something like that would leave an audit trail."

"Something like what?" Kinkaid asked.

"Combs's staffie got some hooker into the sack in Athens," Cyril said, "and the station chief had to buy her off."

Nick Straus smiled suddenly, looking at Haven Wilson, who shook his head in sad recollection. The conversation was beginning to sound like one of Brzezinski's covert scenarios for diddling the Soviets in Afghanistan or South Yemen—a few hundred pounds of sugar in the Russian advisers' gas tanks.

"Murph wouldn't have left an audit trail," Buster was saying. "He would have buried it good."

"Sure, but GAO could find it, couldn't they, Haven?" Fuzzy asked. "Those CPA bird dogs could find a decimal point in a barrel of sawdust. What you do, see, is you get it all down—names, dates, everything. Then you stick it in an envelope and mail it to Jack Anderson. That's the way to get it started."

Haven Wilson grimaced painfully, emptying his glass.

"What's wrong with that?" Cyril asked.

"That's not the way it works," Wilson said.

"That's too chickenshit anyway," Buster Foreman said. "If you're going to bust this shithead, do it big, wide open, something that's got a little class to it, like the way they nailed Agnew."

"That's just for openers," Fuzzy continued. "You start with Jack Anderson, see, but that's just the beginning. A few people read about it, remember something else, and then leak it the same way. It snowballs, like Watergate. Pretty soon the *Post* or *Sixty Minutes* get a handle on it."

"Sure," Wilson put in, lapsing again into the vernacular. "*Sixty Minutes*. Why not bring Cronkite back too? You want to grab a few headlines? Why don't you just stick a pipe bomb up his fundament and blow him that way. Get yourself thirty years in the Lewisburg slammer and a lifetime membership in the ACLU, like the Berrigan boys."

"What's a fundament?" Cyril asked softly.

Nick Straus cleared his throat. "Anus," he whispered.

"Come on, Haven," Fuzzy protested. "The guy's a crook, a corn pone sitting there, a natural setup for a lawyer like you. You could burn him big and you wouldn't have to break any laws doing it."

"That's what you think," Wilson said. "Combs may talk slow, like all those Carolina country boys, but he's sneaky fast. The only way you're going to burn someone like that is right out in the open, him doing it without even knowing it."

"Like what?"

"Like always, something stupid. Like Nixon."

"Hey, like Wilbur Mills," Cyril Crofton said brightly. "Sure. You get him skinny-dipping in the Reflecting Pool with some Fourteenth Street stripper, like Fanny Frost or whatever her name was. How about that?"

The table was silent. Cyril worked in the Agency's collection evaluation shop, handling satellite imagery, but he had a tabloid imagination. No one could think of anything to say.

"He doesn't drink," Foreman remembered finally.

"So what if he did," Wilson said. "Do you think that would slow up a squeaky-shoes preacher like Combs? I know him. He'd just tell those Carolina turnipseeds back home he was checking out her skivvies to make sure it was home-grown cotton. Bob Combs always has an answer."

"So how do we do it?"

"Get him laid by one of those freaked-out congressional wives," Cyril continued. "The wiggy Playboy bunny, remember? What was her name?" Embarrassed, they were again silent.

Haven Wilson stood up. "You people are ruining my evening. This place sounds like the old Kappa Alpha house at Charlottesville." He went across the room and into the front bar. Only a few customers were there, watching the football game on the television set in the corner. The nearby dining room held a handful of diners. He called home from the telephone booth near the front door, but there was no answer. Betsy wasn't yet home from her teachers meeting. When he returned to the table in the back room, they were still talking about Bob Combs.

"You want to know how to get rid of Combs and all that crowd," he volunteered after a minute. "You don't need anything fancy, not all this clandestine nonsense. It's simple. Cyril was talking about Fourteenth Street a little while ago. I could go down to Fourteenth Street right now, Fourteenth and U, we all could, and in ten seconds get the answer, and in ten more have the crowd ready to do it, that's how bad things are. It's that simple."

"Do what?" Fuzzy asked.

"Blow up Capitol Hill."

Nick Straus smiled, but Fuzzy was hurt. "Come on, Haven, stop cracking wise, for Christ's sake. I told you, we're serious. Open up your bag of tricks for a change, give us something to work on. We're not thinking about any black bag job, if that's what you're worried about."

"Haven's right," Herschel Kinkaid said. "It'd take something bigger than Abscam to nail Combs and his crowd. Isn't there a game on?" He looked at his watch and got up to cross to the television set.

"We got fed up," Fuzzy said. "Dallas is stomping all over them."

Kinkaid turned to the football game, but it was halftime. Howard Cosell was interviewing a black heavyweight fighter about an upcoming fight and doing all the talking. The boxer was just grunting along after him, like a life-termer from Lorton or Sing Sing reporting in to the screw after a day on the rock pile.

"Come on, Herschel," Buster Foreman complained. "That goddamned dip's worse than the Cowboys."

"What's the score?"

"Cowboys, thirty-four to seven."

Kinkaid turned off the set and returned to the table. The rain was still coming down, sluicing from the shed roof in the rear; the sounds from the front room had grown fainter. They drank in silence. The Vietnamese waiter from the dining room stuck his head in the door.

"Telephone," he called in a thin soprano. "Is there a Mr. Chen with you gentlemen?"

"Sorry," Wilson answered, looking up at the thin face and the thatch of glossy violet-black hair. "Not here."

"Try Chinatown," Cyril sang out without turning his head. The waiter disappeared. Guiltily, Nick Straus put down his glass without drinking.

"This place stinks," Fuzzy announced to no one in particular.

"It's the fish paste," Kinkaid said. "It reminds me of the Camel Bar in Nha Trang."

Haven Wilson knew it was time to go.

"So what have we decided?" Buster Foreman asked, lighting a cigarette. "What are we gonna do to this grade A Carolina turkey?"

"Fry him," Fuzzy said. "Barbecue him the same way he's been roasting Washington and the federal bureaucracy."

"Deep fry," Wilson suggested, reaching behind him for his raincoat. "Deep fat, maybe pork rind—like what you've been chewing for the last hour. Only it's not going to solve anything. Chew it all you want, but you're not going to swallow it. You're just blowing your ears after a day in the pits."

"We're serious," Buster Foreman insisted. "Come on, get your wig on—give us an idea to work with."

"How come you're so hacked off about Combs? He's been around for a few years. He's no worse than a few other senators I could name. He didn't invent Capitol Hill hypocrisy. So why is it Combs you're so bothered about? The Senate's always been filled with small-time chauvinists like Bob Combs."

"Because he's a goddamned self-righteous hypocrite with seven million bucks in his war chest, that's why," said Buster.

"Hell, yes," Cyril agreed.

"You see?" Fuzzy put in quickly. "Cyril's as sore as the rest of us. Nick's mad too, aren't you, Nick?"

Nick Straus frowned, recalled suddenly from reflections which had nothing to do with Senator Bob Combs or the back room at The Players. "Frustrated, I suppose. . . ."

"What's that got to do with it?" Wilson asked, still looking at Fuzzy. "Sore at what? Because Combs isn't cherry and the rest of the Senate is? They're all the same. I know these people. You're the ones who are cherry."

"So how come everyone's hacked off the way they are?" Buster asked. "Not just us, but everyone?"

"It's the way things are," Wilson offered. "Ask Nick—he's the historian. Ask him, he'll tell you." But Nick Straus faltered, unable to say anything at all. "Everyone's fed up," Wilson said. "Not just here. Look at France. Now they've got Mitterrand, but no one's happy. Look at Norway, look at Sweden. It'll be Schmidt's turn next in West Germany, then Thatcher's. Revolving-door presidents and prime ministers, that's what's happening. Everyone's fed up."

"So how come?"

"Because that's what government has grown to—too small for the problems, too big for the people. Now it's amateur night in Washington—four years of it. But no one has any answers, just the same old bullshit. In a couple of years, that'll wash Reagan out too." He pulled his raincoat across his knees and brought out his car keys. "But that's not why you guys are talking this way. Do you know why you're so pissed off, why you're fed up with Combs, with Reagan, with the Democrats, who're so dead in the water no one's even turned the body over yet? Because it's Monday night and the Redskins lost yesterday. It's raining cats and dogs and half a million Redskin fans who're also Washington bureaucrats in their spare time are sitting around the tube, dying again, just like yesterday, watching the Dallas Cowboys kick the hell out of a team that was twenty points better than the Redskins two weeks ago." He looked at Buster Foreman, beginning to smile. "So while that's happening, Bob Combs is sitting there on TV kicking the hell out of a few GS-18s who make more money than you do. That's the problem. The Dallas Cowboys are winners, like Bob Combs and his seven-million-dollar political war chest. The Moral Majority, that's America's team, like the Cowboys, like that California sing-along crew in the White House."

"Now I've heard everything," Fuzzy said.

"So have I," Wilson added, "and that's why we're sitting here chewing the fat, the Monday night losers. If you really wanted to get serious, you wouldn't screw around with Bob Combs. Combs is nothing, just flat beer like they used to have down at Fort Bragg. In a couple of years no one is going to remember Combs any better than Wayne Morse, Dirksen, or the Dixiecrats. If you want to burn someone, go after Reagan—he's the man you want. It's easy. I mean, he's a natural nitwit, a puddinghead, a stand-up comedian. You want to do something, show him up for the idiot he is? I'll tell you how to do it."

He had their attention now. Even Nick Straus sat forward.

"You get him to go on television, right out in the open, say a televised press conference. All one-liners, like the Johnny Carson show. So you get him to go on a national TV hookup and say something stupid—I mean something so dismally stupid that eighty million mom and pop Americans just sit there in their living rooms looking at each other like their ears just fell off. Just get him to go on television and say something like that, say a message to Brezhnev delivered over the CBS or NBC hot line, something like a kindergarten nursery rhyme, something like 'Roses are red, violets are blue, stay out of El Salvador, Poland too.' That's all it takes. Just get him to do that and see what happens."

He stood up to pull on his raincoat.

"But he already said that," Fuzzy pointed out.

"Yeah, I heard that one too," Buster Foreman remembered.

"So you see what the problem is, don't you?" Wilson asked. "When you've got the answer to that, give me a call. Come on, Nick, I'll give you a lift."

The rain had slackened, the subdued rush dulled by the sounds of conversation in the front bar. A busboy was noisily stacking crates of beer bottles in the storage room.

"Turn back to the goddamned football game," Wilson heard Fuzzy say as he and Nick went out.

"Yeah, like always. Shove it," Buster said.

The two men drove out of the parking lot in Wilson's twelve-year-old station wagon, trailing a pall of exhaust fumes over the damp pavement from worn piston rings and a leaky muffler.

"They get a little carried away sometimes," said Nick Straus. "I'd always heard Foreman and Larson were full of eccentric ideas. I never had much contact with them. Frustrated, I suppose, like all of us."

"They're bored, just blowing off steam. What about you? How's the Pentagon watch these days?"

Nick Straus gave the question a moment's thought. "Just as bad—idiotic, like the talk tonight. High-tech fixes, idiot gadgetry, technological determinism to explain Soviet intent—the same old Pentagon mythology."

In the late sixties and early seventies, when Wilson had moved to the Senate Select Committee on Intelligence, Nick Straus had been his mentor, helping him better understand deterrent strategies, nuclear targeting policy, SALT, and the theodicy of the nuclear arms strategists.

"You mean if the Soviets get a new military technology, it means they're going to use it," Wilson said. "Capability equals intent."

"To gain the advantage, that's right. All the political or historical constraints go out the window. The same primitive fears, the same primitive mythology. But now it's more dangerous. All this new Pentagon budget means is that they're reviving the old containment strategy, containment everywhere. It's lunacy."

Wilson eased the station wagon to a stop at an intersection. A fat, middle-aged jogger in nylon raingear lumbered slowly through the headlights, his feet barely lifted from the asphalt.

"He's foolish," Nick said softly, watching him disappear through the rain-ticked windshield. "Does he think he's doing himself a favor?"

"He's training for a cardiac arrest—that and fallen arches. You can tell by how they move whether they know what they're doing or not. That guy doesn't."

"They're everywhere you look these days," Nick said as Wilson drove on. "You catch the Pentagon shuttle across Memorial Bridge at noon and that's all you see—people running all over the place, like it's lunch hour at St. Elizabeths." The rain pattered against the roof. Wilson dimmed his lights for an approaching car and slowed down. After the car splashed past, Nick said, "It's the same thing along the Mall or the Georgetown towpath. There's a major in my office at DIA. He runs ten miles a day. He logs the Soviet SS-19 missiles, the Mod 4 SS-18 with ten warheads, both, but he spends more time on his jogging log. He calculates his daily mileage within two hundred yards." He turned. "Did you realize that there are fewer than a dozen people in Washington who can understand the calculus upon which the claims for Soviet missile accuracy are based? Did you realize that?"

"No, I didn't," Wilson said.

"That's where most of them you see running along the Potomac come from," Nick said, his voice odd, a man hovering between two voids.

"That's the way it is with those guys," Wilson said, trying to evoke the Nick Straus he'd once known. "It used to be handball, then squash, after that, racquetball. I remember when I was in Berlin for a week or two back in the sixties, working on a Senate staff study. I used to play squash with a bird colonel, a short little guy who was still playing regimental football. A forty-six-year-old blocking back with gray hair, scabs on his shins, and a houseful of teen-aged kids. He could never make the adjustment. He had the reflexes of a kid, but he'd always overrun the ball. He'd nearly kill himself every time we got on the court, and the poor guy'd always lose. Then he'd jump in a hot shower, boil himself up like a lobster, put on his strangle suit, and go roaring off to his battle group, ready to blitzkrieg the Wall. He used to scare the hell out of me. I kept thinking to myself: *This guy's our tripwire out here? This nut?* I used to see the same kind in Vietnam, the kind of gung-ho CO that gives pep talks to his troops over the bullhorn, then steps out of his bunker after the lights are out and gets fragged. That's a kind of paranoia too, isn't it?"

He turned off the boulevard and up the hill through the tunnel of trees, conscious of that crude, colloquial voice Nick Straus sometimes drew from him. He didn't know why he was telling him all this. "Anyway, that's the trouble with the Pentagon, whether it's Afghanistan, Poland, or the Persian Gulf. They're always overrunning the goddamned ball."

"They're dusting off some of the old strategies," Nick said, "and not just containment. Fighting a limited war with theater nuclear weapons, for example. I even saw an option paper the other day for reviving the old

Davy Crockett. You remember that? It's a sub-kiloton nuclear weapon, small enough to be carried by an infantryman. Totally destabilizing, totally insane."

Wilson turned off the shadowy lane and into the Straus driveway. Nick sat quietly in his seat, not stirring, still pondering some cosmic destabilization. Finally, he said, "How about a quick one, one for the road?"

"Thanks, I'd like to, but Betsy'll be looking for me. She's home by now."

Nick opened the door but didn't get out, still holding the door open. "Sometimes I think maybe I didn't put up enough of a fight when they wanted to retire me. What do you think?" He sat looking at the old coach lamp atop the post near the front porch. "Maybe I should have stayed on at Langley for a few more years, kept plugging away." In the years prior to his retirement, Nick had been removed from a SALT II delegation, brought home from a Geneva arms control committee, and then eased into bureaucratic limbo after he'd been accused of underestimating Soviet capabilities in the annual CIA assessment. "Do you ever think about it, whether you did the right thing or not, quitting the Intelligence Committee when you did?"

"Not much anymore."

"It worries me. What you said about this administration is true. It's not a joke anymore."

"No, it's not a joke."

"But even if I were back there, back at Langley, what could I do? After a time, people stop listening; you become too predictable. That's what happened to me. I'd used up my capital."

"Most of us did. The rooster that crowed himself to death. Maybe that was me too. No, I think you did the right thing."

"You think so?"

They'd talked of it many times, but Nick Straus's doubts remained, the question always returning. Something had gone out of him, Wilson thought, some purpose denied, something broken or missing, like the old grandfather clock in the downstairs hall that would fall silent for days at a time and then suddenly begin ticking again, waking him with its ghostly chimes as it tolled the hour at five o'clock in the morning.

"That's always the trap," Wilson said, "waiting a few more years. You wait a few more years and then it's too late, there's nothing left. You don't want to go anywhere or do anything, just remember where you've been and how it used to be—Korea, NATO in the old days, all the old myths that don't exist anymore. No, you did the right thing. The problem now is to pick up from here and go on. Maybe we should open a consulting firm.

That's something we could think about—Straus and Wilson, the beltway bandits.''

"Maybe. It sounds like a shoe store." Nick climbed out. "Thanks for the lift. Stop by sometime."

Wilson cranked down the window. "I'm going out to Ed Donlon's place in the Shenandoah this weekend," he called, "maybe cut some firewood, work the dogs. Why don't you come along?"

But Nick Straus only waved as he passed in front of the coach lamp and Wilson couldn't hear his reply. He wondered what Nick had wanted him to say, what he might have told him—someone whose grasp of the issues of the times made Wilson's own amateur ramblings sound like so much warm air from some bush-town hot-stove league.

He drove back through the rain to his own residence a mile away, a sprawling, white-painted brick rambler on a winding lane between McLean and North Arlington. A small creek lay in front of the sloping acre lot planted in oak, maple, and dogwood. He'd bought the house fifteen years ago at a time he could barely afford it. Now it was appraised at quadruple its original cost and he couldn't afford to sell it. With their two sons out of college and living elsewhere—the oldest in residency at a Boston hospital, the youngest in Oregon—Betsy was already thinking about moving to Naples, Florida. She wanted to buy a house on the Gulf near her parents and sister.

At forty-eight, Haven Wilson wasn't enthusiastic. Washington was his city, even if under enemy occupation, and rural Virginia was his country, autumn and winter country, the hillsides blooming with dogwood and redbud in the spring, with yellow and red maples in October, as in the small town in southwestern Virginia where he'd grown up. He didn't like Florida's unchanging season any more than he liked the Miami Dolphins. People who sat in hot weather stadiums should be watching jai alai or the dog races, not football, which belonged to autumn and winter, to the autumn afternoons of the Midwest or the Atlantic seaboard, to the mud and shadows of the old Polo Grounds in New York with the wind sharp, the dusk coming fast, rain and snow both part of its element. It didn't belong on AstroTurf under a plexiglass bubble or in a sun-drenched coliseum full of California sun freaks sitting shirtless in the stands, bellies to the skies, quaffing beer like kids at a rock concert.

After Sunday's Redskins loss, he'd remained in the basement rec room trying to finish the *New York Times,* all four pounds of it, while watching Sunbelt football with half an eye. Two teams in Day-Glo nylon uniforms scrambled over a vivid green plastic carpet under a Polynesian sky. Tired of reading news reminding him only of his own political isolation here in the Virginia suburbs, he'd wandered outside to rake the leaves, but shadows had come to the rear terrace, darkness to the woods. He'd stood in the eerie dusk like a TV cretin, still wired up to the California sunshine by electronic synapses and synthetic replay, like the rest of the country, persuaded that the great golden aurora from the Pacific had flooded eastward to relight the cold kilns of Youngstown, Lorain, and East Chicago, the artificial dawn reinvesting the continent, washing from silicon valley, the mercury lamps of television city, and the golf greens of Palm Springs where the Great Communicator's transcendentalists gathered, or the tacky, all-night fast-food and drugstore emporiums of the West Coast where their entrepreneurship thrived.

Sunbelt football was killing the game he'd once played and loved, the same way the Reaganites were trashing the country.

"I thought you'd be home earlier," Betsy called as he stood in the back hall, taking off his wet raincoat. "How was your meeting with Mr. Larabee?"

"Crummy."

She sat on the orange sofa in the rear study, her legs drawn under her, a book on her lap. Twists of yarn from the half-completed Afghan had been pushed aside, like the knitting bag. Her once dark hair showed streaks of gray now, cut short. The sharp features were still as striking as ever, her skin as firm as porcelain. "Really? What sort of person was he?"

"A nut." He hung up his coat.

"Then why are you so late?" she asked, disappointed.

"I stopped by The Players to see if someone was there who knew Larabee. Then I watched the game. What time did you get home?"

"Just a few minutes ago." She hadn't been to a teachers meeting but to a get-together of the Kennedy Center Subscription Club, a group of suburban music lovers who purchased blocks of tickets for the Kennedy Center music season. Once a month they gathered at a club member's home to listen on stereo to the program for a particularly esoteric upcoming concert. "But I thought The Players was closing. You stopped to watch the football game?"

"Just part of it." He entered the study and pulled off his tie. The television set was turned on across the room.

"I thought you had enough football yesterday."

"I did. Don't remind me."

"You really sit around too much. The Players is the last place I'd expect you to be. It makes you too negative. What did Larabee want to talk about?"

"I'm not sure."

"You mean you didn't ask."

"I mean it didn't interest me."

"Real estate law isn't the answer to your restlessness. I should think you'd know that by now. In the meantime, you should take up jogging, like Dr. Mercer. Maybe that would get some of the hostility out. It's therapeutic."

"So is beating your kids and yelling at the Russians, like that Air Force family down the street. What are you watching?"

"Nothing right now; I'm waiting. Who was at The Players?"

"A few people from the old days. I don't think you know them."

"Ed Donlon called. What did *he* want?"

"He wants me to talk to someone tomorrow afternoon."

"Good old dependable Ed," she said. "I didn't ask him about Jane. How old is she this time?"

Wilson stood looking at the television set. Ed Donlon was an old friend, of whom Betsy disapproved. Separated from his wife, Donlon was living temporarily with a younger woman. "If you're not watching it, why is it on?"

"I told you—I'm waiting. There's an interview coming. Nancy Reagan is going to be on."

"Who the hell cares." He moved resolutely toward the set.

"I do," she said sharply.

"You don't give up on that crowd, do you?"

"You might at least hear what she has to say."

"I know what she's going to say." He moved across the rag rug to the bookshelves next to the fireplace. In a glass case on a middle shelf were a few artifacts he'd brought back from overseas—Roman coins from Izmir, terra-cottas from Tel Aviv, fragments of a Hittite frieze from Anatolia—together with a few Civil War mementos he and his sons had picked up during their forays about the Virginia battlefields when the two boys were growing up: dumdums, a few brass buttons, fragments of an old canteen, the tip of a broken bayonet. Next to them were the burnished brevets his great-grandfather Carver Wilson had worn at Cold Harbor. Beside the glass case was a Civil War atlas, with a half dozen county road maps folded inside. For four years he'd been searching for rural property in Virginia, with the idea of buying an old farm and opening a rural law practice, like his father's old firm in southwest Virginia. During the past eight months he'd talked with elderly lawyers in Winchester, Warrenton, and Culpeper. Betsy, the daughter of a retired professor at Sweetbriar, had grown up in small, incestuous college towns and thought she despised rural life. She was under the impression that he was revisiting the old battlefields he'd walked over with his two sons so many years ago.

He picked up the Civil War atlas and a copy of the new Kissinger memoir, looked again at the television set, and turned back across the room. "I guess I'll go on upstairs."

"What a poor loser," she said accusingly. "It's only Nancy Reagan. Don't you ever stop thinking about it?"

"That's why I don't want to watch. I don't want to think about it."

"This work you're doing with real estate is just an escape. You know that as well as I do. Dog in the manger. If you're not careful, you'll work yourself into a worse state than Nick Straus."

He turned in the doorway. "What about Nick?"

"Ida called. She was worried about him. She thought he might be here."

"What happened?"

"She said he disappeared just before dinner, just walked out without a word, rain and all."

"He was at The Players. I took him home and we talked a little."

"She said he'd been seeing a doctor again—secretly, she said. Did he tell you that? She hoped you might talk to him."

"Politics isn't his problem."

"What is?"

"I'm not sure."

Depressed, he went upstairs and took a shower. Afterward he lay on his bed in the master bedroom, looking at the farm and rural real estate ads from the Sunday *Post* he kept hidden away in his dresser drawer. Finally, he put the ads aside and browsed through the Kissinger memoirs of the early Nixon presidency, reviewing his commentary on a few of those early crises he was involved with on the Hill. He read a dozen pages, but the solemn Teutonic style gave it the dignity of Thucydides. The back-channel traffic he remembered had read like the Borgias, Kissinger playing Lucrezia.

The rain drumming lightly against the dormer window drew his mind away and he finally put the book aside on the night table, turned out the light, and crawled under the covers. He lay in the darkness, unable to sleep, the rain bringing back the memory of Chuck Larabee's ribald face, the obscenity of his ambition, and then Nick Straus's forlorn figure at The Players, the damp spongy feet pushed out in front of him, the shoes that didn't belong on Nick's feet at all. How could you tell a man you'd known for fifteen years that his socks didn't match or that his feet were a stranger's, not his feet at all, the trouser cuffs damp and a little ragged, like the mop man's in an all-night cafeteria in Times Square or over on East Baltimore Street.

What kind of city was it that would abandon a man of his gifts, his insights, and then let him rot away in the basement of the Pentagon? What kind of city was it that bred people like Charles Larabee?

Betsy's weight, lowered to the twin bed next to his, stirred him. "Are you asleep?" she asked.

He was angry then, but drew in a slow, deep, silent breath to contain it. He smelled cold cream and hand lotion. "Just about."

"You don't sound like it." She lay back on the bed, pulling up the covers. She'd hurt her back playing tennis in August. An inch of plywood lay under her own thin mattress. "What were you thinking about? Your bad manners with Mr. Larabee?"

"I didn't do the talking, he did."

"Then what were you thinking about?"

"Tonight at The Players, what we were talking about."

"What was that? Tell me."

Released by fatigue, his anger returned, more satisfying this time. "How we're going to bury the Moral Majority." She didn't answer. "After that, we're going after Reagan."

Her sigh was audible. "It was only fifty dollars," she reminded him softly. "If you'd stop talking about it, maybe I'd consider giving the money back. But you'd have to promise not ever to talk about it again. Would you promise?"

"No," he said.

He'd bet her fifty dollars the previous autumn that the Reagan Republicans wouldn't win the election. They'd just returned from an evening with her music society friends, listening to a Handel opera, and the hour was late as they'd discussed it driving home; but even after they were upstairs, getting ready for bed, she still hadn't understood why he was so convinced that Reagan would never be President.

"It's simple," he'd told her finally, logic and patience exhausted. "You remember a song called 'Pistol Packin' Mama'? You remember it? It was in everyone's head for a few months during the war. Everyone was singing or humming it, on the radio or jukebox everyplace you went, a stupid song that didn't make any goddamn sense to anyone, but caught on anyway. They still sang it, whistled it, hummed it. There was Europe in rubble, all bombed out, the South Pacific a bloody mess, my mother's trying to get me to take piano lessons, and a hundred million Americans are walking around in their zoot suits humming this idiot tune that didn't have a god-damned thing to say about anything."

She didn't remember the song.

"How about 'Flat Foot Floogie with the Floy Floy'? You remember that one, don't you? The same thing."

She'd wondered instead how he could remember all those idiotic songs.

"Because they're idiotic, that's why! Because they don't make any god-damn sense at all, just like Reagan—just a stupid little pop tune that's dancing around in everyone's head all of a sudden. That's all he is, just two weeks on the old *Hit Parade.* He's not an answer to anything. He comes out of the same consumer plastic factories that dreamed up the Hula-Hoop, the throwaway swizzle stick, and the tuna fish hot dog. Sure it's a consumer society and maybe it's getting worse all the time, but you can't tell me that the people of this country don't know the difference between TV plastic and national politics, that on election day they're going to get into that voting booth, drop the curtain, and vote for a celluloid cowboy dashboard ornament like Ronald Reagan for a four-year American President. I just don't believe it. It won't happen. There are too many people in this country who won't let it happen, and I'll bet you fifty dollars against five that I'm right. . . ."

But he'd been wrong. It had happened, the Democrats had lost, and the senior position promised him at the Department of Justice had gone to a Republican attorney from Salt Lake City.

"It's not the fifty dollars," he told her now, still outraged, the rain brisk on the dormer windows. "It's just everything else. Anyway," he added, "we've got bigger fish to fry."

"Like whom?"

His mind drifted on. He was conscious of the rain, the dark streets, and the growing drowsiness overtaking him like a reprieve. He waited until the thunder rolled away, the grim dark laughter that was overtaking them all. "After we bury Reagan, we're going to move in our own man," he said sleepily. "If this country is going down the tubes, we might as well go in full color, with the biggest mouth in the country in the Oval Office, calling the play-by-play."

"Who would that be?" she asked dubiously, sensing an ambush.

He was silent, imagining her face. "Howard Cosell," he said. He waited but he didn't hear her laughter.

With their sons gone, they'd drifted apart, living different lives. The dark laughter was gone.

"Good night, brother Billy," he heard her say.

3.

The morning was gray with intermittent drizzle, the breakfast room dark under the trees as Haven Wilson finished his coffee. Betsy had left an hour earlier for her Fairfax County junior high school, leaving behind a note attached to the refrigerator door by a magnetic holder: "If you're seeing any Washington law firms today about a partnership, try to be civil, and *don't talk politics."* Wet maple and oak leaves lay on the hood of the old station wagon. As he rolled down the drive, he made a mental note to call Nick Straus that evening.

On Dolley Madison near the approaches to the beltway, traffic was slow. Cars crept along at a snail's pace through the murk, their lights on. He listened to the news on the radio, brooding out through the windshield at the submarine landscape. Near Heidelberg, two rocket-launched grenades had exploded behind the armor-plated Mercedes carrying the commander of U.S. forces in Europe. Two thousand Norwegian neutralists had demonstrated in front of the U.S. embassy in Oslo. An Armenian terrorist group had firebombed the flat of a Turkish first secretary in Brussels. In his small office on Capitol Hill a year earlier, someone from the Agency, DIA, or the Joint Chiefs might have been bustling about, eager to brief interested staffers on how these disparate incidents were related, a bunko operation from the Bulgarian Bluto squad, but on this chilly wet morning, Wilson knew only what the radio broadcaster told him, which wasn't very much.

A few thousand tons of assorted scrap iron were flying around the beltway as well at that hour. Tractor-trailers and dump trucks lumbered past, drenching his windshield and dangerously reducing visibility; Volkswagens and Toyotas darted in and out, sprinting for the fast lanes from the access roads or jockeying for the next exit. Car pool sedans and vans sped by. So did oversized sedans driven by white-haired old women in bifocals. Weak wrists that couldn't lift a four-pound sack of cat food from a supermarket checkout counter steered two tons of steel over a rain-slick four-lane highway. He slowed down as a woman with her head wrapped in a communion scarf cut abruptly in front of him and then gave a vague sort of Episcopalian wave of her hand without looking around.

Circling down the beltway exit at Route 50, he slowed to a stop behind a line of cars waiting to merge below. A blue-and-gray Fairfax County patrol car wheeled past him on the verge, blue light spinning, but no siren audible. An instant later, a car banged him from the rear, a quick ugly jolt that moved the old station wagon a few inches forward on the wet pavement.

Jesus Christ, he thought haplessly, unable to see through the mud-splashed rear window. The patrol car swept on down the ramp and turned up Route 50, where a pickup truck had sideswiped a small yellow private-school bus, blocking traffic in both northbound lanes. He set the hand brake and climbed out to look at the damage. The jolt had bent the Virginia license plate and jarred mud and iron scalings from the undercarriage along the line of impact. The car that had struck him had fared worse. One headlight was broken and a deep dent had been gouged in the sharklike snout. It was a silver-gray Alfa Romeo Spider that had seen better days, perhaps ten years old. Through the vector of tinted glass, he saw a blurred, watery face. The cars ahead of him were still stalled, unable to move on down the ramp and onto the blocked boulevard. No one left the Alfa. Maybe a woman, he decided charitably as he climbed toward the driver's window, someone frightened by the rush hour madness, the obscuring rain, and the police car looming up suddenly behind her. He was prepared to be sympathetic, but as he bent to the window, a man's face was lifted toward him, sunglasses masking the eyes, like two teardrop silver blisters.

"You might see better if you took off the sunglasses," Wilson called in annoyance through the closed window.

The driver rolled down the glass aggressively. "Who are you, a beltway cop? I hardly touched you."

"You bounced me a couple of feet. If you don't think so, maybe the police can bring their chalk lines up here."

It was an exaggeration, but so were the life styles of most Alfa owners. Any other driver would have been out in the rain by now, inspecting the damage, but this young man just sat there. He had a thin, hard face and long blondish hair that could have been fashionably cut or just long and dirty. The blade of nose was welted by a small scar high on the bridge. He needed a shave and his breath stank of fatigue, the ashes of a long sleepless night still in his mouth—too many cigarettes and too much whiskey. Spread on the seat next to him was an area road map, half unfolded to the northern Virginia suburbs. Atop it was the leather sunglass case, as if he'd just slipped the glasses on. The interior smelled queerly of rust, as if the Alfa had been closed up a long time out in the weather.

"It was that cop car," he said. "They nearly junked me, coming up like that."

The accent had a jagged metallic edge, as ugly as a South Philly scrap-iron yard. South Philly, or Jersey, Wilson thought, someplace where the lace curtains and the row house steps ended.

"You might have queered up the alignment, yours more than mine," he said. The white shirt was gray along the open collar; the shoulders of the blue blazer were powdered with dandruff. "How about your license?"

"You crazy? It was just a touch."

"I need your license," Wilson said. The blister eyes were as blank as a mantis's, the mouth a thin white line. Wilson had the sense of someone unwilling to give up his license, a predator caught mistakenly in the gill nets of a suburban traffic jam. "A license, a business card, anything. I may have to get in touch with you."

"Hey, pull it over, will you, Ichabod!" A bushy-haired kid leaned from the front window of a coffee-colored van behind the Alfa. "You're holding up traffic, man!"

27

Wilson stepped back. There were plexiglass fishbowls on the sides and star trails in gilt paint along the door. A beltway cowboy. "Keep your shirt on, sonny."

"Yeah?"

"Yeah."

The cars had begun to crawl forward at the foot of the ramp, merging with the northbound traffic. A second police car had joined the first. Wilson gave the young man his card through the window and waited while he searched his jacket and trouser pockets for his wallet.

"I lost it—I lost my fucking wallet," he said.

"Hey, mister! C'mon, for Christ's sake!" the van driver pleaded. "We get the cops up here, we'll never bust it loose!"

"We're trying. Hold your horses." At the foot of the ramp, the policeman directing traffic had seen the two stalled cars and was beckoning them forward.

"What'd he say?" The Alfa driver's movements were less controlled now and Wilson thought he was frightened.

"He said if we get the police up here, we're in for a long morning."

The man lifted his eyes, saw the police motioning to them from the road below, and then found a business card lying on the dash just under the windshield. He passed it quickly to Wilson. "This is all I got. I swear to Christ, I can't find my goddamned wallet!"

The card was gritty, one corner was bent. The card was from a firm called Caltronics, with offices in downtown Washington.

"There's no name here," Wilson said, lifting his eyes, "just the company." He heard the patrolman's whistle from the foot of the ramp. Horns had begun to wail from behind the van.

"Davis," the man said, head turned away toward the beckoning policeman. "Charles Davis. Hey, come on, man. Let's get out of here."

Wilson couldn't see the masked eyes, but he saw the mouth, the Adam's apple, and the thin hand clutching the steering wheel. It was a small thing, of little consequence, one of life's minor mysteries which break the surface of our lives for an improbable second and then just as abruptly are swept away, like the body of the small child he'd seen while floating the rapids of the Rapidan River during the spring of his junior year at the University of Virginia. The canoe was in the chutes, his paddle was lifted, and the small body had boiled to the surface, drifted for a few yards with the plunging canoe in a lifeless imitation of what as a schoolboy he knew as the dead man's float—swollen arms, small swollen fingers, grotesquely swollen feet—and then had disappeared again. He had searched for it for two hours in the quieter pool below and then had gone to the local sheriff, to the state police, and the only local newspaper within fifty miles. No one knew anything of a missing child. The sheriff assembled a grappling crew from the police and fire departments and they dragged the river below the rapids the next day, a Sunday, but found nothing. For two weeks Wilson drove over from Charlottesville on weekends to pursue the search, joined by a young journalist from a weekly paper who telephoned communities all along the Rapidan. No missing child could be found. By the third week, the local sheriff and state police were persuaded that the young canoeist, unfamiliar with the river at spring flood, had probably seen the body of a farm animal—a shoat, a lamb, or even a heifer.

But Wilson knew what he'd seen. He knew it again by the nightmares that haunted him for years, dreams in which the details were as clear as ever—the bright spring morning, the swift brown water, the rib cage of the canoe under his feet, and then the small body lifting, white fingers, white arms, white feet. Only the face was different.

That moment in the drizzle on the beltway ramp was similar in certain ways. The morning mists had parted, he'd seen an averted head, a thin white mouth, and an agonized hand clutching the steering wheel—a man caught up in some nightmare of his own—and knew that he was being lied to. No one would ever convince him otherwise.

The traffic carried him away. Driving down the ramp and into the stream of cars moving northward along the boulevard, he still pondered the mystery. But then the wet autumn morning returned. The coffee-colored van horneted past him on the inside lane with a supercharged roar of its V-8 engine—a kind of reckless triumph, announced not only by the engine's whine as it ripped past but by a denim-clad arm held languidly out the window, giving him the finger.

BMWs, Audis, and Datsuns filled the small parking lot behind the three-story brick building on the outskirts of Falls Church, most of them owned by the insurance brokers in the suite of offices on the first floor. A boy of ten or eleven was wandering about the lot, inspecting the automobiles. As Wilson drove into his parking space, the boy turned to study the battered fenders and the thick exhaust fumes, then brought his hand up, holding his nose, his elbow high, in a kind of rodent leer. Wilson left the car, and the boy ducked his head, disappearing behind a parked Audi, like a gopher dropping into his hole.

The owner of the real estate brokerage on the second floor was a man named Matthews, with whom Wilson had invested some money from his father's estate in the late sixties, buying industrial and undeveloped residential property. The previous spring, Matthews had been approached by a national real estate company and had decided to sell out. The transfer was to take place at the end of the year and Wilson had been handling the negotiations and the legal work.

The young receptionist was gone from her desk at the top of the stairs on the second floor. Two women in the reception room's orange leather chairs were awaiting the arrival of a sales agent. Identically dressed in knit suits, they were smoking and drinking coffee out of Styrofoam cups. One was plump and dark-haired, the other a thin, washed-out blond, rawhide hard, her flocculence of bright hair shrunk to an orange-bronze scouring pad atop her small head.

"Well, you never know, hon," he heard the blond woman say as he hung his coat in Matthews' office. Her whispered voice was full of ancient mistrust and uxorial grievances, as treacherous as a plastic garbage bag full of smashed bottles. "You gotta watch 'em every minute. There's no tellin' what kind of cardboard they're building houses out of these days. I told him after I found out, I told him right out, I said we wanted a wet bar, sure we did, but that didn't mean we wanted no goddamn crik running through the basement. . . ."

Wilson stood behind Matthews' desk, looking at the telephone call slips the receptionist had left for him. For the past ten days, Matthews had been in Florida, arranging a condominium purchase and his upcoming relocation to Sarasota. In his absence, Wilson had promised to keep an eye on the brokerage.

"That woman called you again for about the twentieth time," the receptionist said as she joined him. She was a dark-haired, energetic young girl just a few years out of high school. "The Kramer woman. She had to see you today, she told me—no alibis. She said today was the last day, absolutely the last day."

"That's what she said last week." He found the call slip with Rita Kramer's name on it and sat down. She was a Californian, come east to buy a house. Her husband was a Los Angeles entrepreneur awaiting a White House political appointment. She had been carrying on a guerrilla war with Wilson for over a week now about a house she thought was overpriced, and wanted to negotiate directly with the owner. "Anything else?"

"Mrs. Polk isn't in yet," she said, lowering her voice. "Those two ladies outside have been waiting for twenty minutes. I don't know what to tell them."

Mrs. Polk was one of the sales staff. Her husband was retired, both enjoyed their bourbon, and she sometimes found it hard to get out of bed in the morning. "She'll be in," Wilson said. "Just give her a few minutes more." He picked up the phone and dialed. The hotel switchboard put the call through to Rita Kramer's seventh-floor room, but a masculine voice answered. He thought the accent was a little theatrical, like Rita Kramer herself.

"Might I ask who this is?" the voice inquired.

"Haven Wilson. She called me a little while ago."

"Oh, yes, Mr. Wilson. She's very anxious to talk to you. She just went down to the flowershop. I'll get her. Please don't go away."

He waited. The gray light flooded through the metal sash like seawater. The wind blew water from the trees against the smoky panes. The office walls, metal partitions papered in coconut fiber with metallic threads running through them, were as thin as matchwood. From the desk he could hear the two women gossiping outside the door, the one voice droning on in a grating whisper that fastened to his skull like a cutting edge, peeling hardwood to pulp. He didn't know how Matthews had managed this for so many years, day after day, week after week. He couldn't shut the door without putting down the phone, and so he sat there as the voice drilled on:

". . . an' you can never tell, you know what I mean? There's this here insulation they got now causes cancer, you know? Breathing it in all day? Then you take someone that went an' used acid to clean up asphalt tile, makin' it all bright an' fresh like they do. Well, I remember when we was out at Fort Riley, we had us a little kitten, sweetest little thing you ever did see. Then she went to licking up some spilt milk off the kitchen floor, you know, the way they do. Before we knowed it, her belly went hard, hard as a rock, an' the poor thing dropped over, dead as a doornail. . . ."

"Wilson? Where in the hell have you been?" Rita Kramer was on the phone, angry and out of breath. Watching her cross the lobby of the downtown hotel before their first meeting a week earlier, Wilson had had intimations of Beverly Hills and Rodeo Drive. She was tall and wide-shouldered, with the long arms and legs of an ex-dancer or show girl. Her dark odalisque eyes and wide mouth were so carefully made up that at that distance her face had the artificiality of a Kabuki mask. Her voice was rude, contemptuous, bawdy, and indiscreet. What impressed him most was her sheer physical vitality, relentless and inexhaustible. She reminded him of a high-class stripper from East Baltimore street who'd often shared his table when he was a young draftee at the counterintelligence school at Fort Holabird.

"I've been out, like you. Someone said you called me."

"I waited all day Sunday, all day yesterday, shut up in this goddamned hotel room. You told me I'd hear from the owner—"

"I said I'd pass on your request to talk to her. I didn't say she'd call you."

"Well, she hasn't called. Did you give her my latest offer?"

"I passed it through her lawyer."

"What'd he say?"

"He said no, just as I said he would. I'm sorry."

"Sorry!" Her voice erupted sharply and he held the phone away from his ear. *"Sorry!* Well, that's just nifty, isn't it! You're still hustling me, Wilson, you and that goddamned Matthews, who took a powder to Florida. You think I don't know a hustle when I hear one? My lawyer's here and he wants to talk to you."

He heard the two arguing in the background and a minute later the masculine voice returned, as crisp and mannered as before.

"Edelman here, Mr. Wilson. Mrs. Kramer is very upset about this entire transaction, as I think she has reason to be. It's almost a week now since she offered you a contract on this property—"

"Five days," Wilson said. "It was too low."

"Perhaps, but we'd like to deal directly with the lawyer who's handling the estate or the owner herself. Mrs. Kramer has only a limited time available to her here in Washington, as she's explained. Since you've become involved, we seem to be getting nowhere. Under those circumstances, I think it perfectly appropriate that Mrs. Kramer be placed in direct contact with the lawyer or the owner, Mrs. Ramsey."

Wilson said nothing. Rita Kramer's voice came back.

"You get my message, Wilson? I'm tired of you giving me the runaround. I want to talk to the owner, Mrs. Grace Ramsey."

"She's in Majorca."

"Friday you said Bimini!"

Wilson had forgotten what he'd said. Grace Ramsey floated around the Mediterranean and the Caribbean like a wisp of high-flying cirrus. "Bimini, Majorca, they're both the same—out of the country. Abroad. I've told you that." He lifted his feet to the desk and reclined in his chair, ready for another five rounds. After a week of sparring and brawling, a certain basis for communication had been established. "I'm sorry, but you can find something else in Washington. Try those Georgetown brokers, like I suggested—"

"And how many times do I have to tell you that's *not* what I'm looking for!"

A long silence followed.

"Are you still there?" she asked finally.

"I'm here."

"Good." She slammed down the phone.

A little after eleven, Wilson led the two women from the reception room down the front stairs. Mrs. Polk had a dead battery and was waiting for a booster charge from a nearby service station. She'd telephoned to ask him to deliver her client and her friend to her residence on his way to an eleven o'clock meeting with an Arlington tax lawyer. The dark-haired client, named Fillmore, was the wife of an army sergeant recently assigned to the Pentagon from Oklahoma. Her blond companion was also the wife of an NCO, and lived in the same transient quarters while waiting to move into a house they'd bought in Annandale. The basement leaked. An aggrieved party, she'd joined Mrs. Fillmore to give her the benefit of her house-hunting experience.

Waiting for them in the rear parking lot was the boy Wilson had seen skulking between the Audis and BMWs upon his arrival.

"I was wondering where you was sulking at," said Mrs. Fillmore, her parental tone less friendly than the girlish chatter that had accompanied them down the stairs. She'd told Wilson she was from Arkansas and was a beautician.

A faint red splash illuminated the boy's cheek. At closer range, Wilson saw ghostly fingers from a powerful hand still outlined against the left side of his face.

"I was waitin'."

"Mr. Wilson, this here is my boy Willard."

"Hello, Willard." The name echoed familiarly in Wilson's mind.

"I guess you heard that name before," Mrs. Fillmore said. "Say hello to Mr. Wilson, Willard."

"Hello, Mr. Wilson," Willard said without enthusiasm. The small insect eyes were still stung unnaturally bright.

"I think I know the name," Wilson acknowledged sympathetically. Willard's brightness hardened visibly.

"Well, it wasn't all my doin'," Mrs. Fillmore admitted philosophically. Her brown purse was shoved under one heavy arm as she pulled on her gloves. A filter-tip cigarette was clamped in the side of her mouth. "That boy's a handful, I don't mind telling you, a heavy burden, an' it's not just the name that does the tormentin'." Wilson held the rear door open and Mrs. Fillmore backed in, found the rear seat, settled back for a moment, then lifted her heavy ankles around. "We're not kin, if that's what you're thinking, Mr. Wilson," she confided as they drove out of the parking lot. Willard Fillmore, next to Wilson in the front seat, small shoulders erect, sat alert on the edge of the seat as if being in front were a rare privilege. "Wouldn't that be something?" his mother added in a girlish aside to her suspicious blond companion. "Being in Wash'n'ton an' being kin to President Millard Fillmore?"

"Ha ha," Willard said.

There was a momentary delay from the rear seat as Mrs. Fillmore gathered her ordnance together. Leather creaked and an instant later Willard

Fillmore took a salvo in the back of the head, delivered by a purse swung by its strap. "Don't smart-talk me, mister," his mother warned. "I done told you—I had enough."

"I heard tell of stranger things," replied her companion fatalistically.

"Tell Mr. Wilson what President he was, Willard," Mrs. Fillmore commanded.

"The thirteenth President," Willard answered expertly, "only his name was Millard." He turned to watch Wilson suspiciously.

"Was he Republican or Demo—"

"There wasn't no Republicans in them old days," Willard said, the hostile eyes still fastened to Wilson's face, awaiting his reaction.

"He's sure got it learned by heart, don't he, Mr. Wilson?" Mrs. Fillmore called in her loud beautician's voice, the one she used for talking to a customer under a hair dryer five chairs away. "We was on Okinawa when Millard was born."

"Willard," her son said immediately. "My name's Willard."

"Willard. Did I say Millard? Lordy, I done forgot what I said. There I go again." Mrs. Fillmore chuckled, but Willard's expression didn't change. "Anyway, like I was saying, we was on Okinawa when Willard was born and the names kinda went nice together, you know, the way they do sometimes, bein' on the tip of your tongue that way, like Sears Roebuck. . . ."

Wilson also heard Willard's whispered voice from alongside, a seditious undertow attempting to drag him away from these backseat humiliations: *"Where'd you get this car, sucker?"*

". . . an' then when my husband Albert decided they just went together, that was that. So we named him Willard Fillmore, right there on Okinawa, not knowing all the time it was Millard Fillmore, the thirteenth President of the United States, we was thinking about all that time, something we clean forgot, me an' Albert both."

Mrs. Fillmore laughed. *"You're a loser,"* Willard was whispering, *"same as this here car."*

". . . an' so we just had the birth certificate made up like that, right on Okinawa, right at the base hospital—Willard Fillmore."

"Them Japs don't know nothing," her companion said truculently.

". . . an' it wasn't till we got back stateside that someone in the PX nursery school told me it wasn't Willard I'd been thinking on at all back on Okinawa, but Millard—Millard Fillmore. Don't that beat all, Mr. Wilson? I wisht I'd knowed my history better, don't you? You ever lived overseas, Mr. Wilson?" Her voice drew closer as she held her cigarette out. "Here, pinch that out the winder for me, would you, son?"

"Yes, m'am."

34

Wilson opened the dashboard ashtray but Willard ignored it and pretended to blow lusty smoke rings for the benefit of a passing gray-haired motorist, who immediately fixed her sharp censorious eye upon Wilson. After she'd slid by, Willard quickly cranked down the glass and let fly with the butt aimed at her rear window.

Mrs. Fillmore didn't notice. "Willard's my little computer," she was saying. "He can beat his daddy at Atari, and Albert's a missile ordnance man. Totes up a Piggly Wiggly bill faster'n IBM, don't you, son?"

"Yes, m'am."

"It's not addin' them bills up that worries me," said her thin companion. "It's payin' 'em."

"He can add up a license plate quicker'n you can read him out the numbers. Show Mr. Wilson, hon." She leaned over the front seat, pointing through the windshield. "What's that car up ahead say?"

"Which one?" Willard sat alertly on the edge of his seat, like a dove hunter at the edge of a cornfield.

"The van."

"That's not no van, it's a combie."

A sharp knuckle cracked the skull above the right ear. "All right, but what's it say, dummy?"

"Four hundred and eleven one way, twenty-four the other."

The Virginia license plate read *327-84.* Wilson frowned, trying to interpret Willard's calculus sets.

"You see? You see what I'm telling you, Mr. Wilson?" Mrs. Fillmore sat back, gratified.

"Three hundred and twenty-seven plus eighty-four is four hundred and eleven," Willard explained. "Three and two plus seven is twelve. Add eight and four and see what you get, sucker." He turned to the backseat to look at his mother. "He's moving his lips, same as you an' Albert do."

"Faster'n an IBM, ain't he, Mr. Wilson? He did that all the way from Oklahoma to Nashville, where we throwed a rod. Laid over for three days, but it wasn't too bad. You ever been to the Grand Ole Opry, Mr. Wilson?"

Wilson admitted he hadn't.

"You ever seen the President?" Willard asked.

"No, not much. He doesn't call me into the Oval Office much these days." It was the kind of reply he might have given his own sons over the breakfast table years earlier, but Willard was insulted.

"Tell me something I don't know, sucker," he whispered vehemently. "Who'd ever think I was talking about you being in the White House?"

"What's that you're saying, Willard?" Mrs. Fillmore demanded from the backseat, her Arkansas drawl full of heavy metal, threatening retribution.

"We were just talking," Wilson explained, conscious of Willard's shrinking head and shoulders. With two sons out of college and out of his tool chest, his sock drawer, his tie rack, and his bank account, he had little patience with someone else's gamy little problems, but the error had been his, not Willard Fillmore's.

Mrs. Polk was waiting for them in front of her house.

"Now you say goodbye to Mr. Wilson," Mrs. Fillmore instructed as she left the rear seat, turning to her son, who still hovered near the front door he'd slammed closed with all of his rebellious strength.

"Yes, m'am," Willard said eagerly. Sedition was in the bright little eyes and some NCO club slur was forming itself in the quick little mind, but then his mother moved in suspiciously behind him, brought back by the false octave in her son's enthusiastic reply, and he seemed to change his mind. "Goodbye, Mr. Wilson," he said, and sped off like a scalded cat toward Mrs. Polk's new bronze station wagon.

"That boy's a handful," Mrs. Fillmore declared, retrieving the yarn cap from the front seat. "This here traveling around has got him all jarred loose."

"I suppose so," Wilson said, trying to ignore the small denim-clad rear end that was so energetically mooning him from the back window of Mrs. Polk's station wagon.

4.

Ed Donlon was only half Irish, but he had a certain Irish charm which many women found seductive. He was a prodigious drinker, raconteur, and philanderer, could quote Yeats and more obscure voices by the hour, especially when he was in his cups, and had a sexual vitality that neither alcohol nor advancing middle age seemed to have dulled. He'd grown up in a sedate Victorian house in Trenton, New Jersey, surrounded by maiden aunts, grandmothers, and older sisters, he and his father, a patent lawyer, the prisoners of a spinsterish sisterhood he wasn't to escape until he was sent off to Princeton at seventeen. He'd been taking his revenge ever since, he'd once told Haven Wilson. They'd known each other for years. Both had been lawyers together at the Justice Department, both in the criminal division, where they'd shared an office. Donlon had moved on to the Agency as deputy counsel and had ended his government career as an assistant secretary of defense. He'd attempted to persuade Haven Wilson to join him at the Pentagon as his senior deputy, but Wilson had remained on the Hill, more interested in returning eventually to a senior position at Justice. In the late seventies, Donlon had left the Pentagon after a policy dispute and joined a small but prestigious Washington law firm. Wilson had the impression that he didn't work very hard, kept comfortable hours, and had been drinking and whoring even more voraciously since his wife had left him.

It was a little before one o'clock as Haven Wilson climbed into the front seat of Donlon's BMW 2002 and the two men drove out through Fairfax into the Virginia countryside. Donlon was dressed for the country in gray flannels, a tweed hacking jacket with elbow patches, and red-soled walking shoes. Only the ascot was missing. He was smaller and a few years older than Wilson, but his thinning chestnut hair was barely touched by gray and his fair-skinned, robust face was uncreased by worry. In his company, Wilson sometimes felt as dull as the paint on a bus-station door.

The rain had vanished and the wind had grown colder. The gunmetal sky held the first premonition of winter. On the way out, Wilson mentioned the problems he'd been having with the California woman who wanted to buy Grace Ramsey's house. Ed Donlon was her lawyer, Grace Ramsey the best friend and former college roommate of Donlon's wife, Jane. But Donlon had washed his hands of it once he'd turned the house over to the Virginia brokerage.

"She doesn't care about money, I'm not going to talk to her about money, her New York lawyers won't talk about money, and that's all there is to it," he said. "I don't care about these people from California, she doesn't care about these people from California, and if they won't meet her price for the house, then she doesn't care. She didn't put the price on the house, a broker did, and it took me six months to get her to agree to put it on the market. Grace is strange, flaky. She floats around in a world of her own. Too much money, which is maybe why George drank himself to death."

The road narrowed to a single lane and they drove past rolling unkempt fields and abandoned farms, ruined silos and tumbled barns awaiting the developer's bulldozer.

"This California woman wants to talk to her," Wilson persisted.

"Grace won't talk to her."

"To you, then."

"I won't talk to her. If I talk to her, I'll have to talk to Grace, and I'm not going to talk to Grace about money. I'll talk to her about religion, poetry, buggery, whatever, but not about money. Never."

"So what am I supposed to tell these California people?"

"What you've been telling them. Listen, Grace stayed with us in Georgetown for two months after George died—two goddamn months. It was like living with someone out of *Midsummer Night's Dream,* Jane used to say. Then she left this painting behind. You know what it was? A bloody

Matisse; I'm not kidding. For the house, she said—for the room and the house. It belongs there. When George was drying out in North Carolina a couple of years before that, she stayed with us for six weeks. Six weeks. That's when I learned—she won't talk about money, doesn't know anything about money, and doesn't care anything about money. For her, it doesn't exist. So after George died, that house sat empty up there on the Potomac because she refused to think about that house and money—for three goddamn years. So her New York lawyer and I finally got her to sit down and talk about that empty house. It was like a séance, a séance with a Ouija board—that's the way that New York lawyer and I had to talk to her. She wasn't even there in the same room with us. You don't understand what I'm saying, do you?"

"No," Wilson admitted.

"Well, you won't—not until you meet her. She doesn't live in our world. . . ."

The landscape had changed. The fields were cultivated and the pastures closely grazed within board and stone fences. Old stone and brick houses, circa 1780, lay within boxwoods and azaleas at the end of oak- and cedar-lined lanes.

They had lunch in Middleburg, at a stone inn off the main street. The cellar restaurant was darkly paneled under a beamed ceiling, like a rathskeller, but the old pine tables, the copperware, and the hand-painted hostelry and ironmonger signs were early American. In the rear, a few tables and booths were arranged around an old brick fireplace where a few logs smoked without flame, but the room was acrid with unventilated kitchen smells and they returned to the front room, where a tall young woman showed them to a table. She didn't look like a rural waitress and Donlon noticed her immediately. She wore a cardigan, a flannel skirt, and boat moccasins; her dark hair was tied in pigtails.

"I'll bet she's got a college degree," Donlon said, watching her return to the end of the bar for menus.

"Probably," Wilson said, looking the other way. Two middle-aged women in flowered dresses and garden club hats sat at a nearby table drinking daiquiris. A young couple in riding boots and identical houndstooth riding jackets leaned with their heads against the wall at a side table, talking softly.

"Sure she has." Donlon's smile brightened as she came back to the table.

"Something to drink?" she asked. Wilson guessed she was in her early thirties. They ordered martinis on the rocks.

"What was it in?" Donlon asked agreeably. "Psychology, sociology? Maybe history?"

"What was what in?"

"Your degree. I wouldn't be surprised if you were a teacher."

"Psychology—psychology and English lit, but that was a long time ago. What made you ask?"

"Intuition. You've probably got a horse."

Wilson looked away, embarrassed. Asking a waitress in Middleburg if she had a horse was like asking a skiff owner in rubber boots on Chesapeake Bay if he was an oysterman, but to his surprise the waitress seemed flattered. "Three," she said, smiling.

"Not Appaloosas, either."

"No, not Appaloosas."

She went back to the bar. "I told you," Donlon said, invigorated. "A thoroughbred."

"What time's McVey expecting us?"

"Anytime after lunch. He suggested lunch, but that's no good. The afternoon will be long enough as it is." His eyes still lingered on the young waitress standing at the end of the bar. "She's not bad. What do you think?"

Wilson studied the menu, trying to ignore him. If the waitress had been flattered by Donlon's guess that she kept horses, she was naive enough for anything. The menu specialties were hand-lettered in a flowery, amateurish script, some in French, and the improvised handicraft made him suspicious. "This is your neck of the woods," he said. "What do you recommend?"

"Something quick."

Wilson put the menu aside. "What's McVey want to talk to me about?"

"Discuss some problems," Donlon said vaguely. "He's been in bed with phlebitis; no visitors, no small talk. That means he's pumped up. He just bought some professor's library from Johns Hopkins and has been reading his way through it, the poor bastard. He gets goddamned lonely. When I talked to him on the phone, he wouldn't let go." Donlon looked up as the waitress put the drinks on the table. "What'd the cook get his degree in?" Donlon asked.

"The cook? I'm not sure. Why?"

He handed her the menu. "When in doubt, take the familiar. I'll have the corned beef sandwich."

"You don't trust us," she said.

"Make mine roast beef," Wilson said.

"He's English," Donlon explained.

"And you're Irish, I suppose." She took back the menus with a smile and strolled away, this time more slowly.

"She's not bad at all," Donlon said, watching her hips as Wilson studied the worm holes in the old pine, trying to decide whether they were made by an auger or a Civil War beetle. He drank his martini in silence. Donlon waited expectantly.

"What's wrong with Appaloosas?" she asked as she brought the plates, not waiting for Donlon's opening sally.

"Nothing, except you don't quite look the type. Someone tried to interest me once."

"But didn't." She was bolder now, her shoulders back as she arranged the plates.

"It's not much fun," Donlon said. "You spend your weekends being dragged around at the end of a horse trailer."

"I'm afraid so."

"My pastures are empty," Donlon said shamelessly. Wilson found himself trying to read the legend on a sporting print half a room away.

She laughed. "Really? That's a shame? Where?"

"The valley of the Shenandoah," Donlon said sadly, as if it were a refrain from a Confederate campfire song. Donlon had a two-hundred-acre farm in the valley with an old prebellum house he and Jane had been restoring, but he hadn't been there since the death of his only son, Brian, over a year ago. Wilson was the only one who visited the place. "The high shoe country," Donlon continued. "Do you know Yeats?"

"A little," she replied, surprised.

"'Huntsman Rody, blow the horn,'" he said in a Gaelic lilt. "'Make the hills reply.' But Rody couldn't blow his horn, only weep and sigh." Smiling mysteriously, he drank from his glass while the waitress watched. The two women in flower club hats were studying them. Wilson felt like crawling under the table. "Do you know it?" Donlon asked. "'The Ballad of the Foxhunter'?"

"No, but it sounds very sad."

"It is. How about another drink, Haven?"

"No, thanks, one's enough. For both of us."

Looking sadly at Wilson, Donlon said, "'The blind hound with a mournful din Lifts slow his wintry head.'" Then, to the waitress: "He says no. Sorry; maybe next time."

They finished their lunch. The young woman returned and stood talking with Donlon for a few minutes. Her name was Nancy.

"You never quit, do you," Wilson said as they crossed the street to the car. The day had grown darker and the wind was sharp against their faces.

"If I quit I'd be dead. Anyway, she wasn't bad."

It was always the same with Donlon. His taste in clothes, clubs, and friends was subtle, fastidious, even a little archaic, but his eye for women was indiscriminate. One seemed to have no relation to the other. Secretaries, restaurant hostesses, cocktail lounge waitresses, even a bag girl in a Fairfax supermarket once when they'd been on their way to the farm—they were all fair game for Donlon, who was constantly on the prowl, not for immediate success but for an eventual one. Two, three, maybe four visits, and then on a rainy night, business slow, the customers' faces grown dull, the talk monotonous, the feet tired, Donlon would be there, arriving alone near closing time. Women bored or lonely with their own lives found his more seductive; they brought him alive as well; but to Wilson there was something sad about it. It was hard to tell Donlon's age now—he might have been forty-five or fifty-five—but in a few years the mystery would be gone, the adulterous intent more nakedly revealed by the wrinkled neck, the dab of hair color, or the denture lines around the mouth. And one evening in a bar or restaurant after too many drinks, he would betray himself to a woman happier or more independent than she had any right to be in Donlon's bachelor book; she would react, humiliating him in front of a few late customers, and that would be the end of the Ed Donlon he had known. He wondered who would be left to pick up the pieces.

They drove west for three miles and turned down a narrow lane sunk in a deep roadbed dug out by centuries of carriage and wagon travel. A few miles beyond, they turned into a narrower secondary road that gave way to gravel as it meandered along a wide creekbed. Stone fences lined the verges, grown over with Virginia creeper, poison ivy, and honeysuckle.

"He likes his privacy, doesn't he?" Wilson said.

"It's his freedom."

They drove across a narrow stone bridge, past a gatehouse with a shake roof, where a wooden sign—*Boxhill Farm*—hung from the eaves. The gravel road climbed between two stone fences lined with shaggy cedar trees. Black Angus grazed along the flank of the hill. They passed a pond fringed with dry cattails, an old springhouse and a few weathered loafing sheds, and climbed the slope toward the distant hill where the tall stone manor house stood in a grove of oak, maple, and pine facing west toward the blue-gray haze of the Shenandoah. The road was paved within the second cattle guard and the hilltop partially enclosed by English boxwood that showed their age in the ragged yellow growth at the base of the trunks.

Donlon parked the BMW in an asphalted parking area in front of a three-car garage. A mud-splattered Dodge station wagon, a Jaguar sedan, and a farm truck loaded with cordwood were parked in the open area.

"This is hunt country, so don't ask about the horses or you'll get the tour," Donlon warned as they climbed the stone steps toward the flagstone walk. Down the slope behind the rear terrace Wilson saw a stone guest cottage, a greenhouse, and a stable. A chestnut stallion was being unsaddled by a stablehand in the open door. The fields beyond were cross-fenced and held a dozen grazing thoroughbreds. "We'd be here all night."

As they approached the stone house, Wilson could smell the faint acidity of the ancient boxwoods and the sharp tingle of wood smoke. Rhododendron, azalea, and holly trees concealed the front of the house. A girl in riding jodhpurs and hacking boots reached the flagstone courtyard as they did, climbing the walk from the other direction. Her cheeks were flushed and she carried a suede jacket over her shoulder. Despite the chill, her arms were bare. "Hi," she called. "You just get here?"

"Just now," Donlon said. "Jennifer, isn't it?"

"Sure, just like last time. He's been waiting for you."

She opened the paneled white door under the fanlight and stood aside. "He's probably in the back study behind the library, where he usually is. Don't tell him you saw me; I'm not supposed to come in this way."

Wilson followed Donlon into a warm, dim interior fragrant with wax and wood polish. A gray-coated houseman, as small as a groom or jockey, stood just inside the door. As they passed in, he moved the door closed behind them, pausing finally to peer out at Angus McVey's granddaughter, who was still outside, struggling with her boots. "Come on, Fletcher, give me a break," she said. "I'm late."

He didn't move, looking at her lugubriously. The thick gray hair was parted in the middle and dipped down over his forehead on each side, like gull wings. Beneath the alcohol-coarsened nose he wore a full handlebar mustache. Wilson had the impression he'd just stepped from behind the bar of an 1890 Bowery saloon or the daguerreotype of the original Abner Doubleday baseball team. Under the gray cotton jacket he wore a white shirt without a collar. He was small and gnarled, but the hand closing the door was larger than Haven Wilson's.

"Come on, Fletcher," Jennifer called. "Be a pal. I've got my boots off now."

He relented, opened the door a crack, and peered out. "Last time."

"Last time," she promised.

He swung the door open and she slipped in, ran lightly across the hall, carrying her boots, and up the staircase.

"This is Haven Wilson," Donlon said.

Fletcher nodded mutely and led them back along the center hall below the staircase. "He's been waiting," he said. The ancient pine floors were lustrous and unmarred. Wilson fell in behind Donlon, keeping to the beige runner. Above the chair rail, the white paneled wall held a half dozen brown ancestral portraits, one of whom, Wilson thought, bore a surprising resemblance to Edward VII. On a small cherry table at the rear of the hall was a mounted brass hunting horn under glass.

As they crossed through a rear sitting room with white sofas, white chairs, and a deep-pile carpet, Fletcher broke the silence. He was wearing old white tennis sneakers and moved like a cat, without a sound. "Haven't seen you since the Crofton Cup." His head seemed to float through the dimness. "Had one at Charles Town the other night," he continued, opening a heavy white door. "A sure thing."

"What did it pay?" Donlon asked. They crossed through a formal library, softly lit and silent as a mortuary. A small, white-haired figure was bent over a writing desk. He didn't look up.

"Didn't. Threw a shoe and the jock pulled her up. Threw it clean over the grandstand. Jock's name was Joquita, Chicata, something like that. A real banana. He don't go to Pimlico anymore. I go up to Charles Town by myself, Jennifer and me sometimes. Those mountain Baptists bet the shit out of the short odds, hammer them right in the ground. You're better off playing bingo at a church supper. You a betting man, Mr. Wilson?"

He inspected Wilson with cool precision as they reached the door at the end of the library.

"Not much."

"The quiet life," he said, the blue eyes lingering on Wilson's gray suit, the soft white shirt with the button-down collar, and the solid woolen tie. "Keep it up," he murmured with quiet approval. "He's in here, just up from the barn."

He opened the door. Wilson followed Donlon into a large, disorderly study. Books and book cartons were strewn everywhere. Angus McVey was seated on a small leather sofa opposite the fireplace, where a low fire blazed beyond the brass fender. He arose to greet them, a tall, white-thatched man in his late seventies, slightly stooped. The blue eyes in the thin wintry face were, for a moment at least, as bright and curious as those of his granddaughter. But then, just as quickly, the curiosity dimmed, the head faltered, and he seemed overcome with confusion. He avoided Wilson's eyes as he shook his hand and Wilson recognized the symptoms Donlon had described to him.

He wore a ratty tweed jacket, a faded denim shirt, whipcord trousers whose twill was threadbare at the pockets and knees, and a muddy pair of gum boots whose leather uppers were cracked with age. He'd been removing the latter as they'd entered, his feet carefully positioned on a square of spread newspaper upon which he continued to stand. "Please," he began in dismay, "sit down, both of you. Have you had lunch? What about a cocktail? Would you like a cocktail? Fletcher, what about a cocktail?" His hands seemed to be trembling, his eyes were flushed. He looked only at Fletcher, no one else.

"Yes, sir, whatever they'd like," Fletcher replied calmly.

"Thanks," Donlon said, "but we just finished a couple of martinis."

McVey misunderstood. "Martinis, then. Two martinis, Fletcher. How do they prefer them, very dry?"

He stood in front of the leather couch on a piece of spread newspaper like a scolded schoolboy or a muddy spaniel, a millionaire flushed with an amateur bartender's anxieties as he tried to accommodate his two guests; and Wilson identified in the distraught recluse everything Donlon had warned him about—the morbid sensitivity, the horror of public appearances, and the initial excruciating discomfort among strangers, a man so pathetically isolated within himself that the act of performing some small inconsequential duty, even in the sanctuary of his own study, seemed to bring him agony. But it would pass, Donlon had said. Just be patient and blind.

"I wouldn't mind coffee," Wilson suggested. "If that wouldn't be too much trouble."

"Coffee? Are you sure?" McVey looked to Fletcher for help.

"No trouble at all," Fletcher said, as calmly as before. The serene, old-fashioned face held the wisdom of some universal valet, omniscient and indestructible.

"Three coffees, then," McVey decided. "Yes, three."

Fletcher nodded and went out.

Donlon talked quietly, described their drive up, discussed Wilson's interest in finding a farm, and told of Betsy's dislike for rural life. Wilson joined in after a few minutes. McVey listened in silence, like an eavesdropper. Fletcher returned with a pair of sheepskin slippers, which he put on the floor next to McVey's gray-stockinged feet. Then he picked up the gum boots, rolled up the newspaper, and silently withdrew.

"She teaches school, you say?" McVey ventured at last. "Your wife teaches school? Very difficult these days, isn't it?" His hand trembled visibly as he searched the table next to him for his reading glasses.

"Yes, it is," Wilson said, looking away. The study was lined with bookshelves. The wooden filing cabinets, the tables, and the two antique writing desks were heaped with books. A few were new but most were old, bound three and four together by cord, the seams split, the morocco, calf, and buckram bindings beginning to disintegrate. There were also manuscripts, bundles of old journals, back issues of newspapers, and a few oddly named scholarly quarterlies Wilson had never heard of.

As the moments passed, Angus McVey's tremors seemed to subside as he described the library he'd recently purchased from a dead history professor's estate. He'd taught at Johns Hopkins, but evidently left his best thoughts in the classroom. There was no marginalia among the old volumes, not a word, not an idle thought. He asked Wilson about his experiences at the Department of Justice and on various Senate committees. Wilson found himself talking about his decision to leave, something he'd discussed with no one, not even Betsy.

Fletcher brought the silver coffee service and placed it on a brocaded footstool. McVey sat up absentmindedly, his eyes on the tray. "No biscuits, Fletcher?" He seemed disappointed, an invalid denied his afternoon sweet, but then apologized. "I'm sorry; what you're saying interests me very much. Please continue."

Even Donlon seemed intrigued by what he'd heard. "Go on, Haven; I've never heard this."

"There's nothing unusual about it," Wilson said. "It happens to everyone sooner or later. It's just that what you're doing no longer has any relevance at all to any world you can recognize."

He'd told them that the seed had probably been planted on a dark, blustery afternoon when he'd accompanied two senators from the Senate Intelligence Committee to a secret briefing by the Afghan special action group in the old Executive Office Building across from the White House. By then, late in the Carter administration's only term, its foreign policy objectives seemed in total disarray. After Iran and Afghanistan, it was obvious to him that a new beginning had to be made. The covert special action deliberations had grown more and more unreal, leading them further than ever from the flesh-and-blood national landscapes where these disasters had their root causes to the more and more specious world of the Washington strategy session.

On that dark afternoon almost ten months after the Afghan invasion, he and the two senators had been informed of the most recent punitive measures being cooked up for the Soviets as part of the National Security Council's policy of demonstrating to Moscow that its Afghan initiative couldn't remain cost-free. Afghanistan had mountains, deserts, xenophobic tribesmen and rebellious Muslim fanatics; yet to the NSC briefers sitting about the long oak table that day, Moscow's Afghan adventure might have taken place on the moon, in a wholly friction-free environment in which the Soviets were immune to any of the hazards of the occupying power except for the gimmicks that handful of bureaucrats was plotting.

The briefing was chaired by a senior NSC deputy, a gray-haired academic and theoretician whom Wilson had seen transformed over three years from a rumpled, fussy, indecisive meddler into a frantic activist and busybody, a sorcerer's apprentice, obsessed by the necromancy of the covert assets he controlled. So Wilson had sat there on yet another afternoon, listening to the deputy describe the latest covert scenarios to convince the two senators of the integrity of Carter's aggressive new line toward the Soviets—orchestrating Pakistani military help here, Egyptian gun and ammo support there, Saudi financing for this operation, European support for that, all of them picayunish, irrelevant, and inane, worthy of some third world mediocrity, like the old Savak, but not of the U.S., whose NSC staffers seemed inspired most of all by some squalid imitation of the old Kennedy machismo, but they were two decades too late. Years earlier they could command as much as seventy percent of the industrial world's assets, invoke allegiances, orchestrate alliances, and command loyalties at the drop of a hat. Now they were reduced to Halloween night high jinks to harass the Soviets. They could no longer command the political, financial, or moral assets to play the Great Game, but were as bankrupt as Chrysler, cooking up dollar rebates to buy the Pakistanis, promotional hardware to bring in the Egyptians, and Awacs planes to lure in the Saudis. What would George Marshall have thought? It was obvious. Their era had passed.

Their operations were only gimmicks, quick fixes, like the disastrous Iran rescue mission. That, too, had just been a technical production, staffed out by a small clique of well-intending military experts from the Joint Chiefs and the Pentagon, those new soldier-technicians who inhabited a kind of finite, self-contained, dust-free research cell that might be useful in replicating the environmental vacuums of space for NASA but weren't the kind of laboratories where the *E. coli* of the political world were to be found. The fine dust sent up by the storm in the Iranian desert had found those flaws quickly enough.

So he'd decided to leave. There was nothing complicated or unusual about his decision. It was a matter of choosing the appropriate time. The discussion he had heard that blustery afternoon in the EOB had merely crystallized an uneasiness that had been growing for years. The gimmicks they had described that day, like the ones you could read about today, no longer represented answers to the problems they faced but were an escape from them, the stategies of weakness or cowardice disguised as strength. It was as simple as that.

Wilson had spoken too much and now he regretted it. He finished his coffee, which had grown cold.

"Your own experience could be quite helpful to us," McVey said finally. "The Center, as you may have heard, is in a dreadful state."

"The Center?" Wilson asked.

"Yes; didn't Ed tell you?"

Fletcher filled his coffee cup again.

"It's what Angus wants to talk to you about," Donlon said. "Helping him reorganize the Center down in Foggy Bottom."

"As I said, it's in terrible shape," McVey added. "It seems to have gotten away from us."

Wilson didn't have a chance to reply. Fletcher's cardamom-scented breath breathed against his ear.

"Was it milk or sugar, sir?" he asked with renewed respect.

5.

In 1975, Wilson had heard that someone had offered the Nixon library fund a million dollars if the ex-President would consent to psychoanalysis within fifteen months of his departure from office. The offer had reportedly been conveyed through a former White House aide who'd returned with Nixon to San Clemente after those final disastrous days. The rumor reached Wilson through a senior NSC staff member, over lunch in the White House mess. He'd given it little notice at the time and supposed it another bit of apocrypha dug up from the Watergate wallow, where a few journalists were still mucking about. Within a month the rumor had reached the Washington press corps, which livened it up a bit and fleshed out the details.

According to one press account, the million dollar offer had been made by an obscure little policy research institute hidden away in a handful of dowdy Victorian residences in Washington's Foggy Bottom between George Washington University and the Watergate. Endowed privately in the late forties and the recipient of numerous government grants and research contracts since, the institute was called the Center for Contemporary Studies, and consisted of a small permanent staff and a handful of visiting scholars and annual fellows pursuing research projects funded by the government, by universities upon occasion, and, less frequently, by private corporations. There was nothing unusual about the Center's activities. A dozen similar policy and research institutes were scattered in and about Washington—most of them larger. What kept them from public attention wasn't so much the sensitivity of a few projects but the banality of the remainder, much of which was the usual technical rubbish that various patrons, most often government agencies, are willing to pay large sums of money in sponsoring. Like federal bureaucrats, academic scholars are often uneasy about their work-in-progress, most of which is utterly irrelevant, and if they can't conceal them by a *Secret* or *Confidential* stamp, an impenetrable title will do. A lot of the Center's work was of this nature.

The Nixon story gave the media the chance to invade the Center's privacy. What they found was an obscure caucus of reclusive scholars, dusty offices, dark corridors, and smelly laboratories, all of which seemed slightly subversive. The inquiries were poorly handled by the Center's director and his deputy. The former was an aging Russian specialist, who denied any knowledge of the Nixon offer. A young reporter discovered that he'd worked for the OSS during the war and was subsequently a CIA office director. After digging about for two months, he credited him with an OSS plan, conceived during World War II, to infest the Japanese atoll of Iwo Jima in the Pacific with twenty thousand rabid fruit bats in lieu of the Marine invasion that subsequently cost so many lives. He was also revealed to be the architect of a CIA effort to clandestinely infect the Russian wheatfields of the Ukraine with a species of wheat-stem sawfly immune to parasites and insecticides. The bugs were to be carried to the Soviet granary by the prevailing seasonal winds from the Black Sea launch area. In a letter to the newspaper that carried the story, the director denied both charges, but in such unfortunate detail—the flora and fauna of Iwo Jima, a meteorological description of the Ukraine in the months before harvesting, and the morphology of the wheat-stem sawfly—that any reader curious enough to plod through the text would have concluded that the science of the denial was so much more encyclopedic than the accusation that both propositions had obviously received detailed high-level consideration.

The deputy director was equally inept. In an interview with a newspaperman, he denied that the million-dollar offer had been made to the Nixon library fund. He was a pipe smoker, who happened to be breaking in a new pipe that day. While he lit and relit it, he also made an excellent case for Nixon's psychoanalysis and ended by urging that the ex-President come forward immediately, for posterity's sake, to deliver himself to a well-known California psychiatrist. MAKE A CLEAN BREAST OF IT, DICK! was the banner line, but what the reporter failed to tell his readers was that the deputy was a psychohistorian and a scholar of the neuroses of leadership, Republican or Democrat, Russian, French, Israeli, or American. Most readers concluded that the Center, like many other Nixon critics, was engaged in a deliberate campaign of harassment and persecution of the former President through the public suggestion that he badly needed clinical help.

The press reports had two consequences. A political holdover in the Ford White House ordered an executive review of all government contracts held by the Center, and the veil of anonymity was lifted from the Center's founder and chief patron, Angus McVey.

He was described by one Sunday supplement writer as an eccentric millionaire and horseman who'd long been a heavy contributor to the Democratic party and to various left-wing causes, a sort of liberal equipoise to the many fruity Texas tycoons and their right-wing billions, but a naïf himself who subsidized the Center and its mercenary scholars to cut the canvas of history to his own baroque design. American wealth had traditionally bought up European artworks and resettled them in mausoleums which bore their family names and had become national shrines; why not history as well? The Sunday supplement writer offered two anecdotal insights into the character of the Center and its founder. One was an original letterhead from 1949 which paraphrased below the masthead a Burckhardt quotation suggesting that history was pathological in nature. The second was a comment by the director of another Washington policy institute, of contrasting views, claiming that neither McVey nor his Center was taken seriously by more sophisticated policy groups, such as his own, which referred to the Center as the History Is Bunk Club.

The press accounts were inaccurate. The Center had begun as a serious research institute, well and favorably known by a number of federal agencies. It had been originally funded by Angus McVey in the late forties for the analysis of political behavior, especially that faceless Soviet totalitarianism confronting the uneasy West across the rubble of Europe. The Center's work on the Soviet apparatchiki was original and useful, anticipating by a half dozen years the office for the analysis of personality and behavior in the CIA scientific intelligence division, which the Center helped organize and staff. Much of the Center's original purpose departed with the creation of the latter. By the early sixties, the Center's contracts with the CIA were negligible and the bulk of its government research contracts came from other executive agencies, most of them for highly specialized behavioral studies.

In addition, Angus McVey wasn't the dilettante described by the press. The youngest son of a Nova Scotia–born mining, timber, utilities, and shipping magnate, he was a millionaire several score over, but not a horseman. The Virginia estate had been owned by his second wife, who'd died in the early sixties. He wasn't an amateur scholar but a professional historian, had taken a doctorate at Harvard, where he'd taught for two painful years before he was forced to resign, victimized by that same morbid affliction which had blighted his youth, devastated his middle years, and finally driven him to the Virginia countryside; which made it physically impossible for him to speak in front of an audience, attend a dinner party with more than a half dozen guests present, mingle in any sort of crowd in which he was recognized, or even chair the annual meeting of the Center's board of directors. After he'd fled Harvard, he'd gone to Europe to spend two years in analysis, but had ended up working toward a medical degree in Berlin. Those years had helped him understand his affliction but not control it—the facial paralysis, the shriveled vocal cords, the hyperventilation, but most terribly of all the palsied hands and neck, tremors which inevitably produced spasms so grotesque that the Harvard undergraduates who'd witnessed them referred to him as Old Anguish McVey. Many were convinced he was an epileptic. But the hysteria or delirium to which he was prey had no physiological base. It was his struggle to understand those psychic demons within that led him from the dance of history to medicine and finally to psychohistory, two decades before the term passed into popular usage.

With the establishment of the Center, clinical psychiatrists might have concluded that McVey had achieved a kind of symbolic transference and found the peace for which he was searching. But there was no peace; the music played on, and the mad manic dance continued.

"I recall someone did raise the question of asking Nixon's collaboration," McVey explained, rattling the bone china coffee cup to the saucer, eyes pathetically downcast, "but not for analysis. I recall that one of our consultant radiologists proposed a brain scan, an X-ray of the cerebellum, what they call a computerized axial tomography, but I didn't believe he was serious. He may have discussed it with someone else, outside the Center. Eventually it found its way into print, I regret to say."

"So it wasn't for psychoanalysis at all," Wilson said.

"Oh, no," McVey responded quickly. "I doubt that analysis would have helped at all. I think most public figures reach a point where self-discovery is no longer possible. Any attempt at self-disclosure that required his cooperation would have been totally impossible. I would hope that he's found some peace of mind, Mr. Nixon, that he's rid himself of these self-disguises, but I'm not hopeful." The tremors were fainter now, barely visible.

Dusk was creeping up the hill. The Virginia skyline was a purple seam across the tall windows. The fire clicked with dying heat beyond the brass fender.

"It might be that the endocrinologists could have drawn a useful portrait," McVey added, eyes drawn to the cherry coals. "It seems clear that he was a pituitary-ridden individual with a fairly brisk adrenal development. Or so Dr. Foster thinks. There may have been some pathological complications."

Wilson didn't understand what he was talking about. "Who is Dr. Foster?" he asked.

"The acting director of the Center. A historian, not a medical man at all, but he's very keen on endocrinology as a collateral tool in explaining behavior. It's still very primitive."

Wilson asked about arms control and disarmament studies, and McVey admitted that the Center had done very little.

"I'm afraid we're a little behind the times these days," he admitted, "a bit disorganized. We need to regroup, reorganize. Our Soviet studies were quite good in their time—Khrushchev, Brezhnev, most of the Politburo, Castro too at a very early stage—but now there's an entirely new set of problems emerging. Most of our behaviorist studies these days are for the National Institute of Health—"

"The Center's gotten off the track," Donlon intruded. "The technicians have taken over."

"The technological determinists," McVey said. "Yes, this whole new class has emerged, men who are completely swallowed up by their technological or engineering disciplines but who have absolutely no sense of the historical or political context. Or even the moral one, for that matter. So we need to restructure, reorganize."

"Angus would like you to take a look at the Center, talk to Dr. Foster, a few of the staff, and maybe make some recommendations," Donlon said.

"If you're thinking about reorganizing," Wilson said, "I know someone who could do a much better job. He's a natural."

"Who is that?"

"Nick Straus."

McVey looked to Ed Donlon for guidance, but Donlon shook his head. "Maybe a few years ago, but not now, no. Nick's stumbling over his shoestrings right now. I saw him last week getting off the Bluebird out at Langley with some bird colonel. I don't think he even remembered me. Anyway, he's over at DIA. Angus is talking about a six-month contract, maybe longer."

"Why don't I take a look first," Wilson said. "Then we can talk."

"You might be interested in a monograph the Center prepared last spring," McVey said, rising. "An in-house study for a colloquium the Center sponsored on the Persian Gulf. It was quite good. It shows the kind of problems the President faces these days." He crossed to a small oak cabinet against the wall and opened a small drawer. "I don't have a copy here, but I had Carter index it."

"The other Carter," Donlon explained. "Carter, the in-house librarian."

"It dealt with the Carter-Brzezinski relationship after the Afghanistan crisis," McVey continued, warming to his subject. "The mobile deployment force, the new Carter doctrine, and so forth. Dr. Foster gave it a whimsical title, 'Dorothy and the Wizard of Oz.' I suppose that defines rather well the relationship of the President to his national security adviser, doesn't it? At least until this present White House. You might ask Dr. Foster for a copy when you talk to him." He closed the drawer, wrote the title and control number on a slip atop the cabinet, and handed it to Haven Wilson. "I find Dr. Brzezinski rather curious, typical of the problems we face, not at all like Kissinger, who resembles a male eunuchoid, but thymo-centric as well. That's Dr. Foster's jargon, by the way. He's a student of Kissinger, but his analyses are often hard to follow. Brzezinski is far simpler." McVey turned to Ed Donlon. "You've met Dr. Rankin, haven't you?"

"Just once."

"Dr. Rankin has the Lenin letters. She and Foster didn't get along and I suggested she work out here. She's staying just down the hill. Shall we look in?"

"So you do studies on U.S. diplomatic personalities as well," Wilson asked. "People like Kissinger and Brzezinski."

"Oh, yes," McVey said. "In these times, we must. I suppose they're much more important these days, much more important. It's the pathology we have to come to grips with, ours more than theirs."

He led them through a rear door, across a tile-floored sun porch, and into a small mud room, where he removed the sheepskin slippers and pulled on another pair of high-top gum boots. On an antique wooden rack nearby were a dozen pairs of hacking, riding, and wet-weather boots. A few velvet-covered riding helmets and cloth caps hung from pegs overhead. McVey slipped into a rain slicker and led them outside to the stone terrace. The light had faded and a gray mist hovered in the air.

". . . In a way Brzezinski somewhat typifies this new technocratic class. For them, technological innovation has always represented a kind of deus ex machina that will liberate the West from its current paralysis caused by the absolute decline of its political capital. I mean, what sensible man is a social democrat these days, or even a liberal?"

McVey's voice had grown stronger in the darkness, as if his body had been left behind, hung on a peg in the mud room. Wilson felt the fog against his face as he searched for the stone walk beneath his feet, and for a moment the unreality of the afternoon struck him with depressing famil-iarity. It was as if he were back again in the EOB, listening to the woolly-haired NSC deputy drone on about the latest covert action plan.

". . . He simply has no faith, you see, no secular faith," McVey contin-ued passionately, "except in the technological sense. For him, the Western political imagination is bankrupt, no longer fertile, like the estates of the Polish diplomatic gentry from which he comes. He can't return. This, incidentally, is why I'm wary of émigré policy experts, East Europeans in particular. Their imaginations are a lost childhood, like Nabokov's. In any case, this is why Brzezinski is so fascinated by technology—these are the new feudal estates. So they invent all this pseudoscientific terminology, this laughable mumbo-jumbo. A diplomat-intellectual shopping in the high-technology PX. For such men, technological innovation will do what Western political and social thought can no longer do—rescue the Western world from its spiritual and moral paralysis to prove its superiority in material terms. Through technology, the Western world is free to reinvent itself. The Soviet mind, petrified by the dead hand of the past, can't. A historical fossil. Watch your footing there; the stones are wet. Don't you agree, Ed?"

"I think so," Donlon said, but Wilson doubted he'd been listening. In Donlon's indifference he understood why he'd been invited that day. Donlon had been asked by his law firm to advise its client, the Center, on its reorganization problems. Never one to overtax himself, Donlon had thought conveniently of Haven Wilson. That was the way the old-boy network operated, a system that seldom did justice to anyone.

"But of course the engineers on the joint chiefs think the same way," McVey droned on, his breath a ghostly vapor on the raw, dark air. "So does the Pentagon—engineering solutions, you see. Sensor barriers in Vietnam, MIRVed warheads, and now the MX missile shell game. But they have it all wrong, you see, just as you were saying earlier, Haven. They believe Tom Swift engineering and technological breakthroughs make diplomacy unnecessary. Don't negotiate with the Russians, who are technological primitives, barbarians; simply outgimmick them. But that's the whole point. It was technology as much as pathology that got us into this dreadful mess. We've always had the individual capacity for self-destruction, for suicide; now we have this insane capacity for global annihilation. This new technological class only brings it closer. Being political or social primitives themselves, they concede the social and political realm to the Russians and claim the technological realm for the West. They miss the whole point. It's our very technology that makes diplomacy and political understanding so essential. . . ."

McVey's indignant voice faded away as they emerged out of the darkness and into the soft yellow glow of the brass coach lamps flanking the low doors of the stone guest cottage. He rang the bell, the chimes sounded from within, and he pushed open the door. "Hello," he called. "Am I disturbing you? Anyone home?"

"In here," a woman's voice answered. "Time for a drinkie?"

The hall and living room were low-ceilinged and partially beamed, the old plaster walls bulged here and there. The pine floors were uneven. Two fresh logs lay atop the mound of kindling in the fireplace, awaiting a match. On the low table nearby sat a tray holding a sterling silver cocktail shaker.

"I have two friends with me," McVey called to their invisible hostess.

"Friends?" She sounded disappointed. She joined them a minute later, a short woman without make-up, wearing a shapeless Ragg sweater with the sleeves pushed back, and a tweed skirt. Her dark hair was parted in the middle and teased out in a kind of wiry bush Haven Wilson's wife once described to him as the "ERA frazzle." A pencil was in one hand, a cigarette in the other. A pair of steel-rimmed bifocals was pulled far down on her pug nose.

McVey introduced them and she moved forward to shake their hands without enthusiasm, one shoulder dropped, foot thrust out in its mannish shoe, like the captain of a women's softball team meeting her opposite number at home plate. "Yeah, Donlon," she said negligently. "You're the lawyer going to get the Center reorganized. Why don't you begin by firing Foster?"

"That's not my decision."

"Just a suggestion."

Wilson thought her uncomfortable, her tone and gestures deliberately aggressive, a crude persona; yet her face was as much that of a child as of a woman.

"Pauline is working on the Lenin letters," McVey said. She turned to look at Wilson.

"You're with the Center?"

"No, just a visitor."

"He may help us with the reorganization," McVey said.

She continued to study Wilson. "I don't remember you. What's your field?"

"I'm a lawyer."

"Oh, God, not another one."

McVey looked sheepish. Donlon examined his watch with a sweeping gesture and proposed that they be on their way. McVey was disappointed, but Pauline Rankin seemed relieved.

The gatehouse at the foot of the long winding road was lit now and a green-uniformed security guard left the office and opened the gates as their headlights approached.

"Well, what do you think?" Donlon asked as they crossed the bridge.

Wilson didn't know what to think. McVey seemed to him the naïf he'd heard about, the Center an improbable collection of eccentrics enclosed in their own world, like the National Security Council, and Donlon merely a salaried retainer, attempting to provide a service. Washington's structures didn't change much, even in the private sector.

"What about these Lenin letters and Pauline Rankin?" he asked as they reached the hard-surfaced road. "What's that all about?"

"A woman professor who thinks Lenin's revolution wasn't really his but belonged to a woman named Inessa Armand," Donlon said. "Angus bought some letters from a Soviet émigré in Paris last year—Lenin's letters to her, smuggled out. According to Rankin, the letters prove that Inessa Armand was the brains behind the Bolshevik revolution. She's writing a book."

"I don't remember hearing the name. Who was Armand?"

"Some Frenchwoman who left her family and threw in with Lenin, lived with him for a while. She died in Russia in 1920, I think—typhus. She had Lenin's child, or so Rankin claims. She says the letters prove that too. She's a dyke."

"Who?"

"Rankin. You think I'm kidding?"

Wilson said nothing. They drove through Middleburg without stopping. "She's probably gone home by now," Donlon said, looking out at the illuminated entrance of the stone inn. "It's a shame, it's a shame with a woman like that. Horses. That's a hell of a way to have to get your sex."

"That's a stupid expression," Wilson said. "'Get your sex.' What is it—something a pharmacist hands out?"

But Donlon only laughed and turned on the radio.

Left for Wilson on Matthews' desk in the deserted real estate office that evening were two messages from Rita Kramer at her downtown hotel, asking him to call. He set them aside. Beneath was a flimsy envelope with his name scrawled on the front, barely legible, written in a thick, childlike hand. According to the typewritten note from the office receptionist, the envelope had been given her late that afternoon by a young man who hadn't identified himself.

Inside was a certified check drawn on a nearby suburban bank, payable to Haven Wilson for three hundred dollars. "For auto damages. Out of town for 3 months," read the block letters on the slip of paper clipped to the check. The note was signed *Davis,* but the name was in primitive block letters, not really a signature at all.

He stood silently at the desk, puzzling over its meaning. Three hundred dollars was an extravagance. The old station wagon was barely worth that. The check was strange, so was the signature, and on a misty autumn evening, alone in the office, a phone ringing somewhere downstairs in the darkness, that made him a little suspicious.

Part Two

1.

The lamps in the executive offices of the Pentagon and in the paneled seventh-floor suites at the State Department had been lit throughout the long gray autumn afternoon. A faint mist was still falling in the darkness beyond the draped windows. The lights from the homeward-bound cars and buses stretched down Twenty-third and Fourteenth streets and out across Memorial, Roosevelt, and Wilson bridges and on into the Virginia hills, an endless geometrical beading of white foci, strung and restrung in symmetrical loops along the boulevards and access roads. It had been a drizzly day, a day when affairs of state were susceptible to minor depression, the denial of blue skies and autumn vistas, a day when the powers of abstraction were prey to bronchial complaints, wet shoes and leaky umbrellas, stalled traffic on Capitol Hill and along Pennsylvania Avenue, planes grounded or delayed, taxis unavailable, limousines late, briefing papers damp, and appointments postponed.

Nick Straus had been working alone in the Pentagon suite that evening, shut away in a small windowless clutter of subterranean offices between B and C rings in the bowels of the building. The rooms occupied by the Defense Intelligence Agency's special-watch group lay behind a steel-clad door operated by a cipher lock. They were deserted now except for Straus, who stood nervously at the Xerox machine in the anteroom, copying documents.

The anteroom where the Xerox machine was located was known to the resident intelligence analysts as the Gallery because of its collection of covert posters and artworks tacked or stapled to the acoustical-tile wall above the gray rows of combination safes and bar-lock cabinets. Some were the products of the DIA graphics and visual aids section, drawn up at the request of the special-watch group. Others were less professional, slapstick jibes at the intelligence or policy establishment, dashed off by some anonymous wit. Others had been casually stolen from one of the many bulletin boards along the miles of Pentagon corridor, the original message altered in ways often obscure to everyone but the thief.

One of the oldest dated from the Watergate era, a three-foot-high poster carefully prepared by DIA graphics to the specifications of some watch group wag. At the top left was a grainy photograph of a sweating, beetle-browed, jittery-eyed Richard Nixon, and next to it, in bold letters, two questions: "Who Shafted Dick Nixon?" "Who Was Deep Throat?" Beneath the photo and the questions was an enormous open mouth, like some smoky grotto or subterranean cavern, dark with shadows, at the far end of which, near the epiglottis, sat a small candlelit figure in a rocking chair, a diminutive Whistler's Mother. The poster was scrawled with the conjectures of those who'd passed along the corridor over the years—"Al Haig?" "George Peterson?" "Bill Safire?" and a few other names—but the face that greeted those curious enough to lean forward to identify it wasn't a man's face at all but that of a Victorian spinster, shawl over her shoulders, lace at her throat, a puzzling, abstract smile haunting Pat Nixon's thin lips.

Nearby was a more recent poster, its message hand-scrawled on a Top Secret cover sheet: "CIA Intel Scoop: Why Did Anwar Sadat Really Go to Jerusalem?" The cover sheet, when lifted, revealed a sepia photograph, cut from some ancient European photomagazine, showing a battalion of steel-helmeted German soldiers goose-stepping through a cobbled street in the Rhineland. The answer, a sardonic comment on the DIA/CIA intelligence rivalry, lay in the caption beneath the photograph: "A clandestine reunion of the East Mediterranean directorate of the Waffen-SS." The heads of three of the German soldiers had been circled and identified in the margin: "SS Obergruppenführer Anwar Sadat," "SS Obergruppenführer Menachem Begin," and "SS Obergruppenführer Zbigniew Brzezinski."

Some punster had added a fourth name to a fourth figure, not among the Wehrmacht storm troopers, but in the grainy sidewalk crowd visible across the cobbled street just to the right elbow of the battalion guidon—a small blank-faced, jug-eared blond boy looking on, awestruck, from the curb. The head had been circled and identified in the margin with a felt-tipped pen: "U.S. Obergruppenwunderkind Jimmy Carter."

To the right of this poster was a much-enlarged reproduction of a U.S. satellite photograph taken on a winter afternoon some hundred and forty miles above Moscow. The resolution was not as fine as that obtained by recent satellite imagery but accurate enough so that the digitalized radio pulses revealed a score of figures just dispersing from the Palace of Congresses within the Kremlin walls, astrakhan and felt hats visible, like the Zil limousines and the mounds of snow heaped at the foot of the steps. The enlarged photo had been sent to the DIA special-watch group following an interagency squabble a number of years earlier involving the Air Force, DIA, CIA, and the Arms Control and Disarmament Agency in the interpretation of certain telemetry intercepted from the Soviet missile-testing facility at Tyuratam. The Air Force and the CIA had won the bureaucratic battle, and the gloating Air Force interpretation team had sent the photograph to DIA, captioned "Another Triumph for Air Force Technocracy." The photo had been taken on the day of an important Politburo meeting and Brezhnev was thought to be among the departing figures.

A disgruntled DIA analyst, one of the team losers, had penned in his own riposte, "And Another Victory for CIA/AF Photo-Interpretation!" attaching identities to those heavily bundled individuals meandering toward their limousines: "Dr. Spock (in dark glasses)"; "Joan Baez (carrying guitar case)"; and "Chairman Brezhnev and Jane Fonda (drums and vocal)."

Judged too sophisticated for the golf club literati at Air Force intelligence, the poster had remained in the Gallery.

Further along near the Xerox machine was a large multicolored poster from some long-forgotten Pentagon briefing session for a congressional committee, apportioning global shares of the U.S. foreign military assistance dollar, the largest of which went to Israel. Someone had mounted the graph in the A ring corridor not long after the 1973 Yom Kippur War, when Pentagon resentment at Israel's insatiable weapons demands was growing, not merely because of the political costs to the U.S. in the Arab world, but because many in the Pentagon were convinced that weapons transfers to Israel had seriously depleted U.S. inventories in Europe and elsewhere and had dangerously eroded U.S. military readiness.

A critic of U.S. economic and military support for Israel had scrawled in the caption: "Support Israel! Buy U.S. Savings Bonds." The poster had appeared originally in the corridor outside the office of an assistant secretary, but had been quickly removed by one of his deputies, who was often visited by officers from the Israeli defense attaché's office. It had reappeared in the DIA special-watch anteroom, a highly restricted area where unaccompanied visitors weren't allowed, a special pass was required, and senior officials seldom strayed. Over the years, additional in-house graffiti had been penned in, reflecting a growing cynicism about the Israeli lobby. "Support Golda's Goyim," one exhortation read: "Henry Jackson for SecDef!" Or: "Watch out for Meir's Mafioso on the Hill! Report all Congressional Briefings to FBI!"

But the most recent graffiti was more subtle, more elusive, and, for Nick Straus, more ominous. An early advocate of détente, of nuclear arms reductions and minimal deterrence, he'd paid a price for his policy views. The admonition which most depressed him was one scrawled on the poster just recently by an anonymous hand. It read: "Support Menachem Begin's New Irgun! Demolish Détente!"

He'd had no difficulty guessing its meaning.

But this rainy evening, his mind was on other things. He was copying a series of DIA and NSA intercepts describing Soviet troop movements along the Afghan and Iranian frontiers during the 1979 crisis. He'd already been retired from the Agency at the time, and these months were voids in his historical memory. An archivist by nature, solitary and tenacious, he was convinced that such fragments would inevitably yield a better logic to Soviet depredations than those credited to Moscow by the Carter innocents or the new chauvinists of the Reagan administration. In the overstuffed safes of the DIA special-watch group, he'd discovered a windfall of such documents, some dating to 1970.

He'd been copying them for three months now, choosing them selectively from the cache he'd discovered, but it was risky work. The noise of the Xerox machine muffled the sound of the cipher lock being operated in the corridor, and he'd once been surprised at the machine by a returning secretary who'd missed her car pool. He'd had difficulty explaining why these old documents interested him. What could he tell her—that the official or public version of Soviet activities from Cuba to Afghanistan was inaccurate and that successive U.S. administrations had known more of these clumsy reactive postures than they understood or had dared reveal?

He cleared the machine and looked quickly at a second folder of papers, a collection of intercepted Soviet messages deploying the airlift in 1973 to relieve the encircled Egyptian army trapped on the east bank of the Suez Canal. But these documents were familiar to him, intercepts he'd seen while still at the Agency; and he turned off the machine, relieved, assembled his copies in an envelope, and carried the folders back to the suite of deserted offices. Like the anteroom, these offices were lined with safes and cabinets, leaving barely enough room for the desks. He shared the outer room with two other analysts, one a Russian linguist, like himself, and the other an Air Force major. The two secretaries worked in alcoves just outside the two small rooms belonging to Colonel Dillon, the watch section chief, and his deputy.

On their desks, as on those in the outer office, lay the only conspicuous evidence of the special watch's mission, the daily monitoring of Soviet missile dispersion, movement, and replacement, from which was defined, by others, the calculus of Soviet strategic intent. This evidence stood on individual desktops: missile replicas distributed by a West Coast aerospace giant with a Washington staff twice the size of the Soviet embassy. Each desk in the section held a cluster of miniature missiles, Soviet as well as American, mounted on plastic pedestals and pointing toward the low acoustical ceiling. The small American Minuteman was dwarfed by the massive Soviet SS-20, a bone-and-city-crushing tyrannosaurus rex from the bogs of the Dnieper, all the more ominous when compared with the graceful American bird, a dove from the cities of light, the product of a more sophisticated, more advanced evolutionary lineage. In recent months, the missile clusters had become popular Pentagon desk pieces. A more expensive chrome model, with nose cones opening up to become cigarette lighters, could be found in the larger, more prestigious offices.

Straus had taken the documents he'd been copying that evening from a bottom drawer of one of the safes in Colonel Dillon's office. Dillon was a former defense attaché in Moscow, a man of staff school intelligence and shaky historical memory, and his intellectual vagueness when dealing with anything less certain than the Soviet global design was responsible for the windfall of documents Nick Straus had discovered. The office had become a historical lumber room. Telegrams, intercepts, staff studies, and option papers that should have been retired years ago had been kept to nourish Colonel Dillon's dim historical wick. New safes and bar-lock cabinets had been moved in to accommodate the overflow, squeezing two of the special-watch staff out the front door to an adjacent office down the corridor.

Yet if Nick Straus was grateful for Colonel Dillon's obtuseness, he'd also begun to despair at ever completing his covert after-hours projects. How would he find the time to pilfer the most important documents from this vast archive and to write the definitive history of post-1972 Soviet foreign policy, stripped of its burden of hysteria, secrecy, cant, and executive privilege, like his still top-secret analysis of the Cuban missile crisis.

The project had become an obsession. He had too little time. Always the first to arrive, always the last to leave, he spent twelve to thirteen hours a day in the special-watch catacomb. His weekends were no longer his own. In his race against time, he wasn't aware of the ghost he'd become. His hair was thinner, his face grayer. He was slightly stoop-shouldered. The flannel and tweed suits he'd fancied since his Harvard graduate days had given way to cotton wash-and-wear, whatever the season, the better to ease the dry prickly heat of the windowless, low-ceilinged cubicles that had become his tomb. The pebble-grained oxfords had been replaced by black electrician's shoes with ripple soles, which he'd purchased in an army-navy store in the Pentagon mall on the advice of a Navy chief he'd overheard one day in the Pentagon cafeteria. The chief had been rambling on to his luncheon companion about the ripple soles and how they eased the hemorrhoids, prostate spasms, and muscle aches brought on by the impact of the Pentagon's miles of concrete corridors. Nick Straus, who experienced similar complaints and had been to a doctor to find relief, immediately folded away his

New York Times, pushed his tray back, and rushed down to the mall to buy a pair.

The others in the section saw nothing unusual in his habits. They'd discovered a mild little man who could be trusted to stay behind and lock up after they rushed off to join their car pools or their racquetball partners, someone who would make sure that no safes were left unlocked, no classified documents forgotten in an out box or on a desktop, and that the coffeepot in the anteroom was unplugged, rinsed out, and ready for the following morning's brew. A few of his younger, more vigorous colleagues in the special-watch section, those late to arrive and quick to depart, might have attributed his long hours and his willingness to substitute for them during their weekend or holiday duty hours to some kind of domestic problem, to an unhappy life or an unathletic physique, or simply to that Jewish melancholia they saw lurking in those sad brown eyes. He'd been retired from the Agency, eased out by an aggressive beltway defense consulting firm, four of whose senior staff had joined the Reagan administration, but was rescued by an old friend, Leyton Fischer, a prim, fussy deputy in policy and plans at the Pentagon who was searching for experienced Soviet specialists to improve DIA's analytical base. But it was a nonpolicy position, after all, a humiliation for a man of his talent and experience. So Nick Straus seemed to the others in the section a pathetic case, a man desperate to succeed but who wouldn't, already beginning to fade into inconsequentiality, a man who, had he not become an intelligence analyst, would surely have become a scholar or librarian, and perhaps with better success, a shy, solitary little mouse, hidden behind the wainscoting.

On his knees now in the corner of Colonel Dillon's office, the bottom drawer of the combination safe open, Nick Straus tried to force the borrowed folder of NSA intercepts into the drawer. His face was damp, his palms wet. The phone had rung twice. He thought he heard a footfall in the anteroom, and got up quickly to look. The anteroom was deserted, but he heard footsteps in the corridor beyond. He waited until they passed and returned to Dillon's office. He couldn't force the file folder in: the drawer was crammed with documents. He searched for the metal release on the rear panel that held the files upright, but the panel was flush against the back of the drawer. He pulled the drawer forward as far as he could and discovered a tattered manila envelope, folded double, thrust awkwardly into the end of the drawer. After he removed it, the borrowed folder slipped in. He unfolded the thick envelope to return it to the drawer and saw the red crayon notation on the flap: *Eyes Only Intercepts: No Dissem.*

He couldn't recall seeing the envelope earlier and now he opened it curiously, removing a bundle of tissue copies of NSA and FBI phone intercepts. Puzzled, he carried them to Colonel Dillon's desk and leafed through them. Most were transcriptions of phone conversations dating from the early seventies. Some were direct phone taps; others were NSA intercepts of domestic and transatlantic telephone circuits. The participants included various executive agency bureaucrats, including State Department, ACDA, Pentagon, and White House officials, a few senators and their aides, congressmen, defense industry lobbyists, political pressure groups, and a handful of foreign embassies in Washington.

Among them he recognized the defense consulting firm he'd worked for briefly after he'd been retired from the Agency. The firm's founder and board chairman was there, General Gawpin, who'd been recently selected by the White House for a senior position with the Arms Control and Disarmament Agency. Les Fine, a former Senate staffer, Kissinger associate at the National Security Council, and now the Pentagon's deputy arms control strategist, was also named.

He paused over a phone intercept of a talk between Les Fine and an unidentified military attaché at the Israeli embassy, fearing the worst:

> Fine: We've got to get him off the Geneva delegation right away; he's giving us problems.
> Attaché: I know. We've tried. Why don't you talk to the senator again, get him to call ACDA?
> Fine: I've tried, but he wants to wait. The point is, Afghanistan is box office these days and we've got to make the most of it while we can, finish them off, bury any possibility of reaching any agreement, whether at Geneva or anyplace else.
> Attaché: Box office? (Laughter) Whose line is that?
> Fine: Mine. The point is to use it to the max. We don't want to let them put us back in the box again, like they did in '73; never. We can't live with that. . . .

Straus read on in dismay. He could understand those who opposed arms control, détente, or any easing of international tensions out of ignorance or their own barbaric fears, but he couldn't forgive those far more sophisticated minds who opposed it in pursuit of their own narrow realpolitik, as this attaché and Les Fine were doing.

He didn't know the man the two were conspiring to remove from the Geneva arms talks. It hadn't been Straus but it might have been, and the memory of his own misfortunes returned—first banishment, then retirement, and most recently dismissal. He sat for a long time at Colonel Dillon's desk, reading through the phone logs and finding additional fragments of an informal kind of conspiracy, organized by a few tragically misguided zealots and ideologues working under diplomatic or humanitarian cover.

As he left the suite that night, his eyes rested for a moment on the old poster hung near the Xerox machine:

SUPPORT MENACHEM BEGIN'S NEW IRGUN! DEMOLISH DÉTENTE!

He decided, as he closed the door, that he might have to do something about that.

2.

Rita Kramer had been waiting alone in Wilson's borrowed office when he returned from the Fairfax County courthouse that afternoon. Her raw presence was already in possession of the second-floor suite, as inescapable as the scent he'd identified in the stairwell and in the gold-carpeted reception room. She seemed more subdued that day. Her dark eyes and wide mouth were as flawlessly made up as before, but she was tired. Her auburn hair was drawn severely from her forehead and temples, small shadows lay like bruises under her eyes, and the harsh light of the office betrayed a coarseness high on the cheekbones that cosmetics couldn't disguise. She'd arrived in a taxi and wanted to see Grace Ramsey's house for a final time. It was the only house she'd seen that interested her, even if the price was too high, and if she didn't negotiate a contract soon, her husband would arrive from Los Angeles. She didn't want to spend another week looking at houses and she had no faith in her husband's taste.

"We'd end up in some blintzy bachelor condo, and that's not what I want," she said. "Maybe Artie's got a lot of things going for him, but taste isn't one of them."

They talked for a while in Wilson's office and waited for Mrs. Polk to return, but Mrs. Polk was delayed and Wilson drove her out to the Ramsey house himself.

"I might have known you were a Democrat," she said as she saw the bumper sticker on the old station wagon. "Where'd you get this bomb? Something left over from the Carter campaign committee?"

The day was partially sunny, with broken clouds overhead, driven from the north.

"I didn't mind getting away from L.A. for a while," she told him as they drove away, "but I'm not that crazy about Washington, not yet, anyway. I told that Georgetown broker Artie wanted to be on the Potomac and she showed me Alexandria, Georgetown, and Capitol Hill. Artie wouldn't live there. He wants to see the Potomac when he gets up in the morning— that's the last thing he said to me before he put me on the plane in L.A.

He's patriotic that way. He wants the goddamned Potomac in his back-yard, wants the Washington Monument and the Lincoln Memorial there when he gets up in the morning, like some grade school kid."

"You could find something in Georgetown."

"Washington's a jungle after dark—don't you read the papers? I don't want to get mugged; I don't want potheads or black guys jiving me when I walk down the street, either. I looked at this town house on Capitol Hill, did I tell you? There were mom and pop tourists from out of town parked all over the place—these tacky campers." She opened her purse and took out a cigarette case. "What I want is a little privacy, someplace with a little class where Artie can entertain his political and business friends and feel good about it, not like some little Lithuanian fur trimmer who'd cut his wrists to break into the big time. It's about time word got around. Artie's arrived."

"Georgetown's got privacy," he said.

"Are you kidding?" she said. "There's no privacy down there; they'd kill him in Georgetown. Basically Artie's a very low-key guy, very informal. He'd walk down to the deli on a Saturday night in one of those crazy sports getups of his and someone would bring him home in a doggy bag, potato salad and all. Don't you read the papers? Anyway, I spent four days with those Georgetown real estate women. They've all got Bryn Mawr accents, like the old Kennedy crowd."

"Bryn Mawr. Is that where you're from originally? Pennsylvania?"

"No. New Jersey. Why?"

"Just curious. Where in New Jersey?"

"A small town; you wouldn't know it."

"I'm from a small town myself—down in Virginia."

"Goody for you. So what's that explain, your small-town manners?"

She was holding a cigarette between her fingers, unable to find a light. "Sorry." He gave her a package of book matches.

"Where do you live, anyway?" she continued, her voice gathering disap-proval as she remembered her futile attempts to get in touch with him.

"Out in Virginia. It's an unlisted phone."

"That's what I mean. A real estate lawyer with an unlisted phone. You're a little weird, Wilson, like that Matthews who shows me the Ramsey house that day and suddenly takes a powder to Florida, like this lawyer for Grace Ramsey who won't show his face." She watched him, waiting for a reply, but Wilson said nothing. He didn't intend to get into another brawl about the price of Grace Ramsey's house. "Anyway," she said, "maybe Artie would seem a little weird to that Georgetown crowd. They'd break his heart down there. No privacy, no views, back gardens about as big as a hot tub, and all your neighbors looking in. . . ."

Her voice died away and they rumbled on in silence. Traffic was light at that hour of afternoon and Wilson had had the same curious feeling that had frequently come to him since he'd left the Hill that he ought to be someplace else—in a staff meeting, taking notes at a hearing, marking up a piece of legislation.

"What kind of business is your husband in?" he asked.

"Don't get nosy." Surprised, he laughed, and she turned immediately. "What's so funny?"

"You tell me he's Lithuanian, an ex–fur trimmer who wears crazy outfits and might get his heart broken by the Bryn Mawr crowd down in George-town and you tell me not to get nosy."

"You mean I'm inconsistent. Maybe. Artie says the same thing some-times, that I'm too impulsive, too personal, that I talk too much some-times. But that's just the way I am. Artie does a lot of things. He's got a garment factory in L.A., only it's not really a factory. He has an interest in this computer software firm out in Van Nuys, a couple of nursing homes, an FM station. Real estate too, out in Palmdale. I can't keep track." The car had grown warm. She lowered the window and let the fur coat slip from her shoulders. "But he's also very patriotic."

"You've said that a couple of times," Wilson recalled. "I've been trying to figure out what you mean."

"Just that, patriotic. He wants to come to Washington to help out. What's so strange about that?"

"Nothing. You mean help the government?"

"The administration—help get things back on the track." She was watching him suspiciously. "What'd you think I meant?"

"I wasn't sure. There are a lot of California patriots in town these days— ex-actors, ex-producers, ex-advertising people. All of them want to help out, like this former movie man with the big hit a few years ago, the one that expressed the Republican mood out in California. Reagan was so impressed he brought him to Washington to head up the U.S. information service."

"What film was that?" she asked mistrustfully.

"*Snow White and the Three Stooges*," Wilson said. "Now he does all his filming in the White House cabinet room."

She smiled but didn't laugh. "Very funny, but I wouldn't want Artie to hear a crack like that. Edelman told me you used to be a government lawyer. What did you do—harass the taxpayers for IRS?"

"No, just a nine-to-five bureaucrat, like most of the people around here."

"That's a pretty grubby life, isn't it?"

"Not bad."

"Where'd you work?"

"The Railroad Retirement Board."

Her gaze was still steady, her silence hostile. "What'd you do?"

He shrugged. "A claims adjuster, ballast bed and firebox casualties."

"You're a goddamned liar, Wilson. You know who you remind me of? I even told Edelman after that first day: 'That Wilson reminds me of someone; I know I've seen him before.' Finally I remembered. You remind me of my Uncle Frank."

"Is that a compliment?"

"In a way, maybe. He was my mother's brother."

Wilson was beginning to feel at home behind the wheel. *You ever been to the Grand Ole Opry?* Mrs. Fillmore had asked.

She told him her uncle visited them every summer in the small town in New Jersey when she was growing up. He was a bachelor and a traveling salesman—hardware, screen doors, embalming fluid for a time, floor wax, fire insurance; she'd forgotten what else. He would take her for summer drives in his company coupé, down to the dairy plant for ice cream or out to the country for fresh corn, sometimes a watermelon, and even more infrequently, cantaloupe, a rarity for her in those days. She would never forget the smell of fresh cantaloupe on the seat beside her as they were driving back to her parents' house.

"When we were out driving, he'd always make up these crazy stories about where we were going. He was always dressed up in a coat, a seersucker coat and a straw hat, sometimes in what my dad used to call an ice cream suit, with a little bow tie. He was shy, except when he was with me. I was ten or eleven, and he'd make up these crazy stories. I think he liked kids better than adults—oh, God, I'm not going to get into that. Anyway, that's all he had, the company coupé, the ice cream suit, and all these crazy stories. Just a bachelor all his life. I was working a club in Reno when I got a telegram about him—Jesus, why'd I ever start this?"

"What happened?"

"A little river town in Ohio. He jumped off the bridge. Why'd you have to ask me? It wasn't until I got into analysis that I understood. Anyway, all those crazy answers were what reminded me. You're a Democrat too, just like my dad was. You people never learn."

"Learn what?"

"That you've got to do it yourself, that no one else is going to do it for you—free enterprise, not carrying the government around on your backs all these years, the way Artie's been doing. What's this place?"

"Rosslyn," he said. He drove down the ramp and onto George Washington Parkway along the Potomac. A few oaks along the slopes still held their autumn color, the last to go. The Georgetown skyline across the river was splashed with sunshine here and there, roofs, turrets, and spires bright against massed purple clouds pregnant with rain. "You could probably find a small place over there," he said, watching her turn to look. "The Ramsey place is pretty big."

"It suits me," she replied. "Just the two of us, but it suits me." She gazed down at the river. "Do you have any children?"

"Two. Grown up now."

"That's nice. Artie's frisky, but not in the family way." She noticed his expression. "Don't be shocked, you'll disappoint me—someone with no come-on, just some down-home bullshit, driving a hand-me-down car. You're not like the rest of this real estate crowd, so don't try to high-hat me. You're a taxpayer too, so don't be so hard on this California administration. What happened—did the Reagan crowd push you out, tell you to take a walk?"

"No, it wasn't like that."

"So you just decided to take a walk anyway and end up in a real estate brokerage with interest rates at twenty percent. Sure, honey, don't kid me. You're probably one of those bureaucrats that got dumped, some expert at spending the taxpayers' money. What kind of legal expert were you?"

"Just the usual Washington expert."

"A lawyer, that's what Edelman said. Like who in particular? Come on, tell me."

"Like any of them—the people over across the river in the office buildings, the guys back there at the Pentagon, the ones that spend all day calibrating their delivery systems for a five-thousand-mile ICBM crunch, right on target, and then go out to the parking lots and can't find their cars."

"You really are cynical, aren't you?"

"No, I just live here."

The winding lane led from Chain Bridge Road to a set of locked iron gates set within stone pillars. Young junipers and older spruce lined the long drive to the parking area in front of the stone-and-redwood house built atop the cliff a few hundred feet above the chutes of the Potomac. Wilson was curious about the house, which he'd never seen, curious too about Grace Ramsey, whom he'd never met, although he'd known her husband, a senior deputy at the Agency. A groundkeeper in worn dungarees was on his knees in a flower bed, planting bulbs. He alternated with another groundkeeper from the Maryland farm belonging to Grace Ramsey's brother-in-law to tend the house and garden five days a week. At night and during the weekends, the two were replaced by a guard from a

Rosslyn security service. In the ancient black pickup truck parked in the drive were three rhododendron shrubs, their roots in burlap.

The air was chilly, still damp from the late morning rain. The vapor brightened the thick carpet of lawn that stretched toward the enclosing woods. A tennis court was concealed by an ivy-covered trellis just at the treeline. She stopped on the walk to look back toward the dark palisade of trees.

"Privacy," she said.

"Nice."

She glanced at him reproachfully. "Nice doesn't describe it."

A sunken living room with a soaring ceiling looked out over the river, but the room was too large and too cold. The glass doors of a small sun room opened to a terrace that seemed to hang suspended out over the gorge of the Potomac. In the far corner was a swimming pool, covered with a blue nylon tarpaulin. A few odd pieces of furniture remained in a few of the rooms and some showed signs of an occasional occupancy. Wilson was surprised. He'd supposed the house was empty. In the long dining room was a seventeenth-century French table with a single chair. A mat, a plate, silver cutlery, and a wineglass sat in front of it. A collection of pewter was still arrayed on the matching sideboard. Above it hung an old oil painting, the woman's face dim with age, the features as blank as a mushroom, the gender known only by the white cap the woman wore.

On the upper level to the north was one of several bedrooms overlooking the river. This one was fully furnished. Fresh linen was on the bed and a few books stood on the night table. A package of cigarettes lay next to an enamel cigarette box. Rita Kramer told him that during her previous visits the upstairs bedroom had been locked, like the small study downstairs.

"So she comes and goes, like a ghost," she said, standing inside the door. The bedroom was furnished in white—a deep white rug, white shutters and drapes, a white French Empire bed and dressing table, a white marble bath. She crossed the room on tiptoes, stopped to look around, seemed to relax again, and then, curiously, opened the door to the dressing room closet. A few garments still hung there. She pulled one sleeve from the rack and then another. "Expensive," she said. "Chic too, but a little out of style. But she certainly has taste." She closed the door and moved on to the white marble bath, where she studied the tub set in the marble shelf, turned on the faucets, picked up a sliver of soap to sniff, and then opened the medicine cabinet. A few barbiturates sat on the shelf with some Valium and benzodiazepine vials. "I don't much like that," she said, shutting the cabinet door. "I can tell you one thing, honey," she said as they returned to the bedroom. "No man ever put his feet up in this room." She crossed to the night table and picked up the two paperbacks lying there. "I know the schmuck that wrote this," she said, removing an Air France boarding pass from one of the paperbacks. It was titled *The Congressman's Courtesan*. On the glossy cover, a balding man in a cutaway coat was being comforted by a young redheaded woman in a black negligee. "He's a friend of a friend of Artie. I wonder why she'd be reading this trash." The second book, by the same author, was called *The Geneva Quadrangle*.

"Maybe a friend of a friend gave it to her," Wilson said. Rita Kramer started to open the bedside drawer, but he said, "Come on now. It's still her house." She looked up, hesitated, and slid the drawer closed without looking in. As they left the room, a silver frame on a small table behind the door caught her eye. The photograph within showed a woman's graceful shoulders, a slim neck, a strand of pearls, but no head. The print had been torn in two. She glanced at Wilson, started to say something, thought better of it, and went out.

"You think I'm nosy?" she asked as they went downstairs.

"I think you're curious, like most women."

"And you're not, I suppose, like most men. You're too predictable, Wilson. How many houses does she have, anyway?"

"A few."

"What's her husband do?"

"He was a lawyer originally. He died a few years ago."

"An old man, or what?"

"Late forties, I think."

"His money or hers?"

"Hers, I think. Most of it."

"Any kids?" She turned quickly. "Don't answer that. I don't want to know."

He followed her into the living room, where she stood in the center of the room, the mink coat dropped from her shoulders, like a stole, long legs apart, hands on her hips as she moved her head to study the high ceiling, the towering windows looking out over the river, and finally the stone fireplace where a few charred logs lay. "Nice for rainy days, don't you think? I hate rain just like I hate snow. Living in Jersey did it—after we moved to Newark. You know the difference between city snow and California snow? Money. Not mountains, honey, money—like Grace Ramsey. This would be pretty comfy in the winter, don't you think?"

"It's a nice room."

"'Nice,' he says again. 'It's a nice room. That's a nice picture, Mr. Picasso. That's a nice nose job you got, Mr. Nasser. This is a nice house you got, Mr. Rockefeller. Your drink nice, lady?' Sometimes you've got a bartender's vocabulary, honey. Nice isn't what I meant. Try to reach out a little. This wasn't her room, anyway; it was his. You're about as discriminating as Artie. This house would sail over his head like the Concorde." She turned and led him up the two stairs to the center hall and back to the small study whose door had been locked during her previous visits. Like the bedroom, it was fully furnished. The small fireplace had recently been used. A white sofa and armchair stood near the window. She circled about cautiously and knelt on the couch in front of the bookcase to study the titles.

"What is it interests you?" he asked. "The house or Grace Ramsey?"

"Both," she said, reading a few titles aloud. She frowned. "Snodgrass? Who's he? Lowell? Wallace Stevens? You ever heard of him? Neither have I." She pulled the book from the shelf and opened it. "Maybe you're right. A poet. But not Artie's kind." She replaced the book and stood up. "Artie thinks he likes poetry, like that California fag poet, what's his name?" Wilson didn't know. "You know who I mean—the guy who sells millions with the stuff that doesn't rhyme, just nice fat words, like some ad for toilet tissue or feminine hygiene in some slick paper fashion magazine. Pure shit, except homogenized. Sorry, no offense. You're not Baptist, are you? Episcopalian, I'll bet, like my broker." She moved to the closet door. "All right if I peek in?" She didn't wait for his answer. The record library and stereo equipment were inside. Paneled in acoustical tile, it looked like a miniature recording studio. On one counter were turntables and amplifiers. Overhead were screens for the closed-circuit television system monitoring the front and rear entrances. Floor-to-ceiling shelves of long-playing records and tapes were racked in the rear. She called out a few titles to him approvingly and finally came out, shutting the door. Then, remembering something, she reopened it and searched for the light switch.

"It's probably a pressure switch," he said. "It goes on and off when you open and close the door."

"Thanks, I thought it was another ghost. This house is full of them, have you noticed?"

"Which kind?"

"I'm not sure," she said. "Come on, let's go look at the terrace."

The gardener was planting a rhododendron shrub down the hillside and Rita Kramer sat on the stone wall at the edge of the terrace, watching him silently as she smoked a cigarette. From time to time she lifted her auburn head to study the lines of the house soaring above her against the broken clouds overhead. The afternoon had grown darker and the headlights of the homeward-bound cars stirred through the gathering dusk across the river. Wilson thought she'd wanted to see the house again because it interested her, as much as Grace Ramsey interested her, that she'd wanted to come out here the way some women, shut up in a downtown hotel room in a strange city, might have gone to a museum or an afternoon movie. She hadn't mentioned offering a new contract on the house. At last she leaned over to pick up the cigarette she'd ground out on the flagstones, wrapped it in a Kleenex, and dropped it into her purse.

"Let's go," she said abruptly, "before I get a goddamned Georgetown accent."

She was edgy as they drove back down the parkway, as nervous as a cat, shifting position constantly, stretching her legs, leaning forward to peer through the windshield as if about to say something, then collapsing back silently. Only as she saw the familiar silhouette of the Watergate and the Kennedy Center across the Potomac did she finally speak. "You've really screwed my brains, honey, you really have. It's depressing, that house back there, you're depressing, this whole goddamned town's depressing. Artie's got to work for a living, not just drift around like a tooth fairy between a half dozen places in Bimini, the south of France, or wherever else it is. Let's stop kidding ourselves. Money always depresses me, doesn't it you?"

"Not much. Stop worrying about it."

"What do you expect me to do? Besides, he doesn't even have this political job nailed down yet."

"I'd wait, then." He turned up the ramp and across Roosevelt Bridge.

"Wait for what? Until he gets here and sticks me in some blintzy place I can't live in?"

She didn't speak again until he stopped the car in the small circular drive in front of her hotel. "The price she's asking is too goddamned much," she said. "You know it and I know it, so let's talk sensibly for a change and stop screwing around. Park it and let's have a drink. Let's work it out."

A doorman came to hold open the front door.

"Matthews will be back from Florida next week. Why don't you wait and talk to him?"

"I can't wait. Artie's coming this weekend."

"I wish I could help you, but there's nothing I can do. The price won't come down. I've talked to her lawyer about it, asked him to talk to you, but they won't budge, none of them."

"That's on the level, you're not hustling me?"

"On the level."

She sat for a moment on the edge of the seat, ignoring the doorman. "All right," she said. "I'll think about it tonight, call you in the morning, maybe even tonight."

He watched her stalk toward the glass doors, her head thrown back, remembering again the dancer from East Baltimore Street who'd shared his table and his nights when he was a greenhorn draftee just out of college, engaged to a shy young senior at Sweetbriar.

Too long ago, he remembered. For sixteen weeks that winter and spring, she'd taught him his life. Now he'd forgotten her name.

72

Short and plump, with thinning brown hair, lightly oiled, and a seamless face chubby with baby fat, Shyrock Wooster prowled the fringes of the crowd gathered that autumn evening in the main reception room of the New Congress Coalition, one of Senator Bob Combs's mail order foundations. He wore a dark-blue gabardine suit, and blue-and-white-striped silk tie, and lustrous mahogany-colored shoes with heel taps. Carried in his right hand was a glass of Beaujolais disguised as cranberry juice. The fat little finger of the fat little hand that held it was daintily elevated, demitasse style, and decorated by a ruby pinkie ring.

What he saw, he approved. The large parquet-floored room in the new Georgian building was similar in many ways to the East Room of the White House, visited that day by many of the out-of-town guests whose private tour Wooster had arranged. The room was elegantly furnished, the chandelier was crystal, the draped windows were tall and imposing, the ceiling medallions were reminiscent of the Tidewater aristocracy, and the only black faces in evidence belonged to the service and housekeeping staff, who, in white coats similar to those of the White House mess, were serving ginger-ale-and-cranberry punch. A small bourbon bar was discreetly located down a small corridor to the rear, but its presence wasn't publicized. Those South Carolinians who preferred bourbon and branch water could find their own way.

Nearly a hundred guests were present, not all of them members of or subscribers to the New Congress Coalition but all of them shareholders in spirit to Senator Bob Combs's congregations of the Moral Majority. Two groups were present, one a chamber of commerce tour from one of the larger South Carolina cities, and the other a group of touring bankers, insurance agents, real estate salesmen, and retailers from New Hope, a suburban community on the fringes of South Carolina's largest city. Invited to share a few refreshments and shake hands with the senator himself, they were what Shyrock Wooster, Combs's political strategist and senior aide, would have called an "ecumenical" gathering. Since "liberal" was a word Wooster had sullied far too often to ever reclaim for his own brand of folksy pragmatism, "ecumenical" was the word he'd coined in his dog-eared strategy notebook when he'd conceived of a group slightly to the left of right-wing zealotry that might be organized as yet another political action foundation to help Combs retire his campaign debts and attract more funding for the battles ahead. The New Congress Coalition was the result.

"What you got here," he'd told Combs at the time, "is your basic Presbyterian and Episcopalian, maybe a few white-shoe Catholics, the golf-playing kind, maybe a few upwardly mobile Baptists in social transition. What I mean is, it's more your chamber of commerce and country club crowd, the kind you see down in the gallery at the Masters in April."

Moral Minutemen, on the other hand, another merchandising outlet for Bob Combs's mail order politics, was made up almost wholly of religious fundamentalists, Methodists and Baptists for the most part, generally rural, like the early catalogue patrons of Sears Roebuck. At a Moral Minutemen reception a week earlier, held in a smaller, less ostentatious building on Capitol Hill, the refreshments had consisted of nothing more elevating than orangeade, hard cider, and prune juice. "Good for moral constipation," a *Washington Post* photographer had cracked when he'd seen the prune juice. "Better than the liberal runs," Wooster had thought aloud five minutes later, but by the time he'd run to the front foyer to deliver his riposte, the photographer had vanished.

The guests Wooster now saw about him in the New Congress Coalition reception room—some smoking, many with bourbon and water—wouldn't have felt at ease in that kind of tabernacle grimness, no more than the iron-britches Moral Minutemen fundamentalists would have felt at home in the opulent Georgian setting of the NCC. Yet the goals were identical: ban legalized abortion, busing, welfare government, sex education, pornography, and permissiveness; bring back prayer to the public schools, discipline to the budget, laissez-faire to the marketplace, tax exemptions to segregated Christian schools, and superiority to the national defense. If all these things were done, then the moral fiber of the nation would be in large part restored and the country would again resemble that city on the hill sought by the founding fathers: New Hope, South Carolina.

To small groups of the Moral Minutemen, Shy Wooster might say, voice lowered to that funeral parlor unction he adopted in moments of moral gravity: "Basically, what we're talking about is faith in Jesus Christ, our Savior, as opposed to the Satans of intellectual confusion that're running loose these days and the Babylon of Big Gov'nment they built up. They're whisperin' in your ears these days, folks, everywhere you turn, same as in the Garden back yonder, at the beginning of time."

To a group of knit-suit Presbyterians from the New Congress Coalition, the same message would emerge more urbanely, delivered in Wooster's chamber of commerce voice: "Basically, what it comes down to, friends, is faith in God, Country, and Free Enterprise as opposed to the polytheism of secular humanism you see everywhere you go these days, from Big Government in Wash'n'ton to pornography in the public schools. If we could just handle our national problems the way you people down in New Hope handle yours, we wouldn't be in all this mess we're in. . . ."

74

A soft Southern voice called to him and he turned back across the parquet floor to join a group of women standing and talking together. All but one were middle-aged. The exception was a plump, dowdy, sharp-eyed younger woman in her middle thirties, who was drinking bourbon. Next to her was a short lady in a blue-flowered dress who'd been in charge of the entertainment for the chamber of commerce delegation.

"You all enjoying yourselves this evening?" he asked.

"Indeed we are and we do thank you for it. It's a lovely reception."

"How was your White House tour? Everything fine?"

"Indeed it was," said the older woman.

Although Shy Wooster still had the scrubbed antiseptic look of a University of South Carolina or Clemson undergraduate—he'd attended both schools and graduated from neither—a vein of Old Testament carnality ran through that porcine wholesomeness like a strip of lean through a flank of salt pork. He preferred the healthy, lusty blond cheerleader type, like those he'd hankered after so miserably during his undergraduate days, a plump freshman sitting high in the nosebleed section of the bleachers, unattractive, unpopular, unpledged, and unscrewed. He'd left college after two years with his virginity intact. In time, he learned to settle for less, like his first wife, a legislative secretary at the state capitol with an appetite as robust as his. He'd gotten her into bed on their second date, but a month after their quick marriage, he'd discovered that the staffs of at least three legislative committees had been there too, including one red-eared rube from the piny woods who had the habit of winking lewdly at Shy Wooster on the morning elevator during those first months of marriage. They were divorced after less than two years, but Wooster had learned his lesson well. "Never get your meat where you get your potatoes," a nimble bachelor senator had told him one weekend at his rural hunting camp, spreading his trousers carefully out beneath his mattress. His white hairless legs were as scrawny as a rooster's, his hair was thin and silver, but his gymnastics that night on the front room couch with a woman from down the road had led Wooster and his partner to take refuge on the kitchen floor. After a few early lapses in Washington and overseas with Senator Combs, Wooster had learned to be more discreet.

He had seen little at the reception that evening to tempt him.

"We were very impressed with what the senator had to say this afternoon," offered a gray-haired woman who'd been in the Senate gallery that day. "He had some very interesting things to say."

"Doesn't he always," added the sharp-eyed woman. Her dark hair was teased out in a riot of unkempt curls. Wooster, who had a quick eye for such things—the libber's hair, the lack of make-up, and the aggressive posture—tried to ignore her.

"School prayer is something we all feel real strong about," the older woman continued.

"I sure am glad to hear that," Wooster responded.

"I should say so," put in the oldest of the group. She, too, had been in the gallery. "He had all the answers right there on the top of his tongue."

"It's the same old speech, he's given it before," said the younger woman. "What'd someone once say? 'Give Bob Combs a mouthful of birdseed and he'd whistle a chicken hawk off a ten-pound rooster.'"

"I've never heard that particular line," Wooster said.

"You have now. Ten dollars and it's yours."

"Sally wrote it," a woman explained. "Sally's the tour scribe. She's going to do an article on our trip for the chamber of commerce magazine, maybe even the paper."

"Is that right," Wooster said. "Well, I declare."

"Maybe I should be talking to you," the woman said. "Where exactly do you fit in, I mean in the hierarchy?"

"I'm just a staff aide, you might say."

"Oh, Mr. Wooster's much more than that. He arranged the White House passes."

"Maybe I *should* be talking to you, then," the young woman persisted.

"Well, to tell you the truth, I'm not much for giving interviews."

"Come on, I wouldn't be too hard on you."

Wooster chuckled. "That's what they all say."

"Say I'm an unwed mother. Take that for a sample. What is Bob Combs going to do for me?"

"Find you a preacher," Wooster said, winking at an older woman. "She's some journalist, isn't she? Comes right at you with her knife out. That's what we like to see. Show 'em a little jujitsu of our own."

"Sally went to Chapel Hill. She was a journalism major."

"Well, I declare," Wooster repeated, his smile dimming as he understood a little better the source of her viciousness.

"You know Chapel Hill?" she asked. Across the room, the assembled guests had begun to clear the floor in front of Senator Combs, who was preparing himself to offer a few words of welcome.

"You could say I've been there," Shy Wooster admitted.

His first foray to Chapel Hill had been a humiliating one. His first year at Clemson, he'd taken the bus to Chapel Hill to see the annual Clemson–North Carolina football game. It was homecoming for the Tar Heels and, as was customary during those years, the Clemson Tigers had been crushed on the football field. Shy Wooster had spent an hour or so after the game rubbernecking about the campus, an orange freshman beanie on his head, two inches of gaudy orange sock showing below his chino trousers. Returning alone through the autumn twilight to the bus station for the long trip back to South Carolina, he'd been overtaken by a carful of drunken Chapel Hill fraternity brothers returning from a victory beer bust. They had with them a libation intended for the Clemson band bus, but that target had been denied them by the campus police. They'd discovered Shyrock Wooster instead. They cornered him under a Honey-Krust bread sign, treated him to a vigorous scalp massage, and then shampooed his head with two bottles of Skrip blue ink. So Shy Wooster had returned to the scrub country of South Carolina that night, sitting alone at the rear of the bus, a newly baptized Tar Heel, blue-faced and blue-scalped, his damp eyes leaking blue tears, another South Carolina hayseed victimized by the tweedy cosmopolites of Chapel Hill's Tudor-style fraternity row.

He knew what these people wanted—not only victory but humiliation. The University of North Carolina at Chapel Hill, like the Council on Foreign Relations in New York, the *Washington Post,* the desk officers at the State Department, or the subcommittees on foreign relations on the Hill, was the instrument of everything betrayed in his native region and in the country at large, a collection of carpetbagging intellectuals and effete patricians in pin-striped suits or tweedy jackets with elbow patches, prattling on in their drawling nasal voices about everything under the sun except what was good for the country. Their devouring rationalism had first betrayed the small-town ethos, that sense of community from which the nation had sprung, and now had moved on to corrupt the national fiber.

Looking at this frazzle-headed woman with the arrogant smile, the condescending quip, and the viper eyes, Shy Wooster knew she was his enemy. He even knew the slur she was now preparing in her quick little mind. "How'd you know I was a Clemson man?" asked the old joke describing the meeting of two Carolinians at the Cosmos Club in Washington. Shy Wooster had heard it three times during his first year on the Hill. "Easy," replied the suave Chapel Hill graduate, hoisting his brandy and soda as the Clemson grad lifted his bourbon and Coke. "I saw your class ring when you were picking your nose."

"Well, it's a mighty fine school, Chapel Hill," Shy Wooster said as the familiar voice of Senator Bob Combs lifted from across the room. The other ladies had moved in his direction, but the younger woman had lingered behind.

"I don't suppose you've got any pull with any of those Senate committees, do you?" she asked. "I've been thinking about finding a job here."

"Well, I just might," he admitted, admiring her bulky sweater beneath the small jacket. "What might be your particular line of endeavor?"

"You must write the senator's speeches," she said, eyes lifted toward Combs. "I haven't heard that line in years. I'll bet you used to sell Fuller brushes. Political science, part-time journalism, like I'm doing now."

Up yours, sister, he thought tardily as the barbs quivered home. "Try the *Washington Post,*" he offered instead.

The irony escaped her, as his quips usually did with the literati. The only music they heard was their own. "I wouldn't have a prayer," she said. "That's why I was thinking of the Hill. I wrote them some letters last year, through the local congressman, but I didn't hear squat. What kind of pull do you have?" She was standing on tiptoes, head lifted toward Bob Combs, whose voice was barely audible. "Jesus, don't tell me he's going to start that again. How many times has he given that speech, anyway?"

"The folks I know over on the Hill wouldn't much appreciate that kind of remark," he said, smiling.

"What's wrong—don't you know any Democrats?"

Wooster chuckled. "Sugar, lemme tell you something. Handing you over to the Democrats would be like giving your own mugger a Saturday night special. I wouldn't do that to my worst enemy."

"Don't worry, I can go either way."

He chuckled again. "I'll bet you can." An English transvestite he'd met in a smoky Soho nightclub during his first trip to London had told him the same thing. Wooster had thought he was in a singles bar. "You sure got spunk, I'll say that for you. That's what it takes to get ahead in this town."

"I need the experience; I'd work anywhere. I'm in a rut working part-time for this chamber of commerce rag."

"I know what you mean." He leaned closer and said softly, "Only fast lanes down there are on the track over at Darlington." She didn't retreat.

"What about Combs's staff? Doesn't he need someone who could write fast copy?" They were quite close, moved together by the guests behind them who were pressing toward Senator Combs's mumbled valedictory.

"Only trouble is he's got them standing in line," said Wooster, encouraged. "There's an awful lot of folks that want to go to work for Senator Bob Combs." But that was only part of Wooster's problem. After Wooster's escapades in Athens and Rome had drawn State Department notice, a State security officer had had a quiet confidential talk with the senator and Shy Wooster had been duly warned. Now when Wooster helped young women find Hill employment, he scattered his wares in the various office buildings, caching them about squirrel-like, where they wouldn't be obvious to the predators about.

"Yeah, I suppose so," she responded. He leaned forward again, subjecting her to the second Shy Wooster shrink test. If a woman held her ground and didn't flinch from physical contact, whether it was their shoulders touching, or his face near her ear, close enough to brush her hair, she was the kind he might put a third move on. She didn't budge, but instead seemed drawn to the contents of his wineglass. She leaned down and sniffed it, then dipped her finger in the contents. "You hypocrite," she said. "That's not cranberry juice, it's wine."

"Well, I'll be," Wooster declared, sniffing the glass himself. "I reckon it is. Someone musta switched glasses with me. How do you like that."

"I'll bet." But her expression wasn't one of disapproval or even disappointment. She seemed to understand.

"Better finish it off before someone notices," he said. He drained the glass quickly. "Sure went down like cranberry juice, didn't it?"

"Yeah, it sure did." She opened her purse and now was sorting among its contents. "Tell you what," she proposed. "People like us have got to stick together. Especially overweight people like us. You give me your card where I can get in touch with you and I'll give you mine. Someone like you has got to have the right connections in this town."

"You can never tell," he said, searching for his card case. "Like they say around here, 'The opera's never over until the fat lady sings.' What hotel are you staying at, little lady?"

Fifty feet away, Senator Combs droned on in his deep but not always audible voice. Of medium height, with a smooth face and wide blue eyes, he wasn't an imposing figure and was in fact rather ordinary-looking. There was little hint of intelligence in the wide blue eyes. They were usually expressionless, sometimes vacuous, as lifeless as the stiff neck and shoulders, or the wooden face in which only the small cherub's mouth moved, as pink and wet as a baby's. His detractors said he had no style, no wit, and no grace, and they were right. In the South Carolina legislature, where he'd begun his career, he was referred to in private by his critics as "The Sunfish" because of the goggle-eyed stare and the fixed rapacity of his ugly little mouth—a small-pond fry too limited for the oceanic prizes for which he hungered. Even to his sympathizers he was often as dull as a Methodist vestryman standing at the back of the church, lips moving unconsciously not in devotion but in pharisaical calculation as he counted the house. Only when he was demeaning his opponents did the eyes become animated, but the gray glint was not amusement but sullen malice, like the churn of a brackish old pond filled with alligator gar. Because he steadfastly refused to compromise with his Senate colleagues on legislation of high principle, he was ineffective as a lawmaker, not so much a politician as a moralist, not so much a man as a set of rigid, inflexible attitudes, as familiar as the pasteboard figures in a child's card game. Sophisticated analysts of government, perplexed by his popularity, were usually the victims of their own techniques. There was no mystery to Combs's appeal among the people who voted for him. The confusion existed only in Washington or in those other insular communities of expertise where government and its study was a way of life and even the barbers in the federal office basements were on the government payroll. For the country beyond, Bob Combs was the spokesman of those who knew nothing about politics or politicians but their abiding contempt for both. Bob Combs, the antipolitician, was the exception who proved the rule.

Most of those listening to him that evening had voted for him and would vote for him again. They were average people, decent, law-abiding, and hard-working for the most part, people for whom politics was not a way of life but an unwelcome intrusion. For them, the fundamental reality was the one they faced every day in their jobs, their office or plant communities, in the cars and buses that took them there, in the house or apartment to which they returned, as well as in the locations where they spent their leisure hours and their children spent their classroom days. For them, attempts to make other kinds of reality more a part of their daily lives seldom succeeded. Distant or complex events, like Washington political chicanery, the London gold market, some popular uprising in Nicaragua, astrophysics, or the efficacy of the MX missile, had only an abstract relation to their livelihoods and intruded only randomly upon the burdens that crowded their lives to the limit. Most of them were skeptical of the plea that government was the guarantor of their individual liberties or that politicians were necessary for their preservation. For them, the reverse was true. Government intruded to make their lives more complicated, not less; and politicians, like government bureaucrats, lived a kind of parasitic existence battened upon their own lives, dignity, and income.

One of the earliest jottings in Shyrock Wooster's political notebook was an entry made following a trip to Charleston, South Carolina, after Bob Combs's election to the state legislature. Combs had been invited to inspect a port authority project, but at the luncheon afterward had been treated contemptuously by the lawyers and businessmen, who saw him as just another political pumpkin from the state capital, with the red clay from the hill country on his tan shoes and the white sidewalls of a county seat haircut on his rube head. In the dog-eared spiral notebook that was to become a kind of *Poor Richard's Almanac* for Combs's political ambitions, Shy Wooster, sensitive to such slights to his patron, wrote:

> Americans are, by & large, contemptuous of politicians. There are few cabdrivers, barbers, small-town hardware clerks, city editors, fancy-pants industrialists, or ambulance-chasing lawyers who can't edify you

about the basic crookedness of American politics and who don't spend a lot of time sneering, making jokes, and looking down their noses at politicians.

They don't raise their sons to be politicians. They want them to be lawyers, doctors, engineers, or baseball players. Ask a farmer what a politician is and he'll tell you it's what's left in the corncrib or the silo after everything else has been busheled out.

To this was added these observations made a few months later, after he had observed the South Carolina legislature in action:

Any fool knows that someone who spends all his time talking about something isn't doing anything about it. In the factory, the garage, the office, and the classroom, the fellow with the biggest mouth is the one quickest to get fired or thrown out when hard times come.

So if you're going to be a successful politician with the people, don't talk like one. If you're going to talk, talk about things there isn't any doubt about—God, or country or patriotism or all those things people know in their hearts are true.

Also, when you talk to the folks back home, don't get too fancy or talk like an expert. It's plain old common sense folks will listen to when they won't listen to anything else.

When he wrote those words, Shy Wooster had in mind audiences like the one now listening to Bob Combs. Decent, proud, practical people, they didn't have the time or the leisure to reflect often or deeply upon the larger problems confronting the country, and when they did they didn't address those problems in the same way as the intellectuals, journalists, historians, or professional politicians who lived on the peripheries of the American office or workshop experience—unlike those who made up Bob Combs's constituency—and whose sole justification for existence was the words they wrote and the expertise to which they pretended. That déclassé group of rationalists and libertarians so atomized the metal of hard fact by their infinitesimal questions and answers that they succeeded only in dissipating the national will.

As practical men and women, those listening to Senator Combs that evening weren't indifferent to distant or complex problems, but unless these intruded upon their private lives in some immediate way, their consciousness of them was occasional rather than systematic—a marginal awareness of national uncertainties and foreign events less as imminent dangers than as lurking threats. Like a bothersome tooth that one day might require a trip to the dentist's office, remote problems had a kind of nagging claim on their daily attention, but until a crisis was immediately at hand, they would hope that the discomfort would heal naturally, whether in Poland or in El Salvador, the nagging pain relieved by whatever natural remedies were inherent in the mysterious international anatomy itself and in those hidden subcutaneous processes that keep presidential aides scurrying, soldiers alert, and the historical engine noisy but intact. But until that time came, they were prepared to live with the uncertainty. In the meantime, they would turn away from the headlines and the editorial pages, where nothing is ever settled, and find relief in the Dow Jones averages or the sports pages, where doubt is eliminated, victories are affirmable, tactics relished, and heroes identifiable.

During Bob Combs's campaign for the U.S. Senate, Shy Wooster wrote in his notebook:

> Intellectuals have doubts, leaders have answers, voters have jobs to keep, mortgages to pay, troubles all day long.
>
> Never add to a voter's problems. When you tell your voters about a problem, tell the answer too, and make it simple enough so they can understand it on the spot.

Spot answers were Bob Combs's stock-in-trade. By the time he'd taken his seat in the South Carolina legislature, he'd had considerable experience in product merchandising. He'd put together his savings-and-loan and automobile empires in South Carolina through effective radio and television advertising, promoting quick answers to daily problems: "Five Minutes for Five Hundred Dollars! That's a Bob Combs Signature Loan!" "Credit Risks No Problem at Bob Combs' Auto Mart!" "Trade In! Trade Up! Bob Combs' Chevrolet!"

The fine print on car liens, second mortgages, and home improvement loans, as well as his usorious interest rates, might have required something more than five minutes, even for a Federal Trade Commission lawyer, but these details, like the more technical language of some of his subsequent Senate legislation, didn't dim popular enthusiasm. Similar techniques were used in his first campaign for the South Carolina legislature, during which he demonstrated how timely was his grasp of those complicated social issues that left many South Carolinians of good conscience troubled and uneasy.

He found his opportunity in the social and political turbulence of the early sixties, when his speeches on the hustings were invariably directed against the same targets: those outside agitators attempting to organize the Carolina textile mills, and the civil rights carpetbaggers sowing sedition among South Carolina blacks. His appeal was that of a righteous man in a society under siege, defending its institutions and its birthright, which were also its privileges, against out-of-state subversion aided and abetted by Washington's meddlesome bureaucrats and jurists and those rootless liberals whose intellectualism had led them to the same treachery as liberals everywhere—the betrayal of their origins. As rationalists, they'd first separated themselves from God; as liberal reformists, tinkerers, and politicians, they had now separated themselves from community and country.

Once elected a U.S. senator, he found the same opportunity. The uncertainty, disillusionment, and fear which he'd preyed upon in his first campaign appearances before crowds of lower- and middle-class white Carolinians in the sixties now had a national constituency. South Carolina's parochial confusion now seemed the nation's. Despite the new vocabulary which his better-educated foundation ideologues had invented to give gloss and respectability to its jingoism—"pointy-headed intellectuals," Combs's redneck epithet of the sixties, had become, in the mahogany-paneled suites of his foundation board rooms and the slick paper essays of his national conservative journals, "secular humanists"—the message was the same. The nation was now under siege, corrupted from within by those same liberals who had once betrayed South Carolina and who still dominated the media, the Eastern banking and foreign policy establishment, the halls of Congress, and Washington executive councils; and threatened from without by those same agents of international subversion, centered in Moscow but now spread throughout the third world, that had once infiltrated the NAACP, the cotton fields, the textile mills, the bus counters, and the rural tabernacles of South Carolina.

So Bob Combs's political revivalism was little more than South Carolina chauvinism brought to Washington, the same fears and uncertainties now writ large across the map of the United States, a nation that, like South and North Carolina, Mississippi, Georgia, and Alabama twenty years ago, was defending its institutions and its birthright, which were also its privileges, against the conspiracies of the political levelers from within and without.

Those gathered there in the reception room of the New Congress Coalition were not fully aware of this, nor would they have fully endorsed divine principle as a policy guide in these times of uncertainty—with an obsolete economy, an overvalued dollar, crime and drugs in the streets, and a sinister, armed-to-the-teeth Soviet Union, whether or not it was the Antichrist. They were interested in answers, not doubts or ambiguities, searching for the same practical solutions they sought in their offices or workshops. In the middle-class South Carolina communities from which they came, they clerked in the stores, managed the banks, sold the real estate, paid the taxes, and elected the officeholders. Someone from their ranks returning home slightly intoxicated from a neighborhood bar or a country club dance had little to fear from the town constable, if stopped, or the judge, if tried. They were of the same community, where the freedoms they enjoyed, like their immunities, didn't count as privileges but as rights. They would have been perplexed, perhaps even offended, if someone from outside that community had told them that simply by their status they were secure from fear, that simply in their indifference they wielded political and economic power. Yet this was exactly what they wielded, and the reassurance they heard in Bob Combs's political nostrums was the promise of how that privilege could be maintained.

"All I can say is what common sense tells me," Senator Combs was saying now, talking about the defense budget. "If your worst enemy gets himself a gun, get yourself a bigger one. Get yourself ten of 'em. Don't go talking about parity or equivalence or any other of these fancy words for surrender. So we've got to be bigger and stronger than they are, that's what this defense budget is all about. That's the bottom line. Anyone who tells you different is just trying to pull the wool over your eyes. . . ."

The remarks got no response from the audience, and Shy Wooster waited, disappointed, hoping that Combs would read the signs and conclude with the remarks Wooster had prepared for him for the Moral Minutemen reception a week earlier.

Combs hesitated, then began again. "'Course you hear a lot these days about this nuclear freeze business, people saying we've got to have a freeze. They're saying Moscow wants peace too, as bad as they do. I reckon they do—a piece here, a piece there, a piece yonder. . . ."

The laughter came first, then the sprinkling of applause, which gathered strength as it swept on toward where Wooster was standing.

"That's an old joke," the frazzle-haired young woman said disdainfully.

"It's not the joke, sugar, it's the timing," Wooster told her. "Did you hear the one about the Arkansas farmer looking for a new rooster?"

"No, I don't think so."

"Come on over here," he said, taking her arm. "I'll tell it to you."

And so saying, he led her off to a solitary corner to submit her to the Shy Wooster obscenity test, which separated the cacklers from the layers.

4.

The pale morning sunshine shimmered in a slight haze over the city. Haven Wilson parked his station wagon in a two-hour parking zone, locked it, and dropped a quarter in the parking meter. He was thirty minutes early for his appointment with Rita Kramer and he turned away from her hotel, crossed the street, and headed north. In his coat pocket was the dog-eared business card given to him on the beltway ramp a few days earlier. Clipped to it was the cashier's check for three hundred dollars.

Potomac Towers was an eight-story office and residential building only a few years old, an L-shaped angle of structural concrete and ugly glazed tile that towered over the neighborhood of detached and semidetached Federal and Victorian residences of Foggy Bottom. A ladder of metal-railed balconies climbed to the garden apartments on the upper floors, where potted plants, deck chairs, and an occasional barbecue smoker were visible through the railings. A small circular drive led to the double glass doors under the overhang. No doorman was in sight, not even a security guard. Cheaply built and cheaply maintained, the building smelled of uncured concrete. He crossed the foyer and walked down the carpeted steps to a small shopping arcade. The small glass-fronted shops selling imported rugs and Indian brass, women's scarves and overpriced haberdashery, weren't open yet. A gray-haired building carpenter with sawdust on his bifocals was rehanging a glass door to a narrow cubicle with the name *Embassy Car Rentals* painted on the glass. The arcade curved in a dogleg to a poorly ventilated coffee shop that held a handful of customers, hunched at the counter over their coffee cups and morning newspapers.

The building directory between the stainless-steel elevator doors listed *Caltronics* in a fourth-floor suite. Lush FM music was piped into the upholstered elevator, which whispered its way upward. "Dentist office music," his younger son used to say contemptuously. Wilson felt as if he were on his way there now. The silent fourth-floor corridor was carpeted in bright orange. As he searched for directions, a thin strawberry blonde in custom jeans and spiked heels passed him carrying an automatic coffeemaker. He trailed after her and found the Caltronics suite just around the corner, the raised vermilion lettering on the door identical to the print on the card the man called Charles Davis had given him on the beltway ramp. The carpeted office within was empty, the door propped open by an aluminum freight dolly. He continued down the corridor, pausing at two other doors marked *Caltronics,* but both were locked. The next door down the corridor was marked by another name, *Signet Security Systems,* but it was also locked. He'd just turned away when a voice called to him, "Looking for someone?" A tall, heavyset man in a beige coat and a black astrakhan hat shambled up the corridor, carrying a briefcase.

"Caltronics."

"Back the hall."

"I thought they might be moving."

"Not this way they're not; back there." The voice wasn't friendly and neither were the suspicious green eyes directing him back down the corridor. His brown hair was thick and curly under the ludicrous wool cap, his cheeks were scarred, and his heavy mustache was flecked with gray.

In the Caltronics suite he found two black movers in gray overalls pulling drawers from file cabinets and stacking them on an aluminum lift cart. The name of a Washington office equipment firm was stitched in red thread across their backs.

"Is anyone around?" he asked.

They told him that there were just the two of them, come to pick up the furniture. They didn't know where Caltronics had moved. The other offices were also empty. In the inner corridor that joined the three private offices, a copying machine stood against the wall; taped to the front was a notice from the firm from which it had been rented, warning that it wasn't to be removed. Behind the machine was an interior door. He opened it, squeezed between the wall and the copier, and peered into a dim interior reeking of silver nitrates and photographic emulsions. He flicked on the light switch to his right and in the red glow of the unmasked bulb saw a photographic workbench, a wall of steel shelves holding a few empty film boxes, and a rack of empty videotape spools.

Another door stood at the end of the corridor. On the wall nearby was a hand-lettered admonition: "Don't Tamper with Telex," but the carpet below was empty; all that remained of the telex machine was the rectangular depression left by its weight. He opened the door and looked into a large, bright room illuminated by a haze of sunlight flooding through the bank of windows along one wall. At a long table against the far partition, a man half-sat, half-leaned, a set of headphones on, his head turned toward the strawberry blonde Wilson had seen outside, and who was now seated at a word-processing console, earphones on as she transcribed on the keyboard the tape to which both were listening.

The man turned, saw Wilson, and stood up, jerking off the headset. Wilson recognized the same burly man he'd spoken to in the corridor.

"Sorry," he called. "Wrong door."

He stepped back, but the man wasn't mollified. "Hey, Mac," he called angrily. "Hey, Mac! Wait a minute!"

"Sorry."

The strawberry blonde had turned too, looking at Wilson in surprise.

"Hey, Mac, what are you doing, huh? You walk in the fucking door like that, into someone's private office, and you just say, 'Wrong door' and walk out. What the fuck are you doing? I mean, who the shit do you think you are?" His mood was ugly, his voice growing uglier as he crossed the cluttered office, pushing his way angrily through boxes of electronic gear that blocked the aisle in front of a long workbench overhung with fluorescent lights, where a TV monitoring camera lay disassembled. Over the door to the outside corridor Wilson saw a bracketed camera, cocked downward, like the one over his head. A small table to the side held a curious-looking camera and two night optical devices.

"I opened the door, Bernie," the blonde called. Her eyes were darkly fringed by artificial eyelashes.

"You opened the door?" He turned brusquely. "What the fuck for?"

"I unlocked it when they took the telex out this way. The movers asked me after they checked out our telex and I said O.K. I guess I forgot to lock it."

Just inside the door next to Wilson stood a teletype machine, connected by metal conduit to the same feeder line that had powered the machine on the other side of the partition.

"So what? The movers are gone. It's not our problem." He turned to Wilson again, no longer moving forward. "Who are you—the fucking telex man?"

"I was looking for someone from Caltronics."

"So you come nosing around here. I told you already, didn't I tell you already? You got the wrong door. What the hell are you nosing around here for? Hey, Mac, wait a minute—"

"Wait for what?" Wilson said, annoyed himself. "I got in the wrong door, like the lady said. You want to make a federal case of it?" He stepped back and pulled the door closed behind him.

"Yeah, well, just stay the hell out, then. O.K.?" He heard the man's voice from just beyond the door; a moment later a set of heavy tumblers fell into place as the security lock was set.

Wilson meandered through the suite a final time, still annoyed with himself, and went out the front door. The movers were dragging their handcart down the hall toward the freight elevator. Wilson went back to the public elevators, but as he stood waiting, eyes lifted to the illuminated number of the floor indicator, he changed his mind, pushed through a nearby exit door, and skipped down the concrete steps to the basement parking garage.

The office equipment firm's truck was backed to the loading dock. A few desks, cabinets, and chairs stood in the shadows, awaiting transfer. Among them were an executive desk and a heavy combination safe/filing cabinet. The safe drawers had been swept clean, but the desk drawers still held the rubbish of office routine, including a handful of business cards. A truck door slammed closed as he searched through the side drawers.

"Hey, watcha doing, man?" a sleepy voice called from the garage floor. A black truckdriver stood looking up at Wilson as he pulled on his work gloves.

At the back of the middle drawer, a few pleated pages were caught, hung up between the middle and bottom drawers. "Looking for an address," said Wilson as he removed the drawer. The truckdriver lifted himself to the freight dock, and Wilson pulled out the caught pages. "You know where Caltronics is moving?" he asked as he put the pages in his pocket.

"We're taking this load to Rosslyn, office over there."

"That's where they're moving?"

"Have to ask the boss. He say doan let no one take nothing."

The freight elevator had settled to a stop at the end of the freight dock. Wilson went down the concrete steps to the garage floor. "I'll check with the office manager."

"Hey, ain't you got it loaded yet?" he heard one of the movers call to the driver.

"Only one o' me. What you talking about?"

Wilson continued across the garage floor, past the parked cars in the reserve area, up the ramp and out into the pale morning sunshine. Only as he crossed Virginia Avenue toward the Watergate did he remove the folded papers he'd taken from the desk. As he stepped to the curb, he stopped to look at them more closely. The two crumpled pages were Xerox copies of a guest or invitation list. A few names were underlined, three were heavily circled, and two had question marks after them. He moved to a nearby postal storage box and smoothed the pages against the iron crown. Some of the names he recognized—prominent politicians, government officials, show business personalities, and local lawyers and dignitaries. In the center of the third page the list was interrupted by the caption "Smithsonian," and beneath it the list began again, in alphabetical order. Looking at the names, firms, and political affiliations cited in brackets, he suspected the Xeroxed pages were a partial invitation list for a cocktail party or reception given by Caltronics earlier in the year.

He tore up the list and dropped it in a waste receptacle. As he stopped at the parking meter to put another coin in the slot, his hand dug in his pocket, he saw a man turn away from the curb across the street. His back was now to Wilson as he moved up the pavement, but the move had been too abrupt for Wilson to ignore and too late for the man to disguise. The hat was different, but the face and mustache were the same, those of the man whose back door he'd gotten into by mistake.

Rita Kramer, wearing a crimson suit and a white blouse, sat at a window table in the hotel coffee shop, her silk-lined mink coat shed like a shell on the leather lounge seat behind her. Her expression was as inscrutable as ever. She was a woman of moods—hard, sullen, or yielding, as she'd been during their trip to Grace Ramsey's house, but always tyrannical. She alone controlled the tempo. It was a little like playing tennis with an overpowering opponent, a semiprofessional, Wilson thought as he approached the table: she always dictated the pace, past performances didn't count, and each day on the court was likely to be a totally new if not totally humiliating experience.

"Sorry I'm late," he apologized, shedding his raincoat.

"It's about time," she said tonelessly. "This is a friend of Artie, Mr. Strykker."

He hadn't realized the man sitting somewhat ambiguously near the next table was with her. Strykker immediately stood up and offered him a soft, damp hand. Short and henna-haired, he was wearing a gray silk suit, a gray shirt with a white collar, and an oyster-gray silk tie. A dark-blue cashmere overcoat was folded carefully alongside him. A few large rings decorated his small fingers, and a vulgar little mustache, spiny as a caterpillar, outlined his upper lip. The eyes were lively and inquisitive, but there was something sad about them, as if trapped within this carefully chosen facade was a coarser but simpler man, struggling for recognition.

"I thought maybe you were giving us the runaround again," Rita Kramer said with a trace of hoarseness.

He sat down gracelessly. "Sorry, but I got tied up."

"I'll bet. For someone who's about to close a very expensive deal, you look pretty nonchalant."

"I've got a miler's pulse rate," he said. "Inside, I'm running wild." She didn't return his smile and Strykker sat studying him somberly. "Breaking the sound barrier," Wilson added, aware of Strykker's mystified gaze. "Are you from California, Mr. Strykker?" he asked graciously. With this meeting, and with Matthews due back from Florida on Monday, he would be out of the real estate business.

"From L.A., where else?" Rita answered for him. "Where's Grace Ramsey's elusive Washington lawyer, Edward Donlon?"

Wilson searched the room for the waitress. *"In situ,"* he said, remembering a scrap of law school Latin. Rita Kramer had that effect on him. So did cat-whiskered California entrepreneurs in shiny suits. "He can't make it."

Rita Kramer sat up. "Can't make it? What are you talking about?" The waitress came to the table and he asked for coffee.

"Too short notice; he's tied up."

"Now look here, Mr. Wilson," Strykker began.

"Shut up," said Rita Kramer, leaning toward Wilson. "What the hell do you mean, not coming? You said we could close this morning. Strykker's got the goddamned check—"

"I'll close for him." He took an envelope from his coat pocket and passed it across the table. "There's your contract. If you have the cashier's check, I'll sign, and you've got the house." The waitress brought a Pyrex coffeepot and Wilson leaned back as she filled his cup.

Rita Kramer still watched him in suspicious silence as Strykker studied the contract through a pair of black-rimmed glasses, head resting on a cushion of double chin. As Wilson lifted the coffee cup, he was aware of the fragrance of baby oil, pressed to his fingers by Strykker's plump hand. He reached for his handkerchief.

"What's it say?" she asked, turning to Strykker. "Is it legit?"

"It looks all right."

"So it's O.K., then?"

Strykker was silent as he turned a page with a wet thumb. "There are a few points I'd like to check," he observed sagely, the way a man of affairs would. He removed his glasses, cleared his throat, and sat brooding ponderously, his glasses removed.

"For Christ's sake," Rita Kramer said.

He put the glasses back on. "Maybe we'd better go back to the office and talk to Edelman."

"Forget it. Go call him if you want to, but don't drag me across town to talk to Edelman again."

"Maybe I could telephone him," he reconsidered. "Artie too." He looked at his watch. "He might be up by now."

"Not Artie, either. This is my money and I want to finish it now, understand? Right here, right now, or I'm leaving this goddamned town on the next flight."

Strykker lifted himself to his feet with a sigh. "I'll give Edelman a ring," he murmured, his voice carrying a faint, weak protest.

"Why all this hassle," she asked dejectedly after he'd gone, "wearing me out like this?"

"You wear yourself out," he said. "Why all these people? Edelman, now Strykker. Who else? Who is he, anyway?"

"A partner of Artie's, a kind of financial consultant. Anyway, you don't know the half of it. When you live with Artie, you live with a houseful. He carries a crowd around with him, night and day."

"Maybe you should have checked with him before this."

"Artie? He said the house was my decision and it's my money—most of it, anyway." They sat in silence as she watched the door, waiting for Strykker to return. After a few minutes, she said, "I hope you've played it straight with me. That's what I told everyone—that you played it straight. I hope you don't disappoint me. I've never handled a sale like this, that much money involved."

"You did fine. You couldn't have gotten the house for any less; she would have kept it. Stop worrying."

"You don't know Artie. He's flying in this weekend to see what I've been up to. Friday night, maybe Saturday. To tell you the truth, I wanted to do something on my own for a change, make a decision without him looking over my shoulder all the time."

Strykker was entering the coffee shop. Watching her face as she saw him, he was surprised by the quickness of the transformation. He observed the same hardness he'd identified when he crossed the coffee shop thirty minutes earlier. It was Strykker. She didn't like him. As she picked up her purse their eyes met, and in that moment of silent contact she seemed to know what he'd seen. He smiled in reflex, but she wasn't amused.

"Don't try to read my mind," she said coolly.

"Edelman seems to think it's all right," Strykker announced, a little out of breath as he sat down. She had dropped her eyes to her purse as she searched through it silently. "Not quite what I would have preferred, but this is his territory, not mine. Are you sure you don't want to call Artie?"

"Forget it," she said, ignoring him as she brought out a pen. She signed the contract, gave Wilson a cashier's check for $150,000 with the balance due in thirty days, and invited him to meet Artie on Sunday afternoon.

On his way out, Wilson passed a florist's shop, stopped, and went in. He ordered a dozen yellow roses, signed Grace Ramsey's name to the card, and asked that they be sent to Rita Kramer's room.

5.

Dr. Foster, the acting director of the Center for Contemporary Studies, was a pudgy little professor of forty-five or thereabouts, wearing horn-rimmed glasses thick enough to so distort his eyes that he seemed not so much to peer through the glasses as to hide there, a reclusive soul seeking refuge from the anarchy of the world. His voice was as relentless as rain, a tireless falsetto that held the light, dry gossipy patter of some graduate school faculty lounge. He was dressed like a mildly bohemian professor, in a rumpled corduroy suit, a tattersall shirt, a wine-colored tie with a dis-colored knot, and scruffy down-at-the-heels loafers.

He received Haven Wilson and Ed Donlon in his first-floor office a little after ten o'clock on a wet Friday morning. Thunder boomed over the rooftops as they made their way up the walk to the old ivy-covered building at the heart of the complex just off Twenty-third Street and only a few blocks from George Washington University. The main building, once a Victorian residence in a neighborhood of nearly identical structures, sat behind a six-foot ivy-covered brick wall and was joined to the other build-ings in the complex by brick and concrete walks well planted along their verges by shrubs and flower beds, as symmetrical as a college quad.

The administration building was darkly wainscoted, the light dim in the reception room, where a gray-haired secretary sat at a desk behind a wooden railing. Dr. Foster's office was brighter. It had once been a parlor.

A long oak conference table occupied the center of the high-ceilinged room, which was painted a pale green. Against the exterior wall was an ornate mantel and a gas-fired heater. Two tall bay windows flanking the fireplace overlooked the side garden.

Foster stood at one of the windows, an architect's plot of the Center unrolled on the window seat as he identified through the rain-streaked panes the buildings across the quad.

"The thalamus group works in that building there," Foster said, pointing across the garden, "the newest one, relatively speaking. The canteen is there too, in the basement. We have a dining room here, on the far side of the center hall, but it's seldom used since the fire. The kitchen fire, I mean. The cook—well, not quite a cook . . . a resident fellow intrigued by the culinary arts. A baked Alaska went amok in the dumbwaiter. Our board dinner. Why anyone would put a baked Alaska in a dumbwaiter, I haven't the slightest. So now we have the meals catered. The annual board dinner is held there. There's also a private library next to it, where we assemble for afternoon tea. The fireplace is real, not gas, like this one, so the atmosphere is quite congenial. Collegial too, although few of the thalamus group attend, and we don't make it compulsory, nor should we. I'm not a thalamus myself, although if I had the opportunity to begin over, I might be. A historian's logic is more in the rhetorical seas in which he swims, isn't it? But I've broadened my perspective, thanks to the Center, and learned to look at history more purely in pathogenic terms."

Dr. Foster smiled, slightly winded. Wilson thought he seemed under strain.

"Thalamus?" Wilson repeated, eyes lifted through the watery panes. "Maybe you'd better explain."

"The endocrine people," Foster said. "But not just endocrines. Biopathology, if you will. The chemical basis of character, success or failure, Napoleons and Lincolns, Mussolinis and Stalins. We call them the thalamus group for short—those that work at that sort of thing."

"I'm not sure I follow. What's it prove?"

"Prove?" Foster seemed surprised.

"Give me an example."

"Lincoln was deaf," Foster said, "hence the majesty, the remoteness."

Ed Donlon turned abruptly from the window to look at him.

"Theodore Roosevelt was the child of cholera morbus," Foster continued, "a neurasthenic weakling who transformed his hyperactive will into ours. Empire."

"You mean that explains it," Wilson said.

"Oh, yes. Convincingly. Woodrow Wilson was poisoned by his mastoid, a septic cadaver. . . ."

Wilson, lips pursed, said nothing, brooding out across the rain-pocked pools of the quadrangle, not daring to look at Ed Donlon.

"A grisly cartilaginous King Tut, dead in the mummy's case at fifty."

"You have a way with words," Wilson said. *Another nut,* he thought dismally.

"One must," Foster answered, "since the scholarship is so purely conjectural. What is needed is a more solid empirical base, and this is what we're attempting at the Center. Much of the theorizing is rubbish. I'm giving you the extreme cases, *simplex munditiis.*"

"So what's the point?" Wilson asked, frowning. "How is it useful?" In the watery distance he saw a queue of raggedy unshaven men standing near the door of the thalamus building.

"You can quantify political behavior," Foster said. "Take Brezhnev, for example. What's his illness? We're not sure. Or Molotov. There we might have had some answers, although we're too late for it now. Was his fall purely political? Doubtful. He may have had the Hallermann-Streiff syndrome, a rather rare disease which is hereditary and could account for the small, piglike eyes. Or take Alexander Haig. A heart bypass creates a terrible kind of metabolic stress. We know he's taut, even seething. What's its nature? Philosophical? Not likely. Physiological? Probably. That's reason for concern. I'm sure Moscow thinks so." Foster smiled, pleased.

"Interesting," Wilson said. Donlon still hadn't uttered a word. He despised psychiatry, Wilson remembered, as if it cast a sickly clinical shadow over his robust infidelities.

"Indeed it is, but what it lacks is a more detailed empirical base," Foster resumed, encouraged. "Where we possess an adequate data base, the results can be quite conclusive. The classic case is Napoleon's."

"In what way?" Wilson wondered, turning.

"His defeat at Waterloo. That can't be explained in military terms. British valor doesn't explain it. Neither does French irresolution, not at all. No, the cause was physiological. The Napoleon who conquered Europe wasn't routed by Wellington. He wasn't even on the field of battle that day. The British surgeon's autopsy tells us everything—the fatty deposits over the hips, an inch deep over the sternum, two inches over the abdomen, the body as hairless as a child's. His dynamism was gone. A thymocentric male eunuch, a hermaphrodite, you see. The evidence is absolutely clear." Foster paused. "His pituitary had failed."

"So he got laid at Waterloo," Donlon said, finding his voice. "Buggered by the bloody Duke of Wellington, is that it?"

Coloring, Foster said, "Not precisely."

"But that's what you meant, isn't it?"

"I suppose one could put *that* kind of interpretation to it," Foster said prudishly, "although it hadn't occurred to me."

"But that's what you meant." Donlon was incensed. "What are you, a Freudian?"

"A historian," Wilson broke in. "What's your field, Doctor?"

"Diplomatic history," Foster replied, his face flushed. "Recent history, the cold war, that kind of thing." The eyes had retreated behind the gray, oyster-thick glasses.

"Don't mind Ed," Wilson continued easily. "He likes to stir things up. What are you working on now?"

"Not much of anything these days, unfortunately—not since I took over the director's duties. I told Angus McVey I would be willing to help out during the interregnum, but it's been three months now, three ghastly months. . . ." The frightened eyes roamed toward Ed Donlon, who stood with his back to them, staring resolutely out the window.

"It won't be long," Wilson said consolingly. "McVey's speeding up the search. You'll be back in your old office pretty soon."

"I certainly hope so." Foster's voice had diminished to a whisper. "Would you like some coffee? We could walk over to the canteen if you like."

"Sounds fine," Wilson said.

Foster appeared relieved. "Let me get the keys. We'll drop by a few offices on the way."

He disappeared through the door, and Ed Donlon turned and joined Wilson.

"That's absolute academic bullshit," he said. "All of it."

"Don't make it so tough on him," Wilson said. "Stop browbeating him. You've got him nervous enough as it is. I want to hear what he has to say." He lit a cigarette and walked to the window, looking again at the ragtag queue gathered along the iron rail leading to the basement entrance of the thalamus building. "What do you suppose that's all about?"

"Why shouldn't I be nervous?" Donlon complained, moving after him. "I chair the admin committee, I sign the goddamned checks every month." He studied the men still assembled in the light rain. Some of them held scraps of newspaper to their heads. "I don't know. I don't know what it is."

"It looks like a Salvation Army soup line."

A cheerful falsetto sang out from the doorway. "We can go now, guys," Dr. Foster called. Turning blankly to look at the plump face, those false words still echoing in his ears, Wilson was conscious of the dual or even multiple identities confronting him in the acting director, whom he doubted endocrinology could come to grips with at all.

"I had Kissinger's seminar at Harvard, but I really don't know the man personally," Foster explained as they descended the long dark stairs from his top-floor office in the history building. The large, dim room had showed the neglect of Foster's transfer from his scholarly duties. The desks and tables were dusty; books were piled everywhere, along with Senate hearing transcripts, scholarly journals, and month-old newspapers. On Foster's worktable, Wilson had seen four volumes by Kissinger, two by Brzezinski. Foster explained that he was working on a scholarly study entitled "The National Security Adviser as Foreigner."

"In one of his seminal books," Foster continued, "Kissinger tells us that history is the memory of states. That's not an American concept at all, but European. That's precisely their problem. Neither is American and both are total strangers to the American experience, European émigrés who know nothing about American pluralism. They're terribly ill at ease in our small-town political tradition, which neither understands. For Kissinger, freedom is the voluntary acceptance of authority, not its absence. He can't reconcile himself to the American belief that our society transcends our political structures. His version of the state is European, derived from Metternich and Kant, not from Locke. The state is supreme, can make no concessions, you see. That's why he couldn't reconcile himself to the Vietnam protesters, why he felt justified in his duplicity and deceit. . . ."

"What do you think of his recent books?" Wilson asked.

"Completely predictable," Foster continued, more at ease now in this flush of scholasticism. He led them out the rear door. "It reminds me of the Egyptian pyramids, those enormous tombs built to perpetuate a pharaoh's grandeur, a mountain of stones—in Kissinger's case, words. A public tomb. A sarcophagus to his reputation. But he isn't buried there—oh, no." He gave up a smile. "The public myth is. This way."

They circled a hedge, cut across a triangle of wet turf, and crossed through the rain toward the thalamus building. Wilson saw a few gulls from the Potomac floating over the rear wall. "Kissinger's greatest gift is his intuitive sense, which is quite keen, actually. In every other way, he's little more than a fashionable platitude. He best defines himself in relation to his audience, like a morbidly sensitive woman. That's where his thymocentric personality emerges, you see, and that's what it is—the persona of a morbidly sensitive woman. He seduced the Washington press corps like Salome, didn't he? Of course he did. Kissinger the seductress. . . ."

Ed Donlon glanced at Wilson, who tried to ignore him. Wilson had the impression that Foster might have been talking about himself.

"It shows best at his press briefings, which I used to attend," Foster continued as he waddled along beside them. "The State Department is just a few blocks away, you know. There, Kissinger's feminine wiles were always on display—that combination of coyness and flirtation, offering those seductive little peeks at the secrets of state, the verbal lip-play before factual intimacy, the caressing little tongue games before physical capitulation, namely"—Foster couldn't suppress a giggle; he drew a breath to continue—"namely, the disclosure on background quote unquote of Salome's SALT I and Vietnam secrets. . . ." The final giggle came like a hiccup.

Donlon had stopped abruptly. "What is this shit?"

"Sorry?" Foster stopped too.

"What sort of smut are you peddling, anyway?"

"Henry's 'Dance of the Seven Veils,'" Foster said, coloring again. "Salome."

"So what's it mean?"

"Mean?" Foster faltered.

"You're a closet Freudian, Professor. No wonder you came up with all this psychoporno drivel."

They walked on, Foster mortified. "All I was trying to do," he protested weakly, "was to extrapolate from Kissinger's presentation self the man within. That's the practice in psychohistory. You recall Kissinger's disastrous press conference with the Italian journalist Oriana Fallaci, don't you? That's conclusive proof. As a very attractive woman, she evoked from Kissinger a crudely masculine persona, you remember? The tough guy, the lone gunman riding into a Western town. What happened, you see, was that Fallaci had preempted Kissinger's traditional role as seductress. He was forced to switch parts, and he'd never been on a horse in his life. It frightened him to death and he said some very stupid things. It was a disaster, the wrong horse, and he betrayed himself. Kissinger as the Lone Ranger? Totally wrong. As Lady Godiva, possibly, but not the other. Totally wrong, totally unconvincing, and everyone laughed at him. . . ."

"'Prius dementat,'" Donlon said, eyes to the heavens. "'Those whom God wishes to destroy, he first makes mad.'"

Haven Wilson changed the subject. "Where do you keep your archives, your old classified material?"

"In Maryland," Foster replied, wiping his glasses and then his forehead. "A security vault out there. We have a sensitive area here in the basement of that building across the way."

They reached the rear of the thalamus building, where Wilson saw by a plaque on a corner column that it was officially known as Erasmus Center. The group of men had vanished from the nearby basement entrance. Wilson said that he'd noticed a queue along the railing and asked what it was about.

96

"Queue?" Foster turned across the porch to glance over the stone coping. "They're still here." Wilson followed and found a dozen tattered men in the shelter of the areaway. Most were bearded, their hair long and dirty; the fingers that gripped the newspaper and plastic-bag rain covers were grimy with dirt, the fingernails broken, the knuckles cracked and cobwebbed with scaling skin.

"Who are they?" Wilson asked as they entered the building. Foster led them down the stairs and toward the basement canteen. The smells of his university chemistry and biology laboratories were in Wilson's nostrils, the air deadened by odors as oppressive as a windless salt sea at low tide.

"That's the Friday morning registration for the coming week's experiments," Foster said. "We attract quite a crowd here these days, especially with the downturn in the economy. Two years ago we just attracted the derelicts off the streets—the winter people, as we call them. Now we get a much better mix. We could always rely on a few students from GW or Georgetown, trying to earn a little pocket money. They can earn up to five dollars an hour, depending upon the difficulty of the experiment."

"What kind of experiments?"

"All kinds. Psychological tests, routine opinion sampling, some biochemical experiments, a few pharmacological tests, very rigidly controlled—but that gets very technical, a bit out of my line. The past year we've been working on a few studies for the National Institute of Health, like our vasopressin work."

"Vasopressin?"

"A peptide released by the posterior lobe of the pituitary," Foster said. "It seems to trigger a hormone into the bloodstream that significantly improves memory. Our volunteers have shown memory improvement of anywhere from forty-five to sixty percent."

"So you test people here."

"Oh, yes, our volunteers. They're paid, of course. Test performances are compared before and after the vasopressin's administered. Our people have scored significantly higher than the NIH volunteers, although that's not surprising. Probably the Washington winter people would have much more to remember than college undergraduates." He smiled again.

"Oh, sure," Donlon said irritably. "Drunks and winos."

"No, we have very strict medical requirements. Derelicts, yes, provided they've a clean bill of health. Excuse me, I want to look in here." Foster carefully opened a door, peeked into the darkened interior, and then disappeared, pulling the door closed behind him.

"The gentleman is a fruit," Donlon said, "a fruit and a nut both. That makes him a gay cupcake and that's not what we need. No wonder everything's so screwed up."

"He's nervous, that's all. Give him time. How long since McVey's seen all this?"

"Maybe ten months. He got discouraged."

"No wonder. Where have you been all these months?"

Foster reappeared, his moon face damp with the warmth of the closed room behind, in which a dozen shadowy figures were seated. "Sorry, but the testing hasn't begun yet. I thought we might observe."

"Memory testing?" Wilson asked.

"No, audience reaction. This way." They continued down the corridor and past the open door of a biology laboratory. A tall cadaverous man in a white laboratory smock leaned against a worktable, stirring a cup of tea as he gazed out the barred window at the ragged figures from the queue as they huddled in the areaway. Foster stuck his head in the room. "Chosen next week's candidates, Dr. Dobler?"

He shook his head, still gazing out the window. "Have you ever seen such creatures of Tartuffian extravagance?" he murmured, blinking his eyes slowly, like a basking reptile.

"Not recently. We're on our way to the canteen. Care to join us?"

"No, thanks. I've got a group waiting next door. Have you seen O'Toole?"

"No, not today."

"He was here, but he wandered off. If you see him, tell him to report to the groundkeeper. He's in no condition for any testing today."

"I'll do that." They followed Foster's pear-shaped figure down the corridor. "O'Toole's an interesting case," he explained over his shoulder, "a perfect testing volunteer in many ways, a *tabula rasa*. We often try out our new testing techniques on him before we send out a call for a group of volunteers. In the meantime he does odd jobs about the Center, a kind of handyman. No one knew much about him, but the vasopressin peptide seems to have recovered quite a bit of lost history. It turns out he was a Catholic brother in some seminary in upstate New York, seminary or monastery, I'm not sure. In the carpentry shop. His name is William O'Toole. They call him Billy." Foster stopped as he turned the corner, waiting for them. "If you've ever passed a few of Washington's winter people, sleeping on a Metro duct or a bench in Lafayette Park, you've probably wondered where they came from. In O'Toole's case, vasopressin told us, but much too much."

"Too much?"

"That can happen too. In the eccentric cases, like O'Toole's, the vasopressin seems to combine with some other neuropeptide, so far unidentified, to form a quite powerful neurotransmitter, activating massive numbers of brain cells previously dormant, something like Sodium Pentothal. It's prodigious in its effects, virtually uncontrollable, as in Billy's case—so much so that it seems to create a secondary character disorder or neurosis."

"You're pretty up to date on all this medical jargon," Donlon said acidly. "What ever happened to the historian's simple behaviorism?"

"Oh, we have that too," Foster quickly replied, "but not so much here. The last citadels of behaviorism are here in Washington, of course—the White House, the State Department, Defense, Congress, the whole ball of wax."

The false note echoed in Haven Wilson's head like a gong. Foster continued: "There's no doubt about it. They're all primitive behaviorists, from Reagan on down. So was Carter, so was Nixon. The higher you go in bureaucratic hierarchy, the more primitive it becomes. Have you ever seen a presidential option memo? I came across one the other day in a Freedom of Information case. Professor Skinner himself might have written it. General LeMay expressed the syndrome best. 'Nuke the Chinks.' Here we are."

Foster held open an enameled swinging door and they entered a brightly lit canteen crowded with Formica-covered tables. A stainless-steel counter and steam table stood at the far end. In the far corner, a solitary figure sat at a table with his back to the wall, hunched over a coffee cup, mumbling to a black woman in a pink nylon dress who was clearing the nearby table.

"What use could vasopressin have?" asked Wilson as they crossed to the coffee urn.

"A number of uses. We know athletes use anabolic steroids to build muscle mass. Thinkers might call upon vasopressin to expand efficient brain mass—figuratively speaking, of course." They drew coffee from the urn. "So it might have any number of practical uses. It would improve court performance, political leadership, competence in Congress, wisdom in the White House."

Foster led them to a table in the center of the canteen, but left his coffee cup there and crossed to the hunched solitary figure. Wilson heard him tell the man to report to the groundkeeper. The man nodded without comment. He was a slight man with brownish-gray hair and a face weathered and cracked by the outdoors, as puckered as a winter crab apple. The blue eyes had the steady fixed resolve of an addict of some kind, distant yet near, veiled yet piercing. His collarless white shirt was wrinkled under a faded serge coat, held together at the throat by a safety pin. Attached to the lapels of the jacket was a chain of paper clips, something like inverted campaign ribbons, traveling down to the first buttonhole.

Seeing the piercing eyes, Ed Donlon had taken the chair with its back to the figure. Wilson had no such luck and found himself the target of that high-frequency radar glare, eye contact unavoidable.

Jesus Christ, he thought in despair, where do these people keep coming from?

"Maggoty thoughts weren't unknown to me," the man called as that initial contact was made. Wilson moved his eyes away.

"It's interesting that you should mention the behaviorists," Foster continued as he sat down, "since I've done some work on that very problem as it applies to foreign and defense policy—"

"You think I'm lying!" the man shouted.

"That's O'Toole," Foster whispered. His voice grew louder. "Public life is full of the breed. Behaviorists, I mean. Just about everyplace you look these days—"

Wilson was more conscious of O'Toole's staccato bursts from the far corner. He sounded like a word-processing machine that had run amok.

"Resurrection is all right, Doc, but how much sleep do you think I'm getting? Two, three hours a night? Less these days! Sure you wanna get the truth out, but there's a mountain of rubbish that's gotta be moved first. . . ."

"As I said, most Washington policy experts are behaviorists," Foster was saying, "but then so is most of Washington—"

"Washington's the wrong place!" Wilson heard O'Toole call to him.

Foster's voice grew even louder. "When you look at it closely, you realize that, conceptually considered, détente is nothing more than a primitive behaviorist system of rewards and penalties, pleasure or pain, a kernel of corn or an electric shock—the same tools the Skinnerites employ with rats and pigeons. But in the case of détente, the Soviet Union is the laboratory rat being disciplined by our white-frocked globalist psychologists, Kissinger, then Brzezinski, now Haig, from their diplomatic laboratories. 'Linkages,' they say, but is Soviet ideology truly as primitive as that—a brain mass which is nothing but reflex, driven by the avoidance of pain?"

"You've seen the ones with the beards," O'Toole shouted, "the beards and the turbans. Maybe they've taken over the planet already, Doc, faking this 'No spika the Inglesa' you get up on Pennsy Avenue near the World Bank. World Bank! Hey, Doc, whose world?"

The surging voice crept closer and Wilson erred in moving his eyes from Foster's face. He discovered Billy O'Toole's manic eyes locked to his like a heat-seeking missile sensor, quite close now, just a few steps away. "So they're faking it," O'Toole told him, his voice dropped to a more confidential register, "all the while owning the planet already, staking out oil and minerals rights in your head. You know the old saying, don't you?

Keep the land and your skulls, give us what's in it." He sat down next to Haven Wilson. "I know you from somewhere. You ever been in Rochester?"

"I don't think so," Wilson answered, half-smiling.

"Maybe you forgot."

"Maybe I did."

"It's not easy to forget Rochester," O'Toole said.

"No, I guess not," Wilson agreed.

Foster had lapsed into frightened silence. O'Toole glanced at him, looked at Donlon, looked at his coat and tie, and returned to Wilson.

"One night in the middle of November, nineteen hundred and forty-nine, I had an argument with my sweetie in Rochester." He paused, searching Wilson's face as if to assess the effect of this revelation. Then he studied Wilson's tie.

Wilson nodded. "That's too bad."

"It was on the floor of the DeMolay Ballroom in Rochester that I had the argument. She was taller than I was and had signed up the last dance on her card with Ben Fitzgerald, the 'See You in My Dreams' number. That's always the best. He was six one. How tall are you?" He was still studying Wilson's tie, as if the fleur-de-lis were a hieroglyphic on a Masonic apron.

"About that," Wilson said.

"He was six one. The 'Dancing in the Dark' number was mine, but the lights were out for that one, you know what I mean. In the 'See You in My Dreams' number, which closes the evening's formal entertainment, the lights come on real slow like, the saxophone players stand up, and the DeMolay banner drops down from the ceiling, real slow and nice. Only this night, it got hung up on the chandelier, someone told me afterward. It comes crashing down like a line fulla wet wash, but that don't matter. The way it's supposed to be is that it comes floating down real easy, everybody steps back from his sweetheart, looking around at everybody else and clapping, but I was five feet seven and my sweetie was five feet nine and she can't hide it, even with her shoes off, you know what I mean?" Wilson nodded. "I thought she was your basically pure DeMolay type, the girl of my dreams, but after she shows me her card where she'd signed up Ben Fitzgerald for the last dance, she says to me, 'Nix on the "See You in My Dreams" number, short stuff. I'll make it up to you later and it won't be any dream.' She gives me a wink and I speed off. Are you with me?"

"I think so," Wilson said.

"What she meant was in the sack."

"I suppose so."

"Me, I didn't know anything about sex at the time. I was an RC. What people did I thought they did out on the dance floor, waltzing to Wayne

101

King. It was two years before I found out. So I'm humiliated, that's all I'm thinking of. I speed off but I don't come back, see? I leave her standing right there in the middle of the DeMolay Ballroom in Rochester and keep rolling, down the stairs, across the lobby, up the street. I get back to my room at the Y and throw off the rented tux, the starched shirt, the rented tie, everything right down to the underwear. I look in the mirror behind the closet door and I don't like what I see. I get out my cashbook to find out what the evening's cost me, and I don't like what I see there, either. I'm burned up. I decide it's time to make a change. On the inside cover of the cashbook, I write, 'From now on, you've got to live with the facts, short stuff, and this book will tell it like it is.' So that cheers me up. I feel like I've got a handle on something now, some real heavy stuff. I'd made a new beginning that night and the way I felt, I could have gone back to the DeMolay Ballroom in my underwear, the trap seat dropped, my ass hanging out, and it wouldn't have made any difference, you know what I mean? Only it's a hard book to keep and I'm no Edgar Allan Poe. The next night I go back to the Y and enter up the daily cash flow—no breakfast, a cup of coffee at ten, two bits for carfare, a cheese sandwich and a half pint of milk for lunch, bean soup and a cottage cheese salad for dinner, and the four dollars I'd spent for my ex-sweetie's gardenia the night before. You see what happened, don't you? Only twenty-four hours later and I'm already bankrupt, wiped out. There in the cashbook where I'm going to tell it like it is, the St. Thomas Aquinas of the DeMolay Ballroom, I get wiped out by a five-foot-seven runt vegetarian who bills me four dollars for a stale gardenia and a buck-fifty worth of rabbit chow. You see the problem in Rochester?"

"I think I do," Wilson said. "You've got quite a memory." Dr. Dobler stood just inside the swinging door with a worker in coveralls from the groundkeeping crew. O'Toole ignored them. Cap in hand, the groundkeeper crossed to O'Toole's chair and took him by the arm. "Come on, Billy. We got gravel to spread."

"I could have gotten her in the sack that night, like Ben Fitzgerald," O'Toole said, rising obediently, "but it was two years before I knew what the shit she was talking about."

"That happens sometimes," said Wilson sympathetically.

"That's been my problem all my life, someone else always standing in my shoes, someone like Ben Fitzgerald." The crew chief led him on. O'Toole turned back. "I never caught up, either. If you're ever in Rochester, stay away from the Y; they put saltpeter in the rice pudding." The chief pulled him toward the door. "If you see me down on Pennsy Avenue in a Lincoln limo with two platinum blondes in the back seat, say 'Howdy,' right? I'll still be here." They dragged him through the door.

"Is that what's going to wake up the White House?" Donlon asked as they left the canteen. "This vasopressin you were talking about? I can see the Pentagon juiced up on that."

"As I said," Foster added uncomfortably, "O'Toole's the odd case."

Wilson and Donlon spent another forty-five minutes at the Center, examining a list of current projects and talking with a few of the resident scholars. Wilson wasn't impressed. It was noon as they passed through the front gate. The rain had vanished and the skies were clearing.

"Well, what do you think?" Donlon asked delicately.

"Why'd the law firm stick you with this problem?"

"They thought I might know something about it. Angus McVey's an old client. He came to us for help and I said I'd see what I could do."

"So you did," Wilson said. "They let it get away from them, didn't they? Just like Nick Straus over at the Pentagon, the same problem."

"What's that?"

"The monkeys are running the zoo."

Near Donlon's BMW, a young man passed them wearing a George Washington University sweatshirt with a few Greek letters below the logo. Red-faced and out of breath, he was returning from a campus political rally, carrying a crude, hand-lettered sign. A few letters had been partially dissolved by the rain, but they could still make out the words:

TIRED OF REAGAN, RIP-OFFS, AND REACTION?
RENT AN ANARCHIST
CALL HAL 632-8111

Wilson turned to Donlon, as if to say something, but Donlon, embarrassed, warned him off. "Don't say it," he advised. "Just think about it some more and we'll talk next week. Let's go over to the club. I need a goddamned drink."

6.

Buster Foreman thought he knew something about Signet Security Systems and was surprised Haven Wilson was asking about the company—a rather odd coincidence. He'd made some discreet inquiries himself about the firm—not the firm but the man who owned it—the previous July after a legislative aide on the Hill had told him a bizarre story. Senator Combs was involved. Buster had always disliked Combs. What he'd heard from the legislative aide had made him suspicious as well.

It was late on a Friday afternoon and the three men sat in the incomplete front offices of a concrete-block building on a side street along a railroad spur in Arlington. Traffic was heavy on the boulevard a block away, where the falling sun glazed the windshields of the homeward-bound automobiles. Like Fuzzy Larson, sitting lazily behind his dusty desk, Buster was dressed for an evening of amateur carpentry—an old sweatshirt, wash-faded jeans that showed a few paint splatters, and ragged jogging shoes. A pair of saw horses sat at the end of the room, a carpenter's toolbox beneath. A Skilsaw, plugged to an extension cord, leaned on its side under the table on which Buster sat. Neither man looked particularly anxious to go to work.

Buster and Fuzzy had leased the building six months earlier. They'd hired a carpenter to remodel the rear, where the working laboratories were located—a ballistics cabinet, a few kilns, a chemical and toxology lab, even a small pathology unit run by a Pakistani pathologist from a local hospital who moonlighted for them several nights a week and on weekends. They contracted lab work from county and rural police departments, but also took on assignments for a few overburdened government labs, like the Bureau of Alcohol, Tobacco, and Firearms at Treasury, which they'd been helping with some demolition cases. The front offices, which they were remodeling themselves, were far from finished. The shell of wooden studding was only half covered by Driwall, and the concrete floor, as yet untiled, was powdered with a fine gypsum dust that lay over desktops, file cabinets, and chairs.

"So tell me what you know about this Signet Security," Wilson suggested. "Tell me who's behind it."

"I'll tell you, but one thing you've got to understand," Buster said. "It's not all bullshit, like you were saying the other night when Bob Combs was on the tube. This thing has been bothering me for a couple of months, since last summer when I talked to this guy on the Hill."

"All right, but what's it have to do with Signet Security?"

Buster had gotten a telephone call that summer from an ex-next-door neighbor in Alexandria, a staff aide to a Louisiana congressman. A Baptist, he'd discovered what he believed were controlled substances in the backseat of the family car one Sunday morning. His son had used the car the night before and he was worried, not so much about his son, but about the habits of the boy's high school friends, one of whom had just returned from Thailand, where his father had been assigned with the Agency for International Development. He knew about the drug problems in Bangkok, particularly among the young AID and embassy dependents. He'd asked Buster to analyze the substances. The lab analysis showed the green berries to be decorations from a florist's corsage and the pills to be a harmless medication, probably from a girl's purse. Buster hadn't charged him for the analysis, and the relieved father had taken him to lunch.

"He's feeling real good about his son, but it turns out he's down in the dumps about his job," Buster said. "The congressman he's working for is a hack, a Louisiana wild turkey, way back in the bayous someplace, and my friend is looking for another staff slot, up front where the action is, like with Combs. Then he tells me he had a talk with Combs about filling a staff vacancy."

"When was this?"

"Just after the election last year. Combs's senior aide is thinking about taking an assistant secretary's job at State or Defense—"

"Shy Wooster," Fuzzy interrupted. "Shyrock Wooster, the jerk that got that Greek broad into the sack in Athens, remember? Superdick." Wilson didn't turn. "Hey, Haven, are you listening?"

Wilson nodded. "Yeah, I know Shy Wooster."

"Just like you knew him the other night when I couldn't remember. How come you didn't say?"

"Shy Wooster isn't worth bothering about. Go ahead, Buster."

"So anyway, he tells me that after he talked to Combs about filling this staff vacancy, a guy comes around to see him, like an FBI interview. This big guy walks into his office one day, flashes this official-looking badge, and starts banging away with the questions. My Baptist friend is a little shook up about the questions this guy is dishing out—a real body-bag third degree. It turns out this guy isn't FBI at all, but an ex-FBI tough who's the security adviser for Senator Combs and his right-wing money machines. . . ."

Wilson waited, watching Buster's face.

"Signet Security," Fuzzy announced. "Signet Security belongs to him."

"His name's Bernie Klempner," Buster said.

"What kind of questions were they?" Wilson asked.

"You name it. Gambling habits, organizations he belongs to, sex life, any crazies in the family, does he know any homos—that kind of garbage. So my friend is a little bent out of shape. My friend thinks Bob Combs is the best thing to come down the pike since prohibition, but by the time Klempner works him over, he's feeling like he's been punched out with his pants down in the men's room by some vice squad undercover team—"

"That's what your friend said?" Wilson asked warily.

"My friend? Oh, no, this guy's a Baptist—he's got Listerine breath all day long. He just said he was upset— 'unclean,' I think he said."

"Did he get the job with Combs?"

"No, it turns out Shy Wooster doesn't want the State or Defense slot, backs off at the last minute, and my friend is out in the cold. He gets a nice folksy letter from Senator Bob saying he'll keep him in mind if something opens up. . . ."

Wilson listened silently. None of these revelations seemed significant. He was more curious about Signet Security.

"But my friend's still a little pissed about this Klempner third degree," Buster continued, popping the lid of a beer can from the six-pack beside him. "So one day he's having coffee over in the Senate cafeteria and he bumps into one of Combs's secretaries, a blue-haired old biddy who's been with Senator Bob yea years, ever since he had those car agencies down in South Carolina. She's a Baptist too, takes a summer retreat down in Spartanburg or wherever it is, and has bunions on her knees to prove it. So she gets to talking about how sorry she is my friend won't be joining Combs's staff."

Wilson was conscious of Fuzzy Larson's omniscient smile from behind the desk.

"My friend asks her about Klempner," Buster said, "and she gets real confidential all of a sudden, like she's afraid the goddamned table is wired up. So she tells him how come Combs has to be real careful and why these foundations of his, Moral Minutemen, the New Congress Coalition, and these other peckerwood outfits have to have a security expert like Klempner to run their background checks. She tells him how many crackpots and crazies write to Combs, hate mail, a lot of it, some so bad they have to be turned over to the FBI or the executive protection service. Klempner has real tight contacts with the FBI, she says, and he handles the liaison work. But that's not all. She says some of this mail is from wackos on the far right, the oddballs who really get juiced on this right-wing snake oil Combs is hustling and want to set up political action committees, get jobs with his foundations or even come to Washington and work free for Senator Bob and his crusade. She tells my friend Combs could really get burned that way—the crazies from the lunatic fringe, the idiot John Birchers, the old Klansmen who want to turn in their bedsheets for one of Senator Bob's red-white-and-blue Uncle Sam suits. Crypto-Nazis, fascists, America Firsters, anti-Semites, you name it—"

Buster's indignation had carried him away and Wilson broke in patiently: "Is that what she said? Combs's own secretary? Klansmen?"

Buster reconsidered. "No. 'Misguided patriots,' maybe, I don't remember exactly, maybe some kind of code word, but that's what she meant—"

"You mean you think that's what she meant."

"What she was saying," Fuzzy volunteered impatiently, "was that all of this publicity Combs has been getting is bringing a lot of weirdos out of the woodwork."

"I understand that."

106

"So Klempner checks them out," Buster resumed, "checks them out to make sure they're on the up-and-up, that they're not going to give Senator Bob a bad name. But that's not the hooker. The hooker comes at the end, when this old biddy tells my friend how Combs has to be careful, how he has to watch his step to make sure he isn't sandbagged by someone working for him or one of his foundations—she said embarrassed, maybe, not 'sandbagged'—the way his poor brother Dorsey almost did him in yea years ago when he went off the deep end."

Buster had stopped, his silence pregnant with mystery. Wilson waited patiently, watching Buster get up from the table and step through the skeleton of studding into his adjacent office, where he dug through the drawer of a filing cabinet.

"Dorsey Combs," Fuzzy said, "the senator's half-brother. You ever heard of him?"

"No. I didn't know he had a brother."

Buster returned with a folder and dropped it in front of Fuzzy. "No one else knows much about him, either. That's when we decided to take a look. Go ahead, Fuzzy, read him the story."

Fuzzy read from the file folder on his desk, detailing a long chronicle of misdemeanors and arrests, beginning with aggravated assault and disorderly conduct in Selma, Alabama, in the late fifties and moving on to Montgomery, Birmingham, and Atlanta. The charges included assault with a deadly weapon, inciting a riot, pandering, indecent exposure, and transporting a minor across state lines for purposes of prostitution. Charges had been brought in Laurel, Mississippi, Ozark, Alabama, and Nashville, as well as in Washington, D.C., in 1968.

"That's what Buster was talking about at The Players Monday night," Fuzzy said, "only no one asked. The guy's a jailbird, a record as long as your arm."

"What's it sound like?" Buster asked. "What's it read like?"

"The civil rights trail," Wilson said. "Is that what it was?"

"You're goddamned right, all the way. Every lunch counter, bus ride, prayer meeting, sit-in, or march by the Freedom Riders, Dorsey Combs was there, lying out in the high weeds with his knuckle duster and ax handle. I'll bet brother Bob wasn't far behind, either. But that isn't all. Bring him up to date, Fuzzy."

Larson read from the folder. "'Inciting a riot, Spartanburg, May '80. Charges dismissed.' 'Detained, Knoxville, August '81, suspicion of transporting a minor across state lines for immoral purposes.' This guy's really got obnoxious habits, doesn't he? 'Charges dismissed.'" He closed the folder. "What do you think, Haven, busy or not?"

"Busier than a monkey with two peckers," Buster said. "How about it, Haven? Are we just blowing smoke rings or have we got something?"

"Where'd you get that?"

"A friend," Fuzzy said.

"A friend where?"

"I've got a buddy with the Bureau, an old skeet-shooting pal," Buster explained. "Last September, Fuzzy and I got to talking about all this shit I'd picked up and I had this friend do an indices check for me, a name check. They've got those computerized indexes and he rolled the tape—"

"That's privileged information—"

"For God's sake, Haven," Buster said. "He did it with his eyes closed, O.K.? Come on, that's not the point. You notice anything funny about this Dorsey Combs?"

"You told me, the civil rights trail."

"Nothing else? Come on, Haven, get your wig on. Think a minute."

"The charges were dismissed," Fuzzy said. "From the late fifties until '72, this Dorsey Combs spent about twenty-eight months in the slammer; nothing since."

"So?"

"So? His brother's big-time now," Buster said, "real big-time. He can pull strings."

"You think that explains it? Tell me more about Signet, this man Klempner. That's what I want to hear about."

Klempner had started Signet Security five years earlier, specializing in industrial security and surveillance systems for a few large pharmaceutical firms protecting their research laboratories against industrial espionage. He'd expanded into similar systems for computer manufacturers. He was technical adviser to a few companies designing surveillance systems hardware, and security consultant to a number of local think tanks and private foundations, like those of Bob Combs. But his ties to the FBI were a little ambiguous. Foreman had heard that two years earlier Klempner had worked a trick with Treasury, Commerce, and Justice that had resulted in three indictments for high-technology export violations. Signet had played the middleman and the U.S. Attorney had gotten three convictions for shippers of U.S. high-tech surveillance equipment to Latin American and Middle East destinations.

"He quit the FBI after a few problems, I heard," Buster said. "Strong-arm stuff, an illegal entry—something like that; I'm not sure. All I heard was that Klempner was working a case, steps on the wrong toes, and someone files a complaint. They put him on leave without pay and have an investigation. It turns out Klempner was bending the law, but the white-shirts in the front office were too polite to ask. He tells them to stick it, resigns, and the Bureau gets off the hook. How about a beer?" He opened another can.

"Forget about Klempner; it's Combs we want to talk about," Fuzzy said.

"No beer, thanks," Wilson said. "So maybe Signet is an FBI front?"

"I don't think so, but it comes pretty close," Buster continued. "This friend at the Bureau tells me Klempner can get a hunting license anytime he wants it. So I came right out and asked him. 'You mean Signet Security is an FBI operation, a front?' 'Not exactly,' he tells me. 'O.K., how close?' 'Like white on rice,' he says. 'He can get a hunting license anytime. Anything he turns up, he lets the Bureau know, and vice versa.' I figure that means black-bag operations. Klempner can go in and do a job without a court order, the stuff turns up on an FBI desk the next morning, they attribute it to a good source, and get an investigation started before the upstairs lawyers know what hit them."

"It's not that easy," Wilson said, getting to his feet.

"Let's get back to Combs," Fuzzy said impatiently. "Buster's got an idea."

The sunlight was beginning to fade from the wooden trusses and the skylight overhead. Wilson moved across the floor to look at an oilskin map of Washington hanging on the wooden studding. A few orange-headed pins were grouped in a small pattern near an Alexandria suburb. "What are these pins for?" he asked.

"Some maniac's loose," Fuzzy said. "We've got six stiffs back in the cooler. Our Pakistani is doing the autopsies. Some really grim shit."

Wilson turned. "What kind of maniac?"

"A suburban cat killer," Buster said. "Let's get back to Combs."

"What's he do, this Dorsey Combs?"

"Minister of the gospel," Fuzzy said. "He's with some Pentecostal outfit down in Knoxville, doing rehabilitation work. The Knoxville cops hung a 'driving under the influence' charge on him a month ago, but he got himself paroled to the custody of this local Sunday school."

"What's it called?"

"The Pentecostal Church of the Open Door."

Wilson smiled. "This man's too good to be true—a drunk, a bigot, a racist, a few morals charges, and he takes up the collection plate every Sunday." He returned to the deskside chair and picked up his coat. "Someone's pulling your leg. How come the press hasn't gotten wind of Dorsey Combs? They'd like to spike Combs's mail order artillery as much as you would."

"They don't have the tapes to roll," Buster said.

"If the press hasn't been digging around in Bob Combs's backyard, I doubt if anything's there," Wilson said. "I wish I could be more enthusiastic."

"I told you he'd say it's bullshit," Buster told Fuzzy.

"I didn't say it was bullshit; I said it sounded a little fishy."

"What isn't fishy if it's not the Combs crowd?" Buster said. "Ask yourself sometimes, the way Fuzzy and I did—where did all these guys come from? What were they doing back in '65 during the Voting Rights Act, or even before that; who were they tied in with politically? Like Fuzzy said, a lot of them are weirdos who just crawled out of the woodwork. I'd like to know more about them."

"He's got an idea," Fuzzy repeated.

"Don't tell him," Buster said. "He'd say it's a wild-goose chase."

"What's your idea?"

Buster was flying down to Atlanta the following week to attend a conference of local law-enforcement officials from the Southeast. He was considering stopping by Knoxville on his return to look up Dorsey Combs, maybe buy him a few drinks.

Wilson, looking at Buster's doleful face, couldn't think of anything helpful to say. Traces of white paint outlined the nails of the hand holding the beer can and were embedded in the knuckles. Weekend carpentry, a little painting, a few odd jobs around the house. They were outsiders now, their plugs had been pulled. The vast omniscient government information machine they'd once tapped into daily—a kind of heart pump or pacemaker that lifted the pulse rates and metabolism of half a million Washington civil servants every morning and lowered them with the thermostats every night—throbbed on without them. They were just ordinary citizens again. The global and domestic struggles were decided without them, like the NFL scores, and they sat on the sidelines every evening in their armchairs, waiting for Dan Rather or Roger Mudd to total up the scores.

"It might be interesting," Wilson conceded sympathetically.

"Yeah, but maybe it's a wild-goose chase too," Buster said, rousing himself from the table. "Come on, Fuzzy, let's start putting up wallboard before you get so goddamned crocked you can't see the chalk lines."

7.

Nick Straus had a headache from the two-hour meeting in the sixth-floor conference room at the State Department. The meeting had been convoked at the request of State's Bureau of Political/Military Affairs to persuade the Pentagon to soften its conditions for opening arms control talks with the Soviet Union. Les Fine, the deputy Pentagon arms control strategist whose phone taps Straus had discovered, had been requested to appear, but he'd sent his assistant instead. Colonel Dillon had been asked to sit in on the Pentagon side as an intelligence adviser, available to answer any questions as to the Pentagon's interpretation of any recent Soviet testing of their SS-18 and SS-19 multiple-warhead missiles. As Colonel Dillon left his office in the DIA special-watch section, he'd insisted that Nick Straus accompany him.

So Straus had been forced to attend, carrying Colonel Dillon's briefing book, a stenographic notebook, and an envelope of recent satellite imagery. He was terrified that Les Fine or someone else whom he'd worked with on arms control negotiations in the past would recognize him in this reincarnation and wonder what in the hell he was doing there.

He sat at the rear of the conference room, trying to conceal himself behind the bulky figure of Colonel Dillon, dreading discovery each time the door opened and someone else arrived, not absolutely certain that Les Fine wouldn't appear unannounced and take over the meeting himself or that some other ancient enemy from another government agency wouldn't arrive, discover him in the back of the room, and raise the same hue and cry: what was Nick Straus, the planetary humanist, the tireless old advocate of minimal deterrence, SALT I and SALT II, doing there on the Pentagon side of the house?

The meeting began on schedule. Once it commenced, Nick's fears were that Colonel Dillon would be called upon to explain some technical point and the colonel, slow on his feet under the best of circumstances, would turn to him in confusion for the briefing book answer. The eyes of everyone in the room would then be settled upon Nick's dim figure seated off in the shadows. Exposure would be inevitable.

But, to his relief, no technical points were raised. Instead, the meeting addressed the central issue: the Department of State's complaint that the Pentagon was imposing impossible conditions for commencing arms control talks with Moscow. As the price for strategic arms negotiations, the Pentagon was insisting that the Soviet Union dismantle seventy percent of its largest missiles, the SS-18s, and seventy-five percent of its multiple-warhead SS-17s and SS-19s. For the intermediate-range missiles in Europe, the Pentagon strategists were insisting upon the dismantlement of the Soviet SS-20s as the price for not deploying the U.S. Pershing IIs and the cruise missiles, "the zero-zero option."

Totally unrealistic, the State Department critics pointed out. One State analyst complained that the Pentagon was asking the Soviet Union to return to its European nuclear posture of 1958–59, in exchange for which the U.S. would refrain from introducing a new missile force. It was as if Detroit were asking the Japanese to recall all post-1960 cars, he suggested, in return for which U.S. automakers wouldn't put into production their own compact models still on the drawing board. As a basis for meaningful negotiations with Moscow, the Pentagon strategy was ludicrous.

One critic made the point Nick Straus would have made had he been a participant—that the Pentagon hard line was pushing the Soviet Union into escalating their strategic nuclear force just at the time they were leveling off—but no one picked it up. None of the Pentagon's critics made the assumption Nick had made long ago, even if it was implicit in their comments: namely, that the Pentagon strategy was exactly what it appeared—a strategy for failure. The Pentagon wasn't serious about opening arms control talks with Moscow, which would reject its demands out of hand. Soviet intransigence could then be cited as proof that Moscow was seeking the dominant power position to dictate the terms of the "peace"— Les Fine's threat of nuclear blackmail again—and the Pentagon strategists would be free to pursue their true intent: achieving nuclear superiority and converting it into effective political power, a chilling reversal of all previous nuclear doctrine.

Yet no one said a word about that. Instead, tedium settled over the meeting as it became clear that Les Fine's assistant had been given no flexibility. He merely listened to the arguments, made a few polite comments, explained why the Pentagon had no intention of softening its conditions, and insisted, quite rightly, that the Pentagon view would prevail at the NSC and the White House.

Pleading a sick headache, Nick Straus escaped Colonel Dillon's suggestion that they visit with a few of their colleagues at State. He threaded his way through the standing figures, head averted, and slipped out the door. The diplomatic entrance six floors below was crowded with television reporters, cameramen, and technicians awaiting the descent of a visiting foreign minister from the Secretary's seventh-floor suite. A group of curious onlookers had also gathered there. Crimson ropes closed off the middle doors and a gallery of klieg lights and microphones was set up near the private elevator.

He moved hurriedly through the spectators, pulling on his coat. The last shuttle to the Pentagon was due in a few minutes, and he had a neurotic fear of missing it, of being left stranded here on the far bank of the Potomac in the Friday rush hour madness. Taxis would be impossible to find; the Metro, whose entrance was five blocks away, would be sultry and packed, the vapor of white lights overhead enough to induce nausea as the underground car hurtled under the river. In the last week or so, he'd come to despise the Metro, which he'd once enjoyed, to despise it as much as the overheated morning buses from McLean, the windowless catacomb between B and C rings in the basement of the Pentagon, and the miles of dim corridor, all of which had seemed to evoke in him these last terrible days the sickly, long-suppressed claustrophobic illnesses of childhood.

As he moved through the glass doors to the side and into the gray light of the dying afternoon, a pair of sharp familiar eyes under bristling brows met his through the smudged glass of an adjacent door, held them for an angry instant, and then were swept past. Quickly he moved away but immediately collided with a tall figure striding up the pavement.

"Sorry—"

"My fault," Nick muttered in embarrassment.

"Nick? Nick Straus?"

It was Harry Squires he'd collided with, wearing an old storm coat and a cockeyed tweed hat.

"My God! Nick! I'd never have recognized you, old boy!" Tall, imperious, and every inch a fool, Squires was a foreign service officer Nick had known for many years, and last encountered in the mid-seventies during a visit to Rome. "Where have you been all these years?"

Nick yielded a dim smile. They'd never been friends, despite the familiarity in Squires's booming voice. From the door Nick had just left, he saw the small, energetic figure of General Gawpin emerge, the brows drawn together furiously.

"Where'd I last see you?" Squires asked. "Rome?"

Fools like Hank Squires were Nick's fate—in grade school, at Horace Mann High School, at Columbia, and at Harvard. Had he been on the *Titanic* or the *Lusitania,* or on the *Hindenburg* when the dirigible erupted in flame over Lakehurst, New Jersey, in 1937, Hank Squires would have been his lounge companion, prattling on about salmon fishing or the improvement in his backswing as the water closed over their heads or the fiery universe collapsed in upon them. If ever a 747 would be blown up by a PLO bomb in flight, with Nick aboard, or a car bomb demolish the U.S. embassy entrance in Paris just as Nick drew up in a taxi from Charles De Gaulle, Hank Squires or his facsimile would be his cabin or backseat companion. Whatever final catastrophe awaited Nick and denied him his life, his body, his mind, the last millisecond of the final moment would belong not to him but to a man like Hank Squires, to whom Nick would be politely listening as still he talked of spaniels, backswings, or haberdashery, while Nick's own consciousness curled like a blackened leaf and drifted off into the great void, indelibly imprinted for all eternity by those final words.

"I had the impression you'd retired," Squires continued, almost accusatorially.

"I suppose I did—in a way. How about you?"

"Just back from Malta. So where are you these days?" Squires's voice was terribly loud.

"Over at Defense," Nick whispered, his cheeks flushed. The Pentagon was anathema to a diplomat of Squires's pretensions.

"Defense?" Squires boomed, very shocked. "At Defense! With those chaps! You're not serious!" Squires had been a diplomat with great dramatic flair, superb style, but little substance, Nick recalled—the Douglas Fairbanks, Jr., of the European Bureau, his detractors said. General Gawpin, having followed Nick out, had now circled somewhere to the rear, eavesdropping out of view. Nick felt his hostile presence.

Two naval officers in white caps left the diplomatic entrance and hurried toward the curb.

"I have to catch the shuttle," Nick said apologetically. "It's the last one."

"The shuttle? But look here, we should get together. Where can I get in touch with you? The Pentagon, you say?"

"I'm in the book. Why don't I give you a call?" An Army officer jogged past. "I have to run, Hank. Sorry."

"We'll get together," Squires shouted. "You're in the Pentagon book?"

"That's right." Nick turned away and trotted quickly down the drive and out into the street. The Pentagon shuttle, an olive-green van with white letters on the side, moved toward him through the dusk. The five waiting passengers had already queued up and were boarding one by one as Nick desperately searched his wallet for his Pentagon pass, still conscious of General Gawpin's hovering presence. He was alone now, standing in front of the open door, still searching frantically for his Pentagon ID. He couldn't find it. The black driver waited impatiently. The seated passengers watched him in disapproval. Their car pools were waiting.

"Come on, man," the driver called out. "I ain't got all day."

Nick found the plastic I.D., but as he plucked it from his wallet the contents scattered across the asphalt. Bending quickly to retrieve them, he saw a few credit cards scattered under the van, and lifted his head toward the driver in a silent plea for patience. The door closed, the engine throttled forward, and the van crept away—not to enable him to recover his cards, as he'd thought, but to continue down the street. It turned the corner and disappeared into the darkness.

He retrieved the last of his possessions and stood up, face burning. The last shuttle was now gone and he crossed the boulevard without turning. Taxis would be impossible to find, so he plunged down the hill, across Constitution Avenue, and moved on through the darkness—past the Lincoln Memorial and out across Memorial Bridge, beyond which there were no footpaths, no walks, just the unending stream of cars moving past, their headlamps reflected against his anguished face like the bright shuttling windows of a speeding passenger train passing across an abandoned station, now black, now white, now black again.

It was there, at the far end of the bridge, that he finally stopped, unable to go farther. He struggled to get his breath, struggled to get control of himself, and as he did, plagued these last few days by some inner agony, by some forgotten guilt that evoked childhood illnesses and sickroom claustrophobia, he knew how fatally he was divided within himself and that something was terribly, terribly wrong.

8.

Haven Wilson drove to Ed Donlon's two-hundred-acre farm in Shenandoah County that Saturday morning. The autumn light had the deep tarnished luster of old pewter and the color was dying on the hills except for the dull coppers of the ancient oaks. A brisk wind drove broken cumulus from the north. He was alone in the station wagon. Nick Straus had begged off apologetically, remembering he had to complete a draft paper for a Monday deadline at the Pentagon. Betsy had shown no interest at all. "It's a little chilly today; maybe next time," she'd said, the way she usually did.

Much of the westbound traffic that morning was made up of vans and pickup trucks, some with camper shells in their truckbeds. Decals of ducks or of bass breaking water decorated their aluminum sides, with an occasional owner's name on the back in magnetic tape: *Bob and Nell, Hank's Hideaway, Furman's Folly.* Hunters and fishermen owned many of them, suburbanites headed for their A-frame cabins and prefabricated bungalows in the mountains. After two hours he climbed into the Shenandoah valley and turned south along the interstate, where traffic was heavier. Tractor-trailers rumbled past, down from the Pennsylvania Turnpike and headed south. Sedans and station wagons with Pennsylvania and New York license plates crept by, luggage under canvas on their roof racks and their backseats piled with cartons and plastic coolers, bound for jobs in the Sunbelt or late autumn holidays on the Florida beaches.

Ten miles south, he glided off the ramp and followed a narrow state road parallel to a spine of hogback mountain along a wide, shallow creek, heavy with autumn rains. White water boiled over the limestone ledges. He cruised through Tolerance, an unincorporated settlement where mud-scabbed pickups sat in front of weathered clapboard houses and cabins along the hollow. The hulks of abandoned school buses and logging trucks lay rusting in the autumn weeds behind boarded-over service stations, garages, and tabernacles. Smoke lifted from a few paintless cabins, where a neat back-stoop woodpile or wash on the line showed a woman's presence.

Two miles beyond, he turned west into the valley leading to the Donlon farm. The property line commenced a few hundred yards up a narrow gravel lane from the secondary road. Half the farm lay in woods up the mountain, the lower half was partially fallow in rolling meadows gone to clover, weeds, and wild blackberries. The best pasturage was along the floodplain of a wide creek on the eastern boundary, where the cattle belonging to a neighboring farmer, Ish Hopkins, cropped the winter fescue. The old barns and lowing sheds were in ruins, but the graceful two-hundred-year-old house was intact, as sedate as a Richmond dowager on the green damask shoulder of hillside between woods and pasture, facing south along the valley. The winding wagon road that led to it was once semi-paved but now had crumbled to gravel as it climbed from the stunted pines and cedars of the secondary road across open hillside, through cross-fenced fields, and into the ancient grove of hickory and oak.

He entered the old house through the kitchen, carrying the groceries to a crude plank table in front of a smoke-blackened fireplace. The dim aroma of scaling carbon and soot-impacted brick from the wood fires of the past greeted him, bringing back ghosts from his childhood, of stories told him in a house similar to this down in southwest Virginia. It was his grandfather's house, where he'd spent the summers as a boy, the same old house from which his great-grandfather Carver Wilson had been summoned on a warm summer evening in 1865, five months after Appomattox, and had walked out to the gate under the pear tree, his napkin still in his hand, his wife and children left behind at the supper table, summoned by those mounted figures at the gate who claimed they'd come to join the Tazewell County scouts organized under his command to end the brigandage and horse thievery in the region. It was near dusk. Some of the mounted men were in gray, some in blue, some in mountain linsey-woolsey, his wife had said. She'd watched from the window. They weren't mounted volunteers but marauding guerrillas from the mountains, who'd heard of his boasts. They'd shot him down under the pear tree.

The old pear tree had still been there during his boyhood, unpruned, the bark coarse, the fruit so hard it slashed his gums, drawing blood. Carver Wilson's oil portrait still hung in the parlor; the story of his murder drew his great-grandson to the pear tree evening after evening during his first summers there. The memory haunted him as he lay upstairs in the feather bed at the top of the rear stairs, the house in darkness, time stopped, memory stopped, his own heart stopped as he reconstructed the summer evening in 1865. It was his first encounter with history, the first taste of that long, dark chronicle that had spilled family blood, but at the time it was only a darkness where his mind and imagination hovered, senses denied him, trapped in a past he couldn't understand at all. The war was over, his great-grandfather had returned from Shiloh and Cold Harbor, had sat for his portrait in Roanoke, and then these men had come. Who were they, these guerrillas from the mountains?

For his grandmother and his great-aunts, the moment had long since faded into lavender and musk, the memory perished in those brittle lines of newspaper verse published by the county poetess the month after his great-grandfather's death and kept by his grandmother in the family album, like scraps of yellowing lace:

> The body on the knees was found,
> The head reposed low on the ground,
> No more to fight guerrilla bands,
> In Tazewell's vales and hilly lands,
> Where Godless rebels kill and thieve,
> Leaving widowed hearts to grieve.

His own memories had never been surrendered in that way. The mystery was the same now as it had been then, as he lay upstairs in the summer darkness and watched the heat lightning shimmer across the valley, or heard the reverberations of an August thunderstorm which brought those marauding voices nearer, standing just below the open window, but this time calling his name through the August darkness: *Haven Wilson! Haven Wilson! We've come for you. Your turn now!*

These familiar ghosts survived in the musk of Ed Donlon's smokeless chimneys. The old brick house in Tazewell County was gone now, like the great-aunts, the grandmother, his mother and father. "Sometimes I think you're only a family memory, Haven," Betsy's father had once told him, "but I suppose that's typical of Southerners. The tradition seems to be passing, doesn't it?"

He inspected the empty rooms, as he always did, examining the windows, the ceiling for seepage, the wiring. Except for the kitchen, no furniture remained. Jane Donlon had withdrawn the antiques after Brian's death. The old pine mantels and the banister that rose three floors from the downstairs center hall were all of value that remained, and were sought by antique dealers and by the thieves who plundered unoccupied old houses.

He had a solitary lunch on the side gallery, sitting with his back against the bricks, out of the wind. The day was darker now, growing more overcast. He would have felt a little foolish had anyone found him there, even Betsy, contemplating fields he didn't own, pastures needing lime and reseeding, fences needing new locust posts, thickets needing bush hogging, and sheds and barns requiring new beams and roofs if their decay was to be stopped. He knew how he would do these things, where he would begin and where he would end, just as he knew what it would look like after three or four years.

But the fields faded, he felt the wind, and was conscious of the rough mortar against his back. Betsy would never live out here. The silence would make her uneasy and in the end she'd fall prey to her solitude, terrorized the same way Jane Donlon had been after Brian's death.

He lifted himself from the gallery deck and gathered up the wax papers and beer can. As he turned toward the door, he saw a group of forgotten objects on the stone coping below the window—a plastic guitar pick, a broken string, and an old medicine bottle with a few dried flowers stuck in its throat. They'd been left behind by Brian Donlon and Sue, his live-in companion, who'd once sat on this same gallery in the evenings and played their guitars.

He took them back to the kitchen and left them on the mantel.

In the drive, he filled the chain saw from the gas can and carried it back along a fence toward an old red oak that had lost two of its lower limbs during an ice storm. As he approached the tree, the silence was broken by the crack of a rifle from high up the mountain.

He stopped, head lifted. Two more shots followed. Deer season hadn't opened yet. Rifle fire this time of year came from either poachers or the beer-drinking gun addicts from Tolerance or Henshaw. A handful of young drifters and dropouts had settled in both communities, most of them self-styled hippies ten years behind the times, some with long hair and beards, others with shaved heads or scalp locks, Mohawk fashion, indifferent to organic gardening and communal effort, devoted instead to guns, beer, pot, and souped-up cars. They trapped or snared fox, raccoon, and quail illegally, flashed deer by night with their pickup trucks and 30-30s, and grew marijuana in hidden meadows high up the mountain for high school and college consumers in the larger towns and the urban suburbs. One group lived in an abandoned schoolhouse near Tolerance—the ones Brian Donlon had fallen in with during his final stay at the farm.

Theirs had been the trucks and Mustangs Donlon and Wilson had found in the drive that Saturday morning they'd arrived with the new chain saw Ed Donlon was eager to try out. Their empty beer cans and roach-filled ashtrays covered the kitchen table, the chairs and hearth; their reeking bodies were sprawled in the front two rooms, sleeping off an all-night beer and pot party, sexes still intermingled under musty blankets.

Wide awake, freshly shaven, wearing his new Bean's brier-proof pants and an Irish hat, Ed Donlon, the country squire, was outraged. His son wore a wispy golden beard, was barefooted, his stringy hair matted. Over his thin shoulders was a soiled scrap of Navajo blanket. Sue, the thin redheaded companion, joined them sleepily in the kitchen, also bare-footed. For Donlon, the experiment was over, his patience exhausted. He was furious. Brian had less and less to say. Pink-eyed, embarrassed, and confused, he finally lit a cigarette, took a puff, and passed it to Sue. Then, still listening to his father, he'd wandered to the refrigerator, removed a can of beer, and popped the lid. His father reached him in two steps and knocked the can from his hand. It was nine o'clock in the morning.

Haven Wilson turned and left. He walked back to the lifted trunk of the BMW, where the new chain saw lay, and stood looking at it, ashamed. He could hear Ed Donlon's shouts from the kitchen. He closed the trunk, but a few minutes later Donlon came out of the house, grabbed up the chain saw, and headed for the woods. Wilson went back to the house, but Brian had gone upstairs with the girl and he followed Ed Donlon instead. When the two men returned from the woods just before lunch, the house was empty, the potted marijuana plants had disappeared from the kitchen windowsills, and Brian and Sue had vanished in her yellow Volkswagen.

Father and son had had disagreements before, but none as final as that one. At the beginning of his sophomore year at Haverford, Brian had left school to find secret refuge on his father's farm, living first in the house and then in a small cabin he'd built in the woods higher on the mountain. Haven Wilson had stumbled upon it not long after Brian's death, a small, crudely built shed constructed from boards salvaged from a partially col-lapsed barn. A few forgotten books lay moldering on the rough shelf—a book of Sufi, Tagore, Herman Hesse, and a water-marked Gordon Light-foot songbook. On the plank sills sat the ubiquitous medicine bottles with straw flowers stuck in their throats. To the side of the cabin lay an over-grown plot, hacked out by hand, where Brian had cultivated his marijuana plants.

After Brian had run out of money that first autumn, he'd telephoned his mother, who secretly sent him money orders from a Washington post office. When the first snows came to the valley, he returned to his parents' house and he and his father reached a temporary understanding. He lived in the Georgetown house and found work as a dishwasher in a restaurant on Pennsylvania Avenue behind the Capitol. Waiting tables at the same restaurant was a young woman a year older, also a college dropout, but more traveled. She'd tended goats on a communal farm in Idaho, picked peaches in Oregon, where she'd studied art, and owned a battered yellow Volkswagen with Colorado license plates.

That February Brian moved in with her, sharing a two-room basement flat on Capitol Hill. The two drove to the Shenandoah farm a few times that winter, helping Ed Donlon with the restoration of the house. After

Brian lost his job and couldn't find another, he'd gone to his mother with a proposition. He and Sue would move to the farm and help with the restoration until autumn, when they both planned on returning to school. They had ideas for an herbal garden and a goat house, and would earn extra money selling herbs and feta cheese to Washington restaurants. Ed Donlon was skeptical but Jane was enthusiastic. She was a potter and sculptress and had had plans drawn up for converting one of the outbuildings into a studio-workshop. Instead of hiring a carpenter from Tolerance to begin construction, she offered the project to Brian at ten dollars an hour.

Brian and Sue moved to the farm in May. By midsummer the shed that was to become a studio-workshop was still in ruins. The lumber delivered from the sawmill near Fenshaw lay weathering in the high weeds near the barn. A few fields had been partially cleared but the blackberries were reclaiming them, as tangled as the abandoned herbal garden on the hillside above the silo. The most well-traveled path was the one across the pasture and up the mountain to the cabin where the marijuana grew in luxurious solitude, nourished by the thick compost brought up through the woods by Brian and Sue from the floor of the ruined silo.

Haven Wilson and his youngest son, Paul, occasionally joined the Donlons during their Saturday renovations. They seldom saw Sue, who would melt away with the Donlons' arrival, retreating up the pasture toward the hidden cabin, not to return until dusk, when supper was being cooked on the charcoal grill. Ed Donlon had spoken no more than a dozen words to her. Jane Donlon's attempts at conversation—family, school, her future plans—were turned away with the vaguest of answers, but Jane seemed to understand. She was a dreamer, like her son, drawing substance from silence.

Brian was always there when Haven and Paul Wilson arrived, smiling softly, holding a coffee cup or a beer can, his eyes lit up by that curious glow Haven Wilson could recognize but not completely understand. He was a conscientious worker. His movements with a hammer, a saw, or a wrecking bar were lazy but sure. It was as if Brian, as they worked, saw designs hidden from the rest of them—lights, shadows, texture: the weathered whorls of an ancient oak board that didn't need nails at all, the leaning hickory post that wasn't made stronger by wire, already unique in its own way by the rusty nails embedded in it, by the wild grasses nearby or the abandoned chickadee's hole at the top of the post.

On the beam of an old barn, Paul Wilson once found a heap of rusting iron, old wagon bolts, hand-forged hooks and horseshoe nails, gear cogs, and teeth from a sickle bar—junk, nothing more, to Paul Wilson, the political science major at Georgetown; but they were arranged in a curious way, bound together by a curl of wire from a broken wagon spring. As Paul lifted the objects into the burlap trash bag, Jane Donlon stopped him. "No, those are Brian's," she'd said, as if she, too, had recognized what her son had found there.

They grew accustomed to finding such clutters of rusted objects around the outbuildings as they cleaned up, Brian's totems of rustic sculpture gathered in the corner of the old blacksmith shop, along a beam in the smokehouse, or in a box behind the kitchen range. They were Brian's collections, Brian's objects. Jane Donlon thought she understood them. She saw in her son's indolence the beatitude of an artist, intent like Klee or Miró upon hieratic meanings—rusty shapes which light transmogrified, green beetles like Egyptian scarabs on the unweeded corn tassels, the haiku ideographs of the bore weevil on a panel of rotting oak board Brian had set aside, unable to burn.

Haven Wilson, like Ed Donlon, thought only of a pastoral Eden—too much beer, too much marijuana, the effortless sensuality of those hot summer days and the girl named Sue. Neither of them knew much about drugs. Paul Wilson, who did, had nothing to say. Had Haven Wilson discovered those purple bruises on Brian's arm, he might have thought they'd been made by a falling beam or a slipped crowbar, like the scab on his shin.

But as the weeks passed and the herb garden went back to weed, like the front yard, and nothing got done except when Ed Donlon was there on a Saturday or Sunday, Ed's patience began to tatter. The discovery of a houseful of drunken layabouts in the old brick house that morning was the last straw:

"Get out and take what you have with you! Everything, both of you! Don't come back until you've straightened yourself out! If that takes ten years, then it's all right with me!"

Brian and Sue disappeared. They heard nothing for two months. Then in late October a postcard came to Brian at the house in Georgetown, postmarked from Durango, Colorado. The card was from Sue, enrolled again at the small junior college she'd left three years earlier. "I hope by now you've kicked it or whatever," she wrote, "got it back together, because if you haven't, it'll get harder all the time."

Jane Donlon thought she recognized the warning and believed it intended for her. She went to the police, who promised to look for him, and visited two halfway houses with the family physician, searching for information. She learned nothing.

The first week in December, she received a telephone call from Brian. His voice was thick with rheum and his speech was slurred. He told her he was working at a restaurant in Largo, Maryland, and didn't need money. He'd called because it was Thanksgiving and they would be having turkey

121

and cranberries. He'd thought of sending them a bottle of Madeira, like the bottles his grandfather uncorked at the house in Connecticut, but hadn't been able to find the right label. He said he wanted to wish them a happy Thanksgiving and hung up. Thanksgiving was five days past. She and Ed visited every restaurant they could find in Largo, Maryland, but Brian wasn't employed at any of them. That was the last they heard from their son.

The second week in January, Jane received a call from the Washington police, narcotics division, asking to speak to her husband. She lost control of herself and the detective said he would call back in thirty minutes, after her husband was home. She was unable to reach Ed at his office and called Haven Wilson instead at the Senate office building, still semihysterical. He telephoned the narcotics division, spoke to the detective, and then drove to Georgetown to pick up Ed Donlon. At George Washington University Hospital, Donlon broke down in the parking lot and couldn't leave the car. Wilson met the detective alone inside. The body lay on an emergency room receiving table in the morgue, covered by a sheet, one foot exposed. As soon as Wilson saw the old man's foot, grayish-yellow, wrinkled, vein prominent below the ankle joint, the sole carbon black, he knew the police had made a mistake; but the error was his. Wasted and sallow from hepatitis, Brian Donlon lay under the sheet, dead of a drug overdose. Heroin and cocaine had been injected in combination into a vein bruised with needle marks. He was nineteen years old. He'd been dead for six hours when the landlady of a rooming house near Dupont Circle found the body next to the bed in his furnished flat.

"You never talked to him, never! You never talked to him!" He stood in the downstairs hall of the Georgetown house that evening, listening to Jane Donlon upstairs, where her husband was trying to comfort her. Wilson had visited Brian's furnished room alone and had returned with those possessions the narcotics squad had been willing to release. They'd found a quantity of marijuana in the rear closet and suspected Brian had been retailing it from a source in rural Virginia. Everywhere in the room he'd found evidence of Brian's paralysis—the dozens of letters begun to his parents and to Sue but never completed, the fragmentary drawings and sketches in the artist's pads, the aimless prose poems of the composition books, and the wooden box of rusting objects from the farm lying in dust beneath the bed.

A sudden stranger in the Georgetown house, he listened to Jane Donlon's anguished voice, to her husband's hoarse words of consolation, and returned to the living room with the portfolio of Brian's letters and sketches. In the armchair next to the floor lamp, he sorted through them again until he found the most recent one. It was dated January 11, the day before, and he'd found it lying in full view on the table. As incomplete as the others, it was addressed to his mother:

> I always thought Dad knew something special, knew something he'd tell me one day, but he never did. This was what I always thought, even after I went to Haverford. It was always in the back of my mind whenever we were together, whether it was working on the farm or doing something else—that maybe this was the day he would tell me.
>   But that day we had the argument, I knew he was never going to tell me, that he was keeping it all for himself or he just didn't know, and so I knew the time had come to find it for myself.

"You never understood him, never! You refused!"

Jane Donlon's voice was exhausted now, only a throb of brightness dissolving in her throat, like water into coarse sand. He hesitated, still holding the letter under the lamplight, trying to decide. He was still considering the letter as the chimes sounded. The Donlon family physician was at the front door, summoned by Ed Donlon. Wilson admitted him and after he'd gone upstairs, returned the letter to the portfolio. These were Brian's words; Wilson was a stranger., He had no right to withhold them.

Two months later, the Donlons separated. Jane went to Connecticut and apprenticed herself to a potter and sculptor.

9.

Artie Kramer was ten years older and an inch shorter than his auburn-haired wife. His gray hair was long on top, combed back neatly from his tanned forehead, but puffed out like goosedown over the small ears. He looked like a man who spent a few hours a day under a sunlamp. His skin had an orange-yellow luster that didn't so much resemble sunburn as it did margarine coloring. He wore a blue blazer, a white turtleneck, and flared gray trousers. Worn over his shoulders like a cape was a creamy-white car coat with more flaps, epaulets, zippers, and brass rings than an Italian flying circus. For all this sartorial tidiness, fashion had done nothing to improve the face, which was as sour and rumpled as a club fighter's gym bag. His voice was loose, rumbling, and derisive, delivered out of the side of his mouth, like the windowman's at a Coney Island hot dog stand.

But he'd stopped complaining now and sat in the center of the flagstone terrace overlooking the Potomac, in a wicker chair fetched by one of his factotums from the game room of Grace Ramsey's cliffside house. His steady gaze drilled the sunlit spaces somewhere beyond the river. The nostrils of the battered nose were somewhat flared, as if still outraged by the headful of bad odors brought back with him from his private tour of the house. He also continued to ignore Haven Wilson, who sat on the stone wall nearby, his back to the river, regretting his decision to join them.

He'd been waiting for the group when they'd finally arrived, thirty minutes late, driven out from Washington in a limousine-service Cadillac preceded by Edelman's diesel Mercedes and Strykker's white BMW. In the Cadillac with Kramer were Rita and two men who had accompanied him from the West Coast. One, named Chuckie Savant, was a plump little sycophant who scurried about with a headwaiter's briskness and self-importance, and the other was a glum, goat-shouldered moron named Franconi, who had no voice at all and whose eyes were hidden behind dark glasses.

Kramer hadn't acknowledged his wife's introductions as Wilson met them in the front drive. He hadn't even turned in Wilson's direction. Rita Kramer had been left standing alone, embarrassed. Chuckie Savant and Franconi had stared at him sullenly and then moved away too, following the two Kramers as they toured the grounds and then disappeared into the house. Edelman, tall, gray-haired, with a pharmacist's pallor and dry white lips, had introduced himself but found he had nothing to say. He removed his glasses, wiped them silently, and strolled after his clients. Strykker didn't leave his car. He watched somberly through the window, said something to his woman companion, and drove quickly away.

Wilson had waited alone on the terrace, listening to the voices from inside—Rita Kramer's first, followed by her husband's, harsher, crueler, growing more ugly, his taunts unanswered. Then he'd heard no voices at all, just footsteps, the slam of a door, the slam of another, this time louder. It was after one of these explosions that Edelman appeared suddenly on the terrace alone, as if blown through the door by the concussion. He said nothing, prudently ignoring Wilson as he stood at the end of the terrace, studying the river and polishing his glasses again. Chuckie Savant and Franconi emerged a few minutes later and strolled together toward the nylon-covered swimming pool, deep in conversation. Five minutes later, Rita and Artie Kramer appeared.

"You don't know, you just goddamn don't know," Kramer was saying as he emerged into the autumn sunshine. "The sleazebags, the goddamn sleazebags." Rita Kramer's face was flushed, her eyes averted. "Where the hell are the goddamned chairs?" Kramer grumbled, searching for a place to sit in the sun. Chuckie Savant hurried inside and returned with two basket chairs. One remained unoccupied. Rita Kramer disappeared around the corner of the house and her husband sat in silence, nostrils flared, gazing suspiciously out across the river toward the Maryland hills.

Now Rita Kramer had returned with a wicker picnic basket from the limousine and was unpacking the catered lunch. She unwrapped the tea sandwiches, uncovered the salad and plates, and began filling the plastic glasses from a bottle of chilled Chablis.

The day was clear, the azure sky unbroken by clouds. The terrace, warm in the autumn sun, was cool in the shadows.

"Where's the Washington monument?" Artie Kramer grunted unpleasantly, bestirring himself.

His wife moved to the stone wall. "You can almost see it," she said, leaning out over the cliff and pointing upriver with a salad spoon.

"Almost. Always almost," her husband said. "Almost shit." He made no move to look. Instead he turned to Chuckie Savant. "What'd that PR flack say about almost?"

"Which flack?"

"From the studio. You know, *cojones*. Almost."

"That was 'if.' If your mother had *cojones*, she'd be your father." Savant chuckled. "But it comes to the same thing."

"Sure it comes to the same thing," Kramer said. "What do you think I said?"

"What's *cojones?*" Franconi asked.

"What do you think it is if your mother had them she'd be your father?" Artie answered. "Where's Georgetown?" He looked across the river.

"The same way," Rita answered, again pointing with the spoon.

"What's that over there?" He nodded across the river.

"Maryland," Edelman replied. No one spoke for a long time. Rita Kramer went back to the wine bottle and finished filling the glasses. She served the others and then Wilson, who seldom drank wine in the middle of the day, but had no heart to refuse her.

"We drove through Georgetown last night," Artie Kramer said to no one in particular, shoulders hunched, knees drawn together like an invalid as he scratched his ankle. "Last night and this morning. It was crowded, all jammed up—wall-to-wall hookers, niggers, and junkies. Franconi didn't go."

"I hadda date," Franconi said.

"Sure, Frankie had a date. A two-hundred-dollar date. How can anyone live in that place? Where's the privacy, huh? That's where you hang your hat, isn't it, Edelman?"

"Not really, but there are some attractive locations in Georgetown," Edelman replied.

"We didn't see them, did we, Chuckie?"

"Naw, we didn't see them."

"Only I didn't say Lake Tahoe, did I say that? All the way out here? Lake Tahoe?" Kramer's head was turned as he spoke to his wife, who knelt at the picnic basket behind him, but he couldn't see her face. She didn't lift her gaze from the plates she was preparing. "Did I say Lake Tahoe?"

"No," she answered, her head still lowered. "You didn't say that."

"O.K., then, you shoulda waited like I told you to—"

"I wanted to save you the trouble—"

"You shoulda waited, goddammit!" His voice lifted cruelly, but she didn't stir, still crouching out of sight, searching for knives and forks from the basket.

Wilson had seen and heard enough. He rose silently, looking at Rita Kramer.

"Two days, that's all," Kramer muttered, turning back toward the river. "Just two days, two crummy days, an' I woulda been here myself, handling these sleazebags."

Rising, Rita leaned over from behind him, put a paper napkin on his knee and then a paper plate. He moved the wineglass to his left hand and took it. "What is this stuff?" He picked suspiciously at the corner of the sandwich.

"It's chicken and lettuce, all white meat."

"That's mayonnaise. That stuff looks like mayonnaise to me—"

"It's butter; just butter, salt, and pepper, that's all—the way you like it."

Gingerly Kramer picked up the sandwich and began to chew, his mouth partially open, the sounds audible to everyone. Wilson carried his wineglass back to Rita Kramer's picnic basket.

"I think I'll move along," he told her. "The security man can lock up after you're finished." She lifted her head, her eyes wide, like a punished child. It wasn't the face he had grown accustomed to.

"Please," she said.

"Stick around, Wilson," Artie Kramer called loudly over his shoulder, still smacking his lips. "I haven't finished with you yet. You think I forgot about you, watching over there all this time like some kinda Mister Invisible? You think I'm just sitting here enjoying the scenery? I seen better scenery in Bakersfield. I wanna talk to you."

"Please," Rita whispered.

Wilson returned to the stone wall and sat down.

Artie Kramer finished his sandwich and gazed out over the river, butter still on his lips, his cheeks pouched like a chipmunk's. His jaws still moved rhythmically. He washed his mouth with Chablis, put paper plate and plastic glass on the flagstones at his feet, and wiped his face, neck, and ears with the napkin. "Maybe you think I didn't notice," he resumed, tossing the wadded napkin toward the picnic basket. He missed and it rolled into the cool shadows. "Hey, babe," Kramer remembered, watching his wife retrieve it, "I forgot to tell you. Howie Dickson bought a place up near Carmel. Paid what—eight hundred thou, Chuckie?"

"Eight hundred thou," Chuckie said.

"That's nice," Rita said.

"Wait'll they hear about this. Wait'll they hear Rita bought a wired-up house built by the head of the CIA—right, Chuckie?"

"Wait'll they hear," Chuckie said, turning to look at Wilson.

"Only we wanted to come into Washington real quiet, didn't we, babe? Real quiet. No bank dicks at the front gate, like this one has got, no one blowing off sirens, no closed-circuit TV unless we put it in ourselves. You a friend of his, Wilson? Is that why you were giving Rita all of this hassle about this house, checking her out like you were looking for something? What are you looking for? You wanna see my tonsils, you wanna see my gall bladder scars?"

"Let's not start that again, Artie," Rita said.

"Start what? I'm talking to Wilson, O.K.? I'm not talking to you! I'll get to you, don't you think I won't. This guy's into me for a hundred and fifty Gs already, like you are! You mean I can't talk to him like he's my pal? If I was into someone for a hundred and fifty Gs, I'd be his pal, O.K.? How about it, Wilson? You a friend of his?"

"Who are we talking about?" Wilson asked.

"Who'm I talking about, listen to him. Who'm I talking about? The guy that built this house, that's who I'm talking about. So what's all this hassle, all this shit with Rita, with Edelman there? All those guys in uniforms out at the gate, all this hardware inside? I may not have a pedigree like you creeps, but I'm not stupid!"

"I don't know what you're talking about," Wilson said. "Grace Ramsey owns this house."

"She inherited it from her husband," Edelman said. "He died a few years ago."

"So what'd her old man do?" Kramer asked Wilson. "Let's hear it! What'd he do?"

"He was a lawyer."

"He was a fed, like you! CIA, wasn't he? C'mon, Wilson, don't fuck with me."

"I knew him as a lawyer," Wilson said. "But maybe your information is better than mine; it makes less sense. That's the way it usually is."

"What'd he say?" Kramer asked Edelman.

"He said your information is better," Edelman said dryly.

"It sure as hell is," said Chuckie Savant.

"What's your angle, Wilson?" Kramer continued. "You and this lawyer

Donlon that don't show his face. He was CIA too, wasn't he? How come is it you're giving us all this grief? What is it—you think our pedigrees won't wash? C'mon, Wilson, what's this all about? You're a fed too, aren't you?"

"Artie, please," his wife said.

"What the hell are you after?" he continued indignantly. "All this nosing around. My wife comes east to buy a house real quiet like and a couple of feds try to hustle her this one. A couple of days later, someone's frisking my offices in L.A. The immigration dicks send a couple of snoopers around to my dress plant, looking for Mexes, then I get a raid and gotta lay off two lines. Then pretty soon some twerp from IRS is giving my accountant some shit about my '78 and '79 returns and says I'm gonna get an audit. So what the hell's this about, Wilson? Who tied you to my tail? What do you think—that I'm washing someone's dough to buy this place, that I'm gonna put slots in the front room, a couple of roulette wheels in the basement?"

"I think you're a little confused about something," Wilson said.

Kramer turned to Edelman. "Tell him!" he demanded.

Edelman removed his glasses, took out his handkerchief, and wiped his glasses very carefully, looking out across the river. "Mr. Kramer feels he's been victimized by some very clumsy scrutiny recently, ever since his name was mentioned for a political appointment. Something of a pattern . . ." He smiled wanly, as if to dissociate himself from his client's suspicions.

"What does Grace Ramsey's house have to do with it?" Wilson asked.

"Since Grace Ramsey's husband was at one time a senior deputy at the Agency, as was this lawyer Edward Donlon, he draws a connection—"

"That's not the whole story," Chuckie Savant interrupted. "You got it all wrong."

"Shut up," Artie said. "Let's hear what Wilson has to say. C'mon, Wilson, lay it on us, the way you did in the old days when you were a fed over at Justice. Maybe you're still a fed, huh? Working some sting? C'mon, Wilson, we're not stupid. Who's pulling your string these days? What's this shakedown all about?"

"Please, Artie," Rita Kramer pleaded quietly. "This isn't the place."

"I think Mrs. Kramer is right," Edelman said.

"Who the hell cares what you think! I'm talking to this fed here! C'mon, answer me, pal. Tell me about all this hassle you've been dishing out."

"I don't know what you're talking about. The only problem was the price. That caused the delay, nothing else—"

"Lemme tell you about the price," Kramer broke in. "You wanna talk about price? O.K., we'll talk about price! For all these Gs you took Rita for, it don't even have no screening room, not even a place to put one! Nothing! It hasn't got no sauna, no hot tub, nothing but a crummy little bar and a pint-sized pool you couldn't even get five fat ladies in! You know what that kind of dough will buy in L.A., Wilson? You know what it'll bring? No, you don't know. You don't know nothing, Wilson, because you got shit in your ears, same as Edelman here, who I told not to do nothing without checking with me, same as I told Rita when I sent that telex from Palm Springs telling her to hold up till I got here! You think I can't smell some kind of shakedown in all this shit you an' this lawyer been dishing out?"

Kramer's composure, like his grammar, had broken apart. Confused or not, the anger was genuine, Wilson thought, looking at a white-faced Rita Kramer. "You received a telex?" he asked.

She shook her head. "I never got it," she whispered.

"I said it, didn't I?" her husband shouted. "Didn't I say it?" He looked angrily at Wilson. "What do you want, an affidavit! I got a copy. Give him the copy, Chuckie."

"It's in my briefcase."

"Well, go get it the fuck outta your briefcase."

Chuckie Savant hurried across the terrace and disappeared around the walk. Rita Kramer still knelt near the picnic basket, but her hands were idle, her shoulders slumped. Edelman brooded silently across the river, his arms folded, his back to Artie Kramer.

Wilson stood up and opened his briefcase. "The house isn't worth all of this," he said. "If you don't want the house, I'll void the contract."

Rita Kramer looked up; Edelman turned in surprise.

"Don't shit me, Wilson," Kramer said suspiciously.

"No, I'll void it, the sooner the better—"

"Sure, listen at him," Kramer said. "He cuts off my balls and when I get rough he calls it a vasectomy." He laughed, looking around for an echo of assent, but Chuckie Savant wasn't there. "Then I get a lawyer and you tell me I can have 'em back, gold-plated. I can wear 'em around my neck. Just smooth, sure, like it never happened."

Wilson removed the copies of the contract. Clipped to the top was the certified check for $150,000 he'd been holding for Matthews' return from Florida the following day. "Like it never happened," Wilson said.

"But you got bad memories, right?" Kramer continued. "Real bad memories. How much to take away the pain?"

"A receipt," Wilson said, "a receipt and a statement withdrawing any claims." He gave the documents and check to Edelman, who looked at them, still surprised, and then at Artie Kramer, who was impatiently holding out his hand. "Lemme see 'em." Rita Kramer stood up and went into the house without turning. Her husband didn't look up. "Sure," he agreed finally, handing the contract and check back to Edelman. "Write him out what he wants, but no residuals, O.K.? Nothing left on the books—right, Wilson?"

"Nothing on the books."

"No fingerprints, nothing."

Edelman followed Rita Kramer into the house. Chuckie Savant hurried back along the walk, carrying a briefcase, and handed Artie a sheet of telex newsprint, which he studied silently. Then, beckoning for Savant's brief-case, he took it on his lap, opened it, and searched for something, while Savant hovered by in embarrassment. "What's this shit?" Kramer asked, taking out two nudist magazines and waving them accusingly at Savant. "What's this—a tit show, a nooky rag? You oughta be ashamed, a man your age, playing with himself like this. Go get yourself a two-hundred-dollar date, like Frankie." He put one magazine over the newsprint, like a straightedge, and tore it in two. One section he handed to Savant. "Show him this, show him his affidavit."

"It's all right; I'll take your word," Wilson said.

"What's wrong, you don't trust us?" Savant said. "Read it for yourself."

Wilson still declined. "You sent it from Palm Springs, you say?" he asked. "When was that?"

"Listen at him." Kramer laughed. "Listen at him, would you? What'd I tell you? These guys don't forget. Last Sunday, yeah. I was in Palm Springs last Sunday, playing golf. You wanna know my handicap? On the eighth green, I get to thinking about Rita, worrying about her, how she might make a mistake. I send for my secretary, who's waiting for me in the clubhouse, drinking tomato juice on account of his ulcer. It's a foursome I'm not gonna leave for nothing. I got five grand riding on the next hole. So my secretary hustles out in a golf cart and I tell him to send this telex to Rita. So he calls L.A. and sends the telex. What else do you wanna know?" He was still smiling. "I got contacts, Wilson. You think I don't have contacts? I got your number, you and this here lawyer Donlon."

"This was last Sunday?" Wilson said.

"Yeah, Sunday. Give Wilson some bubbly, Chuckie."

"Where'd she hide that bottle?" Chuckie Savant finally found the Chablis under a napkin in the wicker basket and refilled Artie Kramer's glass, but Wilson declined. Edelman returned from the house with a neatly printed legal document which Kramer signed and passed to Wilson, who read it, folded it in his pocket, and stood up.

"Cool—right, Edelman?" Kramer said, watching Wilson. "Look at him. He turns over a hundred and fifty Gs and don't bat an eye. You got class, Wilson. They must be playing you big, real big. They must be working you on a million-dollar gig. C'mon, we're pals now. I'll show you a little class too. C'mon, whose pants are you guys trying to get into?"

"Isn't there something for him to sign?" Chuckie Savant said.

Kramer turned in annoyance. "How about the Rams game?" he asked. "Aren't they playing?"

"It's on at four," Franconi said.

"Yeah, go watch and see. I wanna talk to Wilson. You too, Edelman."

"I've got an appointment," Wilson said. "I'll take a raincheck if you don't mind. Some other time."

"I thought you had balls, Wilson," Kramer said. "C'mon, relax. Have a little bubbly and let's talk. . . ."

But Wilson left him sitting there, with Chuckie Savant and Franconi standing nearby, no longer knowing what was expected of them.

Edelman followed at Wilson's heels. "It's a little confusing for you, I suppose," he offered as they emerged from the walk and climbed the steps in front. "Artie Kramer is a self-made man," he continued as they reached the station wagon. "He's jealous of what he has and not particularly at ease with those he doesn't know, particularly government people." Wilson nodded, watching Rita Kramer leave the front door. "I can't always explain his logic," Edelman continued with a sigh of self-absolution. "His contacts with the government have generally been confrontational. By some instinct of self-preservation, he measures others purely in—" he hesitated, as if conscious of violating a client's confidence—"in adversarial terms."

"You mean he's a paranoid," Wilson said, as Rita Kramer approached. "Who told him I used to work at Justice?"

"He did some inquiring, I'm not sure how. Any interpretation he gave was purely his own. . . ."

Rita Kramer joined them. "I'm sorry," Wilson said.

"I could have handled it," she said. "If you hadn't given back the check, I could have talked him out of it—all those goddamn crackpot conspiracy theories of his, all those crummy reasons he dreams up for everything that happens, and him the first to know." She was still annoyed. "Sometimes I think he ought to be locked up."

Surprised, Edelman discreetly moved his eyes away, studying the blue spruces.

"It seemed the best thing to do."

"Maybe it was," she said. "I'm the one who's got to listen to him all day long. If what he said today didn't make any sense, wait till you get him talking about the Kennedy assassination—Oswald, Jack Ruby, and Castro, even the KGB. Or the Bay of Pigs. Or Iran. You want to see a volcano about to erupt, ask him about Iran." She paused, dismayed by her own voice. "Anyway, he thinks everything in this town is wired up by the CIA, the FBI, or the White House. If it wasn't so pathetic, it'd be funny, but that's the way he grew up, a street-wise kid from Brooklyn who's never really made it out of the tenth grade. He's still reading comic books, but now he makes them up as he goes along. He thinks being street-wise can explain everything. He's patriotic, that's no joke, and maybe that's what makes it so pathetic. Can you see him on a White House appointment list?" She looked at Wilson, who didn't answer. "Neither can I. That's what makes me think something funny's going on. . . ."

Franconi emerged from the terrace and came up the steps toward them. Seeing him, Edelman displayed a lawyer's prudence and moved discreetly away. They watched him disappear into the house.

"So now you know why I wanted this thing nailed down before Artie came," Rita continued as she watched Franconi open the rear door of the Cadillac and rummage about in the back seat. "The worst part is he makes me suspicious sometimes. That's what hurts."

"Suspicious in what way?"

"Raising all that fuss back there was just the excuse. I picked out the house; it was my idea, not his. For someone like Artie, he decides, no one else. When he doesn't get his own way, he cheats on you until he does. Now he's got his own way. What are you looking for?" she called impatiently to Franconi, who remained at the rear door, his movements very deliberate.

"The doctor bag. Artie feels a migraine coming on."

"It's in the front seat on the floor."

"That's just the way it is," she said. "I was in analysis once and I thought it might help him. It didn't." Franconi had lifted the bag from the front seat and was searching through it. She watched him suspiciously. "Did you find it?"

"Yeah, I got it."

"Then get out of here, you creep."

They watched Franconi go down the steps and onto the terrace.

"It must all seem pretty infantile to you, doesn't it?" she said.

"Not particularly. I'm sorry it worked out for you this way. I know how much you liked this place. It's too bad. If he changes his mind, give Matthews a call."

"He won't change his mind. We've got a hotel suite downtown now; we can have it as long as we need it." She turned to look at him. "Do I get to keep the roses or should I send them back?"

"No, I think Grace Ramsey would want you to keep them."

"Grace Ramsey?" She gave a small laugh. "You're a goddamned liar, honey, but thanks anyway."

Betsy was sitting on the rear couch in the study as he came in the door. She was wearing a set of foam rubber earphones as she listened to a new

Bach recording brought by Dr. Mercer, also wearing earphones, who sat on the ottoman nearby. He was wearing jogging togs. He was slim and spare, a nonsmoker, nondrinker, and vegetarian, an ascetic gray-haired bachelor who taught community college physics and astronomy. Wilson had seen his ten-speed bicycle propped against the breezeway post. Lanky arm lifted, Mercer gave him a friendly wave. Betsy lifted her head in a delighted smile. Silently, he retrieved the *Post* and the *New York Times* from the table and went downstairs to the game room. The Redskins were playing the Cardinals in St. Louis, but he didn't turn the television set on. He read through the first sections of both papers, sitting in the leather armchair, but finally, out of curiosity, turned on the game to hear the score.

The Cardinals were up by nine, but the Redskins were driving late in the fourth quarter. He feigned disinterest, fiddling with the tuning knobs. On the third play after he'd adjusted the picture, the Redskins wide receiver caught the Cardinal secondary changing coverage, broke free on a fly pattern, took the deep pass over his left shoulder, and loped into the end zone without breaking stride, not a Cardinal defensive back within five yards.

He sat there in astonishment. "Did you see that goddamned pass?" he heard himself say.

There was no one, of course—just himself in the sun-filled game room. Over the stereo behind him hung his sons' pennants, travel posters, beer signs, and high school letters. Nearby was a map of the world suspended from a narrow wooden box—they'd found it in a secondhand store—racks of long-playing records, and a covered pool table. Upstairs, Bach was playing. Outside, the bright sun lay on the patio, not a California synapse but a magnificent autumn afternoon along the Atlantic seaboard, yet the leaves were still unraked and the sack of pine mulch was still unopened near the garden shed.

The moment had lived for him, miraculous in a way few others had been these recent autumn days. He sat on his heels in front of the television set, awaiting another miracle.

Ten minutes later the phone rang upstairs, but he ignored it. Betsy was halfway down the stairs, calling to him. "Didn't you hear the phone?"

"I heard."

"It was Ida Straus calling, looking for Nick. She thought he might be here. Have you seen him?"

"Not recently." The Cardinals had moved the ball twenty-five yards in three plays, keeping to the ground as they ran out the clock.

"She sounds very worried."

A blitzing Redskins linebacker was trapped inside; the Cardinal ball carrier broke two arm tackles and rambled for nine more yards.

"I really don't want to get involved in their arguments, Betsy," he said, "not just now."

He stood up, the spell broken. He turned toward the stairs, but she'd disappeared without a word. Looking back at the television screen, he hesitated and then switched it off.

Betsy heard the basement door slam and waited for the car to start, but the sound didn't come. Curious, she moved to the study window to look down onto the terrace and saw her husband standing below, wearing an old corduroy yard jacket, holding a fifty-pound sack of pine-bark mulch. He was as motionless as a garden statue, holding the heavy bag in his arms as he looked toward the woods. He didn't move, still looking down into the woods. Then he dropped the bag to the flagstones. It split open, but he had already turned away. A few minutes later, she heard the car start.

Thank God, she thought.

10.

Although the inner courtyard of the Pentagon was now in full shadow, in the windowless warren of offices between B and C rings the sterile white lights burned on, day and night interchangeable, the air within as unchanging as a tomb.

Nick Straus sat at Colonel Roscoe Dillon's desk in the inner office, exploring his chief's pending file, a folder crammed with staff studies and policy recommendations forwarded for comment by other Pentagon offices or bootlegged to Dillon by his network of cronies scattered about the building. Leaning against the wall behind the door was a new poster, prepared that week by someone in DIA graphics for inclusion in the Gallery but removed by Colonel Dillon, who had once been assigned to NATO headquarters in Brussels, and thought it a slur against his former commander in chief.

The caption on the poster read: MAFIOSO MOUTHPIECE PLEADS FIFTH AMENDMENT in banner headline fashion, but the picture below, enlarged tenfold, hadn't been taken at a recent Senate hearing on labor racketeering but at testimony before the Senate Foreign Relations Committee. It showed a taut, seething Alexander Haig in a dark pin-striped suit, head thrust forward belligerently as he ranted about El Salvador.

The poster had drawn no smile from Nick Straus, who had turned his attention that day to the review of current Pentagon projects, his old obsession put aside. It was a race against time. On Colonel Dillon's desk that afternoon he'd found two telephone call slips left for him by his secretary on Friday afternoon, requesting him to call General Gawpin on an urgent matter. He had no doubt what Gawpin wanted to discuss.

The documents he'd found in Dillon's file had been much more troubling, raising doubts that went far beyond his own welfare. One was a Top Secret options paper proposing that U.S. line officers in Europe be given "pre-clearance" for the battlefield use of tactical weapons in Europe—in effect, the yielding of that gravest of presidential responsibilities, the launching of a nuclear attack, to field-grade officers in Europe. A second document was equally frightening. A CIA study passed to DIA for comment concluded that Soviet strategic rocket forces were in the process of changing their readiness posture and would shortly be prepared to launch their missiles at the first sign of hostile intentions, a new "launch on alert" policy that would leave no margin for error. Each side would only reinforce the other's paranoia. Much of the world would be delivered to nuclear terror by the electronic glitches of technology or the brutish muscular spasms of a few front-line field commanders, as primitive as that nameless Berlin battle group colonel Haven Wilson had recently described to him.

The final document that had drawn Straus's notice was a faded Xerox copy of the most recent additions to the U.S. nuclear warhead strike list of Soviet targets. Each nuclear warhead in the U.S. strategic inventory was assigned a military or industrial target in the U.S.S.R. or Eastern Europe. Since the nuclear warheads had by now far exceeded the legitimate targets available, the National Strategic Target List Division had begun to show considerable ingenuity in assigning targets to the newest additions to the U.S. strategic warhead inventory. Nick Straus recognized the Russian place names. They were no longer identifying targets; they were inventing them.

He carried Colonel Dillon's folder to the Xerox machine and began copying those documents that most frightened him. Four pages had been copied when the operating light went out and the machine stopped. Straus pushed the start and reset button, but the machine didn't light up. He reset the plug in the receptacle and pressed the button, but the circuits didn't respond. For months the machine had been his accomplice, sharing his solitude, its voice the only one he trusted, that soft secretive whir-and-whisk that so cleverly flipped the documents out. Its mind had been his mind, a perfect analogue, but now it was dead. Why?

Lifting the cover again, he peered down into the glass but saw only a dim repellent face peering out, eyes as exhausted as his own, lacerated with cowardice and guilt. The hands on the cold gray cabinet had a strange pallor—the transparency of those eyeless fish from an underground grotto—but they moved as he moved.

"Traitor," the machine said. *"Judas and thief."*

He left the office, his briefcase empty. The corridor he passed through led him by a half dozen deserted DIA offices, where the lights burned and the desks sat empty, their in boxes turned on their sides. At the DIA guard desk, the blue-uniformed security officer was talking to a sweeper from the weekend utility crew, who leaned against a trolley strapped with canvas bags full of unclassified waste.

Straus signed the register and disappeared up the ramp toward the river entrance. A watch officer from the Joint Chiefs passed him on the escalator. "Hey, Straus!" he called. "I thought you guys didn't come in on Sunday!" He wore dress blues. Nick looked at him as if he'd never seen him before in his life. Outside the mall entrance, he paused in the gathering dusk and stood at the top of the steps as if waiting for an official sedan from the motor pool. Then, remembering how he had arrived, he went down the stairs, crossed the road, and found his Ford, parked in a reserved area, a parking summons on the windshield.

"Nick? Is that you?" Ida called to him from the living room as he entered the house. He didn't answer, standing in front of the hall closet as he returned the briefcase to the top shelf. "Nick?"

He went upstairs, still wearing his overcoat, and rattled through the bottom of his dresser, uncovering some Xeroxed documents; then he took a folder of classified material from the bottom of the cedar chest, found an old wool cap there too, one he thought he'd lost in Nova Scotia, pulled it on, and returned downstairs. From a cabinet in his basement office, he retrieved several dozen additional documents and stuffed them in a paper bag.

Ida met him at the top of the stairs.

"Nick, someone's here to see you. In the living room with me. He's been waiting."

He didn't answer, his head turned to one side, as if listening for something. The blue yarn cap was pulled down over his ears, a pile of documents was under one arm, and a grocery bag of crumpled papers was under the other.

"I can't take this anymore, Nick. I just can't take it." Her voice broke and she began to cry.

"It's all right. It won't be very long now."

He went out the back door, stood for a moment on the rear patio, and then descended the stone steps to the back garden. Still holding the bag and the papers, he stood at the brick barbecue pit. There were no matches in his pockets and the can of combustible fluid for lighting the charcoal was put away. He stood in the darkness, holding the parcels, and then, as if he could go no further, sank down on the redwood bench and remained there, head lowered, like an old man returning from a grocery, collapsed at the bus stop, waiting for a taxi.

He was still sitting there when Haven Wilson opened the kitchen door and joined him. Ida Straus watched nervously through the kitchen window. Thirty minutes later, they adjourned to the basement office.

It was after eleven o'clock when Haven Wilson left by the front door—left a little unsteadily, Ida Straus thought. She was upstairs in bed by this time, most of the anxiety relieved by Nick's increasingly awkward trips up the basement steps for replenishment. She'd left sandwiches for them out on the kitchen counter and they'd disappeared, but so had the bottle of Bordeaux from the top of the refrigerator.

As he came into the bedroom, she expected him to say nothing, to crawl into bed in silence, the way he usually did, the only conversation her own questions, all of which were usually turned aside. But this night, he needed no prompting:

"Did I ever tell you about the time I got stuck at the top of the Ferris wheel with Roy McCormick, the dumbest kid in my class?" he began. A shoe dropped.

"No, I don't think you did."

"The only time I ever went up in a Ferris wheel was at a class picnic and Roy McCormick talked me into it. I was sixteen. He was the dumbest in physics, in chemistry, in Latin, and in everything, I'm the winner of the Bausch & Lomb medal, the physics whiz kid, and I let the dumbest kid in class talk me into going on this Ferris wheel and we get stuck at the top. He's a Roman Catholic; if we spill out, he goes his way, I go mine. That's what he told me at the top."

"I've never heard that story."

"I was telling Haven about it. Fools are my fate. I've never said this before, but it's true. I'm not unique, I'm not special. I've never pretended to be special, never. But it's true. Fools are my fate. He's had the same experience."

"Really?"

"It was the same that time in Geneva when you weren't with me. I'm invited out by this couple at the U.S. mission in Geneva—a weekend. I let them talk me into going on the gondola, the cable car. As soon as we get in and the door closes, I see my companions. They are all very heavy German tourists—Bavarians. Very fat Bavarians. As soon as I see them, I know. Oh, I know. I didn't want to go out that weekend with this very nice couple from the U.S. mission in Geneva. I want to read a little, to walk a little, to talk to the Russian, Kuimov. But I cannot say no. I'm too polite, too *gentil*, to say no. Now that I see these very heavy, these very fat German Bavarians, all Catholics, like Roy McCormick, gossiping away in the same German language my grandfather—well, never mind the language—*I know*, how can I not know? Do you understand what I feel? If I am going to be smashed to smithereens on the rocks below, I don't want it to be in the company of a gondola car full of shrieking Bavarian tourists or an addle-brained couple from the U.S. mission in Geneva. . . ."

"Oh, Nick . . ." she said piteously.

"So fools are my fate, but it's my fault." Another shoe dropped. "So Haven and I were talking about it."

"Talking about what?"

"A number of things. I want to be with my own kind. . . . No, I'm not going to Israel. In Israel, my own kind is a minority now, growing smaller. I'm talking about another kind. It's time to say no to the Roy McCormicks, to silly people from the U.S. mission, to the Hank Squires and the Roscoe Dillons and the Les Fines. They're not going to get me in their Ferris wheel or their gondola car, never. Neither will the Pentagon or those people across the river. That's what Haven and I were talking about."

"So what are you going to do?"

"We don't know yet," he said. "We will."

Part Three

1.

The Pentecostal Church of the Open Door in Knoxville had a substitute parson that night, a short middle-aged man with sad gray eyes who'd taken over the late evening prayer meeting when the regular mission evangelist, Reverend Tolliver, had been hospitalized with pneumonia. His name was Dorsey Combs.

It was cold in the streets outside, a shadowy, decrepit section of the city near the river, not yet reached by urban renewal. A spittle of rain tattooed the storefront windows of the tabernacle as Mrs. Tolliver began the services.

"I see we got a right smart group of folks here tonight," she announced, "so let's do right by them." She was a tall, matronly woman dressed in Baptist black. Her strong face had a tallowy tint to it, like lye soap, untouched by rouge or lipstick. She sat down at the old upright piano, turned back the leaf, briskly rubbed her hands, and began pounding out "Our Hope, the Lord, Is Here Tonight" as the Yellon sisters and Elroy Yates, an evangelist and gospel group, stood up in front facing the gathering of drifters and winos who'd come in to escape the frosty streets outside. Elroy was tall and horse-faced, with a gospel voice contrived from a chronic adenoidal condition that had been the misery of his high school days, a rain-barrel baritone that didn't sound like the real thing to anyone outside Elroy's head. As he sang, he was spared the audience's facial spasms by his own muscular contortions, which lifted his eyes to the ceiling and kept them there, fastened to a few strips of crepe paper still hanging overhead, a dusty memento of some long-past harvest sale when the tabernacle had been a Goodwill clothing store.

The coal stove in the rear hadn't heated up yet, despite the flickering brightness through the mica window, and the room was chilly. The Yellon sisters wore coats over their bright-blue taffeta dresses. Elroy Yates had a scarf wrapped around his rooster neck. The congregation was slow to warm up to the Bible songs and Mrs. Tolliver left her piano to stand at the lectern to read from the Scriptures. Satisfied, she turned back to the piano, hoisted her black skirts, and began another inspirational song.

After the revival music, she returned to the front to tell her listeners where Elroy Yates and the Yellon sisters would be appearing the following week—a social note intended to flatter the gospel singers, not entice their audience. Had any of them the carfare or the will to get out of town, they wouldn't have headed for the Bethel Church in Kingsport or the Elks Club in Johnson City, but would have been long gone down the highway for work in the Texas or Oklahoma Sunbelt.

Buster Foreman sat on a folding chair in the back row, eyes impatiently roaming the muslin curtain hanging behind the old piano. Gusts of cold night air blew across his neck each time the door opened; the steady trickle of damp current along the floor made him conscious of his cold feet. Numbed by the cold, a few of his earlier companions had crept forward to the chairs nearer the stove. He sat alone with an elderly black man who leaned forward from time to time, as if to stifle a cough, but in fact to quickly warm himself from a half pint of muscatel hidden in his mackinaw.

It was a little after nine o'clock when Elroy Yates and the Yellon sisters filed out through the muslin curtains and Mrs. Tolliver introduced the middle-aged man who had silently emerged from the rear. They were fortunate, she said, to have Mr. Dorsey Combs on hand to carry out Reverend Tolliver's work during his hospitalization. She described Dorsey Combs as a lay preacher of the gospel who had once had his own radio program, *The Bible Answering Hour,* when he had been "The Bible Answer Man" to thousands of Christian homes in the region. He had studied at Bible colleges in North and South Carolina, and published articles on the Scriptures for church publications in Atlanta and Nashville.

The subject of Mrs. Tolliver's eulogium stood just behind her, a man in his late fifties with gray-black hair, bushy eyebrows, and secretive gray eyes that seemed to be wholly indifferent to the hungry, ravaged faces studying him from the shadows. His dark suit was rumpled, like his shirt and tie. His black shoes were scruffy and unshined. Across the front of his vest hung a gold watch chain. A man without an iota of self-consciousness, he was calmly searching the small pocket of the vest with his fingers as Mrs. Tolliver introduced him. As she finished, he brought something to his mouth and bit down just before she turned. Buster Foreman guessed it might be a plug of tobacco.

Mrs. Tolliver retired to the piano stool after Dorsey Combs replaced her at the lectern and began collecting her music. Dorsey Combs began by talking about St. Paul and Foreman listened, less conscious of the words than of the face. Had the hair been thinner and the face plumper, flushed to a cherubic warmth by the glow of television lights and a boisterous claque in the back of the Senate hearing room, he might have been watching Senator Bob Combs. His half-brother was merely a small-town facsimile, Foreman decided, a small-time tabernacle sponger and hypocrite, with sawdust on his shoes, silver in his tongue, and larceny in his heart.

Mrs. Tolliver softly closed her piano, arose, took up her sheet music and evangelical notes, and slipped on her coat. As she tiptoed out through the rear curtain, she paused to send a small gratified smile back toward the audience, and then disappeared. Dorsey Combs looked around, nodded, and then leaned forward against the lectern. With his foot he prodded something from beneath the base, leaned forward even farther, lips working, and spat into the spittoon. "I seem to have lost my train of thought there," he began again, wiping his mouth. "Maybe Mrs. Tolliver carried it away with her, maybe it's getting too late now and all of us are pretty tired." He closed the Bible and lifted his eyes toward the front windows. "Looking out in the streets yonder, I can see all the winders around here are dark now, only our own lights lit, which kinda makes me uneasy. How do you folks feel about it? That worry you any?" No one spoke. "No? You ain't worried? Well, maybe I ain't worried either—"

"He ain't from Tennessee," came a drunken voice from the middle row.

Combs looked up. "Maybe I ain't, but that don't mean I haven't been where you folks are. I been there too, and I didn't have any answer man to help me." He gazed at the drunk, waited patiently, and then resumed again, his voice lifted in a parody of a revival tent evangelist. Very loudly, he cried, "Seems like all you gotta do these days is reach out for the telephone to get you an answer, reach out for the telephone or the TV knob, whether it's the hard times, the Good Book, the whiskey, or Brother Satan that's a-jumpin' up an' down on you, a-hootin' an' a-hollerin'. You all hear what I'm saying? How many of you's awake?"

The room was silent. Combs studied them silently, shifted the plug of tobacco, and then draped himself over the lectern, speaking very softly. "It's a sorry mess when you can't even tell me if you're awake or not. I count three or four maybe, like that big fellow in the back row yonder. I count two more like that fellow over there, sneaking a little somethin' out of that bottle he's got hid in his pocket. It ain't sin. If it ain't sin, how come he's a-sneaking it?" Someone snickered. "It ain't funny, it's downright pitiful, that's what it is. I ain't talkin' fire an' brimstone, if that's what you come to hear. I ain't talking all that trash to you just on account of that bean soup an' crackers you come to get."

He looked around the room very carefully, still draped over the lectern, and stood up. "All right. Lemme put it to you simple like, so as even a mo-ron can understand. You boys been talked at too much. The time's come to do something. You boys need to get yourself organized, get yourself a union. Does that reach you?" The room was silent. "I see it don't," he said, disappointed. "I'm trying to do right by you, but you ain't making it easy. You boys are all wore out, wore to the bone, like everyone else who's got any sense these days. You fellows just gotta get yourself woke up good, that's all. Let's see what the Good Book says."

He opened the Bible and read a passage from St. Paul. "A man's life is mortal, that's what Paul is telling you, same as I'm telling you." He closed the book. "But let's take a step away from the Good Book an' see what we can come up with on our own." He stepped out from the lectern, standing at the edge of the small platform. "A man's life is all mixed up with other lives, you an' me all thrown together into this life, you follow me? This ain't the TV you're watching. It ain't enough to just sit out there all the time listening. Look at it this way. I bet we got some carpenters out there—carpenters, hod carriers, maybe some masons. 'Hewers o' wood an' drawers o' water.' You boys ain't drawing any water. How come you're just settin' out there, all messed up, like a load of lumber, like a mess o' bricks or buildin' stones, all jumbled up? I tell you why. Because you haven't got yourself organized. You're not organized, when folks come to building something, they're just gonna grab holt o' you any which way, toss you here or there any which way, the way the hard times do, the way the textile mills do, an' they're just gonna slam you into this job or that, any which way, and when there ain't no jobs they're just gonna leave you rot out there in the high weeds where you folks are rotting, any which way. You hear what I'm a-telling you now?"

The room's silence was broken only by the fiery rumble from the coal stove. Many were asleep.

" 'Course now, some folks come out o' hard times pretty good," Dorsey Combs continued mildly. "Sure they do. Some of us get toted up to the steeple, get carried up there high and mighty, up there at the top of the spire, where the sweet music plays. But there ain't much room up there, you notice that? You ever notice how small it is, up there high and mighty, ridin' on everyone's shoulders up above the pigeons even, where the sweet music an' chimes play all day long? But you fellas out there, you ain't lucky at all. You're hid out in the cellar, spread out on the walks, pounded into sand by every Tom, Dick, and Harry on his way to Sunday school, his big fancy automobile parked at the curb, feet and tires trampin' on you all day long, you see what I mean? And another thing if you're lower down, which is what I been trying to tell you since I stood up here, is that being that far down, it's not just the Tom, Dick, and Harrys, either, because even the pigeons are gonna shit on you, that's how bad it's got. That's the difference between high and low style, boys, and that's what I'm here a-telling you.

Until you boys get yourself organized, you folks are low down, no count, low style, ornery mean, like I'm a-talking, and the pigeons have shit on you good—"

Someone laughed. Dorsey Combs ignored him.

"So you know what I mean, don't you? Now you're beginning to get woke up. So lemme tell you something else. It's not just the pigeons I'm talking about—"

The sound of the rear door being opened stirred those in the front row with the expectation of bean soup being brought from the kitchen behind the alley, but it was Mrs. Tolliver, her face stung by the cold, returning to fetch the prayerbook she'd forgotten on top of the piano.

Dorsey Combs's expression changed immediately. "Take your beginning from Ezekiel," he sang out, his voice lifted to its revival tent register. "'Awake, awake, put on thy strength, O Zion! Put on thy beautiful garments, O Jerusalem! I give my back to the smiters and my cheeks to them that plucked off the hair! Who is he that shall condemn me? Lo, they shall all wax old as a garment! The moth shall eat them up!'"

Mrs. Tolliver smiled, but then her eyes dropped to the spittoon at the foot of the lectern. Dorsey Combs smiled too, a sad, weak smile. "'Come and sit in the dust, O virgin daughter of Babylon,'" he continued, but the cold cheeks turned away, to disappear through the curtain. After they heard the rear door close, Combs dropped the quid of tobacco into the spittoon and nudged it back under the base of the lectern. Foreman watched him bring a small medicine bottle from his inside pocket, twist off the cap, and take a long pull. "'How much less man, that is a worm, and the son of man, which is a worm,'" he muttered huskily, his eyes shining as he replaced the bottle.

Someone guffawed. "That ain't no bean soup," another called out. The audience was awake now, aroused by Mrs. Tolliver's intrusion, and disappointed that the soup hadn't appeared. They had also seen Dorsey Combs's bottle.

"How about passing it around?" a younger man yelled.

"Don't be a-laughing now," Combs protested, but it was too late. His grip had slipped; sedition was in the air.

"Where's the bean soup at, preacher man?" a hoarse voice asked contemptuously.

"Boys, if you're gonna whip old Satan, you gotta play Satan's game," Combs said, but the laughter only grew louder. "It's not old Satan we're messing with, anyways. He's gone out the back door to get him a job over on the Savannah River. Don't go depending on the Good Book. Step away from it, step up to yourself for a change, get organized, get yourself a union—"

A tall, gaunt man in the middle row stood up. "You got yours," he called out. "Gimme some o' ours!"

Combs yielded. "All right, it's a-coming," he promised haplessly. "Just hold down the ruckus. I need me a head count first. You fellas that are first-timers, step up to the front. I need me three to serve an' three to wash up. I don't want any wash-up gang sneaking out the back door like they did last night."

The crowd grew quiet again and Dorsey Combs counted hands. "You boys done pounded me into sand," he said as he left the platform. Buster Foreman saw a small, weak man, eyes flushed with humiliation.

The wash-up crew disappeared, as Dorsey Combs had feared, and Foreman stayed behind to help Combs and the cook wash the dishes.

"I figured you for a federal man soon as I laid eyes on you in the back room," Dorsey Combs confessed, wiping his eyes after a long swallow of whiskey from the coffee cup. He sat with Buster at an all-night truck stop on a highway east of Knoxville. It was called Colonel Tom Pepper's. During the drive out from the city in Buster's rented car, Combs had described the proprietor as an old friend from his South Carolina days. "Saw it right off. How come you looked me up? I got those charges dismissed, but you can't tell sometimes. Maybe you heard about them."

"Which charges are you talking about?"

"Federal charges," said Combs, leaning forward with a sigh as he returned his handkerchief to his hip pocket. He had a small potbelly, an encumbrance that forced him to give breath when he bent, stooped, or stirred himself too energetically. "Transportin' a minor across state lines. You try to keep foolishness like that hushed up, whether it's one lie or a pack o' lies." His gaze was elusive, a little shy, the sad gray eyes no longer so secretive. His hand trembled as he reached for the cup. Two coffee cups were on the table in front of him, one filled with coffee, the other half-filled from the medicine bottle of blended whiskey he kept in his pocket.

"I heard something about that," Buster said. At the storefront church he'd heard the public orator, but at the wash sink and in the car driving out he'd had a sense of another Dorsey Combs, this one the small-town fabulist, the barbershop and courthouse-steps raconteur. It was difficult to tell where the life ended and the stories began.

"It was all on account of that trouble over in South Carolina," Combs said, "where we were organizin' that textile plant I was telling you about. I was living in a boardinghouse, and the company union went and bought off the woman that runs it. Said I'd run off with her daughter. Lemme tell you sumpin' about that daughter, too. It wasn't carnal knowledge that got that girl's clothes tore up. A pure case o' self-defense. She wasn't any minor, either, like her mama was claiming. She was twenty-five if she was a day, that girl was, but her mama dressed her up like that, dressed her up like she was a china doll, fourteen years old. You ever run into a widow lady like that? Keeps herself and her daughter dressed up like they was still both virgins, thinks no one'll know?"

"I don't think so," Buster said. Only two truckdrivers sat in the midnight silence of the truck stop and one of them turned to look at Combs. The air was tart with griddle fat and boiled coffee. A CB radio crackled from the shelf behind the cash register, carrying truckers' warnings of radar traps, icy ramps, and one-lane traffic on the interstates into North and South Carolina. "Who brought the charges?"

"Her mama done it. The daughter knew I was coming to Knoxville to visit Colonel Tom over there and ast could she ride along to see her uncle. When we got here, turned out there wasn't any uncle. I gave her bus fare to get back home an' took her right on the gravel out in front there to catch her a Greyhound. That's where we had the argument. Got her clothes tore an' so did I." He lifted his arm to show Buster a gaping hole where the sleeve had been ripped. Then he stood up and peeled off his coat. The right sleeve of his white shirt was missing. He wore only a starched cuff. "Tore the sleeve right off, coat and shirt both. Woulda jerked my arm right out the socket. I got the coat sewed back on. Can't hardly tell, can you?" He put on the coat again, pulled the cuff down on his wrist, and resumed his seat. "What happened was, on the bus going back she tore her clothes up some more, and after she got home made up the damndest pack o' lies you ever heard. Her mama swore out a warrant. I wouldn't o' touched that girl, wouldn't have harmed a hair on her head—not with that face. Ugly? Lordy. You oughta see it. You think you know ugly?"

"Some ugly, maybe," Buster said warily.

"The worst ugly, what's that?"

"That's hard to say."

"Toad soup," Combs suggested smartly.

"Yeah, that's ugly," Buster conceded.

"Ugly as toad soup, that's what she called herself." Combs reached for the coffee cup. "Just as mean, too. Two days after that, I tore up my machine in an accident out on the highway there. Been here ever since, high and dry. My car's out back. No place to go, nothing to get there with, only shank's mares. The Church of the Open Door's got a rest home for folks like that." He smiled dimly, looking at Buster Foreman from beneath the bushy eyebrows, as if he recognized a kindred spirit. "They dry 'em out, Miz Tolliver does. Hang 'em up and dry 'em out, sunshine clean, like country wash, only it's the psalm-singing and prayin' does the scrubbing, sure as lye soap. She's done a right smart bit of praying in her time, Miz

Tolliver has—had to, married into that family like she did. She's done some praying for me, too, along the way. First knew her in Bible class down in Georgia and I was the Bible Answer Man, like she said. Used to call me up at the station. I could do voices then—livestock reports, produce market, even did a baseball game once. She was a pretty young girl then. Went down to see her one weekend. We kept in touch over the years. Did too many voices to suit her, that's the trouble." His voice trailed away and he drank again from the cup. He smelled of whiskey and tobacco, the aroma so powerful that Foreman knew it wouldn't have escaped Mrs. Tolliver that night or anyone else sitting in the first two rows at the storefront tabernacle. "Should have stayed in radio," Combs said sorrowfully.

The tractor-trailers came whining down the grade out front, bound for the interstate. Combs seemed to listen, his head turned away. The two truckdrivers paid their bill and left.

"How come you looked me up?" he began again, after a minute. "You said you wanted to have you a little talk. What in particular you got on your mind?"

"Nothing in particular; just find out a little more about the Combs family," Buster said. "You told me you were a union organizer. When did that begin?"

"A long time ago, longer'n I wanna remember."

"So you've given it up now."

"I'm wore out. I been through it all an' I'm wore out. I've turned myself in, you could say, come to the end of the line and turned myself in to the Church of the Open Door. There was a time I could do it, but not anymore. They broke me down, this country did. Wore me out. Look at that."

He held out his hand, palm down, stubby fingers spread, but this time it wasn't the alcoholic's tremors Buster Foreman noticed. The fingers were scarred and bent.

"Where'd it happen?"

"Happened everywhere," Combs said. "Look at it. They busted my fingers and they broke my head. I've been beat up, scalded, pistol whipped, and stomped on. I got my ear half-chewed off once by a bus driver and had a bucket of cold horse piss poured on me once down in Laurel, Mississippi. They did it every way but legal, but they done it. No, I'm wore out. You saw me down at that church tonight. Time was I could take a bunch of folks like that, worse off than I was, and get 'em all fired up, ready to go, like in the old days, but you saw what happened. What you heard tonight was my old Ozark, Alabama, speech, 'cause that's where I made it, down in Ozark, twenty-one years ago. What'd you think of it?"

"I was a little confused," Buster said.

"Steeples an' spires," Combs said, as if he hadn't heard. "It was in a

Methodist church outside of town and we were gonna march, but we couldn't get that colored congregation to join in. So I heard about it—I was the champeen talker of that particular group we had down there—an' I went over that Sunday night and had me a few words with 'em. I talked to those folks a long, long time. I told them about organizing, standing together. I told them about the steeple and the spire, how small it was, how the sweet music plays all day long but just for a blessed few, and how even the pigeons got a better roost than they did. It wasn't easy. When you stand up an' say 'shit' to a Sunday night Methodist congregation like they was, you'd better either have quick feet or a quicker head, 'cause they'll come after you like a bunch o' bees, run you right out of your britches if you don't watch. But I had the word in those days. I had something to say and they'd listen, something that carried me along. Even now, I can feel a little of it coming back, the way it was in the old days, but they're all gone now, the movement's all broke up, all scattered. Oh, Lordy . . ."

He faltered, his voice heavy with emotion, and Buster Foreman watched the brightness gather in his eyes as he leaned forward once again to take the handkerchief from his hip. "But I'd do it all over again, I sure would," Combs continued huskily, "do it all over again tomorrow." The chair creaked as he touched his wet cheeks with the folded handkerchief. "They broke me down quick tonight, didn't they? Got to me fast. Wouldn't have done that in the old days. I get upset, thinking about it. They're all gone now, all of 'em, just like the feelin's gone. When we lost the feelin', the movement broke up, and the wind carried it away, just like that dust bowl they had out in Oklahoma back in the thirties. . . ."

"The civil rights trail," Buster said, no longer puzzled. He and Fuzzy had been wrong. The long record of arrests and convictions hadn't been for lying out in ambush in the high weeds with his ax handle or knuckle duster. He'd been one of the marchers.

"Those were the best years I gave to anyone, the best years of my life," Combs was saying. "I couldn't tell you how far I walked, how many places I went. The first time was from Selma to Montgomery, walked all the way, and got my head busted open outside the Jefferson Davis Motel, I think it was. There was some kind of honky-tonk next door and some trash standing out there alongside the road, a-hooting an' hollering. Closer we got to town, the worse it was, and so we had to close up a little. I was walking on the outside, right along the edge of the highway. Next to me was a Catholic priest, next to him a Congregationalist lady from somewhere up in Massachusetts. All of a sudden, I heard someone call out my name, call out just clear as a bell. 'Hey, Dorsey Combs, what are you doing with them niggers, carpetbagger?' this fella yells at me. It was a used-car salesman I knew from up in South Carolina and I couldn't figure out what he was doing with that trash standing up alongside the road. So I tell the folks around me to keep moving, but I go over to him real quiet like, on account of those were the rules we laid out before we left Selma—no talking, no laughing, no heckling back—but once I step off the pavement I'm back with my own folks again, I can talk their talk, they can talk mine. So I say to this car salesman, 'Who you callin' carptetbagger, you redneck pecker-wood sonofabitch.' I never saw who it was cold-cocked me first, whether it was him or someone else, but when I woke up, I was in jail, me and that Congregationalist lady both. First time she'd ever been in jail."

"But not the first for you," Buster Foreman said.

"Could be; I don't remember now." He studied Foreman curiously. "How come you know all this? You used to be government, son. If you're not now, you used to be. I seen too many of 'em not to know. What is it you wanna find out about?"

"What Bob Combs was doing all those years."

"Go ask him. Haven't spóken to him in twenty-two years; not him, not the rest of that family. He's a half-brother—not real kin where I come from. Me, I'm my daddy's side. He worked in a textile mill, same as I started out."

"When did you get into the movement?"

"I went up to the Highlander Folk School in Monteagle, Tennessee, training to help organize the textile mills and the coal tipples. There was some folks from the NAACP up there at the same time and that's where I met up with them. Rosa Parks. You remember Rosa Parks?"

"I don't think so."

"December 1955. She started up the Montgomery boycott. Wouldn't sit in the back of the bus and got fined fourteen dollars. Just fourteen dollars to get it all started up. Find something you can get started up with fourteen dollars these days. Couldn't even get a hotel dinner in Nashville." Combs waited for Buster Foreman to answer, but he had nothing to say. "What do you do—work for a newspaper, digging up dirt?"

"No, not a newspaper; just curious."

"So you're looking for dirt," Combs replied. "Lemme tell you something before you get started. You go butting into Bob Combs's business, you're buying yourself a whole lotta trouble."

"What kind of trouble?"

Dorsey Combs picked up the whiskey cup. "The kind of trouble that don't need asking. Bob Combs is like that textile mill over in South Carolina that run me out of town—big business." The CB crackled from behind the counter, a trucker's voice warning of a disabled truck on an exit ramp, but there was no one there to hear.

"Let me try something on you," Buster said, "just see what you think. If Bob Combs's politics are pretty bad today, they were worse twenty years ago. What would you say to that?"

Combs nodded silently, looking toward the front windows. "There's a whole lotta folks smarter than you an' me that never figured that out, did they?"

"So when you were active in the movement, what was he doing?" Foreman asked.

"You're wasting your time," Combs said. "If he was up to no good, who's gonna say so? If you find out, who's gonna change him? The only way you're gonna change him is change the country, and that's not the way things are moving. You saw those folks tonight, buried so deep in misery it'd take more than anything I know to blow 'em out, an' I don't see anything like that walking down the road, not in my lifetime, not in yours. No, these here are the days when you gotta find your own way back, son, every man for himself. Not politics, not gov'ment—nothing. No one else is gonna help you, no one at all. . . ."

"Who do you know up in South Carolina who could tell me something about Bob Combs?"

"It's bad," Dorsey Combs continued, ignoring the question. "Maybe it's been worse, but it's bad. Worst I ever had was when I got myself picked up down in Laurel, Mississippi—'60, I think it was. I didn't know anyone down there, just the advance man that come in by bus from New Orleans, but he hit the road before I got there, scared clean out of sight. Used to be a YMCA fella. I called on a few colored folks, but they wouldn't hardly talk to me and I couldn't blame them. Two hours after I got into town, the police picked me up. That was the worst week I ever spent. Two nights straight they took me out in a car, just me and these two deputies, packin' pistols and a riot gun, riding around the back roads—just the three of us. They had me hog-tied in the back seat. I never knew whether they were gonna bring me back or not. The place they had me locked up didn't have any winders. They took away my belt, my shirt, my pants, even my shoelaces. I thought it was all over. They woke me up one night with a bucket of cold horse piss poured over my head. Things have got pretty bad when they got you so far down you don't even have nothing to hang yourself with when you're ready to go. What you got left after that?"

Dorsey Combs raised his sad, glistening eyes to the small figure squeaking toward the table in a pair of grease-colored shoes, carrying a steaming mug of coffee. He wore a counterman's paper hat, a dirty white T-shirt, an apron and white trousers stained gray by a day at the grill. The cap and T-shirt carried the same logo as the electric sign outside, the menu, and the gilt-lettered signs that decorated the walls: *Colonel Tom Pepper's Fried Fritters.*

Dorsey Combs introduced Tom Pepper. "Colonel Tom and me go back a long way," he said.

"How come you're out here?" Tom Pepper asked. "She run you off again?" He was small and wire-thin, with muscular arms as pale as lard. The yellowish-gray hair was long on his neck and the scanty sideburns reached far down his jaws. Two tattoos, a black panther and an American eagle, their blue ink faded with age, clawed their way up his forearms.

"Me and my friend wanted someplace to talk."

Tom Pepper looked carefully at Buster Foreman. "Where you from?"

"Washington."

"He's come down to sample your fritters," Dorsey Combs said dryly. "Fried any which way, take your choice. Got corn, chicken, oyster, okra, and I don't know what all. Colonel Tom's got a place up near Gatlinburg, right on the road where all the rubberneck tourists come rolling through. Must be worth a million dollars a year, all that free advertising. He's gonna get him a national franchise that-a-way."

Tom Pepper looked again at Buster Foreman. "You in the fast-food business?"

"No, afraid not."

Pepper called across the room to a small, dark-haired woman who was wiping the stainless-steel splash plate behind the grill. "Hey, Cora, you got any batter fresh?"

"All finished," she answered without turning.

"With fritters it's all in the batter," Tom Pepper said, "same as it is with fried chicken or pancakes. What I got is an old family recipe."

"Handed down in the family Bible," said Dorsey Combs. "Come with his chicken fricassee and his Confederate colonel's commission."

Tom Pepper didn't move his eyes from Buster Foreman. "You know any fast-food folks up there in Washington?"

"No, sorry."

"Colonel Tom used to be in the car business in South Carolina," Combs amplified, refilling his cup. He stirred the coffee and whiskey together with a spoon. "Had him the Hupmobile agency in Spartanburg. Had the Kaiser-Frazer distributorship. Had the Packard franchise. Had a Studebaker lot. Would have had him the Edsel too, only someone took it away from him."

"Shit," Tom Pepper said. "I wouldn'ta had no Edsel agency. I knowed it was a lemon first time I laid eyes on it. I started me up a foreign car business in Darlington, doing real good, until some sonofabitch stole it offa me. You notice I ain't mentioning any names." He looked at Dorsey

Combs, then back at Foreman. "After that, I got into the restaurant business. You a car man?"

"Not much."

Tom Pepper turned and called to the woman at the grill. "Hey, Cora, hon. Reach me one of them cards under the cash register."

The woman put down her rag, moved to the cash register, stooped, and then held out a card.

"Reach it over here," Tom Pepper said.

Her shoulders dropped, she put her hands on her hips in annoyance for an instant, but then left the cash register and crossed to where they sat. Her dark hair was bound in a snood and there were deep shadows under her eyes. "That's not reaching, that's walking," she said as she put the card on the table. "Your feet aren't any more wore out than mine. How come you're out here so late?" she asked Dorsey Combs sympathetically.

"He's resting up," Tom Pepper told her.

"Did she throw you out, or what?"

"We're talking business," Tom Pepper told her. "You go mind your own."

She looked at her husband disapprovingly. "Dorsey comes drinking himself into trouble out here again, it *is* my business. I won't tolerate any trouble with that tabernacle woman."

"You'll tolerate trouble with me, you don't git on back there where you belong," Tom Pepper warned without looking up. He passed the business card to Buster Foreman. "This here's my new card," he said in a friendly voice. "Just had 'em made up."

"That'll be the day," Cora said.

"You and her both," he threatened.

She laughed wearily. "I'll bet. She'll come out here and raise a knot on your head you could grow hair on, then she'd take those skinny bones of yours and scramble them up in that batter so fast you'd come out not knowing whether you was okra or pork sausage."

"I don't have any pork sausage," Tom Pepper said, insulted.

"You would by the time she turned loose of you."

Tom Pepper ignored her, concentrating on the card he'd passed to Buster Foreman. "'Course this here isn't the only outlet I got," he said politely. "There's one on the road to Gatlinburg, like Dorsey said, but this one here is the number one store."

Buster Foreman nodded, studying the card. Like everything else in the truck stop restaurant, it was another advertisement for Colonel Tom Pepper and his fried fritters. In the lower-right-hand corner, it announced that franchises were available.

It was after one o'clock and the dark streets were deserted when Buster Foreman drove Dorsey Combs into Knoxville. At Combs's direction, he turned through the downtown commercial district and into a shabby old residential area now gone to furnished rooms and boardinghouses.

"Just a little Bible reading an' hand holdin' is all," Combs was murmuring drunkenly, his mind now running free, disengaged from that caution that had restrained their earlier conversation. "Find yourself a good woman an' hold on to her, that'd be my advice. Find one an' stick to her. Don't go running around like I did. Up at Highlander in the fifties, met a little woman from Boston. College teacher. Unitarian. Smart too. Talked the way the books talk, right off the page. I mean, if you could take an' let the words walk off the page the way they were written down, that's the way she talked. Like a goddamned dictionary." He hiccuped and drew a deep breath. "But it was all wrote down. Book learning. When it come to bed learning an' you had her in the dark, had to be hand taught. She was some woman. Maybe she'd put up with it, all the women trouble I had. It's right up there," he advised, pointing up the street with an unsteady hand. "That porch where the two lights are on."

Foreman saw only one porch light. "A boardinghouse?" he asked. He'd been tempted by Dorsey Combs's condition to draw him out further on his half-brother, but couldn't bring himself to do it.

"Tolliver's. Rest home, they call it. Got a tax-exempt license. Where folks that have strayed can find a helpin' hand. But you've gotta be Pentecostal. You a Pentecostal?"

"No. I don't know much about it."

"You an Odd Fellow, Order of Odd Fellows?"

"Don't know that, either. Why?"

"Ought to look into it for your old age. Odd Fellows got rest homes all over, old folks' homes, places where you can sit out the last years in peace an' quiet." He hiccuped again. "Take care of you, take care of you good, better than any Medicare or social security, which they're gonna close down anyway. Only it's just for the Caucasian race, like the Republicans these days, that's the trouble. Coloreds have their own. You'd qualify. I'd rather be a new-baptized Pentecostal—better than a goddamned Democrat these days." His fingers fished in the vest pocket for the tobacco plug. "She can put up with tobacco if it's snuff or chewing, but not much else. She's a right hefty piece of work, Miz Tolliver is, but she's got a hateful problem." He bit down on the plug."

"What problem's that?" Buster asked, drifting toward the curb.

"Her husband," Combs said. "Stone cold dead in the britches. Just ease up here and I can slip out, quiet like, no doors slamming, no loud talk, hear?" He clapped Buster on the shoulder and eased the door open. "Nice talkin' to you, son," he whispered. "I got your card. Something turns up, I'll send a picture postcard."

Foreman watched him go unsteadily up the walk, pause at the foot of the wooden steps to collect himself, sway for an instant, smooth his rumpled jacket, and then start to climb. He staggered twice and stumbled back to the sidewalk. On the third attempt, his hands reached forward to touch the risers, like a crawfish; he gained the top and stood up to creep very slowly across the porch.

The hall light was dim. Dorsey Combs took off his shoes inside the door and tiptoed past the open staircase to the second floor, past the dark parlor, smelling of faded altar flowers, past the cheerless sitting room and the closed doors of the transient guest rooms, and on to the tiny cold bedroom at the back of the house. An old iron bed occupied half the room; against the walls were a wooden dresser and a cardboard wardrobe where his other suit hung.

Sitting on the bed, he removed his coat and the shirt and staggered across the hall into the small bathroom. As he stood at the basin, he heard the creak of the back stairs and straightened. As the second squeak from the steps reached him, and then the third, as stealthy and ominous as the first, he turned out the light and fled frightened back across the hall and closed the door. He had pulled off his socks and was stepping out of his trousers when the door was pushed open and Mrs. Tolliver stood there. She was still dressed in black, her face as white and cold as a somnambulist's. The smell of hospital corridors and sickrooms was still in her garments.

"You've been drinking," she said coldly. "I smelled it then, I smell it now."

"My chest was worrying me; it was all knotted up—"

"Liar," she said, stepping into the room. "Liar and hypocrite. Drunkard, defiler, blasphemer—" She brought the leather belt from behind her back, raised it high over her head, and struck him savagely. The first lash drew blood high on the cheekbone, the second blurred the vision in his left eye. He could no longer look up, no longer think of the words he wanted to say, but was driven to the floor, hands over his head, his drunkenness no longer shielding him from the pain of the slashing belt.

Her expression didn't change. She seemed hardly aware of him at all, even as she turned finally to go out, switching off the light, closing the door, and leaving him in darkness. He crouched there for a long time, naked shoulders and face burning with fire. At last he lifted himself and crawled blindly into bed with his pain, but he tried not to think of his agony, only hers. He tried to imagine how she might one night be released from it—he drunken and weak, she standing there with the belt, merciless and strong, but then finding him for the first time in his lifted eyes. She would know then what had become of her, what had become of him, and she would drop the flail to gather him in and cleanse them both. . . .

Come down and sit in the dust, O virgin daughter of Babylon, he recalled through his agony, as if waiting for her to come. But that night, as on other nights, he heard only the creak of boards as she undressed for bed in her lonely room on the second floor—she the warden of his bondage, he the prisoner of her faith, as dark and windowless as that jail cell in Laurel, Mississippi, so many years ago.

Buster Foreman drove east through the gray overcast Saturday morning, the thoughts of the previous night's conversation dissolving in the mist and smoke as the miles rolled by under his wheels. But outside Gatlinburg, one last memory of that long evening aroused him. He saw a roadside stand, perched on a clay bank, offering souvenirs. A hundred yards beyond was a second stand, its facade scrolled in a kind of bargeboard, like the gingerbread porticoes of the old riverboats that once paddled along the Savannah and Tennessee rivers. The red letters, dim and peeling with the corruptions of the seasons, advertised Colonel Tom Pepper's fried fritters, but winter was in the air, the sky was dark, and the gravel shoulder of roadside deserted. At the front of the lot was a rusting sign mounted on an iron frame, declaring that the stand was closed until spring.

But something else caught his eye, a name even more familiar by now. The car radio was playing "I'm the number one fan of the man from Tennessee," a guitar was strumming relentlessly, and a tractor-trailer's air horn was blowing furiously ahead of him; yet the small printing in hard enamel on the iron base sprang out at him like the towering *See Rock City* advertisements visible on every granite face he'd passed since leaving Knoxville.

The sign in the weeds at the side of the road had once belonged to Bob Combs's car emporium in South Carolina.

At the next intersection, the cloud-hung mountains of the Great Smokies still in the distance, Buster Foreman turned around and headed back to Knoxville.

Tom Pepper admitted grudgingly that he'd once worked as a used-car salesman for Bob Combs marketing cars from Combs's wholesale lot to small operators in Georgia, Alabama, and Mississippi, but he attached no importance to it.

154

"How come you're asking all these questions?" he complained loudly, but his aggravation was more for the benefit of the two truckdrivers who sat listening at the far end of the counter, waiting for their order. Tom Pepper's cap, apron, and trousers were clean, he was freshly shaven, his hair damp, but the smell of grease and boiled coffee was very much the same. "Maybe he done me dirt once, maybe he didn't, but that's between him an' me. I didn't steal that sign no ways; I borrowed it. I ain't looking for no trouble now; got a franchise business to sell. Bob Combs has done a lotta good in Wash'n'ton and that's all right by me. I ain't into politics no ways, nohow. What are you, a newspaper fella?"

Without Dorsey Combs's mediating presence, Buster Foreman was just a meddlesome stranger, in off the road. The two truckdrivers sat watching him. Tom Pepper saw their glances.

"Bob Combs is all we got going for us up there, ain't that right, boys?" he said smartly. One nodded in sullen agreement, still studying Buster Foreman. "Goddamned right," Tom Pepper said. He picked up his cigarette from the edge of the counter, puffed on it, then drank from a coffee cup as he waited for the hashed brown potatoes. "I'm into fast food, not fast talk. They're all fulla shit anyway, all them goddamn politicians. Ask them boys what their road taxes are. You wanna hear some loud talk for your paper, ask 'em about that."

"I didn't say I was with a paper," Buster said, getting up. Through the small serving window he saw Cora Pepper bent forward, looking sternly at her husband.

"Even if I had anything on him, which I ain't, I wouldn't go talking to no stranger about it. I got enough troubles without the government tormentin' me. Get some little sucker from IRS on my ass, I'd really be up shit crik."

Buster Foreman paid for his coffee and went out. As he reached his rented car, he saw Cora hurrying around the side of the building from the kitchen, a cardigan sweater drawn over her thin shoulders. "Lemme tell you something," she called out. "Hold on a minute. You wanna find out something about Bob Combs? You go talk to Miz Birdie Jackson over in South Carolina, hear? A colored woman over there. You wanna find out what Bob Combs and some of that trash of his done? You go talk to Birdie Jackson. You tell her Cora sent you. Her name's Bertha Jackson, Miz Bertha Jackson. She's in the phone book. If you can't find her, go out to Frogtown and talk to Deacon Caldwell Taylor of the Mount Zion Reformed Baptist Church. He'll know what I'm talking about, only don't tell no one except Birdie I sent you."

She took the card Buster Foreman gave her, turned without looking at it, and hurried back around the building.

2.

Painters, carpenters, and electricians appeared that week at the old Victorian complex in Foggy Bottom. Refurbishing the offices in the main building had been Angus McVey's idea, come to him that Tuesday evening over drinks at Ed Donlon's house after Haven Wilson told him he was willing to take a closer look at the Center's problems and submit his recommendations for its reorganization, if that was necessary. He also said that he'd need help and that he'd asked Nick Straus to assist him, not on a full-time basis, since that was impossible at present, but as a consultant. Ed Donlon had been surprised but had held his peace. McVey was agreeable to anything. Wilson proposed a sixty-day study, McVey six months, and Ed Donlon had offered the compromise, a ninety-day contract.

The subject of a permanent director was also discussed and Wilson told them he'd begin the search and make the recommendations in his final report. Wilson had Nick Straus in mind; Donlon, Haven Wilson; and McVey? It was difficult to tell. They had dinner at the Cosmos Club and afterward toured the deserted Center, accompanied by Fletcher. McVey, who'd avoided the Center for almost a year—since Foster's stewardship, he'd admitted: the man made him profoundly uncomfortable—was dismayed by the grimness of the offices in the late evening cold.

The Center's architect appeared a day later and the painters, carpenters, and electricians soon followed.

Wilson began at the Center the same week, installed in a small office behind the director's suite, which was converted into a conference room. There, all the various Center committees held their meetings, which Wilson attended as a silent observer, and there, too, he met each morning with individual members of the Center staff, inquiring about projects, schedules, and organization, as well as soliciting ideas. His afternoons were usually devoted to organizing his morning notes, to dictation, and, as the weeks continued, to interviewing candidates for the directorship.

His meetings with the various specialists of the thalamus group left him uneasy. He knew little about the behavioral sciences and decided he should learn more. The relevance of some of the special studies the Center was conducting for the Institute of Health and a few other government agencies escaped him completely.

"Like much that goes on in Washington, you have to take it on faith," Dr. Foster advised him one morning as they were discussing it.

"That really doesn't answer the question, does it?" Wilson had said. "The fact is, the Center, as Angus McVey conceived it, is now doing things that have absolutely no relationship to its original purpose."

"The condition of modern life," Foster said sorrowfully.

156

"Sorry?"

"The condition of modern life," he continued, "is to live with questions so complex that the questions are as obscure as the answers. Life lives on the margins." He'd smiled, pleased with his aphorism, but Wilson had grown tired of Dr. Foster's evasive tautologies. Foster had returned to his old office in the building across the quadrangle and had left behind a cabinet drawer filled with unresolved administrative problems, including the coming year's budget, appointments of fellows, and three folders of unanswered correspondence. Wilson had sat him down one morning and gone through the folders item by item, suggesting how Dr. Foster, still the acting director, was to respond. By the end of the second week, those daily administrative sessions with Foster had become part of his routine.

"Simplicity," Nick Straus had counseled. He'd taken up evening residence in a dark office across the hall from the director's suite. Once set aside for Angus McVey's use, it hadn't been occupied for over a year. A large oak desk sat at the rear of the room, in front of a wall of empty bookshelves. At the other end of the faded Persian carpet was an arrangement of leather chairs grouped about a gas-fired hearth. In the corner behind the desk was a pair of combination safes, now filled with the confidential and secret material Nick had transferred from his house in McLean. Wilson had a vague idea of what they contained, but asked no questions. Nick still clung perilously to his job with the DIA special watch, waiting for the ax to fall. He hadn't yet worked out a strategy for bringing to public attention what conscience demanded of him, and Wilson, besieged by other problems, left him to grapple with it alone. Nick's advice on the Center was straightforward enough—simplicity. Haven Wilson should cut boldly through the entanglements that obscured the Center's activity—including the dismissal of the entire thalamus group—and return it to its original purpose.

Rita Kramer called Wilson unexpectedly one dark, windy afternoon, a curious reprieve.

She was waiting for him near the front entrance to the Watergate Hotel, standing out of the raw wind, shoulders hunched, knees together the way some women stand when they're cold and miserable.

"You sure took your time," she said, her jaw stiff, her watering eyes leaking a shadow of mascara down her cold cheeks. "I'm freezing. Which way?"

"There's a coffee shop over there," he told her, looking down the street toward the familiar orange roof of the motor hotel. They didn't speak as they walked, heads averted from the punishing wind. He had no idea what she wanted to talk about. Inside, she disappeared into the powder room while he got coffee from the serving line. Her make-up was intact when she joined him at a booth in the rear.

"Artie wants to talk to you," she said as she opened her purse and took out her cigarette case. "He's going back to L.A. for a few days and he wants to talk to you. He said something about a rain check."

"Matthews is back now."

"So I heard. He doesn't want to talk about real estate."

"What's he want to talk about?"

"Just talk." She lit the cigarette and studied him, disappointed. "Try not to look so enthusiastic."

"The last time I talked to him, it didn't make much sense."

"Don't be a nebbish."

He had nothing to say, and so they sat in silence, looked disapprovingly at each other. "Don't be so thin-skinned," she said finally.

"I'll try," he said.

"Maybe he's not your kind—"

"I didn't say that."

"Yeah, but I know what you're thinking. Maybe he fractures the king's English, maybe he's a little hard to take sometimes, but give him a chance. What do you want me to do—turn him off?"

"Is that what you wanted to tell me?"

"I wanted to make sure you didn't brush him off if he called, like everyone else seems to be doing these days." A couple seated nearby arose and her eyes followed them. "I've had it with this place. Maybe you can make sense of it; I can't."

"What's the problem?"

"A lot of things. This political appointment, for one thing. It's not getting anyplace." She turned to look out the window at the gray figures passing along the sidewalk, bundled up against the cold. "Edelman told me you were supposed to get some big job at the Justice Department if the Democrats won."

"It was a possibility, nothing definite."

"So when it didn't work out, you just walked away."

"I'd been thinking about it for some time."

"Just walked out and didn't let them tear you to pieces. It must have been pretty hard. I know how some things can tear you up like that." She waited for his reaction, but he said nothing, still watching her. "You don't make it very easy, do you? Always in the driver's seat. Edelman says you've got a lot of contacts in this town."

"He does too, probably."

"Artie doesn't trust him; not these other amateur political flacks he's been talking to, either."

"Is that what he wants to talk about?"

"Maybe. He thinks you showed a little class that day at Grace Ramsey's house."

"I thought I was highly pissed."

"Stop making fun of him."

"That's what my youngest son used to say, 'highly pissed.' That was when he was a high school freshman. His word for moral outrage. He lived in a kind of three-tone universe those years. I wasn't making fun of anyone."

She stubbed out the cigarette emphatically and then picked up her purse and gloves. "I can see you've got other things on your mind."

"If he wants to talk, I'll talk to him."

"How about tomorrow night, stopping by for drinks?"

"All right," he answered after a minute, but then hesitated, as if he finally understood her purpose. "What do you want me to tell him?"

"Stop trying to read my mind," she replied coolly.

"You said that before," he recalled. "Are you ever the same person two days in a row?" He slid out from behind the table and stood up.

She'd started to get up too, but now hesitated. She gave the question some thought, her eyes lifted toward him, as if no one had ever asked before. "No," she decided finally, rising. "Who can afford to be?"

3.

To Haven Wilson, the voices of the three Californians held the querulousness of in-laws shut up too long together in the same room. He'd begun to regret he'd come.

"I appreciate what you done," mumbled Artie Kramer, resuming his monologue, "handing back that check like you did. Times like this, it wasn't easy. What are you doing?" He looked up from the deep couch where he was reclining, shoes off, toward Chuckie Savant, who was idly twisting the dial of the radio on the table beside him.

"Changing the station. I got tired of that disco."

"It wasn't disco, it was classy music. Turn it back."

"I thought you weren't listening."

"Sure I was listening. Wasn't I listening?" he asked Wilson. "Sure I was listening. My foot was tapping. Didn't you see my foot tapping?"

"You got your shoes off."

"So what if I got my shoes off. Am I a tap dancer, I gotta have my shoes on when I listen to music? Hey, babe," he called to his wife, just entering from the kitchenette of the hotel suite with a plate of hors d'oeuvres. "What's the name of that black singer I go for, the one that plays the piano?"

"Roberta Flack," said Rita Kramer, looking at Haven Wilson. "Are you ready for a drink?"

"Yeah, Roberta Flack. Jesus, can that broad sing. She was singing now and Chuckie turned it off, the stoop. Sure Wilson's ready for a drink. Bring him a piña colada."

"He doesn't drink piña coladas."

"Anything's fine," Wilson said. "Beer will do."

"How do you know what he drinks?" Artie said. "Sure he drinks piña coladas. How do you know he doesn't?"

"He's not the type."

"You think it's a pansy drink because your faggot hairdresser goes for it?"

"He's not a faggot and he drinks wine these days, like me."

"Yeah, white wine. That's all you see these days," Artie said. "Take a doll to lunch and what's she want? White wine. That or that fancy soda water, that French stuff. That's the trendy drink, even in L.A., just like that broad last week. Sure, white wine—"

"Like what broad last week?" Rita asked.

"Just a figure of speech."

"Yeah, what kind of figure, what kind of speech?"

"Nothing, O.K.? Just nothing, see? Go get the man his cold beer."

"What's he talking about, Chuckie?" she asked, turning.

"Nothing!" Kramer said, rising from the cushion. "Just a figure of speech, like I said, so climb off my back, where you been all week." She turned abruptly and went back to the kitchen. "Give him some imported stuff, O.K.?" he called after her. "The stuff Franconi got." He sank back again. "Where the shit was I?"

"You started to say something about Kansas."

Chuckie Savant got up and silently crossed the carpet toward the rear kitchen. "Yeah, Kansas," Kramer said, his eyes following Savant. "A lotta people don't understand me, figure me all wrong. What they don't understand is the way I think, how I grew up. It wasn't in Kansas." He stopped, listening to the voices from the kitchen, Chuckie Savant's first and then his wife's, angry and loud. The kitchen door closed violently and Kramer put his head back against the couch, looking at the ceiling. His coat had been cast aside, like his shoes, and his tie was loosened. The room was in shadows and the cones of lampshades at each end of the couch drew concentric shadows against the recessed ceiling. Through the gauze of drape at the windows, the lights of Washington flickered within the darkness. "It's a nice suite," Kramer said after a minute, "real class. A friend of mine leased it last January. Pete's a beautiful guy, Pete Rathbone. He's down in Acapulco for a month, told me to use it while I get this political job lined up. He spends a lotta time in Washington. You heard of him?"

"I think so," Wilson said. Peter Rathbone was a Washington lawyer and PR man who'd served under the Nixon administration and had settled on the West Coast.

The kitchen door opened and Chuckie Savant returned with a beer and a glass for Wilson. "What'd she say?" Kramer asked as Savant sat down to put on his shoes.

"She's hot. What'd you say that for, taking a broad to lunch last week?"

"It's my problem, O.K.? Don't put your nose in."

"I think I'll go downstairs," Savant grumbled, "let you guys talk."

"I gotta wait here for my L.A. call," Kramer said. "Did she ask who it was?"

"She said she didn't give a shit anymore," Savant said as he pulled on his coat. "See you later."

Artie Kramer watched the door close. "She'll be O.K.," he said after a minute. "What this is all about is I know a doll who runs this ad agency in L.A., so I take her to lunch. We do business that way, but Rita gets hot. I give her a little ad business, but it's just peanuts and she's got two kids to support, so I buy her lunch. A few other dolls like that, but Rita still gets hot. You married?"

"Yes, I'm married."

"Yeah, well, you know how it is, then." Kramer sat back, listening for sounds from the kitchen. "That's the reason I asked you about Kansas, if you ever been there," he resumed again, pulling a cigar from his pocket. "The reason I know about Kansas is because I grew up in Brooklyn, never mind where. The worst, the pits, just a jungle, see—a fucking jungle. Where do you come from? You talk a little funny. Not funny; different."

"A little town down in Virginia."

"That's what I figured A nice place, I'll bet. Guys like you don't know. Maybe you being a fed once, maybe you know, but not most of them. Like this Pete Rathbone; a beautiful guy, but he don't know. Guys will tell you, 'That goddamn Artie Kramer's a paranoid,' but they don't know, either. It was just a jungle, which is maybe why I come on strong to a lotta people. Kids have playgrounds now—swings, jungle gyms, backyard pools. Where I grew up was just the goddamn jungle without the gym, you know what I mean? I mean, you'd be surprised by a lotta people I meet that think they know everything there is to know about this country—Yosemite, Yellowstone, Big Sur, all those places. A guy who's lived in California all his life, what's he know? If you don't know Brooklyn—only now it'd be the South

Bronx or Harlem, maybe—you don't know shit about this country. You ever been to Brooklyn?"

"Once or twice," Wilson said.

"Well, you gotta grow up there to know what I mean. When you're a kid, a shrimp like I was in a place like that, you grow up scared. In your apartment, the streets, in school, in your own goddamn bed. When I was eight, nine, there was this widow lived across the hall, an Italian. She had a son who'd been in the slammer, up at Sing Sing. So he came back and I used to hear them talking about him, this Ferruci guy. 'The Sing Sing Canary' was what they called him, but I was eight or nine and it didn't mean shit to me. So one day he brought home this washing machine for his old lady. This was about two weeks after he got out of Sing SIng. It was one of those wringer types, you know? It's got an arm that swings around and it rolls around the kitchen or wherever it is on casters. You know the kind I mean?"

"I think so."

"It's no big deal, right? So this was December and this guy Ferruci was in the kitchen putting that goddamned wringer washing machine together for his old lady and I'm across the hall, looking out the window. I'm all alone. It was snowing outside, a blizzard's what I mean, and if it hadn't been snowing like that, I woulda been across the hall in the kitchen, watching this stoolie—only I don't know he's a stoolie, right?—watching this stoolie put this goddamn washing machine together. I always had a mechanical aptitude that way, only I never did anything with it. Wasted it, like Rita with that dancing act she used to have. So I'm standing there at the window, watching all this snow dumping down, like it does when these old sanitation trucks used to dump it in the East River. I mean, there it is, all this snow falling in the street, beautiful stuff, like they got up in Central Park or out on Long Island, real Christmas snow, like Saks Fifth Avenue, and here's this dumb nine-year-old kid watching it through the window, like it was a real miracle, see, just three days to Christmas, and maybe two, three blocks away a bunch of Dago street cleaners are shoveling it up like crazy in these dump trucks they got and hauling it off to dump in the fucking river. I mean, that's got to be ironical, don't it?—like in a Frank Capra movie or something. The goddamned East River too, which is about the filthiest goddamn sewer in the world, O.K.? . . ."

Kramer paused as he sucked at his wet cigar, his eyes narrowed against the smoke as visions of Brooklyn sugar plums danced in his head.

"So I'm standing there at the window, watching the snow, see. That's the only thing I'm seeing, nothing else." His voice was quiet, very deliberate, and Wilson knew that the scene was with them, in this very room. "The apartment house is real quiet, like it is when you've got this heavy snow, like it's got a blanket wrapped around it. But while I'm standing there, there were these two hoodlums, these two animals, come walking up the stairs real quiet like and into the Ferruci apartment and back into the kitchen where he was putting together that washing machine, both of them wearing these black overcoats, and they back Ferruci up against the back window and blow him right through the glass with a sawed-off shotgun. But I don't know anything, see, like the sanitation trucks around the corner, shoveling up the snow. When I get there and then the police, there's Ferruci lying over the shed roof over the back where an old Lithuanian family lived, like my old lady. There's Ferruci, all twisted up down there, his legs bent under him, wearing this big bright-red Christmas necktie all over his face and neck and chest, only it isn't no necktie. It's Ferruci's brains hanging out—brains and everything else, like someone just threw a bucket of slops from the back door of the butcher shop. But it's still snowing, see, only now it's blowing in the window that's all smashed open. And you know what I'm thinking? I'm thinking, 'It's sure gonna be cold in here tonight for old lady Ferruci,' because I know she don't even have the dough to get her goddamn heels on her shoes fixed. I know because I followed her up the stairs a couple of times that week and she told me about it. So that's what I mean. It'd make a classy film shot, wouldn't it?"

"I expect it would," Wilson acknowledged.

"Only that's not all. 'Sing-Sing Canary,' that's what Ferruci was, right? A squealer, what the Mafia calls *omertà* in Italian—the code of silence. Only what does a kid of eight or nine know about that, a shrimp? Nothing. It's just the world out there, all of it in big black coats that could just come walking up the stairs like that, tracking up your kitchen the way they did old lady Ferruci's, and blow your fucking head right out the window. 'Canary,' that's all I hear, but that's a clue, all right. That tells me some-thing. 'Canary'? Canaries sing, don't they? Whistle? Sure, any kid knows that. Listen, Wilson, I didn't pucker up my goddamn mouth for two years. 'How come you didn't whistle you was waiting?' this dumb kid over in the next block asks me when I come knocking on his door instead. Is he fucking crazy? I'm gonna stand out in the street whistling for him and a day later my brains turn up in a garbage pail? No chances, see? A kid gets it all mixed up. The next time it could be me, you, anyone. So that's what I mean about growing up in a jungle. In Brooklyn where I lived, you'd never know whether you'd make it or not, all these crazy ideas in your head, running all the time, your mouth stinking dry, shit in your pants, a bagful of busted glass in your chest. So that's the way you grow up and people from other places don't understand that. Harlem, the South Bronx, they're the same now. Not jungles, Wilson—prisons, just like Sing Sing. You're a fed or you used to be, so maybe you understand too. That's why I asked you about Kansas. Lemme tell you about Kansas. You get this down on film and you got a classic, like that scene with the snow coming down, the trucks around the corner, shoveling up the snow, and Ferruci lying on the goddamn shed roof, wearing his brains for a Christmas necktie, only the idiot writer I had working on this script never got it right."

Rita Kramer returned silently from the bedroom, her glass of white wine now replaced by a whiskey. She curled up silently in the armchair, her face bathed, her auburn hair freshly brushed, watching silently as her husband lifted himself from the couch to pad across the floor to the foyer, where he turned the night lock and latched the chain.

"So I'm out in Kansas for the first time," he resumed as he sat down, "eighteen or nineteen, my ass drafted, O.K.?, on my way to Fort Sill, which is an army camp in Oklahoma."

"You think he doesn't know where Fort Sill is?" said Rita Kramer.

"I'm talking to Wilson. So anyway, I'm—"

"That's what I mean. You think he doesn't know where Fort Sill is?"

Artie Kramer hesitated, shut his mouth, and then sighed. "You know where Fort Sill is?" he asked Wilson.

"I think so. In Oklahoma."

"You satisfied?" Kramer asked his wife.

"You don't have to explain everything," she said.

"O.K., I'm on my way to Fort Sill. On a troop train, you know—just a cattle train, that's all it is. One boxcar, that's the mess hall, another's the kitchen, and the goddamn soldier boys are all jammed up in the seats. O.K." He sat back again, puffing on the cigar. "It's hot as hell in the middle of August and the heat's coming off the metal like a goddamn frying pan. Every time a regular train comes whistling through, they pull this dink troop train off on a goddamn siding, like these sojer boys are just animals. So I'd never been on a train before like that, never been no place except Staten Island, but I've heard about these places, and I've got a blade in my pants—I shit you not, Wilson."

"Talk about animals," said Rita Kramer.

Her husband ignored her. "So we're standing on this siding waiting for this passenger train to come whistling through and it's about an hour late, so I'm outside, hanging over the vestibule door—you know how it half-opens?—waiting, taking a smoke. I've come halfway across the country and haven't seen nothing yet—you know what I mean?—not a goddamn thing. Just little hick towns and hick hills and hick rivers and hick railroad crossings you pass through so quick you don't know what the shit's sitting out there on the road behind the windshields you see, whether it's some broad or a bunch of rednecks with sawed-off shotguns."

164

Rita Kramer sipped from her glass, carefully studying Haven Wilson's reaction.

"So I'm hanging over this half-door, see, my collar loose, my mouth dry, trying to look tough, only I'm scared shitless about this work camp they're sending me to called Fort Sill after that reception center in Jersey. I spent three days on KP, they shaved our heads, so I'm just a five-day private in the U.S. Army and already I look like a goddamn convict from Attica or Sing Sing, some kind of European DP like my old man musta looked like when he come off the boat at Ellis Island. Only now I'm hanging over this door, looking out at this hick Kansas field that's as flat as a pool table and nothing there except corn. Just corn, that's all. Nothing. Then I see this old man, this farmer, this old fart sitting on a front porch on the other side of the road, just about as far from me as that door over there. His chair's tilted all the way back and he's wearing these old overalls, and he's got on this straw hat. He's chewing tobacco, chewing it big, real heavy, but I pick him up real quick. I'm waiting, see, like he's got my number, my whole family history—some punk from Brooklyn with a blade in his pants who doesn't belong out here—and he's about to let me know, the way they would over in the next block in Brooklyn. I figure he's about to rip one off in my direction, a whole mouthful of toad juice he's getting pumped up there. *Splat!* That's for you, punk. *Splat! Splat!* There's two for your old lady, a couple of Kansas oysters. Big and brown. They don't wash off. Yeah, O.K. It's juvenile, like Rita says, but what do I know? I'm eighteen, nineteen. But anyway, this old guy finally gets rid of this big one he's been sucking up—*Phooey! Plop!*—right off the side of the porch."

Artie Kramer sat back. "Shit, Wilson, this old guy doesn't even know I'm there. He's not looking at the train or all those loudmouth skinhead draftees. He doesn't give a shit. He doesn't have to. You know what he's looking at? The goddamn corn. The corn and the soybeans or whatever that green stuff was, the cows out there in the field, the railroad tracks that are empty right on down the line, like in that flick *High Noon*—no shivs, no bicycle chains, no zip guns, no sawed-off shotguns, no punks from Brooklyn getting stomped under the back stairs. So that wakes me up, seeing that, and I know what it must feel like to live that way, just clean and wide open, like that old dude sitting in his straw hat looking at his corn."

"So he decided to get out of Brooklyn," said Rita Kramer, watching Wilson.

"So I said to myself, 'Screw Brooklyn. I'm gonna buy me a ranch in Texas.'" Kramer laughed raucously, lifting himself from the couch with his empty glass. "That's where I thought I was—Texas. It'd make a great movie shot, wouldn't it? But you'd have to get the panning right, get the camera angles right." He wandered across the room toward the kitchen, still in his stocking feet, his pants drooping low on his small hips below the slight paunch.

Rita Kramer watched Wilson silently, still curled up in her chair. They heard the blender go on in the kitchen and she said, "Did he tell you about the snow scene, the flat in Brooklyn?"

"He told me about it."

"It's his favorite, except he can't get the writers he's worked with to get it right. Remember those paperbacks we saw at the Ramsey house—*The Geneva Quadrangle,* that garbage?" Wilson remembered. "He even got him to work on it." She put her head back against the chair. "I'm not sure now whether it actually happened that way or something else. It's hard to tell with Artie sometimes. Sometimes he gets the real world and the celluloid one mixed up."

"A lot of people from California have that problem."

"Don't kid," she said, her head still back. "I don't feel like kidding."

The blender went off. "I didn't realize he was in the movies," Wilson said. Her eyes were lifted toward the ceiling.

"He's not." Her voice was flat, perfectly emotionless. "He just thinks he is. He gets all these hot ideas and gets someone to write a film script around them. He's dropped a bundle that way. He ought to be in comic books." She sat up, moving her eyes from the ceiling toward the door as her husband came back.

"Only they got problems in Kansas too, Wilson," Artie Kramer continued, as if he'd never left. He collapsed down on the couch with a fresh drink, a creamy concoction Wilson couldn't identify. "After Fort Sill, they sent me to Fort Riley, Kansas—to leadership school. This was during the Korean War. Junction City, Kansas, O.K.? A real sweatbox in summer. So one night in Junction City, I make a pass at a bar girl, but she freezes me out. So I come out at twelve, one o'clock, half-crocked, really snockered, and these three local rednecks are waiting, and they pound the shit out of me on account of one of them's her husband, a real animal. One of them's got on a pair of asbestos gloves, the other's got his fists all taped up with inner-tube rubber, which is something I'd never seen before, not even in Brooklyn, where they got bicycle chains. So what are you gonna do? 'Screw Kansas too,' I told myself, and went to California."

He laughed again, but his wife wasn't amused. "So what about our guest?" she asked. "Doesn't he get a drink too?"

"Sure, if he wants one. You want another beer, Wilson?"

"I don't think so, thanks," Wilson said, looking at his watch. "I'd better be on my way."

166

"Street wise," Rita Kramer said dryly, getting to her feet, "not social wise." She picked up Wilson's empty beer can. "You see the White House's problem?"

"He said he didn't want anything, that he's gotta go," her husband compained. "So what do you want I should do—break his arm?"

"Don't be a klutz," she said.

"Who's being a klutz? You're the klutz. I start talking about white wine and you get hot about some doll that don't mean nothing to me. What the hell's wrong now?"

Standing in front of the couch, Rita Kramer had dangled her head forward to mimic his speech, her jaw dropping cretinously, the words drooling out. "Doan mean nuthin' to me." She picked up Wilson's glass. "You don't have to talk like that."

"That's the way I talk, O.K.? If it's not some broad, it's the way I talk. O.K., I've heard you talk like a slut too. Remember that time down at Malibu, that fancy party, and this guy put the move on you? You think my ears weren't burning, all those classy people standing around? What the shit's wrong with you, anyway?—always on my back these days."

"Tell him about your problems with the White House," she said, turning away to flounce silently across the room, her hips swaying in some exaggerated parody of a nightclub waitress or cigarette girl.

"Who's that supposed to be?" Artie Kramer shouted as she vamped her way toward the kitchen. "What do you think you're doing, showing off like that? If it's supposed to be that doll I took to lunch, she doesn't walk that way, all right! She's got some class, not like that two-bit chorus line you used to show your legs with!" But Rita Kramer ignored him, hips swaying, like a stripper on a ramp, as she disappeared into the kitchen. Artie Kramer, who'd hunched forward as he'd called after her, sank back again. "Jesus, that woman," he complained. "Thinks she's got all the moves, thinks she's got all the answers. Did you ever meet a broad like that? You can't keep up. What was I talking about?"

"She was saying you were having a few problems here," Wilson said, "problems about this political job."

"Yeah. Oh, yeah." He sighed unhappily, holding the cold cigar, gazing out across the room as he had that first afternoon, sitting on the sunny terrace above the Potomac. "It's a long story, Wilson, lemme tell you, and I thought maybe you knew something about it—that fancy house out there, a sting, you know what I mean—but Rita says you're on the level—"

"He is," she said as she crossed in front of the couch to hand Wilson a glass of beer. "So tell him."

But Artie wasn't enthusiastic. "What's it matter?" he said morosely. "I'm not looking for no shoulder to cry on."

Rita Kramer winced, closing her eyes. Her husband didn't look up. "There wasn't any sting," she said as she returned to her chair. "You're just a babe in the woods. Maybe you're top banana with your pals out in L.A., but this is Washington and you're just a babe in the woods. Wilson isn't."

"Edelman isn't, either," Kramer said, "and Edelman doesn't know shit. What you know wouldn't fill up the Hollywood Bowl, either." She didn't answer, curled up again in her chair, holding her drink and gazing silently at her husband, who'd turned again to Haven Wilson. "Lemme tell you one thing. This isn't any ego trip, taking a job in this administration. No way. I don't need the bucks because the bucks aren't there, right? It's costing me. Sitting here right now is costing me, when I've got a whole deskful of problems waiting for me back in California. But I'd made up my mind I was gonna help out, do something, make a contribution, like they say. Remember that old Kennedy speech—'Don't ask what your country can do for you'? Remember that? Well, lemme tell you, I made a promise. I was mad—Jesus, was I burned. I musta lost—what?—thirty pounds? That's when I decided we had to get this country turned around again and I was gonna join up, do whatever they wanted me to do. . . ."

It was the American hostage crisis in Iran that had awakened Artie Kramer from fifteen years of civic indifference. He'd watched the first television footage in disbelief—American marines and diplomats herded from the U.S. embassy like prisoners of war, blindfolded and bound by their gloating captors. Beyond the front gates, a hysterical foreign crowd roared for their blood. As this national humiliation dragged on, weeks and months of it, the disgrace had become his own. It was as if he, too, were among the hostages, but even more as if all the old newsreels of World War II and Korea had gone berserk, as if the dim grainy historical footage of the past forty years had been reedited, respooled, and replayed nightly, but with a different ending—America the vanquished, the defeated, the disgraced, America the great Satan, led about in its prisoners' rags every evening on the television news to be taunted and reviled by the foreign rabble America had once given freedom.

"I saw these bastards, these crummy little sleazebag scum over there, burning our flag, holding our people in cages, like animals, like Nazis, and the idiot administration in Washington just sitting there, not doing a fucking thing. Then they had those demonstrations, those yippie Iranian students—remember?—in Washington, in L.A. even, where they burned the flag, just burned it, those scumbag maniacs, and we didn't do nothing, just like they let those helicopters get blown up in the desert over there. Then there was Carter, him and that shit-eating Howdy Doody grin on TV, and that's when I knew he had to go, him and all these rest of the idiots that got us into this mess. What Reagan and others were saying was true—a third-rate country, that's where we were headed, getting pushed around by all these pipsqueak countries that don't have any more gross national product than San Bernoo, and if we didn't do something quick, it'd just be down the tubes. . . ."

"That's when he decided to get into politics," Rita said.

"Yeah, that's when I decided. But it wasn't just Iran, it was everyplace else you looked. Take my mother, who I've got to keep locked up in this fortress condo down in Miami where she won't get mugged or pistol-whipped by some crazy drug freak down there. Or this coke they found in some Minuteman missile silo out in Montana—coke, heroin, acid, you name it. Then you got these new Russian missiles Reagan was talking about, drop 'em right down those missile silos, this window of vulnerability he proved was right—"

"Reagan?" Wilson asked. "How do you mean, Reagan proved it?"

"Yeah, Reagan. He said it, didn't he? Him and all those defense experts—"

"But it was Iran that got Artie started," said Rita.

Her husband sat forward. "I tell you what I did, Wilson," he said. "We have this screening room in our place out in L.A. where we show maybe three, four flicks a week. Sometimes we ask our friends in, and most of the time everyone's laughing it up like crazy, talking and drinking, but this one night I get a different idea. I show them a whole evening full of nightmares, you know what I mean? I show them this Iranian TV footage I'd made on the Betamax—CBS, NBC, ABC, the whole ball of wax—and then had the film division over at Caltronics help me edit—"

"Caltronics?" Wilson interrupted again.

"Yeah, Caltronics. They've got a small film division and they gave me a hand, but I showed him how I wanted to edit it. So anyway, I show my friends this whole two hours fulla nightmares about Iran, and after it was all over and everyone is sitting there really pissed, really burned, I told them to get their checkbooks out, I was taking up a collection. I did everything but sing 'God Bless America.' You know how much I raked in?"

"No, I don't," Wilson said, still remembering Caltronics. The business card given to him that rainy morning on the beltway was still in his wallet, together with the cashier's check for three hundred dollars.

"Fourteen grand. Would you believe it? I took in fourteen grand that night, I shit you not. I'm a goddamn one-man political action committee, right? So I say to Rita the next morning after we added it up, 'What the shit am I gonna do with this?' I was thinking about this one congressman I was going to help, but we can't give him more than a thousand on account of the law. So I get someone to help me spread it around, and that's when someone asked me if he could put my name up, a political appointment."

"Who helped you spread the money around?" Wilson asked.

"I got in touch with a few people—Pete Rathbone, mostly. He was doing some big fund-raising for the Republicans out there. He's got a piece of Caltronics now, helping to get it reorganized, go public."

"What is this Caltronics, what's it do?"

"Artie's got a small piece of it," Rita Kramer said, "a small piece. Nat Strykker used to own most of it, but it's being all changed since Rathbone took over—"

"That's not what he asked," Artie said. "He doesn't know Strykker. He wanted to know about Caltronics."

"I met Strykker," Wilson recalled, "that day we signed the contract on the house."

"Don't remind me," Rita said.

"Computer software," Artie said, "that's Caltronics. Software management systems, inventory control, purchasing, you name it. They design the systems, sell them, teach them, then walk away—lock-and-key jobs. They grossed maybe a hundred million last year."

"Big business, then."

The phone rang and Rita crossed the room to answer it.

"That's just the skin off the banana," Kramer said. "It's gonna take off. This new management team Pete Rathbone is bringing in has got some computer whiz kids they're bringing aboard. We're gonna go public, get new financing. The sky's the limit, Wilson, I shit you not. Who was that?"

"Your call from L.A.," Rita said, returning to her chair. "I told them to call back in five minutes."

"I'll be on my way, then," Wilson said.

Kramer leaned over to pull on his shoes. "It's not an ego trip, like I said, being here in Washington, but I can't get any answers. I don't understand what the shit's going on."

"You mean about this political appointment."

"He's getting the runaround," Rita said.

"You got good contacts, I heard," Artie continued. "If I'm stepping out of line, people don't want me here, O.K., I understand. I'm a sport about it." He stood up. "Only let them tell me straight out, not all this runaround I've been getting. It's been four, five months now. A guy like you should know—right, Wilson? Someone that's been around this town as long as you, one of those invisible guys that don't ever change. You're not like these amateurs that have been giving me the stall. Hey, I gotta tell you about this fella I knew in Vegas, went down to Cuba back in the sixties, doing some work for the CIA—" His face had brightened, but his wife cut him off.

"Save it for next time. I'll go down and get a table. Don't be too long. You might change your shirt while you're at it."

"Just between the two of us," Artie Kramer told Wilson as they stood at the door. "We'll keep in touch; you and Rita when I'm not here, how's that? We can play this game same as they can. . . ."

Rita was silent as they went down together in the elevator. Wilson was troubled that her husband may have misunderstood his reasons for coming. They stood together near the street entrance as he pulled on his coat. "Street wise, not Washington wise," she said. "You see what I mean?"

"These things always take time. If you're impatient, the way your husband seems to be, you're bound to worry—"

"You sound like Edelman."

"I don't know Edelman."

"He's like all these Humpty Dumpties around here, afraid to stick his neck out. None of them will come right out and say what's taking so long. I don't care for myself, I'm ready to leave this town anytime. It's Artie I'm thinking about. He raised all this money, told all his friends back in California he was going to take a job with this administration, and now they're leaving him high and dry. They'll tear his heart out back there. . . ."

"I'll see what I can find out," Wilson said. "Do you know how a background investigation works?"

"No, not really."

"It can get complicated," he said, watching her eyes.

"What's that mean?"

"Has he ever had any trouble, any arrests or convictions?"

"You've got some nerve."

He pulled on his gloves. "That's what I meant. If you can't give me a straight answer, why do you expect anyone else to?"

"If he found out I ever mentioned it, he'd break my neck."

"Don't, then."

"It was in Brooklyn, he and his uncle. Receiving stolen property. Some furs his uncle bought."

They were standing in the corridor of traffic and he moved her to the side. "How long ago was this?"

"When he was twenty, twenty-one. Thirty years ago. You think that might explain it?"

"Was he convicted?"

She nodded. "A suspended sentence."

"I doubt if that's the problem. Anything since?"

"Not that I know of. If someone wanted to hold this over his head, could they?"

"It depends upon the position the White House has in mind."

"He's afraid maybe that's it."

They stood in silence as she searched her memory for something to add, but there was nothing more.

"I can't promise anything, but I'll see what I can find out," he told her. "It probably won't be very much. If he's impatient about a few months' delay, Washington isn't his town. You ought to tell him that."

"I have. You don't know Artie. Thanks for coming."

The faint, cold rain that had fallen at dusk had stopped now, but hovered in the mist lifted from the wet pavement by the passing cars. Outside the hotel, Wilson took a cab to Ed Donlon's detached Federal-style house in Georgetown. Cars lined the curbs on both sides of the narrow street. Ivy shimmered with rainwater under the brass coach lamps and a note was stuck through the door handle. Donlon had gone to put in an appearance at a cocktail party down the street and Wilson should wait inside. Wilson found the door unlocked. A single lamp was lit in the living room, a log burned in the grate, and two drinks had been abandoned on the mantel, half-finished, their ice cubes dissolving. On the rim of one was a trace of lipstick, probably that of Mary Sifton, Donlon's off-again, on-again companion these recent months.

Wilson took off his coat, called Betsy and told her what time to expect him, and returned to the wing chair near the fireplace. As he opened his briefcase, he saw a hand-blocked card leaning against the lamp base:

POTTERY AND CERAMIC EXHIBIT
JANE BODLEY-DONLON
THE OLD KILN CONN.

Below the invitation Jane had printed a few sentences, but without a salutation: "Emil, Greta, and I are excited about this, especially the new glazes, which are an absolute miracle. Positively delirious about their possibilities. As for everything else, much the same. As for my intentions, am tired of thinking of *us, us, us,* and am entirely in metamorphosis. Must wait and see what exotic new creature emerges. . . ."

Wilson read no more, turning away uncomfortably to the typed notes from the Center, prepared that morning, warning of a budget crisis. He didn't know who Greta was, but Emil was the Austrian-born painter, potter, and sculptor to whom Jane Donlon had apprenticed herself after the separation. Wilson was still sitting there, reading the notes on his lap, when he heard the front door open and shut. He got up mechanically, still reading, moving in front of the fire, expecting Donlon and Mary Sifton to emerge from the hall, but then heard a soft tread on the stairs, climbing toward the second floor. Puzzled, he put aside the notes and crossed to the doorway. Hovering above the cold air of the street that greeted him he detected a fine, light fragrance that somehow seemed familiar.

He called out but no one answered. The footsteps moved higher. He went to the staircase and looked up through the spindled banisters toward the second floor. The steps had moved on, though, climbing lightly toward the third floor, where Brian's old room and the guest bedroom were. Wilson climbed a few steps, hesitated, called out, and then climbed again. The fine scent still hovered on the air, as mysterious as before. He called a third time, but there was no answer. Standing halfway up the final staircase, he saw through the third-floor banister a seam of light under the paneled door of the guest room.

Was it Jane Donlon, unexpectedly returned? Mary Sifton? "Ed's not here," he called, deciding on neutrality. "He's down the street. He'll be back in a few minutes."

There was no answer. It wasn't his business, he decided, turning back down the staircase, just as the seam of light was broken by a shadow moving inside. He thought whoever it was would open the door, but a moment later he heard the sounds of horns, pipes, and flutes from a radio or record player and recognized, without knowing its name, a saraband from those Baroque archives so popular with Betsy during her stereophonc séances these long autumn evenings.

He was again sitting in the living room when Ed Donlon and Mary Sifton returned. They came in stealthily, like a pair of thieves—Donlon on tiptoes, Mary Sifton, the Treasury lawyer, carrying her shoes. Donlon didn't realize he'd had too much to drink; neither did she. Wilson thought they looked foolish. Donlon, too, climbed the staircase to peer through the spindles of the third-floor banister, and then returned to the living room, still smiling secretively. Seeing his face, Wilson recognized what he might have looked like thirty years earlier during that wild escapade Donlon had once described to him—a summer weekend during his Princeton years when he was working at a New York brokerage and had returned to Trenton with a secretary he'd met there. The family—sisters, grandmothers, spinster aunts, and father—were at the Jersey shore in the old gingerbread cottage they occupied every August, and Donlon had the old Victorian residence in Trenton to himself, he and a nubile young secretary from Queens whose usual weekend excursion was an afternoon at Coney Island. Twenty-four hours of nude, faunlike chases and nonstop fucking, Donlon had said, in a performance never to be repeated in that corner of

Christendom, not even on the dusty replica of a Grecian urn within the curved glass front of his father's bookcase.

Rattling the martini shaker for another round—but not too loudly—Donlon had no idea of how he looked, Wilson thought. He said he could stay for one drink, no more. Donlon was in no condition to talk about the Center, although he tried, keeping his voice low. The occupant of the third floor, he told Wilson, was Grace Ramsey, come to find refuge again in the Georgetown house after six months of aimless, inconsolable wandering.

4.

The criminal division at the Justice Department was much the same as Wilson remembered it—dark woodwork, dark hall, dark desks, and a wintry, forbidding look on that dark wintry afternoon. On his way to his four o'clock appointment with Fred Merkle, an old colleague from his Justice days, he'd looked in his former office just down the corridor from Merkle's suite. The smell of duplicating fluid was gone from the outer office and a Xerox cabinet stood in the alcove where the old duplicator had been. He recognized none of the secretaries, who all seemed much younger. The room he and Ed Donlon had once shared was now divided into cubicles by metal partitions. The entire suite and its occupants seemed to have shrunk. Standing in the old doorway, Wilson felt like Gulliver among the Lilliputians.

Fred Merkle was reluctant to talk about the case at first, but did admit that he was handling it. His bony face was as passionless as an old woman's, but it was a face without gender. He wore horn-rimmed glasses, his high forehead was touched with liver spots, and his thin hair, silver now, was carefully combed over a bald spot. His hands were small and white, freshly scrubbed, like a dentist's.

It was the hushed voice Wilson found most familiar, still as irritating as ever after all those years, the vehicle of Merkle's agonizing circumspection. During their five-year association years earlier, Merkle had discussed his personal life on only two occasions, both times over a rainy-day lunch in the cafeteria, where Merkle had described in embarrassingly trivial detail National Geographic films he'd seen at the Society auditorium. He had no personal life to speak of. His wife was an invalid, confined to a wheelchair. Over the years, his speaking voice had become an infirmary whisper. His own life was here, in this gloomy office where he received Wilson like an old friend but was reluctant to share the Justice Department's case against Caltronics.

He admitted that they had a case. Caltronics had been under investigation for bribery and corruption after a Caltronics sales agent was suspected of bribing a government contracting officer for the award of a twenty-million-dollar computer time-sharing contract on the West Coast. Wilson, after a week of cautious probing, had learned as much from a friend at the Security and Exchange Commission, who'd given him Merkle's name. He didn't know that Justice had been working on a second case involving the same Caltronics salesman and a Navy procurement officer handling the award of a sixty-million-dollar computer software contract for naval ordnance inventories.

"Ready for the grand jury?" Wilson asked.

"Hardly," Merkle said with an ambiguous smile.

"So you really haven't made either case."

"Right now, that's hard to say. What we had initially looked very good." He hesitated, removed his glasses to draw a small finger across his eyelid, and then looked at Wilson silently. Without the glasses, the face was one Wilson didn't know. "Here it gets a little sticky," he continued, almost apologetically.

The U.S. Attorney in Los Angeles had had sufficient evidence to obtain a court-authorized wiretap—legal surveillance—but only for two months. A California district judge had refused to authorize the extension.

"Before you could complete the case," Wilson said.

"We thought by then we'd found a material witness willing to cooperate," Merkle replied, looking over Wilson's shoulder at the closed door. "It didn't work out, unfortunately." His eyes moved back to Wilson and he put his glasses on.

"What happened to the witness?"

Merkle smiled faintly. "He disappeared."

"In Los Angeles?"

"No, here. In Washington, as a matter of fact."

"A Caltronics employee?"

Merkle didn't answer. The smile may have been intended to answer for him.

Wilson mentioned a few names—Artie Kramer, Nat Strykker, and finally Peter Rathbone. Only the latter's name evoked Merkle's nod of recognition.

"He's new to Caltronics—just took over, I understand," he said. "I know Peter. He was on the transition committee."

"The Reagan committee?"

Merkle was surprised Wilson didn't know. "Oh, yes, he was here until February, I believe, when he went back to California. I thought he might have taken a subcabinet post, but apparently Caltronics made an offer he couldn't refuse. You didn't know that?" Merkle was amused.

"I knew he worked in the Nixon White House but not Reagan's," Wilson said.

"Peter's an old hand at it, one of the best. We'd heard you might be coming over here had the elections proved otherwise. I'm sorry, sorry it didn't work out. A lot of us are, I think."

"You've felt the political heat?" Wilson asked.

"In what way?"

"The Caltronics case."

"Not at all," Merkle said. "Peter Rathbone's too smart for that. We're just not ready to make the case."

"You know who Artie Kramer is and what he's doing in town?"

"We had a wiretap and we have a lot of names," Merkle said. "Kramer's may be one of them, but I can tell you quite frankly that it means nothing to me. That's as much as I can say right now."

That was as far as Merkle was willing to go, whatever his feelings about the current administration.

"Old loyalties do come back, don't they, Haven?" he offered blandly as he accompanied Wilson past his secretary's desk to the outer door. "Do you remember Carl Dowdy, from antitrust? He dropped by the other day too, in to renew old acquaintances. He has a law firm in Chicago. Seems to be doing very well."

But Wilson's visit paid a cryptic dividend. Two days later, he received a call from Fred Merkle, asking him to drop by. When he arrived, the secretary told him Merkle had been summoned upstairs.

"I'm sorry, Mr. Wilson, but he'll probably be gone for an hour at least. Would you like to reschedule for tomorrow?"

"No, I'll give him a call at home tonight."

A large man in an overcoat sat at the end of the table in the alcove, reading a newspaper in the gray light of the high windows. Hearing Wilson's name, he got up, dropping the newspaper aside. His hair was long and curly, a thick mustache grew down the corners of his mouth to his chin, and his rough cheeks were pitted with scars.

Wilson recognized him and waited in the hall as the man followed him out.

"Bernie Klempner," he said, sticking out a huge hand. "You're Wilson. I was gonna ask Fred to get us together sometime. You saved me a trip."

They left by the side door. "I figured you for someone from Labor," Klempner said as they turned up the street. "That day at Potomac Towers and you came busting in my back door like that, I figure you for someone from the Labor Department, maybe the old special investigations section, one of those fucking dimwits over there who blew the Central States pension scam." He laughed raucously and pulled on a cheap furry Tyrolean hat made in some Hong Kong or Korean sweatshop. Settled atop his shaggy head, it looked like a stuffed animal sitting on a bedroom pillow. "What'd you figure?"

"I figured you were annoyed."

"I was," Klempner said sarcastically. "Maybe I still am. That's why I wanna talk. You got a few minutes?"

"I was going back to my office. We can talk there."

"We'll grab a cab, next block over." He pulled a package of gum from his pocket, removed a stick, peeled it, stuck it in his mouth and began to chew, the bulge of muscle flexing like a bicep. Below the dark overcoat his trousers were short at the cuffs, and an inch of dark stocking showed. Metal taps were nailed to the thick heels and they rang out along the pavement like Percheron iron.

"I heard you been asking around," Klempner said, studying the crowded street ahead of them, "asking questions, looking up a few old friends. I figure I better find out why. You're a Democrat, someone told me, headed for big things until the Reagan crowd short-sheeted you. Broke your toes off at the ankles. Criminal division, I heard. Was that it?"

"A possibility. Who told you?"

"This town doesn't keep any secrets, not from me, anyway. I did a little checking after you blew in my back door. I heard some lawyer from Salt Lake City got your job. That's tough shit, man, my heart really bleeds. I was fifteen years with the FBI and I quit cold turkey, like you did. Maybe you heard. I don't bleed easy. Who set you up for this big job at Justice— your pals on the Hill?

"Some old friends."

"You were gonna put things straight, I heard. That's the trouble with all these goddamn political appointees—they've all got big ideas, all of 'em wanna make it big. Me, I don't give a shit—high road, low road, I go either way. You guys that are all gonna make it big are just the same, white on black, black on white. You tell me the difference."

He watched Wilson's face as they walked, but Wilson didn't reply, head down, wondering how accidental their meeting had been.

"They're all gonna put things straight their way," Klempner continued, head back again, eyes restlessly roaming the street ahead of them. "Like Fred Merkle back there, who's as dull as bay oyster and just as honest. Or they roll into town after election day, think they own it and are gonna rip it off, like your pals over at the Watergate or those dude ranch cowboys over at the White House. Me, I like Washington the way it is, my way—just the way you see it. C'mon, there's a cab."

He bounced across the pavement into the crowded street, grabbed the taxi's rear door handle, and pulled the door open before the driver could speed away.

The driver, a Nigerian, protested: "Hey, mon—I'm on call—"

"Like shit you are. You're cruising for brothers. Lemme see your green card." Klempner hovered over him, huge, shaggy, and intimidating. The thin driver conceded and they drove off.

"My car's in the shop," Klempner continued randomly, settling back on a seat covered with dull plastic, very worn. On the dashboard was a display of personal items—tinted photographs, toilet articles, religious medals, and a radio—like a barbershop shelf. "I can take the Metro, catch a cab, either one, I don't care. You a sports fan?" The pale-green eyes showed only conversational interest.

"I follow the Redskins, that's about all."

"I watch them sometimes, but I wouldn't give six bits to watch them play. Hey, who do the Redskins play this weekend?" he called to the driver.

"Giants, mon. New York."

"See what I mean," Klempner said, moving his eyes again to the pavement crowds. "These Afros from overseas try to blend in, jive you like that boogie crowd over in Southeast and think you don't know the difference. Washington's a spectator sport, Wilson, that's all it is. A goddamn spectator sport, and I'm not just talking about that hot-air circus up on the Hill. Who wants to pay twenty, thirty bucks a shot to go out to RFK and watch twenty-two millionaires punching a leather ball on Sunday afternoon, when you've got all this sideshow on the pavement? To a lot of people, Washington stinks, just like the government stinks, but it's my air and I breathe it. Me, I'm right here all the time, the same way, what you see one year to the next. I don't blow away when a new crowd of shysters move in."

He lowered his head to follow someone walking jauntily along the pavement, shoulders bouncing in a brown leather coat. He turned to follow him through the back window. "See that black dude in the high-heel shoes? Carver Mack, from over at Fourteenth and U, the candy man for that crowd over there, a drug dealer."

Wilson looked indifferently out the rear window.

"He used to carry this thirty-eight with a speed loader. They picked him up in Rock Creek Park a couple of years back on a bust, but all they could find was this thirty-eight in his armpit. He told them he was hunting squirrels." Klempner laughed softly. "Talking about squirrels, TV on Sunday afternoon doesn't have a goddamned thing to do with football, just like this California crowd over on Pennsylvania Avenue doesn't have a fucking thing to do with politics. The way this country is, Sunday afternoon comes and CBS could put two kangaroos in boxing gloves on the tube, and all these armchair jocks around the country would still hustle out to the icebox between rounds like they were going to miss something." He prodded the front seat with his knee. "Isn't that right, sonny?" he called to the driver.

"Yeah, mon, yeah."

"See what I mean?"

"Still an Agency front?" Klempner asked as they climbed the steps to the Center. The brick masons and ironworkers who had been erecting the new front fence were putting away their tools for the day. Once it was complete, the high-palinged iron fence would limit access to the front and rear gates. "Still cooking up reptile poison for Castro and some other weird shit, or have you cleaned that up too?"

"What do your friends tell you?" Wilson asked, a little deadened by Klempner's unremitting cynicism.

"They tell me you can pump up a flat economy with hot air, same as the Sisters used to tell us you can get a virgin pregnant with little green bananas." He stood in the reception room, gazing about curiously. It was empty and silent at that hour of the afternoon.

Wilson led him into the director's office, shut the front and rear doors, and paused to look at the telephone messages waiting on the desk. Rita Kramer had called and asked that he telephone before six. Buster Foreman had called twice, wanting to know if he'd made up his mind about going down to South Carolina with him. They could drive down over the weekend. Wilson had forgotten all about it.

Klempner peeled off his overcoat as he stood at the bay window looking out over the quadrangle. "It's a pretty big layout," he said. "Who does your security?"

Wilson said he wasn't sure, still looking at the telephone messages. Then he crossed the room to join Klempner, who offered to do a security survey. Business was slow and he could give him a good price. A complete package: survey, hardware, and installation.

They sat in the leather chairs at the end of the room. "So you're looking for new business, is that it? That's what you want to talk about?"

"I'm always looking for new business. I drive by this place maybe three, four times a week. I see what's happening. I get curious." He smiled, as if savoring Wilson's uncertainty. "It's not hard to figure. Me, I'm like the old dog on the block. Someone new moves in on my sidewalk, I walk around sniffing assholes. Only in your case, it doesn't figure—a guy like you with your background and a pair of clowns like this Strykker and Artie Kramer. What's the connection? They got you on a retainer?"

Wilson lifted his feet to the coffee table and sat back. "I have an interest in a small brokerage out in Virginia," he said. "It handled a house out on the Potomac and Kramer's wife was interested. It didn't work out."

Klempner didn't seem convinced. "Like I say, this is my town and I know it. I see things happening."

"What kind of things?"

"Whatever. Maybe I couldn't get a front table over at Sans Souci or wherever the fast crowd hangs out these days, but I know who does. Maybe I couldn't find the hat room at the Cosmos Club, either, like some of your friends, but I know who's dicking who over on the Hill, same as you do, who's getting coked up or juiced blind, who's hanging out at the gay night spots after the Georgetown dinner parties shut down. . . ."

"Maybe we ought to swap stories," Wilson said.

"Instant replay, Wilson. I've seen it too many times, like you have. Only you don't know these two clowns, these out-of-town cheapies, like I do. So I figured maybe I'd better fill you in, put you wise."

"Artie Kramer, you mean, Kramer and Strykker."

"Artie Kramer's nothing, Wilson," Klempner said. "Real small but he thinks he's big-time. He's nothing. You think he's got connections, that he's smart? He's got an IQ about ten pounds lighter than a rock, nothing heavier, that's what he's got."

"He raised a little money for the Republicans. He's got a piece of this Caltronics, I hear, a few other things."

"So he made a little money out there; so have a lot of dumdums. Only how many of them decide to go big-time, set himself up in Washington with a federal job, like a Bel Air millionaire—maybe a clearinghouse for favors, a little respectability? So he kicks in a few thousand to a couple of congressional campaigns, gets a few of his companies to kick in too, like this Caltronics outfit. He gives a lotta bucks to this one Nevada congressman—a real dull family-type guy; O.K., so what if he is a Mormon turkey?—and he thinks he owns him. Same with a couple of campaign types out there he's mixed up with, one he cut into a real estate deal near Palmdale, where you've got all these Defense contractors and the B-1 bomber crowd picking up options. He thinks he owns them too. But that's Kramer's mentality. The creep doesn't give, he buys."

"To do what?" Wilson asked after a minute. "Just for a political appointment?"

"You figure it out. When all these rube politicians come riding in on Reagan's coattails, Kramer sends them letters here in Washington, trying to pick his slot. Something big, he tells them. He tries to put the heat on the transition committee, but Kramer doesn't exactly come across as a Harvard Law type, does he? Not if you're one of those PR smoothies working over there on Pennsylvania Avenue. So maybe they try to brush him off—some dinky job with the Small Business Administration, the Commission on Maritime, maybe GSA. But Kramer doesn't go for it. He wants to be up front, box seats all the way, like four years of the inaugural ball. Kramer wants to impress people, Wilson—impress them big."

Footsteps passed along the corridor and Klempner paused to listen, eyes moving to the door. Dusk was falling across the quadrangle beyond the old bay window. The footsteps were those of his temporary secretary, going home. He got up to turn on the lamp, intrigued by Klempner's vehemence.

"Impress which people?" he asked as he sat back down.

"The big shots out in California and Nevada," Klempner said, "the movie crowd, the Malibu society bums who never took him seriously—not him, not that Las Vegas hooker he married, not that houseful of lap dogs he keeps hanging around. You wanna know the kind of guy Artie Kramer is, Wilson? I'll tell you. He's the kind of guy who gives movie screening parties out at his place in L.A. and no one comes except his crummy pals. He's the kind of guy whose wife gives alfresco lunches at his beach house and no one shows except his crummy friends. What kind of guy are you these days if the only bums you can get to your fancy parties are your crummy friends, your gin rummy pals? You're nothing, Wilson, and that's what Artie Kramer is—a nothing social-climbing punk with nothing friends."

"How do you know all this?" Wilson asked.

Klempner shrugged, stood up, and crossed the floor to drop his chewing gum in the wastebasket next to Dr. Foster's old desk. "I was three years in L.A. and I've got an acid-proof memory. It doesn't wash out. I know a guy who's still out there—the FBI office in L.A. We keep in touch. A couple of years back, Strykker and his buddy Kramer were dicking around trying to get a piece of a casino in Vegas and they made a book on them." He smiled as he returned to the chair. "You wanna hear something funny, you should hear those wacko transcripts—a Marx Brothers movie." He looked at his watch, took out a cigarette, and sat down, searching his pockets for a match. "You ever met Strykker?"

"Once. He was with Mrs. Kramer when she signed the contract on the house."

"What'd you think?"

"I didn't talk to him much."

"Don't kid yourself. Strykker's smart as a shithouse rat, take my word." He lit the cigarette, filled his lungs, and sat back, gratified. "He used to be the brains, an accountant. A CPA, a ledgerbook magician, now he's out of his class. That's why they brought Pete Rathbone in. Strykker started out as a taxman after the war, a one-horse operation with a sign in his front yard, a desk in the parlor, and his first wife licking the stamps. All he wanted was an orange grove somewhere. Now he's got this big accounting firm, a securities company, and a piece of a couple of insurance outfits. He's spread coast to coast, but so is his paper. He can't catch up. Yeah, he's smart all right, big time, but they'll nail him one of these days. He's been cooking the books for so many of those companies of his for so long, he's got half the CPAs in California cross-eyed. You think I'm kidding?"

"I don't know Strykker. I've heard Caltronics belongs pretty much to him. How'd it get started?"

"Strykker. Ten years ago it was a two-man operation, going broke—two young computer engineers designing software systems out of their garage. Strykker was doing their tax work, saw a good idea going nowhere because these kids didn't have any business smarts, so he raised some money and bought into it. A couple of years later, he took control, bought them out, and the company started to roll. Maybe two hundred million last year. Yeah, Strykker's smart all right, a real hustler, only he's a heavy loser at the tables, real heavy—heavy enough so he doesn't watch it, it's going to bury him, nothing but lead in his pockets. He's been lucky so far; Caltronics is his gold mine."

Slouched deep in his chair, Klempner gazed sleepily at Wilson, studying his reaction.

"You've been keeping your eye on them," Wilson said. "I hear you've got a hunting license these days, working for your old friends."

"Me?" Klempner smiled, like a man who didn't want to be believed. "Someone's been pulling your leg. Can I use your phone?"

"Go ahead. You've got an office next door to Caltronics. If you had a hunting license, that would be pretty convenient, wouldn't it?" He watched him cross the floor to the desk.

Klempner was still grinning. "I was next door because they wanted me there—security work. They got some hot new software designs—algorithms, they call them. A whole new breakthrough, they say. I had a contract."

Wilson listened as Klempner called a downtown garage and asked about his car. It wasn't ready. He called a local cab company, but the dispatcher told him he wouldn't have anything for thirty minutes.

"Why did Caltronics close that office at Potomac Towers?" Wilson asked as Klempner wandered back to the bay window. The winter darkness had settled over the grounds outside and the lights had been extinguished in most of the offices.

"It wasn't working out," Klempner said, hands in his hip pockets, rocking slowly on his heels. "It was supposed to handle government contracts, government relations, but the people running it didn't know what they were doing. It was just a place where Strykker and a few other of the higher-ups could hang their hats, keep their appointment books—a goddamn valet service." He went back to the chair and sat down. "So they turned the account over to this big law firm over on K Street. It cost them a bundle—a hundred and fifty grand a year, someone told me. They shipped the staff back to California—all but one, anyway. That was another reason they closed that office. He cleaned out the local bank accounts and disappeared; almost a hundred grand, I heard. Did Merkle tell you about that?"

Wilson hesitated, unwilling to concede an advantage.

"A guy named Morris," Klempner continued, taking out a package of cigarettes, but then he refrained and put the package back. "He disappeared. Did Merkle tell you about this court order?"

Again Wilson hesitated, wondering if Klempner was more interested in learning what Fred Merkle had told him or in identifying Wilson's own interest in Caltronics.

"He said a district judge had refused the extension of the legal surveillance—closed down the wiretaps."

Klempner sat forward, shoulders hunched. "Sure he did. They were trolling for big stuff, a fishing expedition—don't let Fred kid you they were just setting it up with this bribery rap, but the goddamn judge smelled a rat." His voice had dropped and now, conscious of it, he sat back again. "This is sensitive stuff and this place is too quiet, Wilson. I can hear the fucking walls listening."

"It's me," Wilson said, "trying to figure out what this is all about."

"You shouldn't worry; it's not your problem. Me, I'm buttoned up. If it leaks, it's my ass. I'm just trying to do you a favor, keep you from getting burned." He reached for his hat and coat. "Hey, which way do you go home—out Chain Bridge Road?"

Driving out Whitehurst Freeway, the two men discovered they had something in common. Klempner was from Philadelphia. His mother ran the lunchroom for a parochial school and he'd gotten an accounting degree from St. Joseph's. He was drafted in 1954 and after basic training sent to the army criminal investigation school at Fort Holabird in Baltimore.

Wilson told him that he'd gone to counterintelligence corps school at Fort Holabird.

"So you know what it's like," Klempner said. "It was the CID that got me interested in the FBI. After I was discharged, I went back to La Salle, got a law degree, and joined the FBI. Shit, you shoulda seen me in those days—dark suit, skinny tie, buttoned-down collar, shined shoes every morning. FBI, right? I was starched right down to my asshole."

"I think I know the type."

"Straight arrow all the way, Mr. Clean, a Catholic kid from Philly still trying to polish up the rough edges. After I joined the Bureau, I kept at it—took public speaking at GW, a couple of economics courses, a little philosophy. You know the drill: anything that looks good in your file." He laughed again and dropped his cigarette out the window. "When they send me down to the Atlanta field office, I'm still wet behind the ears. I still had the Philly accent down there with all those Peachtree Street secretaries, all of those broads with the soft mouths and the warm tit, but I'm not making out, not me. That might give the office a bad name. So I'm trying to live up to the John Q. Public image, Hoover's G-man, learning to play golf, joining the Lions Club, polishing the apple with the JCs."

"This was when—the fifties?" The old station wagon rumbled over the potholes, the exhaust pipe banging.

"The fifties, right. Big troubles down there. But that was the first time. I was twice in the Atlanta office. The second time was in the sixties. Anyway, this first time an old inspector comes through from Washington one day and he takes me to lunch down at this club where he always hangs his hat. He's got a voice like a gravel pit, this old guy, a face like a slag heap, tough as scrap iron, you know what I mean; but he's married to the Bureau, just like an old soldier, like Hoover—no family, nothing. He's been through the wars—Crime, Incorporated, up in Brooklyn, Dutch Schultz and that crowd, Philly, Chicago—only now he's an inspector and they're gonna retire him. He's got a little bungalow down near Hialeah near the track, not far from a golf club, right on a boat canal. He's gonna play the ponies and watch the flamingos, shoot a little golf, grow a little garden, pull in the bass off the boat dock. You've heard guys like that who have it all worked out."

"A few."

"So he takes me to lunch. It's the second time he's been through, a Saturday, half day, and we have a couple of belts. 'Listen, Klempner,' he tells me, 'I've been watching you, the way you're going, but you're not gonna make it that way.' Me, I don't know what the shit he's talking about and I'm too scared to ask. So we drink some more and he finally tells me, 'Listen, Klempner, you take your choice,' he says, 'the high road or the low road—the soft-collar lawyer the way you've been playing it or the grungy bastard the way you are. High road or low road.' I figure the guy's got X-ray eyes and knows something, only I play dumb. So we have some more brews. He's loaded up this time, so am I. 'The low road's tough,' he says, his eyes beginning to wobble around, 'and it's slower, and when the other guys get the kudos and their wives take home the roses, you'll still be standing down there in the crowd, looking up their skirts, but that's just for the choirboys. You'll be seeing pussy while the rest are smelling roses. That's what we all come home to at night, not roses but pussy, and that's what you like—isn't it, Klempner?—pussy.' And he gives my leg a squeeze under the table and when he does, I've got his number. I know what this old fart is—a fruit, like Hoover was, only he's not getting any, either, married to the Bureau like that, an old fruit gone dry to the bone, nothing left but a leg squeeze under the table now and then with some kid like I was. All of a sudden I got sick to my stomach, real sick, but I got a lot of things cleared up that day. . . ."

They drove along the canal, carried along by the outward-bound traffic. "The poor bastard," Wilson said after a minute.

"Yeah, that's what I thought. The poor bastard, but he wised me up. This old guy had seen it all and so had I, but I was faking it, pretending I hadn't, trying to forget the way I grew up, how tough it was. I knew what he was telling me—I was listening to my own conscience talking. Like my old man, talking to me from the grave. So I drove him out to the airport that afternoon and when I got home I threw away the fucking choirbooks. From that time on, when I'd work a case, whether it was a white-collar CPA, a Peach Street blonde, or some dimwit redneck from the Klan rolling over the state line with a trunkful of industrial dynamite, headed for some civil rights sit-in, I'd work them from the bottom, low road all the time. Maybe the promotions didn't come as fast, but it paid off. I got more ass than the Georgia Tech campus. Maybe that held me back some too. I got married late." He laughed crudely and lit the cigarette he'd been holding for five minutes. "But I'm almost fifty now and ask me whether I'm sorry, even after they busted me. Christ, no. That's why I know this town the way I do, why nothing in it's ever going to change. . . ."

The house was beyond Chain Bridge on the District side, boxlike, painted white—a miniature colonial replica on a narrow lot. The porch lamp was lit, dimly bathing the small porch and shrubbery in an anemic amber glow. A bicycle leaned against the porch post. A new Dodge station wagon stood in the drive in front of the garage doors. As the lights of Wilson's car swept the front porch, the aluminum storm door opened and a small girl came running out into the cold. The blue-gray eye of a television screen glowed through the curtained windows of the living room; a few small, dark shadows were silhouetted against it.

The girl ran through the headlights of the car, her yellow hair bouncing against her thin shoulders. She was coatless despite the winter nip in the air. "Did you get it, Daddy? Did you bring it?"

Klempner pulled a long, thin package wrapped in white paper from his pocket. "You think I'd forget?" She snatched the parcel away, leaving her father squatting in the drive.

"Are you sure it's the right kind?"

"Chocolate mints, just like you said. Hey, don't I get anything?"

But the girl had already turned through the headlights and back to the porch, the box held out like a trophy.

"It's her teacher's birthday tomorrow," Klempner said through the open window. "You remember how it was—the fourth grade and your teacher's birthday tomorrow. Forget that and all the clocks in town stop, Santa Claus closes down." He didn't move away immediately, watching his daughter go into the house. "Who gives a shit?" he asked after a minute. "You tell yourself that after a while: Who cares? You? Me? If I knew then what I know now, I'd have been on the take twenty years ago—had a two-hundred-grand pad down near Hialeah by now. It's too late for me now." He leaned into the car again. "Just between you and me, like everything else we've been talking about, but these guys are trouble, Wilson. Don't do them any favors."

"I'll try to remember."

"A word to the wise, O.K.?"

Coming from Klempner, the cliché sounded so patently false that he wondered why he bothered.

"Is everything all right?" Betsy asked, coming into the kitchen, her apron still on. He stood in the middle of the floor in his overcoat, not yet entered his house at all, still turning over the events and conversations of the past week, as he'd done all the way home.

"I think someone's conning me," he said. He pulled off his coat and slipped his arms around her waist. "What would you think of that?"

"Impossible," she said.

5.

At the top of the rear stairs at the Center's main building was a small office lined with empty bookcases, containing a desk, a few wooden cabinets, a blackboard, and an electric heater. The room had been recently dusted, the windows washed, and the carpet vacuumed in expectation of Dr. Pauline Rankin's arrival. The study had most recently been occupied by a Polish-born mathematician and linguist who late in life had turned his attention to the quantification of Soviet political behavior based upon an obscure calculus of his own design which was keyed to certain obscure Soviet periodicals. He'd been a resident fellow at the Center for two years, but had departed without publishing a word. A carton of his documents sat in the corner of the office, awaiting forwarding to his new address, which he'd never provided. The carton had been waiting there gathering dust for eighteen months.

The blackboard behind the desk had been scrubbed clean of those obscure calculus sets and symbols which the mathematician-linguist had once pondered by the hour, sitting atop his desk, chalk in hand, warmed by the electric fire which he mounted on the desk during these hours of meditation, like an émigré who still carried in his bones the icy grip of a gulag from which he would never recover.

If the figures and the equations were gone, however, one sentence still remained, drawn in a wavering, eccentric script at the top of the blackboard. It read:

> When nations, like individuals, come to "know" those particular theories which explain their behavior, they escape their bondage by becoming free to disobey them—and they always do.

These words weren't in chalk, as they appeared, but had been painted there in enamel by the resident scholar himself the afternoon of his departure, standing on a wooden chair, being watched by Billy O'Toole, who'd brought him the paintbrush and the can of paint. They might have served as his epitaph. He disappeared the same afternoon, out the door and down the walk, an emaciated figure with stringy yellowish-white hair, wearing a threadbare overcoat and carrying a battered cardboard suitcase, a man not unlike those derelicts who queued up at the back door of the thalamus building each Friday for the coming week's biochemical experiments.

The morning Dr. Rankin arrived at the Center, Haven Wilson was in his office, reading a draft statement Dr. Foster had dropped off. The latter's appearance before a congressional subcommittee hearing on Soviet subversion in Latin America had been agreed to and Foster had nervously supplied Wilson with the testimony he intended to give.

Reading the statement, Wilson understood Dr. Foster's nervousness. The language was too dense, the sentences too long, too elliptical. Remembering from his years on the Hill how short the congressional attention span would be, he took a red pencil from his desk drawer and began to mark up Foster's typescript. The author had hovered in the corridor for a few minutes after he'd left his testimony with Wilson, lingering there as if awaiting a summons. He'd reappeared at the front receptionist's desk, gossiping as he craned his head to look through the open door to see what Wilson was up to. He hadn't been enthusiastic about his appearance before the congressional subcommittee, but Wilson had insisted. Once Foster had seen the red pencil raised against his typescript, he'd quickly clamped on his hat and fled in humiliation out the front door.

A few minutes later, Wilson heard a noise in the corridor and discovered Fletcher, a heavy carton of books in his arms. Dr. Rankin stood with him, a small figure wrapped in a quilted kapok coat that embraced her like a life jacket, hiding her neck and lifting her arms, penguin-like, away from her trunk. Her thick glasses were misted by the warm air of the corridor.

"Is this the office?" she asked Fletcher. "It seems to be occupied."

"Looks like it." On his head was a salt-and-pepper cap, the crown folded forward over the bill. The smell of the hunt country was in their garments.

"Your office is at the top of the stairs," Wilson said as he joined them.

"I really don't like stairs," Dr. Rankin said.

"Maybe we can switch around later."

"I'm really a creature of habit," she said. "Once I get accustomed to an office, I don't like moving. I *detested* leaving Angus's cottage."

"Maybe you'll get used to this one, then," Wilson said. "I'll show you, come on."

She didn't seem pleased by the office. "It's very dark," she said, opening the drapes. Fletcher left the box of books on the desk and went back downstairs to the van. "It's still very dark," she said. "Why is the woodwork so dark?"

Wilson went downstairs to help Fletcher unload the van, but by that time, Billy O'Toole had arrived. He heard that familiar voice rattling on in the same collegial way he'd come to recognize on a dozen occasions during the previous weeks.

". . . even after I got out of the seminary, they still came after me, stayed in my head all night. You ever know Latin?"

"Don't think so," Fletcher muttered as they reached the foot of the stairs, both of them carrying pasteboard cartons of books and papers. Wilson waited for them on the landing.

"You never studied Latin?" O'Toole asked.

"No. Don't remember if I ever did," Fletcher answered.

"If it's Latin, once it gets in, you can't get it out. Like mice in the pantry, you know what I mean? All night long running around in there. In Chicago once, it really had me going. March the fifth, nineteen fifty-three, the day Joe Stalin kicked the bucket. You ever been in Chicago?"

"A few times."

"March the fifth," Billy O'Toole said, stopping on the narrow steps. "I woke up in a doorway in Chicago near the el and I finally figured out who I was. You know who I was?"

"Haven't got a clue."

"St. Thomas Aquinas redundant, the old man himself, writing the *Summa Theologia*. An old parish priest on the South Side took me in, but I didn't fool him. St. Agnes Parish. You know St. Agnes parish on the South Side?" Billy O'Toole still waited on the stairs, holding the box of books against the banister.

"The books go upstairs, Billy," Wilson called.

"Don't think so," Fletcher answered, giving Wilson a brief baffled look.

"St. Agnes helped me out. Went to night school. Would have studied code-breaking, but they didn't have any. Someone was lying. It wasn't St. Thomas at all, but an old priest from my Jesuit school days. Studied the *Summa* so long it came out in his sleep, you know what I mean? 'We proceed thus to the Tenth Article.' You married?"

"Married once; still am."

"I wouldn't mind, but you've gotta find out what you want in life. What is it you want? What is it with all these blackboards, all these books we're carrying, all these words? Wax, like those pears they kept on the parlor room table at St. Agnes parish on the South Side. Couldn't eat them. Try sinking your teeth into that and you've got a mouthful of nothing. Where do you want these here books at, lady?"

Pauline Rankin confronted O'Toole at the door of the small office, her hair springing up like a burning bush in the orange glow of the electric heater on the desk behind her. Lured to the door by O'Toole's surging voice, she stood looking at him curiously, her small hand at her throat. "I can't seem to get the lights on," she said.

O'Toole immediately put the books down inside the door. "You ever been to Sandusky, Ohio?" he asked, unplugging the electric heater and inserting another plug in the receptacle.

"No, I don't think so."

"It's on Lake Erie," O'Toole said, turning on the switch. The room came softly alive.

"I know," she said.

"Try thinking for a while," Billy said, looking around the room. "Try thinking about Sandusky, Ohio. Maybe it's where your parents took you for a summer on the seashore, only you were too little to remember where it was except how big and dark all that water was you've been remembering ever since."

Pauline Rankin turned to look at Wilson in silent astonishment.

"This is William O'Toole," Wilson said.

Wilson returned to his office downstairs, wondering who would give Pauline Rankin the bad news. He and Nick Straus had met the previous week with a white-haired Soviet specialist from the Library of Congress who'd been examining Lenin's letters to Inessa Armand, the French-born Bolshevik feminist. In his hundred-page analysis, he'd concluded that the letters were undoubtedly forgeries, probably dating from the early thirties, when an attempt had been made by certain Soviet personalities to discredit Lenin. Pauline Rankin's obsession with restoring the Bolshevik revolution to its true founder, a forerunner of modern feminism, was thus denied its only historical prop. She'd been possessed by the idea for over fifteen years, ever since she'd done her doctoral thesis at Columbia.

Nick Straus, absorbed in his own secretive research across the hall these long evenings, said that it probably didn't matter to Pauline Rankin one way or the other. He agreed with the analysis and was convinced that the letters were forgeries, but pointed out that after fifteen years, historiography would have little impact on her obsessions and she'd probably continue to write the same book the rest of her life. If she couldn't write accurate history, whatever that meant, she could write pop history, and few would know the difference.

Wilson was more concerned with the reaction of Angus McVey, who'd spent thirty thousand dollars to acquire the Lenin letters.

He also had other things on his mind.

It was shortly after four when he left the Center by the back gate. After reviewing his appointment book for the past several weeks, he'd decided to begin again, focusing once more on those days the confusion had begun.

The building manager at the Potomac Towers was out, but a gray-haired secretary in the reception room supplied him with a dog-eared directory listing the tenants, issued six months earlier. He found no one named Davis under the Caltronics entry. Morris's name was there—the man Klempner had mentioned—but no Davis.

The secretary didn't remember the name, either. "How come you're asking?" she wondered.

Wilson told her he was trying to reach him to return a check.

"The manager probably knows. I think he went down to the coffee shop."

The arcade below was deserted. In the small boutiques, the clerks stood idly behind their glass cases, gazing out the showroom windows, waiting for closing time. A dark-skinned Latin American was leaving the door of the Embassy Car Rentals cubicle. Wilson walked back to the coffee shop, but the stools were empty and the counterman was mopping the floor. He returned to the glass doors in front and stopped as he pulled on his coat, looking out at the windswept drive and the waterless pool filled with blowing leaves. The Latin American was climbing behind the wheel of a gray Mercedes sedan with New York license plates. Wilson watched the car drive away, remembered something, and then went back to the arcade.

The sign in the window of the car rental firm read: *Foreign Cars a Specialty—Discounts for Diplomats.*

"Can I help you?" asked the bright-eyed young girl at the car rentals counter.

She told him they had Fiats and a few Mercedeses for rent, but she wasn't sure about Alfas. She thought they might have one. "I can check if you like." Through the doorway of the small office behind the counter, the toe of a wing-tipped shoe was visible, lifted to the corner of a cluttered desk. A squall of cigarette smoke and the muttered sounds of a random phone conversation drifted out the doorway, idle intimacies being exchanged at the end of a long afternoon.

"Don't bother," he said. "Is the lot outside?"

"In the basement, across the street, and then the reserve lot."

"Where is that?"

"Near Alexandria." She gave him a brochure and a rate schedule. Inserted in the brochure was a yellow flier advertising weekend discounts for excursions to an Atlantic City casino. "Potomac Towers tenants get a fifteen percent discount," she told him.

"You do a lot of business that way?"

"Quite a bit, I suppose."

"What about Caltronics upstairs—did they do much business with you?"

"Oh, yes, quite a bit. They've gone now."

"So I heard. Thanks."

He left. The manager still hadn't returned and he went down the concrete steps to the basement, walking past the cars on the first and second subterranean levels. There was only a single Fiat parked in the rental car area. Across the street, a black attendant was listening to a transistor radio in the guard hutch at the front of the parking lot. The Embassy Car Rentals area was far to the rear, identified by a metal sign wired to the cyclone fence. Twilight was coming on by the time he reached it, and he found no Alfa, but he knew by then this was the wrong way to begin. He wasn't even sure why it mattered.

He went back to the Center. He didn't feel like having drinks with the Kramers that evening, but he'd promised Rita.

6.

A gold-and-white Moroccan bird cage hung from a Moorish post near the circular leather lounge seat where Artie Kramer sat, and he'd summoned the waiter to have it removed. It was unhealthy, he complained, but the waiter told him the birds were only decorative, part of the decor of the Marrakesh Room. Kramer pointed out that there were live cockatoos in the large white cage inside the door and insisted that something with dirty feathers had just moved in the cage hanging near the table. The headwaiter soon arrived, but by then Rita Kramer had gotten up to inspect the cage and confirmed that the perch held only an exotic facsimile of a tropical bird, fashioned from a few feathery plumes.

"What do you mean, making a fuss?" Kramer said to his wife after the two waiters had left. They were both dressed for an evening in a box at the Kennedy Center. "I saw something move, I'm telling you. Who's making a fuss? You ever see those tarantulas come in with those banana boats from South America? It might have been a real bird in there, for all you care. People breathe in that stuff and that's why you've got all that TB in Manhattan, all those pigeons roosting outside. You think a New York pigeon is bad, wait till some Mexican pigeon unloads on you."

"Marrakesh is in Morocco," said Rita Kramer, looking away.

"Who wants to sit in a bird zoo and have a drink, anyway?" he continued to Wilson. "It's like this condo my mother's got in Miami, which is why I don't visit her like I should. It's like living in a goddamn bird cage—worse. On the bottom. My old lady, she eats and sleeps TV in a six-room condo; is that healthy or not? You talk to her and that's all you get—birdseed. Johnny Carson, Merv Griffin, Donahue, the soaps, *Dallas*—all these little dabs of TV shit dropping on you all day long. She wants me to have a house in Palm Springs on account of her asthma, so she can come visit me and tell me what she saw on TV. Rita can tell you. Am I right or not, babe?"

She ignored him, gazing out across the lounge, chin on her folded hands. Her eyes, dark with shadow, seemed not so much disdainful as fatalistic.

"I got a cousin, this musician," Kramer continued, "he plays saxophone with this hotel combo down there and lived with her for a little while. It ruined him, all that talk. He had to get out. You heard about all those sea birds on the beach after an oil spill? Feathers all gunked up with tar and oil? This cousin, he's a musician, like I say, and after six months in the condo with her, that's the way he was. She's got a voice like an ice pick, like a laser beam. You're shaving at the bathroom mirror, door closed. Electric, even. *Zap!* She's got you, right through the walls. A musician, he's gotta have space, he's gotta have quiet. After six months with her, this cousin couldn't write a note, couldn't blow a tune, nothing, like one of those birds on the beach after an oil tanker's dumped on him. She did that to my old man for forty years, dumped on him till he didn't know what the shit was happening to him, why his hair fell out, why he had heart trouble, couldn't breathe at night, lost his appetite. 'Never get married,' my old man told me in the hospital. His dying words." He looked at his wife. "What's the trouble?"

"We're not talking about your mother," Rita said.

"I feel bad about it 'cause there's nothing I can do. What do you want I should do—take sides against a dead man?"

"For Christ's sake."

"So I'm talking to Wilson. Do you want I should put on my pajamas and prayer shawl and go climb on the couch with one of your Jewish doctor friends for five hundred an hour?"

"Finish what you started," she said wearily.

"I got together two hundred, maybe three hundred grand for these wimp congressmen I was telling you about. I don't wanna put a lid on it—the money, I mean. Maybe it was more. But I'm not looking for any payoff, understand?"

"I understand. What did they promise?" Wilson asked.

"Nothing, not in so many words, but we had an understanding, you could say. Then I come to the inaugural ball, put on a white tie, Rita a custom Godolfo dress, and I get the fever again. What do they call it?"

"Potomac fever," Wilson said.

"What's that?" Rita asked.

"It's a respiratory ailment," Wilson told her. "Defeated senators and congressmen get it, so do retired generals and diplomats. It's a collapsed ego, curable only in the Washington oxygen tent."

"Hot air," Rita said. "Oh, sure."

"What'd he say?" Kramer asked, distracted by the arrival of a formally dressed couple at the next table. The woman wore a long skirt and sable, the gray-haired man a tuxedo. They moved with a certain graceful indolence, conscious of the attention they'd drawn.

"Tent city. Why don't you listen when you ask a question?"

"I was listening." His eyes wandered back. "Being in Washington pumped me up again. Things were gonna change after the Carter mess and I wanted a piece of it, so I got the fever. Some of my friends thought I was out of my mind, crazy." His small manicured fingers fondled his cheek and jaw, touching his tanned skin. "You think I shaved close enough?"

"That's not the half of it," Rita was saying. "Strykker was dead set against it. He told Artie to forget about it."

"Yeah, well, he had his reasons," her husband said, his eyes lingering again on the couple in sable and tuxedo. "Some new projects he wanted me in on."

"That's pure bullshit."

"O.K., lemme talk, all right? Don't talk so loud anyway. You may think it's bullshit, but your violin wouldn't fill up Carnegie Hall, either."

Cocktail music was playing in the background and Wilson nursed his drink as he listened to Kramer describe his talks with the transition committee during that week in Washington. One member of the staff had kept in touch with him after his return to California, but in June he'd returned to private life and his replacement had been less forthcoming. Kramer's congressional friends had assured him that the White House appointments staff was working on his assignment. Pete Rathbone, who'd been asked to reorganize Caltronics under a new management team, had told him to be patient. Then, to his surprise, quite a few people in Los Angeles seemed to know about his pending appointment.

"That's because you'd been shooting your mouth off," Rita said, "all over town. . . ."

"I don't shoot my mouth off," Kramer said indignantly. "Do I look like a guy who shoots his mouth off? A blowhard? Not this guy, not me. You can ask my friends, Wilson. Anyway, all of a sudden I'm getting calls from schmucks I'd never heard of, like everything was up for grabs and I was the guy to see. I get calls from a cable TV outfit, a couple of coin companies that want a piece of the action on these coins for the L.A. Olympics, even a couple of garbage companies that are dumping for these chemical plants. Then this guy comes to see me, a guy that's collected some money from Caltronics on government contracts—finders' fees, they call them. He says he's got real good contacts in Washington, where he's got an office—"

"Who was that?" Wilson asked.

"It doesn't matter," Kramer said.

"He was a friend of Strykker," Rita put in.

"What'd you say that for?" her husband asked, annoyed.

"Because he asked."

"We're not talking names, we're just talking, O.K.?"

She ignored him. "You want to know his first name?" she asked Wilson. "It's Chuck. He came out to the house for drinks after he called Artie, using Strykker's name. He just walks in and five minutes later it's 'Artie' this and 'Artie' that, and I'm 'Rita' and he's 'Chuck'—a real greaser."

"What was his last name?" Wilson asked. Neither answered. Rita sat in silence, looking at her husband, who was still sulking, slumped down in the lounge seat and looking off across the shadowy lounge.

"So this jerk came to see you," Rita began quietly, still watching her husband, a sudden invalid, a pouting child. "Go ahead, finish it. We're trying to help."

After a minute, he stirred. "So this guy comes to see me," he said in a weak voice. "I'm not saying who. I'm no rat snitch. He comes to see me on account of he's heard I'm lining up a government job. He tells me what I should go for, the jobs that pay off the best. First, there's this thing called the property disposal board that's going to auction off all this government property. He says I should go for that. There's this here one job on the

194

board still open. He tells me I should go for it. Then he starts talking about the government property they're gonna sell off, like this piece in Vegas, about a hundred acres of sagebrush near the airport, just down from the Strip. It's worth twenty, thirty million. Maybe we can cut a deal, he tells me. Can you imagine this schlemiel? I tell him he's got rocks in his head."

"So what did he say?"

"He keeps on talking. A motor-mouth, this guy. He tells me I ought to think about this GSA outfit, since they do all the government purchasing, handle the property, the leasing, buy all the furniture. He says they even have a computer section and that would tie in good with Caltronics. I'm really hot by this time. I tell him if I'm going to Washington, it's not gonna be as any warehouse clerk—"

"A definite sleazebag," Rita said.

"O.K., but he's Strykker's buddy and did him some favors on government contracts. I don't wanna step on any toes. He's got connections here—"

"For Christ's sake, grow up!" Rita exclaimed. "He's just a cheap hustler, the way Strykker started out. I knew that as soon as he walked in the door." She took a cigarette from the silver case on the table and lit it. "Artie's just being loyal," she told Wilson. "Maybe he can't say it, but I can. Strykker once tried to get Artie interested in this film outfit his brother-in-law picked up. It's a good thing he stayed out. Artie knew then what Strykker was all about, even if he won't admit it."

"It was just small potatoes," her husband grumbled, "rabbit turds— nothing worth getting excited about. Anyway, that was ten years ago."

"Strykker had big plans for this film company," she continued. "real classy—motel room peep shows, funky porn on closed-circuit TV. A real Cecil B. De Mille type, this Strykker."

"That was a bad rap," her husband said, stroking his tan jaws again. "He's got a new image now."

"Oh, yeah. A new image, sure. He got baptized. They baptize them every week that way out in L.A. The district attorney does it. The district attorney and the grand jury."

"Rita's got it all wrong," Artie said. "An investigation, not an indictment. Strykker told me all about it. It wasn't him, anyway; it was his brother-in-law, and it was eight, ten years ago."

"A few smut shops, a couple of outcall massage parlors. Takeout sex."

"Come on, that wasn't Strykker. What'd you have to bring that up for?"

"To let him know what Strykker is all about. He'd sell anybody, just like he'd buy anything if he thought he could get away with it. People like that don't change."

Wilson frowned, watching her face.

"What's the trouble?" she asked.

"I'll tell you what Strykker is all about," her husband continued. "Over two hundred million last year, maybe more. You're always getting hot about something, all the time complaining about someone trying to hustle me. Me, I just take human nature as it is. I don't second-guess nobody."

They sat in silence. The fog of cocktail music had evaporated, uncovering in the far corner a small figure who'd just taken his place behind a piano. His first chords were muted but tender, an anniversary request for two tables of nearby tourists.

"There's a question I wanted to ask," Wilson said, "something I'm not clear on."

"Go ahead," Kramer said without enthusiasm, still wounded by Rita's revelations.

"That day at the house on the Potomac, you seemed to think it was some kind of scam. I didn't understand that, I still don't."

Rita looked at her husband, waiting. "Yeah," he began, "something funny going on. It didn't add up. Not right away. It was something I didn't tell Rita." He turned to her. "This guy comes to see me again, this guy we were talking about, the schlemiel that hears I'm lining up a government job."

"Chuck, you mean?" she asked.

"Names don't matter. I didn't tell you, but I might as well. So what do you think this crumb has the nerve to say to me this second time? It's at my office. He tells me he hears my appointment's got lost. Remember, this is the guy with the Washington connections, the guy that's got those finders' fees from Caltronics. What do you think he says?"

"I don't know," Rita said. "Where was I?"

"You were here, looking for a house, that first week." He turned to Wilson. "What do you think this crumb says?"

"I couldn't guess," Wilson said.

"I'll tell you what he says," Artie continued, sitting up indignantly. "He tells me, 'You wanna federal job, Artie, you got one,' just like that. 'No sweat.' So I remember these government contracts he's gotten for Strykker. I'm talking maybe fifty, sixty million, understand. So that's what comes into my mind. Big dough. So I ask him, 'How much?' 'Ten grand,' this sleazebag says, and I tell him to get the shit out of my office. I mean, here I raised all this money for the Republican campaign committees, these congressmen, maybe two, three hundred thou, and this crum bum in a fifty-dollar suit is asking me to take ten grand for a federal job. Can you imagine this guy? I got Mexican cloth cutters down at the dress factory could hustle me with more class than this slob. I'm burned, really burned. I mean, it takes me the whole morning to get my head together. What the hell do they think I am—some cheap little shyster that'll take a ten-grand fix? That's gotta be peanuts, you know what I mean? I mean, I've got my self-respect. . . ."

Rita looked away suddenly. Wilson was the prisoner of the outraged eyes and the small hand that clutched his sleeve, bathed momentarily in a mist of expensive Scotch, light shampoo, and exotic skin bracer.

Even larceny had its protocol, Wilson thought dismally.

"Then I get to Washington and on Sunday Rita shows me this house out there. Maybe that's O.K. for her, trying to impress a few flaky friends down at Malibu, but what about me? There are a couple of cops in blue uniforms around the gate, the place is wired up like a rock band, and I get the word you and this lawyer were feds at the Justice Department, the guy that owns it is CIA. Something's going on, right?"

Feeling very stupid, Wilson said, "I still don't understand." Rita hadn't turned.

"It's a setup," Kramer said. "That's what I'm thinking—it's a setup. I don't go for the ten grand this schlemiel is dangling, maybe I'll go for something bigger. You've got my hundred-and-fifty-grand deposit, only when settlement time comes, you feds are gonna give me a pitch. I'm your pigeon now and you guys are gonna rip me off, only with more class this time, something that breaks big all over the front pages, like an Abscam." He neatly drew the headline in the air with his manicured fingers. "'L.A. Businessman Pays Thirty Grand for Political Appointment.' You see what I'm thinking?"

"I see what you're thinking," Wilson conceded, "but it's a little primitive, isn't it?"

Rita had turned to look at her husband. "That's the dumbest thing I've ever heard in my life."

"I'm talking to Wilson. You're telling me Abscam wasn't primitive?"

"Possibly. But that means you thought this approach in L.A., the ten thousand, was a government sting," Wilson said.

"I'm nervous, I'm real nervous. What do I know what to think? This guy Chuck has real good connections in Washington. Too good, you know what I mean. Like you and this lawyer, Donahan—"

"Donlon," Rita said.

"What's the difference? But Pete Rathbone tells me not to be nervous, move to Washington if that's what I want, but do it real quiet like, and it'll come through."

"What about now?" Wilson said. "You still think I was going to rip you off?"

"Rita put me wise," Artie said. "Anyway, I'm not a hundred percent perfect all the time." He'd begun to massage his jaws again and finally decided he needed a shave after all.

"You just shaved two hours ago," Rita reminded him, but he left them there and went upstairs anyway.

"You see what I mean?" she asked after he'd gone. "It's embarrassing sometimes."

"A lot of people get confused," Wilson offered.

"Not like that. Have you found out anything?"

He waited a minute before he answered. "I think I may know what's holding things up, but it's too early to say."

"You'd rather not, then. You think he'll finally get an appointment?"

"I'd say so, yes."

"That's what Pete Rathbone told him last night. They talked on the phone."

"Rathbone's the man that's been encouraging him, is that the way it is?"

"From the first, I suppose. What did I say about Strykker that got you interested?"

"When you said he'd sell or buy anything if he thought he could get away with it." He smiled as he thought about it. "Like his friend Chuck."

"Don't be so mysterious," she said.

"I'm not. What was his last name, this man Chuck?"

She thought for a minute. "Like the town in Wyoming, only a little different. Larabee."

Part Four

1.

The Sunday afternoon was still dark, the rain intermittent, the small brick bungalows and ramblers in the South Carolina suburban neighborhood even more dismal in the drizzle, even more forlorn on their tiny patches of dun-colored sod. A few showed signs of home improvement—small chain-link fences, aluminum awning over the front windows, or iron filigree for porch posts—but not the thirty-year-old cottage with the peeling paint and the plastic birdbath in the front garden. Beyond the sidewalk, the front yard was trampled to dirt along the flower beds and porch. A child's tricycle lay overturned near the front steps. A *For Sale* sign stood in the yard next door, where two garbage cans were drawn to the curb, their ruptured black bags spilling refuse from a basement housecleaning.

"Someone's got dawgs," the woman taxi driver complained as she pulled up to the curb. During the drive from the motel, she'd told him she'd been a WAC driver at Fort Jackson. "Lookit that mess laying out there on the sidewalk. Down at Fort Jackson, you couldn't keep no dawgs. Ain't that a shame now. This here neighborhood ain't what it used to be, I can tell you that. You sure you got the address right?"

"I'm pretty sure," Buster said.

Birdie Jackson's cousin had been rudely explicit in telling him how to reach her house: "You come if she say so, but if you're out o' town, get you a cab. I don't want no out-o'-town machines outside my house, hear?"

"It's being lived in too," the woman driver called through the window as Buster withdrew his wallet, "lived in hard as lye. Lookit that wash hanging out there to the side. Who'd go an' hang up wash on a day like this? Looks like she just throwed it up there on her way out the door."

Buster paid her and went up the walk to the porch. The screen door was ajar and the lace curtain behind the glass pane dropped shut as his footsteps thudded across the wooden porch. Before he could knock, the door swung open and a dark, sullen face greeted him silently. A snow-white scarf concealed her hair. On her plump shoulders was a white smock, to which was pinned the star and crescent of a Muslim sisterhood. *Honkie,* the gruff black eyes seemed to say, *Honkie, what you doing my house?*

The living room was dim and feverishly warm. The odor of incense hung in the air. A brown enamel heater hissed away against one wall; the windows were draped in purple plush, and overstuffed chairs circled the linoleum floor. A small television set sat on a metal table and on the wall behind it hung a black-bordered portrait of Malcolm X. An empty playpen stood near the entrance to the dining room, in which the overhead lights were on and the dining table was being used as an ironing board. On the top of the cabinet to the side were two artificially tinted portraits of uniformed black youths taken by some army-base photographer.

"Sorry to bother you this way," Foreman said as she led him through the dining room. He felt embarrassed by her hostile silence.

"You ain't botherin' me none," she muttered coolly, without turning. "Just don't go messin' her up any." She moved in her worn carpet slippers, broad hips swaying, into a small, dark hall where she knocked softly at a door and then gently pushed it open. The room beyond was a sun porch, its windows covered with sheet plastic. Green plants hung everywhere, and Buster Foreman, confused for a moment by the profusion of cascading green, felt like a man peering into the crypt of some zoological garden, trying to find its inhabitant. The elderly woman who awaited him was so small, so still, and so silent that he noticed her no more quickly than he might a finch hidden in dense summer foliage. She sat in a portable wheelchair in the corner, wearing a heavy wool sweater over her green wool dress, which reached well below her knees. Her ankles and legs were encased in dark-brown stockings and one leg was surgically wrapped, larger than the other. On her lap was an open book. Her small head was lifted and she wore tortoise-rim spectacles, like those of a professional librarian circa 1920. Her gray hair was parted in the middle, as neat as a woolen cap, hiding her ears.

"This is him," her cousin told her in a low voice. "Baby Ahmed's sleepin'."

She went out. The old woman was smiling, her dark eyes bright, as if no longer able to suppress her curiosity. "How's Miz Cora?"

"She's fine."

"Did he marry her yet?" Buster Foreman wasn't sure what she meant. She watched his hesitation in disappointment and then moved her head to look at him more closely. "How long you been knowing her?"

"Since a few weeks ago."

The smile faded. "An' she tole you to come see me?"

200

"Just like that. She told me to go talk to Mrs. Bertha Jackson over in South Carolina."

The quick, soft laugh betrayed her disbelief. "She didn't say that, she didn't never say that—not Bertha, not Mrs. either. I never been married."

"She said go talk to Birdie Jackson."

"She said that when you saw her?"

"That's what she told me."

She nodded and pointed to a stool at the foot of the bed. "Fetch it around here so we can talk. I lose my eyes looking up at you like this. You a big, tall buildin', Mr. Foreman. Sit down so I can see you better."

Birdie Jackson laughed for a long time after Buster Foreman told her why he'd come. She seldom thought of them anymore, Bob Combs, Shyrock Wooster, or any of the others. Cora she remembered often—they still exchanged Christmas cards—but she didn't know Tom Pepper very well, just that he was the friend of Cora's who'd taken her away. She was a shut-in, leaving her cousin's house only to go to church when someone with an automobile would offer to stop and pick her up, but that wasn't often now. The old generation, her generation, was passing away. She never passed her old place, the house her father had built and which had since burned, but she didn't miss it. She doubted she would recognize it now. Bob Combs's automobile acreage had devoured her father's three acres. The trees, fencelines, and small cabins that had once lined the old pike where she'd grown up were obliterated, paved over in asphalt or concrete on which stood new glass-and-concrete malls and shopping centers as unfamiliar to her as the new downtown skyline. She seldom read a newspaper or watched television. She preferred the radio. Most of her old friends who knew her story were buried now, like those elders of the Mount Zion Reformed Baptist Church to whom she'd deeded her property after her long trouble with Bob Combs.

From a dusty cardboard suitcase she dragged from beneath the bed, she removed an old cigar box, withdrawing an ancient photograph taken with a Kodak box camera on the dusty pike in front of her father's paintless cabin. A Model A Ford truck stood in the foreground. Two white men in engineers' laced boots and fedora hats leaned against the cab. A short black man squatted between them, his hat off, wearing faded overalls. At the front of the truck, a black youth held a surveyor's transit; next to him stood a small black boy holding a sight rod. The black man squatting in front of the two out-of-state surveyors was Birdie's father, the black boy with the rod, her brother. Both were dead now. The picture had been taken fifty years earlier, when the old rural pike was being widened for the first time, culverts added, and city water brought to the small paintless cabins hidden behind the clay bank among the pine groves.

Birdie thought her father was smiling in the yellowing photograph. She held it toward Buster Foreman for his inspection, but if there was a smile there, Buster couldn't identify it. She took it back to study it again. Yes, she detected the smile. Her father was a very serious man. He was smiling on this occasion for two reasons: first, because he'd never before had his picture taken by a white photographer from the local newspaper; and secondly, because he alone among the small community of rural blacks had the money to pay for the water connection. He was a maintenance man in a downtown hotel and the three acres he owned were free and clear. On a side acre he planted a small truck garden each year and on summer and autumn weekends peddled fresh vegetables from a horse-drawn wagon through the shady streets of the older residential section where his wife and later his daughter did day work as domestics. After a city ordinance banned horses and mules from the residential streets, he sold produce from a small wooden stand at the intersection a mile away.

He died in the early fifties and the insurance money enabled Birdie, his only survivor, to bury him decently and to pay for the sewer connection and the interior plumbing which exempted the small cabin from the condemnation order that soon leveled the other cabins and shacks adjacent to the Jackson property. The old pike lay along one of the principal arteries west of the city, which was creeping inexorably toward Birdie's vegetable and flower gardens. The first suburban shopping center had appeared just a mile to the east. To the west, the approaches to the new interstate were being surveyed.

On a mild autumn day in the mid-fifties, Bob Combs's advertising manager and general factotum knocked on the screen door at the rear of Birdie's house, doffed his coconut hat, and passed his card through the narrow opening reluctantly yielded to receive it. Shy Wooster was barely in his twenties at the time. His face was pink and chubby with baby fat. To Birdie Jackson he seemed like a boy who hadn't yet begun to shave. He was certainly too young for the hat, the wide-shouldered serge suit, and the ingratiating smile. He asked Birdie if she might be interested in leasing billboard space along the front of her property.

She said she wasn't.

She watched him as he consulted a small booklet, as small and as secretive as her bank deposit book with the Farmers and Merchants Bank, smiled again, this time brazenly, and told her that her property taxes would soon be due at the county treasurer's office. He suggested she might be able to use the additional income.

202

She told him that she'd already laid money aside for her taxes, where it was earning interest, gave him back his card, and shut the door.

Bob Combs had that month bought the strip of property bordering Birdie on the west. He planned on relocating his used-car lot from its downtown location and adding to it in time a new suburban garage and showroom for his new-car franchise. In March the move was made. In May, Shy Wooster came to see Birdie a second time, with the same results. That summer, Combs bought the property bordering on Birdie to the east and within a month had moved his paint and body shop from downtown, installed in a pair of corrugated-metal buildings just across the fenceline. By then, construction had begun on a shopping center directly across the pike. To the west, clearing and grubbing had started on the new highway interchange.

During the following autumn, bulldozers and road graders leveled the ten acres directly across the road, filling the air with red dust; by night the floodlights of Bob Combs's used-car emporium glazed the side windows of Birdie Jackson's cottage, where the cups and saucers on her china shelf, the pots and pans under her stove, and the vials and bottles in her medicine cabinet marched back and forth until the midnight hours to the pounding and hammering of the Combs body shop just east of her parlor window.

In November, Shy Wooster came to see her a third time.

"Must get pretty noisy here at night," he informed her through the back screen, "all that bangin' and carryin' on, all that dust an' commotion 'cross the road there."

"I don't notice it much," Birdie told him in her light, dry parlor-room voice. "Work all day in town an' go to bed early, like I always done."

"Some billboards on that bank out front would shut out a lot of that noise and dust."

"'Deed they would," she agreed as she began to close the door. "Shut out the morning sun from my garden, too, when spring comes."

That same month the architect's drawings for Bob Combs's new- and used-car emporium were completed. The bank was satisfied, the zoning commission was satisfied, and the regional sales manager for the Detroit automobile manufacturer was satisfied, but not Bob Combs. He had amplified his original ambition and now wanted to consolidate his real estate holdings and build an even larger car mart, incorporating Birdie Jackson's three acres.

"It sticks out like a sore thumb, that little pea patch out there an' that shantytown crapper sittin' in the middle of it. What kind of trade you gonna attract when you got roosters crowin' and nigger wash hanging on the line all day right next door?" he told Shy Wooster. "We've gotta figure some way to get her to sell out real quick."

This wasn't what he told the regional sales manager. "Well, I tell you," he said. "What I'd like to do is spread out even more with a high-volume trade, but I'm a little hemmed in right now. We got a lil old nigra woman livin' over there, livin' all alone, like she has all her life, an' we kinda feel responsible for her. I don't wanna go uprootin' anybody, just moving them out of house an' home like that. What I did was tell her we'd rent some billboard space out front so she could get a little money ahead an' start looking for a place out there in Frogtown, where all the colored folks from around here have moved to, but she was too proud to take it. That life she's got over there is all she knows. I kinda think it's only the good Lord himself has the right to tell her, 'Time to move on, Miz Birdie. Progress is movin' in on you and it's time to get on down the road.'"

Bob Combs had a seductive voice. Disembodied by radio from the chinless face, the small sanctimonious mouth, the small watchful eyes, and the muscleless flab of his waist and shoulders, it was the voice of reverence and piety, flowing from the purest wells of rural and populist sentiment. He'd discovered it almost by accident during his secretarial college days, when he was selling a variety of kitchen gimcracks and medicine cabinet nostrums to keep himself in books, clothes, and hair tonic. He wasn't quick on his feet, was incapable of spontaneity and as dull as a boardinghouse bathtub. Barbershop colloquy of any length, depth, or subtlety quickly proclaimed him for what he was—a nasty, short-tempered bigot. Sharp-eyed housewives who questioned him too shrewdly about his door-to-door product saw the same transformation—a nasty, red-faced bully stooping to collect his shabby merchandise in front of slammed doors, barking dogs, and, occasionally, abusive husbands. After a winter and spring of failure, he took to the back roads one June in a Ford coupé as an apprentice to a velvet-voiced salesman from a Nashville religious house, peddling devotional materials. By August he had a coupé of his own. He'd learned to lengthen his sentences, deepen his delivery, and to introduce himself by talking about everything under the sun but the product in his display case. He'd also learned to keep to the dingier, less sophisticated side of the tracks. By the end of the summer he'd acquired a resonant baritone that didn't so much enlighten his customers as entrap them, like flypaper, reaching its syrupy, comforting tongue into dim parlors and despondent bedrooms where the lonely, the elderly, or the infirm waited for visitors who never came.

That was the beginning. In time he moved from devotional ware to encyclopedias to Formica kitchen counters, then to automobiles, second mortgages, and finally into politics, returning to that same fundamentalist

204

constituency whom he could now assure that the Gospel—less its devotional wares of songbooks, sheet music, telephone book covers, wall tapestries, birdbath statuary, and mother-of-pearl gifts for the pallbearers from the family of the deceased—was their only political hope, and Bob Combs its apostle.

The baritone had less effect upon Birdie Jackson, who had frequently been the prey of real estate developers, to say nothing of asphalt-siding and burial-insurance salesman who'd heard of her patrimony. She knew the value of her property, just as she knew it would go higher. She'd often discussed the subject with a trust officer at the Farmers and Merchants bank, whose advice followed her own instincts: if she was in no hurry to move, wait until the price was one she couldn't afford to pass up.

The day Bob Combs appeared at her back door, he was smoking a Kiwanis Club cigar. He'd just returned from the monthly luncheon downtown and was feeling particularly benign. He knocked at the screen door, stepped back, cast a tolerant eye over the eclectic clutter of the rear stoop—washtub, scrub board, chopping block, a bag of chicken feathers, plaits of drying onions hanging from a beam—studied more covetously the side and rear acres, and lifted his hat as the inside door opened.

"Howdy, Miz Birdie," he began, with that bounteous smile that was the most prominent feature of his billboard advertising and, his admirers claimed, could charm a cat out of a shrimp bucket. "I'm Bob Combs."

"I know who you is," she said. "Seen your face often enough around town these days." She didn't open the screen door as she pulled on her faded woolen mackinaw. On her feet she wore a pair of men's galoshes.

"I came to see if maybe we could talk a little business, Miz Birdie. Maybe I could come in and we could have a quiet talk about this nice place you've got here."

She was looking at his cigar. "Ain't no smoking in my house," she said. "Hangs in the curtains, chokes my birds half to death, gets into my bread dough. You wanna talk, you stay out in the yard an' we can talk like this. I was fixin' to go out, anyway."

The kitchen behind her was small and neat; an iron stove stood across the floor. Two bird cages hung from the side window. A gray cat was lying on the sill. Combs rubbed the ash from his shoe in the yard, returned the cigar stub to his pocket, and followed Birdie across the path to the coal pile next to the rear shed. She filled the scuttle, her gloves on, and then carried it back to the house, still in silence. He made no offer to help. He thought she had reconsidered, now that his cigar was extinguished, and that she would invite him in. She didn't. She locked the screen door instead, carried the scuttle inside, and then returned to the door.

"If I'd sell, ain't no place my chickens could go," she said. "No place I could carry them. What'd I do with my birds; my cats too? This is the only place they got, just like me. Money don't mean nothing to them, nothing at all. I got what I need to take care of myself." She hesitated, looking at his bright eyes, the cherub's mouth, and the polished light-tan shoes, curious as to what metal this billboard Jehoshaphat was made of. "How much would you be a-paying?"

Combs thought she was being coy. "Five hundred dollars an acre," he announced, generosity rich in his voice.

"Lord a-mercy." She smiled, embarrassed. He smiled too, not unaware of what such a princely sum must mean to this little old darky woman no bigger than a twist of burley tobacco. "Lordy me," she continued. "You do go back a long ways, don't you, Mr. Combs, you an' my daddy both. I ain't heard tell of them prices since the car line out yonder carried you all the way to town for a Roosevelt nickel."

Then she shut the door.

Shyrock Wooster hadn't been with Combs when he'd made the offer, but he knew of Birdie Jackson's rejection. Combs had described the encounter, but with the same vagueness that marked his sales career: the subtleties and the fine print were omitted. He hadn't revealed the stinginess of his offer. He'd said instead that she wouldn't abandon her family homestead, her chickens, her cats and her canaries, and that the small cottage was her refuge against the intrusions of a rootless and changing outside world.

Shy Wooster knew of Birdie Jackson's passion for neatness, order, and propriety. He thought she was giving herself airs, an old black spinster in a broken-down shanty mimicking those Episcopalian dowagers from downtown whose cool parlors she dusted and whose silver tea services she kept polished.

"Break them chickens loose and maybe she'll go where they do," he told a stripman from the Combs body shop one morning as they sat at the linoleum counter of the roadside coffee shop and diner on the pike. "Even better, throw a bucket of pig shit in that front parlor of hers an' I tell you you'd see one fast nigger running down the road out there back to Frogtown, where she belongs."

The diner and coffee shop belonged to Cora Richards, the ex-wife of an army sergeant from Fort Jackson. They'd bought the diner's inventory and lease from the former owner with his mustering out pay, but he'd reenlisted, they'd been divorced, and now Cora ran the business alone— cook, waitress, and proprietor. She was a plain woman, but not unattractive. Her hair was raven black, her figure full-bodied, her eyes quick and friendly, but not with customers like Shy Wooster. Those who sat at the counter or the four small tables inside the door had known her ex-husband, but rarely talked about the divorce. They were for the most part salesmen from the car lot or the body shop across the pike, construction workers or dozer operators from the crews working on the new shopping center next door. Shy Wooster was much younger than most of them. In his whispered counter talk and vulgar innuendos she heard the frustrated sexuality of a college freshman of the times. After her divorce, he'd become obsessed with the idea of taking her out. He'd asked her three times, not over the counter with others present or even alone with her in the diner. The invitations had come by phone late in the evening, just as she was about ready to lock up. In the sly, insinuating voice she heard the same adolescent mixture of contempt, condescension, and sexual fascination she'd seen in his eyes as he'd followed her movements at the grill.

"Come on, you wanna little of what I got to give, honey, just say so," he'd urged during the third and final call. The voice sickened her the way an obscene telephone call would, and she would have responded vigorously this time, more than a match for Shyrock Wooster's fraternity house imagination, but the hour was late and she was tired, and she'd slammed down the phone in tears. Alone with her in the diner that evening was Tom Pepper, a tired, silent, used-car salesman from Bob Combs's lot across the pike. He'd served time in Tennessee for manslaughter after he'd returned from the war, and now lived alone in a weed-grown trailer on an isolated lot halfway to Frogtown.

"Hot stuff, aincha?" he teased her after she told him the story. "Hot stuff, gettin' all them college boys hot in the collar."

"Ornery too," she said, wiping her eyes. "Next time he comes in here, I'm gonna take out after him, fix him good."

"Ornery as me," he said as he wiped off the tables.

"Ornrier," she said, putting her handkerchief away. "You ever two-time me, I'll tell 'em how you can tap-dance, tap-dance up a storm."

He didn't believe her. "You ain't that ornery," he said as he straightened up the chairs. "But don't you worry any about Mr. Rooster. I'll have me a quiet talk with that little sucker."

Shyrock Wooster never called Cora again, and it was four months before he reappeared at the diner.

Standing at the grill that morning, Cora heard Wooster's remark about sending Birdie Jackson down to Frogtown. She bought country-fresh eggs and seasonal produce from Birdie, and the following Saturday morning, as the two women stood in Birdie's back kitchen, she asked if Bob Combs had approached her about buying her property. After she learned that Birdie had rejected his offer, she cautioned her.

"You better watch out," she said. "You know what some of those car salesmen of his that are all the time on the road are mixed up in, don't you?"

Birdie knew. "But don't you worry about my chickens and cats; this place, neither," Birdie told her. "I got someone a-watching."

Cora wasn't reassured. She thought Birdie was talking about the good Lord.

A month after Birdie spurned Combs's offer, the local fire marshal and his deputy appeared unannounced at Birdie's back door, come to investigate a complaint that her two coal stoves were improperly installed, improperly vented, and violated the fire and building code. They found four violations and told her the tin stovepipes would have to be replaced by a brick or concrete-block chimney.

"But that'd mean I'd have to tear out my walls," she protested. "Tear down the walls, you might as well build you a new house."

"I tell you, Miz Jackson," explained the fire inspector, "what you got here is a real fire hazard, real bad, this place built the way it was. First thing you know, that fire could spread and that whole place next door could go up in smoke—see how close it is? Then you got them sheds in back, that old chicken house. What you gotta do is hire yourself a mason and get them chimneys fixed up right."

"That's a whole lotta cash you're talking about too," she said. "I got by the whole winter all right. Be April soon."

"Your cook stove's bad as your heating stove. That pipe there—see how close it is to the wall? Already scorched up. What I'd do if I was you would be get me a electric range an' baseboard heat, forget about them old stoves—"

"I can't afford no 'lectric heat. You know what Judge Hooker pays down on Magnolia Street?"

The fire marshal didn't know. He gave her four citations and thirty days to comply. Only as she was escorting them out the door did she remember. "You talking about fire a-coming, I wanna show you somethin'. Lookit over here."

She led the two men from her rear stoop and around the side to her mulched strawberry patch a few yards from the side wall of Bob Combs's body shop. "Lookit this here!" she called plaintively. "Ain't this a shame." The strawberry plants nearest the fence were yellow and dying. A dozen showed a speckling of vivid automobile lacquers. "Ain't there some kind o' law about that too, them paint smells eatin' up my garden like this?"

Beyond the wire fence, a paint compressor was chugging away on a concrete pad. The doors to the paint shed were closed, but the vapors from inside were even more crudely vented by the jerry-rigged gravity air ducts than Birdie's two stoves, escaping well below roof level. The raw winter air was explosive with the smell of volatile paint fumes. "You smell that?" she asked. "Lemme tell you something else. Sometimes it come so thick an' terrible you know the wind'd take fire too, quicker'n coal oil you touch a match to it. You can't hardly breathe sometimes, it gets so bad, burning your face up. . . ."

The fire marshal had turned to look at his deputy, conscious of the cigarette in his hand. The deputy backed away immediately, holding the cigarette behind his back.

"Ain't there something you kin do about that?" Birdie asked.

In the office next door, the body shop manager, the bookkeeper, and Shy Wooster were all watching as the two fire inspectors had entered Birdie's cottage.

"I'll bet they're gonna stick her good," the manager had said as they left the window. They were still discussing it ten minutes later, after Shy Wooster had telephoned Bob Combs and told him the fire marshal had arrived as scheduled.

"You're goddamned right they're gonna stick her," Wooster declared, leaning back in the bookkeeper's chair with his feet lifted to the desk. "Stick her right in the pocketbook, where she don't have nothing at all, just those skinny old dried-up bones of hers."

"I feel a little bad about it," said the bookkeeper.

"I wonder what she's gonna do now," the manager wondered aloud. "Maybe she'll just wrap herself up warm until spring comes."

"I tell you what she's gonna do," Wooster said. "She's gonna hire her a cut-rate home-improvement company like Oswald's, that's got all those liens on them new siding shacks down in Frogtown. Look me up Oswald's number. I'll tell him I got an old nigger woman'll sign most anything at all for five dollars down an' five dollars a month, sign right on the dotted line. . . ."

But the bookkeeper didn't reach for the telephone book. He and the manager were looking instead toward the service counter behind Shy Wooster, where the fire marshal and his deputy had just entered. They took off their hats and then the marshal put his citation book on the counter, licked his cold thumb, and began counting off the pages.

"Howdy, boys," he said, without lifting his eyes. "How you folks doin', all this cold weather still hanging around? . . ."

"What kinda fool would go an' plant strawberries in a high-rise commercial zone, anyway!" Shy Wooster cried. "Plant nickel corn an' squash in a goddamn shopping center at two dollars a square foot!"

"Same kinda fool thinks she can get away with it," said Bob Combs coolly, turning away from the rear of the paint and body shop. A structural steel rigger and a sheet metal crew had been at work for two days fabricating a new forced-air ventilating tower for the paint shed, lifting forty feet into the air and costing more than four thousand dollars. But this wasn't the only expense incurred by the complaints about Birdie Jackson's coal stoves. Near the front gate, a bright-yellow ditching machine was being loaded onto a lowboy. Behind it lay the freshly excavated trench alongside which lay scattered sections of the new three-inch water pipe for the emergency hydrants at the rear of the lot. The fire marshal had given the body and paint shop eight violations in all, totaling some seventy-five hundred dollars in construction costs, and no thirty-day grace period.

"That nigger done closed me down," Bob Combs said softly as he watched the lowboy trundle out into the highway, speaking now not as the JC or Rotary Club entrepreneur but as a redneck country boy out of the pinewoods down near the Georgia border. "She done closed me down, that nigger did." His temper had two circuits, the first quick, nasty, and red-faced; and the second without animation at all, just a certain sullen grayness in the lifeless eyes, like scorched tin. This was the second. "What's she cooking with now?" he asked Shy Wooster. "Coal oil?"

"I haven't found out."

"We've got to move Miz Birdie on, on down the pike to Frogtown with the rest o' them niggers. She got a lien yet, hired Oswald?" Wooster didn't know. "Well, you better be finding out. We got to move her out before warm weather comes. She thinks she's gonna get me to pay her a dollar a square foot for that patch o' sand burrs and pole beans and skinny roosters, she's been sleeping with her head in a whiskey jar."

On Friday evenings, Birdie Jackson took supper with the ladies' altar guild of the Mount Zion Reformed Baptist Church, driven out to the church by Deacon Caldwell Taylor on his way home from his caretaker's job with a local cemetery. On this Friday, the small cottage was empty except for the birds in their cages and the two cats on their rugs in front of the kitchen stove. A night-light burned on the table just inside the back door.

From the office of the used-car lot next door, Shy Wooster watched the taillights of Deacon Taylor's rusty old Ford disappear down the pike to the west toward the Mount Zion Church, and then hurried out to the side of the lot where the colored handyman, Smooter Davis, had just finished buffing a Cadillac sedan acquired two days earlier from a black undertaker in Decatur, Georgia. Indicted for a numbers operation, he'd needed quick cash. Smooter Davis, a lean colored man in his mid-thirties, had washed and waxed it that day for Combs to deliver personally to a local asphalt paving contractor. Davis was the utility man at the car lot. He'd driven a six-by-six in Italy during the war and had studied to be a diesel mechanic in the East on the GI Bill. His own garage had failed, and he drove the auto carrier for pickups and deliveries in the Southeast, acted as Combs's liaison with a few colored lots about the state, and did odd jobs around the shop and yard. He was unmarried. In Shy Wooster's estimation, Smooter Davis was a man indifferent to anything except cars, whiskey, and all-night pussy from the front porch widows or husbandless wives of Frogtown.

Smooter Davis began humming as Shy Wooster came around the building. As he climbed behind the wheel, the humming grew louder. Then Davis sang a few bars of "Don't Let No Cadillac Woman Make No Flat Tire of You" as he snapped the cloth like a shoeshine boy.

"Talk about yourself," Wooster called through the window, "'cause I'm not getting any poontang these days, not like you."

Smooter Davis was doing his duck walk as he made a few last swipes at the hood. "'I got a woman,'" he sang, pretending to finger a harmonica, "'won't fit in your backseat. . . .'"

Bob Combs was waiting on the back steps of the businessmen's club as Shy Wooster drove up in the Cadillac twenty minutes later.

"That sure is a whole lotta automobile," Combs said admiringly as Wooster climbed out and gave him the keys. "I don't care who owned it. Give Smooter a Cadillac and a shine cloth, he'll really go to town, won't he?" He leaned his head in and sniffed the back seat. "Got the smell out too. You smell anything?"

Wooster opened the door to sniff. "Don't think so."

"Hair straightener? Lily flowers? They sure bury 'em big down in Decatur, don't they? Big an' black. How's it handle?"

"Easy as pie," Wooster said.

"Well, it's sure one fine automobile. What Mr. Collier don't know won't hurt him. Maybe I ought to keep it, find Mr. Collier another."

"Maybe you should."

"Why don't we take a spin, find out how all these thingamajigs work. What's it got? Air, power steerin', power brakes—lookit all that. Gotta be an airplane pilot or an organ player to get it off the ground. Come on, climb in—show me how to work it."

"I got to get to the pharmacy before it closes," said Wooster.

"How come? Someone sick?" Combs took off with a lurch, stopped, and started again. "This is one fine machine, I tell you that; just glides along, don't it?" He turned up the dark street. "We'll just take us a quiet ride down to Doc Coker's pharmacy and see how this Cadillac automobile handles. . . ."

It was a cold, clear night, with a full moon in the sky. At Doc Coker's pharmacy, Shy Wooster disappeared inside while Bob Combs waited in the car, fiddling with the radio, the air conditioning, the heater, the power windows, and the power antenna. The windows slid up and down without a sound, operated by a small console on the driver's door. Ten minutes later, Wooster reappeared, carrying a cylindrical parcel, tightly wrapped. As he closed the door, the lingering breath of some bitter pharmaceutical stirred from the recesses of his coat, a foulness compounded in part from asafetida, sulfur, and rotten eggs.

Combs quickly took the cigar from his mouth and lowered the window. "What the Sam Hill's that?"

Shy Wooster left the wrapped parcel on the seat and scrambled out to rapidly open his coat and thrash the aroma away. Then he got back in. "Buzzard's breath," he said. "I was watching Doc Coker mix it up."

"What's that?"

"Something Doc Coker cooked up for me," Wooster said as they drove away. "Something that hangs in the curtains worse than shit from a sick pig, stomps the bugs right off the wall, turns a dead cat over, belly up."

"What are you gonna do with it?"

"I'm gonna fumigate someone's house for her, fumigate her right out the back door so fast she'll never look back, not until she's ten miles down the pike, holding her nose all the way to the Georgia line."

Combs gave a friendly chuckle. "Well, I don't wanna know about that, but I can tell you one thing sure—that was a right horrible smell I got a whiff of. Where'd you say your car was at?"

"Over at the finance company."

Combs turned again, but this time into the congestion of a Friday night crowd gathering for a basketball game. The street ahead was filled with arriving spectators crossing through the beams of the slowly passing cars toward a brightly lit high school gym. Members of a high school band in bright-red uniforms were hurrying through the shadows, instruments in hand. A policeman with a red-lensed flashlight was directing cars into a parking lot.

The Cadillac gathered speed as they passed the gym and escaped into thinning traffic. Out of the darkness a laggard clarinet player, still struggling into his tunic, bolted across the street. Combs slammed on the brakes. He was catapulted against the wheel, Shy Wooster was slammed against the dashboard, and something popped to the floor.

"Good God almighty," Combs groaned from a bruised rib cage. "What kinda brakes are these, anyhow?"

"Moonshine brakes," said Wooster. He looked queerly at Bob Combs, Combs returned the look accusingly, and a moment later Wooster's hands were scrambling wildly among the cushions. It was too late. An angry sibilance was now audible from the darkness of the floorboards, and a moment later the loathsome contents of Shy Wooster's vacuum-packed grenade exploded in their faces. The slight hint Combs had gotten earlier seemed now like a whiff of roses. The putrefaction was so numbing, so paralyzing, that neither man, having once breathed, could breathe again. Combs's head expanded steadily, like a gas-filled balloon. The lips compressed first, then the cheeks bulged, finally the eyes popped out, like a bullfrog's, but then the whole straining membrane burst, an asphyxiated croak followed, and he collapsed forward over the steering wheel, like a split bladder, slack-jawed and drooling.

Shy Wooster had tried to lower his window and screw his head out, but had failed. Sobbing for breath, he tried the door instead and had managed to partially open it when it was violently welded shut by a passing lamppost. The handle came off in his numb hand as the car climbed the curb, bounced down the sidewalk, and came to rest straddling someone's hedge.

It was there that a summoned patrol car found them—two dark shadows sprawled on the turf, identified by their poisoned, possum-bright eyes, their reeking clothes, and their odd, braying voices. After he'd collected himself, Shy Wooster claimed that they'd been victimized by a stink bomb thrown by an intercity rival as they'd passed the high school gym. The officer approached the Cadillac but then retreated a few steps and put his report book away. Smooter Davis was summoned with the tow truck and the patrol car took the two victims to the city hospital.

Shy Wooster had three broken fingers—judgment enough, decided Combs, who had no visible injuries.

2.

"You say your house burned?" Buster Foreman asked. "Burned because of the stove, or what was it? A Sunday night?"

"Sunday night," Birdie said.

She'd been attending services at the Mount Zion Church the evening it happened. The fire marshal had inspected the ruins the following day and in his report claimed that the fire had started in the kitchen wall, caused by the same flue defect that had forced him to give her two citations ten days earlier. She'd moved to Frogtown.

"So the stoves hadn't been fixed," Buster said.

"One was fixed," she answered, her voice now a little hoarse, "the one in the parlor. Not fixed but started to get fixed." She'd moved from the collapsible wheelchair to a straight-backed rocker Buster Foreman had brought in from the living room. A handkerchief was in her bony hand and was in constant motion—to her throat, her temples, her forehead, but most often to cover her mouth as she smiled like a young girl, remembering an incident she hadn't talked about in years. "Oh, Lordy, Mister Foreman," and she would laugh, "you asking me about a whole lot of foolishness I done forgot a long, long time ago." But she hadn't forgotten at all, and her memory was as clear as a spring fed from an underground fault, untouched by the rancor of the seasons.

"What about the kitchen stove?" he asked, leaning forward again. He desperately wanted a cigarette and something cool to drink. They'd been talking for almost two hours.

"Well, the kitchen stove was working, but I wouldn't say it was fixed yet. That's where I left my cats in the evening, right there in the kitchen. The other stove, in the parlor, they was working on, but I didn't have no fire in the box, not that Sunday evening. The masons was working on it and they left their tools there, still on the floor behind the stove. So the parlor was cold when I left, like the kitchen stove. But they say the kitchen stove took fire right up where the stovepipe went into the plasterboard, but that didn't make no sense to me. I was cookin' on a hot plate Miz Cora let me use. Then they say the curtains went up, then the ceilin', an' after that the can o' coal oil in the kitchen. That's what they tole me, but they didn't know any more about it than I did. There wasn't any curtains on the wall behind the stove, an' there wasn't no coal oil there neither, not when I left. It was out in the coal shed next to the chicken house, but you know what they say: colored don't count, an' I couldn't tell them fire marshals how to do their business, not with them knowing how many shacks and tenant houses out there git burned up ever' winter by a bad stove or someone, some chile, foolin' around with stick matches. . . ."

"So you think someone started the fire in your house?"

She rocked backward slowly, and folded her hands in her lap. "There was some other burnin' goin' on in them days," she said, "burnin' folks didn't hear about, like that foolishness out at Mount Zion Church after Deacon Caldwell Taylor brung that NAACP preacher from Atlanta up to meet with us. They say it was a cross burning, some folks said, burning right in the road out in front of the church, but it was a sorry-looking mess if that's what it was. Looked like two old Christmas trees wired together to me, something some kids would do. So with that goin' on, an' all that marching and singing getting started up down in Atlanta and Montgom'ry an' Birm'n'ham, it didn't surprise me none some devil reached out an' fired up my kitchen curtains that Sunday evening, not with Bob Combs an' his kind being right next door. I knowed sumpin was coming—"

"Because Cora told you?" Foreman asked, his hand again moving to the cigarette package in his pocket. Her eyes moved too, and he took out his pen instead.

"Not with just what she said," Birdie answered. "A whole lotta things. It was a feelin' I had, a feelin' some other folks had too. I knowed Bob Combs wanted to move me out and wanted my place, but I knew he wasn't gonna give me good money for it, so I went down an' talked to 'em at the bank. I told Mr. Giles down there, I told him find me someone who'll pay me a good price, I'm fixin' to move on, but do it quiet like, only I'm not selling out to Mister Bob Combs. So he did."

"This was before the fire?"

"Two weeks before my place burned."

"So you expected something to happen?" Buster asked.

"It was a feeling some folks had, like I said," she replied, as if protecting someone.

"Cora, then," Buster Foreman guessed.

She moved her head to say no, almost imperceptibly, the same Delphic smile on her lips. They sat in silence. Then she said, "Colored sticks together, Mister Foreman; maybe it don't always seem like it, but we do."

No, not Cora. It was Smooter Davis who'd told her that the time had come for her to sell out. He was the one who kept his eye on her cottage.

"Folks never paid much attention to him, snappin' that rag an' walkin' that fool duck walk like he used to do," she said, "singin' them low-down songs, he used to call them. But that man had eyes, had ears, had more sense'n all of that trash over at Mister Bob Combs's car lot put together. He was Mount Zion too, but he never let on. He knowed everything that was goin' on over there at that garage and car shop. It was him that had to clean up them cars on Monday morning, tires all muddied up after they'd been on the road all Saturday an' Sunday or had been taking folks to one of them meetings out in the woods. It was him got the cars ready. He'd have to be a fool not to know about all them telephone calls comin' in an' goin' out over in that used-car office, getting folks together, getting the automobiles, sendin' them off down the road an' heading out o' town, picking folks up on the way—all that trash going down to Montgom'ry or Selma or wherever it was at—all that ugliness that was hanging along the side of the road waiting for them marchers to come walkin' by. . . ."

Her voice faded. "The civil rights marchers?" Buster asked, leaning forward. "The Freedom Riders?"

She nodded, her eyes dropped to her green woolen skirt. She plucked at the wool with her small fingers, the handkerchief still wadded in her palm. "It was over at Bob Combs's used-car office they got things organized around here. They was the ones got that white trash all riled up, got 'em the cars, got 'em the gas. Smooter Davis even knowed when it was they had their meetings out at Mister Bob Combs's huntin' camp—stompin' around the fire, burnin' them torches, listenin' to those devils in their white robes they'd bring in here from down in Georgia an' Alabama—"

"The Klan? These people had ties to the Klan?"

She didn't say it. "Smooter Davis knowed all about that. He'd tell Deacon Caldwell Taylor that maybe folks should stay pretty close to home, not be drivin' around out there in the piny woods on the other side of the county line when they was getting together. So that's how Mount Zion knew. Smooter Davis was watching for us. He knowed everything that was going on over in the car office, who was doin' this, who was doin' that, who it was that burned—"

She faltered in embarrassment. Buster waited.

"Last time I talked to white folks like this was Mister Giles at the bank," she said softly. "He's dead now, but he never did come out to my house, not even when I buried my daddy."

"Times have changed," Buster said.

"Not hardly, they haven't. Some things have got worse. Lookit my cousin out there, all got up like that." Her hands had stopped and she hesitated, drew a deep breath, and then began again, uncomfortably. "You from Wash'n'ton. Maybe you know about this business, maybe you can tell me. It never did make a whole lot o' sense to me. I ain't tole no one this, not a soul, an' I thought I never would, but Smooter Davis been gone a long, long time now, over twenty years, an' no one ever laid eyes on him again, just like the law never laid a hand on Bob Combs and that used-car bunch over there. They say he stole a cash box out of the used-car office that night he disappeared, but I never believed that, neither." She lifted her eyes at last. "I never told Deacon Caldwell Taylor this, I never told Cora this, neither. There was a whole lotta guessing going on about who done it, but that was all it was. I never said a word, just like Smooter Davis tole me not to, so what I'm gonna tell you now is between me an' my own conscience. . . ."

She didn't learn the truth for almost seven months. She'd sold her three acres by then, not to Bob Combs but to an East Coast tire and auto accessory chain searching for local property for a new suburban outlet. Mr.

Giles at the bank had handled the transaction. She'd moved to a small rented cottage in Frogtown, only a half mile from the Mount Zion Church, and it was there that Smooter Davis came to see her one sultry July evening. She had just finished supper and was sitting in the front porch glider when a car came down the sand road from the direction of the church, passed her house, stopped, backed up quickly as the driver saw the light from her kitchen at the back of the house, and stopped at the gate in front. Smooter Davis got out and ran quickly along the path to the front steps. He was wearing a white shirt and a straw hat, dressed the way he usually dressed when he went out on the road for a pickup or delivery around the state for the used-car lot. He told her he'd just been to Deacon Caldwell Taylor's house, but it was dark, like the church. He wanted to use the phone at Deacon Taylor's house or the church. She told him he could use her phone and led him into the front room.

"But before he made the telephone call he went out and moved the car down the road a piece, like he didn't want anybody knowing he'd been there," Birdie said. "He was all hot an' bothered about something, like I'd never seen him before. Then when he got on the telephone to this man in Atlanta, it was like it wasn't Smooter Davis a-talkin' at all. He sounded just like Mr. Giles down at the bank—giving out these numbers, car numbers, an' who was in 'em, a bunch of that trash goin' down to Columbus, Geo'gia, for some big hoo-raw down there, only he didn't say hoo-raw. Then when he started talkin' guns an' dynamite, I just went on back out to the porch again. Then I heard him give out my name and my telephone number, like I could be his witness if somethin' happened. . . ."

She paused to touch the handkerchief to her temples, as Buster Foreman leaned forward to catch the small, quiet voice. From beyond the door behind him, he heard a child begin to cry.

"It was after he hung up my telephone that he told me who it was burned down my house. Shyrock Wooster done it, he said, with someone else waitin' outside over in the car lot, not setting foot inside my fence, just a-watching, the way Bob Combs always did. He done it with a blowtorch, Smooter told me, done it with a blowtorch off the garage bench over at the car lot, fired it up inside my kitchen, and cooked up that wall till it took fire too. Only there was nothin' he could do about it, he tole me, and that was why he hadn't come to talk to me about it. He said I couldn't say nothing about it, couldn't tell no one at all, not a soul. He said Mr. Bob Combs's day in court was coming, his day in court an' his day o' judgment, and when it did I would be readin' about it in the newspapers. He said Bob Combs an' them others over at the car lot had done a whole lot worse than that, mixed up with the Klan down in Georgia and Alabama like they was—"

"He said Klan, then?" Foreman asked. "You're sure of that?"

"He said 'Klan,' said it right out. But he said he had to stay clear of it an' I thought he meant he'd be getting himself into a whole lot of trouble, but that's not what he was talkin' about. He said he had to hold his peace right then on account of there was a whole lot of other things going on—back in the pinewoods near Mr. Bob Combs's huntin' camp, them cars shufflin' here an' yonder on the road all the time, some of them not even with the right license plates, some of 'em packing guns an' dynamite. He said this was a whole lot bigger than that meanness Shyrock Wooster did, burning up my house with a blowtorch. I tole him I didn't know what that could be and he said my house was just city law, state law, and what he was talking about was the U.S. government, like the man down in Atlanta he was just talking to. . . ."

She had leaned from the straight-backed rocker to bring the old cigar box to her knee.

"That was the last time I saw Smooter Davis," she continued. "They found his machine later, drove up behind the Trailways bus station in Athens, Geo'gia, but they never found Smooter. They say he stole a cash box out of the used-car office that night, stole the car too, but that was just ugly talk by folks makin' up lies for what they didn't never understand. 'Stole him a cash box an' tried to swim the Savannah River with it,' that's what Shyrock Wooster tole Cora. Smooter used to get his coffee at Cora's back door. 'Stole him a cash box just like that Emmett Till boy done down in Miss'ippi, tried to swim the Pearl River with that stolen cotton gin ventilator wired around his neck.' That's what Shyrock Wooster said after Smooter Davis walked off the face o' the earth, an' that's when Cora broke a soup bowl over his head. Then he had to go an' say somethin' even worse, about how he used to see Smooter all the time creepin' around the back of the diner an' it wasn't just his coffee thermos he was gettin' filled up. That's when Tom Pepper lit on him—jumped clean over the table to grab him. That was some mess Cora had to clean up. Tom Pepper got fired from his job an' had to go to court. . . ."

She searched among the faded letters, the old ribbons, the photographs and brass keys in the cigar box, until she found a yellowing fold of paper. She adjusted her tortoise-rim spectacles and unwrapped it very carefully to read what was written there.

"Smooter wrote it down for me before he walked off the porch that evening, the name of this government man down in Atlanta that was gonna bring Bob Combs, Shyrock Wooster, an' all the rest of them to judgment in the U.S. courthouse. He wrote it down for me so I'd know if he had any trouble an' this man could come an' talk to me. He said he'd been meetin' with him—out at Mount Zion once, in Athens, even down in Atlanta, where he had his office. You from Wash'n'ton, maybe you know what it was he was talking about. Only it never was in the newspapers, unless it was up there or down in Atlanta. He never did come see me."

Buster Foreman took the old utility bill which Birdie passed to him and turned it over, reading the telephone number and the name penciled there so many years ago by Smooter Davis. The telephone number was that of the FBI's Atlanta field office. The name of the FBI agent was Bernard Klempner.

3.

When Nick Straus was finally told he was being transferred from the special-watch group at DIA, he stopped by Leyton Fischer's office on the third floor of the Pentagon, to question him. No explanation had been offered by the DIA personnel officer.

"They simply feel you'd be more useful in the daily summary shop," Leyton Fischer said cautiously, still fingering the document he'd been reading as Nick sat down. A diminutive man in a gray suit, Fischer seemed dwarfed by the huge desk and the huge carpeted suite.

"Which daily summary shop?"

"DIA's," Fischer said, hiding his contempt for most of DIA's institutions by not looking at Nick Straus. He was a deputy to Les Fine, whose office was next door. "It's in terrible shape, apparently, and they think you're the man who might help improve it."

"You mean I'd be chief of the DIA daily intelligence summary?"

The DIA daily Top Secret summary circulated every morning among senior policy and intelligence officials scattered throughout Washington. Its format was New York tabloid—vulgar headlines and grainy intel photos. The prose, summarizing the DIA intelligence coups of the hour, was intended to be epigrammatic but was usually execrable; yet the summary was widely read in the Washington intelligence community and at the White House, particularly by those overburdened senior officials who hadn't the time or the knowledge to wade through those detailed, highly classified reports from which the DIA summary was collated. The tabloid was often misleading, not simply in condensing the abstruse or the complex to a few sensational paragraphs but in the inclusion of great quantities of raw intelligence, often uncorroborated and unanalyzed. Used this way, the DIA daily brief was the tool of the most hawkish elements of DIA, who exploited the morning tabloid to get their bellicose warnings to the senior policy ranks at the Pentagon, the White House, State, the National Security Council, and a few Senate and House committees, without having them watered down by the interagency clearance process.

"No, not as chief," said Leyton Fischer. "I'm told they couldn't quite manage that."

"As what? Soviet or East European reports officer?"

"To be honest with you, I'm not quite sure," Fischer replied with a trace of annoyance. His principal adversaries that autumn afternoon weren't Chairman Brezhnev, Fidel Castro, an Atlantic Community in turmoil, or an undervalued yen, but an amateurish White House staff. During a meeting that morning in the White House situation room, the national security adviser had so consistently confused Laos with Cambodia and Honduras with Guatemala that the minutes were totally nonsensical, a comic opera farce, betrayed by the document now in Fischer's restless fingers.

"Did anyone tell you whose idea it was?" Straus asked quietly.

"I really don't get into DIA personnel decisions, Nick. It's not my shop, not my turf at all."

"But it was you who recommended my name to DIA."

"That's right, but it was DIA that made the decision to bring you aboard. I gave you the highest recommendation, that's all."

"Whose hit list am I on, Leyton?" Nick asked. "First the SALT delegation, then Geneva, later the Agency, now this. Who's behind it?"

"That's ridiculous, Nick. I'm surprised—I really am. They had to reduce the staff by one, and since you're the most recent on board, it's your position they're eliminating. . . ."

Nick Straus listened, disappointed. Close to sixty, Leyton Fischer had begun on the Hill, moved to State, to the National Security Council, back to State, and then on to Defense. Others his age had long exhausted their political or intellectual capital over shorter periods, like Nick Straus, but not Leyton Fischer, who'd served Democrats and Republicans alike with an unerring sense of self-preservation. Nick had always thought of him as an ideal staff aide, shrewder than the mediocre minds he often served, but now he heard the voice of the sycophant, quick in the advocacy of fashionable causes—détente when it had originated, an honorable exodus from Vietnam but too late, the MX missile system, and now a trillion-dollar defense budget.

If there was a hidden core of originality to the man, Nick thought sadly, watching the slim, fluid fingers, its evidence must lie in the Georgetown house he'd owned for thirty years, in the antiques he and his wealthy wife once collected, in the books he accumulated as a relentless bibliophile prowling the back-street bookshops of Europe, or in the fussy little gourmet dinners he prepared in his Georgetown house before a Kennedy opening for a few select friends or the wealthy intimates of his now dead wife.

He was a mandarin, nothing more.

220

"It's really the best they could do," Leyton Fischer was saying. "I think you should go along and talk to them. I think you should, Nick, really. For Ida's sake."

Embarrassed for Leyton Fischer, Nick had looked away toward the yellow drapes and out through the tall windows overlooking the Potomac. At this distance, the monuments and the skyline dominated by the Capitol looked so small, so tidy, that they seemed artificial, like a Japanese garden. *Ida?* Why Ida? He'd only met her twice. Was Leyton Fischer saying he felt sorry for him? Leyton Fischer wasn't being honest with him. He knew he must decline. He no longer belonged in this building. Haven Wilson was right; he should leave. But that's not what he heard himself saying.

"I'll do that, Leyton," he heard a voice saying as he got to his feet. "I'll go along and talk to them."

"Thanks, Nick, I appreciate it. It would make all of us feel a lot better. I'm sure it will all work out."

This is incredible, he thought as he reached the corridor. Whose voice had he heard? His voice, of course, like that time he'd agreed to go up in the Ferris wheel with Roy McCormick. They had denied him his livelihood for the fifth time, denied him his substance; yet he'd replied as if he had no existence at all. He had said yes so many times that there was nothing left now but these pale, transparent affirmatives. Even a Xerox machine could order him about. That night he and Haven Wilson had gotten drunk together, the resolve had returned, but what had happened since?

He was only a ghost, he decided, nothing more than a ghost. His existence was only what theirs would allow him and since they would allow him nothing, he was simply a piece of amiable bureaucratic ectoplasm, encased in a drip-dry suit and ripple soles that whispered him along these ugly Kafkaesque corridors, like ten thousand of his kind, as if there were no one there at all.

The suite occupied by the staff of the DIA daily intelligence summary was large and well-lighted, located on an outer ring near the cafeterias and the shopping arcade. A half dozen secretaries were busy at their electric typewriters and word processors, typing away at the drafts prepared by the six DIA geographical reports officers who sat in the seclusion of their glass-and-steel cubicles, only their heads visible. The suite resembled the copy room of a middle-size mail order house, readying its winter catalogue for its subscribers.

The section chief and editor was a cadaverous civil servant in his early sixties with yellow-white hair, very long over his collar, an eczematous face and hands, and bitter breath. A product of some moribund prairie normal school, he'd taken graduate degrees at a Midwestern university, but hanging on the walls of his office were certificates of summer seminars he'd attended at Harvard and Columbia. The former's imprimatur hung conspicuously on a panel just to the left of his littered desk, attesting to his enrollment at some national security seminar. Nearby hung neatly framed certificates from the National War College and the Industrial College of the Armed Forces, institutions of clerical ordination, as well as scores of photographs taken by official photographers at U.S. installations around the globe during his annual "orientation" tours. In a much-enlarged recent photograph, he sat in the cushioned captain's chair of an American aircraft carrier on station in the Indian Ocean, a camera about his neck, an admiral's blue baseball cap on his head, a manic gleam in his eye.

The gleam was there during his conversation with Nick Straus. Long in the tooth, he was also long-winded. He knew little about Nick except that he had a diploma from Harvard and wrote well. He'd been shown examples of his drafting by DIA personnel and had been impressed. *Mirabile dictu,* Straus was a wordsmith, a classicist of the three *C*s—concision, clarity, and completeness—a talent woefully lacking among those military officers in their cubicles outside, whose drafts were as innocent of style as an orderly room bulletin board. He needed a deputy with a keen eye and a quick pen to help in the editing of their summaries of cables, memoranda, intelligence reports, and intercepts gathered from the four corners of the globe. As an instrument of policy, the daily intelligence summary had no equal. *Imperat aut servit!* Rule or serve! The daily summary ruled, read by senior policymakers before the *Washington Post* or the *New York Times.*

Nick Straus listened uneasily. The section chief's speech was pedantically florid, ornate with Latin incrustations and Teutonic barbarisms. He saw before him a normal-school Carlyle from the great prairie, a bureaucratic fossil left behind by the glacial moraines of the cold war's coldest days, but living on here in this underground crypt. He watched the long spatulate fingers prowl the desktop, lifting a paper here, an intercept there, sometimes moving self-consciously to the mouth to hide the crooked teeth. He remembered how the DIA daily summary was viewed at the Agency, where it was circulated with the warning that this was a DIA "in-house" product. It was read by senior officials there, like *Pravda,* not for its information but for the pathogenic clues it supplied as to DIA's tactical priorities and the Pentagon's obsessions of the moment.

From the box on his desk the old civil servant brought forth the DIA tabloid for that morning. The red banner headlines read SOVIETS GIVE CASTRO NEW MIG-25 SQUADRON. The sensationalism was characteristic, the bias obvious. The Soviet MIG-25s had been on the ground in Cuba for almost six months and didn't comprise a full squadron at all. The aircraft were new only in the sense that DIA had just decided to publicize them. In fact, they were old aircraft, a few intended originally for Somalia, others for Syria. Two submarines and a Koni-class surface ship were also reported to be on station in Cuba, so a lead item announced, but they had been in Cuban waters for many months. Publication of both items coincided with the new arms package for El Salvador now being aggressively peddled by the Pentagon.

The lower half of the front page proclaimed: SOVIETS SUCCESSFULLY TEST-FIRE SS-16 ICBM. This was also misleading. The special-watch group had monitored the testing for DIA. The SS-16 was the Soviet SS-20 medium-range rocket with a third stage attached, and the Strategic Rocket Forces had experienced all kinds of difficulties in the modification. Testing had resumed after five initial failures. The sixth attempt had been moderately successful, although the various intelligence agencies had disagreed on the extent of the success, but this sixth effort was followed by three more failures. The readership at the White House or on the Hill wouldn't look too closely at these ambiguities.

Looking at that headline, Nick Straus decided, queerly enough, that he might accept the position being offered him after all. He knew, too, why the position was being offered. They were shutting him away, still vowed to silence, like a Trappist in this pontifical ritual-ridden monastery.

4.

The Center seemed curiously active that week, the lights from Haven Wilson's rear office visible through the early November darkness long after the other buildings were deserted. Buster Foreman was often there, returned from South Carolina with a bizarre tale about Bob Combs, Wooster, and Bernie Klempner.

"Klempner's the guy," Buster told him. "He's got something on Bob Combs; that's why he's so tight with his foundations. Combs is paying him off. Maybe he's got something on Caltronics too. He hears you've been asking around about Caltronics, so he drops around to warn you off, afraid you're muscling in on his scam."

"What's the scam?"

"That's what we'll have to dig out. If you can't get by Fred Merkle, I'll go talk to some of the boys in the back room."

Wilson invariably returned to the accident on the beltway ramp, the key, somehow, to much of the recent confusion. Foreman attached little importance to it.

"It could have been anything," he said. "Some guy bangs into you from the back, cops all around, and he gets a little shook. You ask for some identification and he snatches up this card and hands it to you, anything to get the hell out. He's got problems—maybe a suspended license, maybe no insurance. So a couple of hours later, he gets a little worried because of this trouble he's got. He figures you might come snooping around and he's worried you might find out something. So he pays off—three hundred bucks to keep you from getting nosy."

Wilson's logic had led him that far, but beyond that his suspicions had quickly evaporated. Now he heard them being revived in Buster's meandering voice. "Find out what?"

"Could be anything. That he doesn't have a license. That maybe it's not his car. If it's not his car, it's not his card. A hot car, maybe?"

"I don't think so," Wilson said. "If it's a hot car, all he cares about is not getting nailed on the spot. He's going to ditch it after he rolls away, or get the hell out of town. He's not going to hang around long enough to drop off the three hundred. So that means he's still hanging around."

"So you think he's still around town somewhere."

"Probably."

Buster held out his hand. "O.K., let's have the license number. I'll see what I can find out."

Dr. Foster had been in the front office some of those evenings, toiling away on his testimony for his appearance before the House subcommittee, scheduled for the coming week. Angus McVey's granddaughter, Jennifer, had also dropped by, escorting a young man in a long leather coat through the complex. She introduced him as a former college classmate, now a producer of television documentaries, planning a series on Washington policy institutes and think tanks. She'd volunteered the Center's cooperation, but Wilson wasn't sure Angus McVey had approved.

Nick Straus's office was curiously empty.

5.

It was a cold, raw morning and Wilson was wearing a crushed felt hat and a lined raincoat, both taken from the rear closet in the expectation of freezing rain, possibly snow. The commuter rush had eased by the time he reached the industrial zone north of Alexandria. Behind the ribbon of commercial buildings along the boulevard lay a wasteland of razed lots, railroad yards, an occasional warehouse and gasoline storage tank, and weedy or cindered acres behind chain-link fences. It was ten-thirty as he parked his car on the potholed side street in front of a wooden building painted bright yellow. A neon beer sign glowed in the dark window of the bar in front; a padlocked metal grille protected the front door. Next to it stood a clapboard house, isolated on a grassless lot. An old Ford truck rested next to the mesh fence of a diesel fuel depot. A line of drab wash whipped in the wind. A small girl was pulling a rusty wagon along the path to the wooden steps. Seeing Wilson pass along the deserted street, she dropped the handle and called out to him. He watched her pull a bedraggled doll from the wagon and skip toward him, holding the doll out. She hung over the fence. "See," she said. On the doll's cracked pink cheeks were the same plum-colored jelly smears that daubed her own face.

"No school today?" he asked.

"Benny's took sick." She held toward him the heel of toast spread with jelly, but just as quickly took it back to hold in her teeth, as she continued to hang over the fence. The blue vein in her neck stood out; her face was pinched with the cold. No other houses were in sight. A fuel depot, a utility substation, a line of boxcars. A rusty West Virginia license plate hung from the front bumper of the immobilized Ford truck, a derelict from the West Virginia mountains, like the child.

The cold had settled in his feet and stung his face as he crossed the street toward the Embassy Car Rentals reserve and maintenance lot. He went in through the open gate. The office building was off to the side, an aluminum-paneled portable structure mounted on a concrete-block foundation, reached by a set of recently painted wooden steps. He ignored the building, hoping no one would appear, and inspected the dozen foreign cars lined up on the opposite side of the lot. Most were Fiats and Subarus, bright new economy models, recently waxed. The rear of the lot was formed by the high wall of an abandoned brick warehouse and the corrugated steel maintenance garage. Through the high windows he saw the bluish-white glare of an arc welder's torch. An old Ford and a Chevrolet were parked in front.

Buster Foreman had been unable to trace the Alfa, and Wilson didn't really expect to discover it here, but then, beyond the weeds to the side, he saw three old foreign cars resting on blocks, their paint faded, their engines gone, their hulks awaiting the claw of a lifting crane. The hood of one was raised and as he moved beyond it he saw the gray Alfa Romeo convertible. It had recently been in an accident. The hood was deeply pleated and the windshield and driver's window were smashed. Only as he peered in through the broken glass and saw the road maps lying in the bucket seat was he convinced it was the same car. A few business cards were scattered along the dashboard shelf. He reached in gingerly through the smashed glass and retrieved the three he could reach. Two were Caltronics cards, like the one passed to him that morning on the beltway ramp.

He stood up. Below the gray belly of overcast, a 727 was lifting from National Airport in the distance and the fierce horneting sound carried his eyes with it. He should have felt satisfaction but discovered only annoyance, a fatalism as cheerless as the windswept lot beyond. He didn't know what he'd discovered. He didn't even know what he was doing there.

The short, balding mechanic at the metalshop bench in the garage wasn't too cooperative. He was fingering a grimy master cylinder as Wilson asked him about the Alfa. A gangling, dark-haired apprentice was more forthcoming.

"Used to be a rental, but not no more," he said.

"Not worth toting away," said the older man. "Engine's froze up, frame's out of line, not worth shit. Got stole, drove without oil, then wrecked. How come you're asking?"

Wilson said he had a similar one he was restoring. He asked when it had been stolen.

"Six months ago, maybe."

"Cronin fixed it up," the young man said. His thick dark hair was uncombed and his bony, unbearded face was that of an adolescent. Only his height and hands were those of a man; his fingers were large and the cracked knuckles embedded with grime. "Got it running good and drove it around town, a pickup car. Then he wrecked it again, couple of weeks ago."

"How?" Wilson asked.

"Have to ask him; no one's seed him since."

"Yeah, Cronin—Cronin shit," said the mechanic, crossing to a Fiat sedan with its hood up.

"Who was Cronin? A mechanic?"

"Pickup and service man," said the young man. "Used that car all the time after he got it running again. Only one it'd run for."

The mechanic wandered back to the bench for a socket wrench. "Screwy as that car was," he said. "Agent Orange, cowboy, whatever you wanna call him, a real junkie weirdo." He banged a crescent wrench into a metal drawer and went back to the Fiat.

"He was a good mechanic, Cronin was, only a little crazy," the young man continued.

"So he knows the car," Wilson said. "Someone wanted to rebuild it, maybe he could."

"I reckon he could if he had his head straight."

"You know where I could find him?"

226

"I dunno; he never would hardly say. Living with that same girl, I reckon."

"Maybe I'll talk to them up front." He watched the mechanic as he bent under the Fiat hood. "You wouldn't happen to know where this girl lives, would you?"

"No, sure don't. Worked at a pizza place over on Telegraph Road is all I know. She used to call here."

"You remember her name?"

The young man thought for a minute, shaking his head. Then he hesitated and smiled awkwardly in a moment of pure adolescent divination. "Yeah," he recalled. "Wendy, like the hamburger place."

"Screwy, got a screw loose," explained the rental manager in the front office. "Junkie, pothead, I don't know what all." A voluble, middle-aged man, he followed Wilson out of his small office, counting a handful of coins he'd taken from his pants pocket. His pants sagged low on his hips. Pushed back on his head was a pearl-gray fedora with a thin brim. He wore a butterscotch sports shirt buttoned at the collar, but no tie. "Tried to meet him halfway, give him a chance, the way I would any vet, but it didn't do no good. In an' out of the VA hospital, in an' out of trouble, sometimes wouldn't show up at all. No telling where he's running loose at." He paused in front of the soft-drink dispenser in the customers' waiting room, still fingering the coins. "Slept in a cot back in the parts room first month he was here; didn't know it till the mechanic back there told me. Had to put a stop to that. Told me he couldn't get a place. Had to garnishee his wages a couple of times. Still owes me a hundred, but I'm not looking for him. Not looking for no trouble, neither."

He'd told Wilson to write him a letter and offer a price if he was interested in the junked Alfa. He didn't have Cronin's address—he'd kept on the move, one room after another every month and they couldn't keep up—but he was a good mechanic, factory-trained by a foreign-car agency in Flushing, New York. Then he'd had some problems with the VA and come to Washington. The last time he'd seen Cronin was the day before Wilson's accident on the beltway. They'd found the Alfa, wrecked, at the rear of the lot a day later. "He was supposed to be in Atlantic City, picking up a car, but he doesn't show up and we find the car in the back there. What happened was he had a headful of something and come in that night and run that Alfa into the tow truck that was in the back, got scared and took off. When he called in the next day, I fired him. He was drunk on something then. Don't know what it was, don't wanna know. . . ."

His hands had returned to his pants pockets and now he brought the coins out again, separating them carefully. "It's a shame," he said, "that's what it is. The VA hospital puts a man on drugs and turns him loose, no telling what he's gonna do. . . ."

"I appreciate your help," Wilson said, pulling on his coat. "Thanks again."

"No trouble, friend." He stopped to count the coins again as he stood in front of the soft-drink machine. The office was deserted, like the windy lot outside. No customers had called, the phones were silent. In his careful segregation of the palmful of coins, Wilson saw the hebetude of an idle service bureaucracy: car salesmen, clerks at their counters, barbers behind their empty chairs, gas station attendants on the midnight watch—all groping in frustration to unlock their boredom, like a child shaking a useless clock. "Don't know what it's all comin' to," the manager complained. "Try to help someone out and you just get yourself in trouble. But try telling that to some junkie Vietnam vet thinks folks like you an' me owe him a living. Get educated right quick. Better have yourself a baseball bat ready when you do."

He grinned at Wilson suddenly, as if they were fellow sufferers, middle-aged, middle-class, and everywhere oppressed.

Maybe that's it, Wilson thought as he crossed toward the gate.

Telegraph Road was a long, dreary boulevard. The rain began, stopped, and began again. He counted four pizza parlors along the way. At a phone booth outside a drugstore he called two before he located one where a girl named Wendy had once worked. She'd left several weeks earlier. The order clerk who told him this hung up when he learned Wilson wasn't phoning in an order. He drove back to the pizza parlor, a new building painted in bright colors, like a carnival midway's version of an old trolley car. The counter clerk wasn't helpful, but the young blond girl who took his order in a rear booth had just come on duty. Her pink gingham dress was crisp and clean, her eyes bright, and he was her first customer. She brought him a pizza and a draft beer and said she thought one of Wendy's friends still worked in the kitchen. As she gave him his check, she supplied a street name but no number, just a neighborhood not far away—an intersection with a traffic light, a gas station on the corner, then a furniture refinishing shop, a duplex next door with rooms in the back.

He found himself on a rain-darkened walk between two clapboard houses. Beyond a sun porch whose windows were hung with green plants was an entry door, the gray paint worn with passage. Two of the four metal nameplates on the post held no cards; the names on the others weren't familiar. Inside was a small hall, a set of chairs, and the doors to the unfurnished downstairs rooms. One door was open, but the room inside, painted an electric blue, was empty except for a mattress in the middle of the floor. He heard the sound of a television set within the door facing the front of the house. A dog began to bark furiously as he knocked and he heard its nails scratching against the linoleum inside as the door opened a crack and a pair of dark-brown eyes peered out.

He took off his hat and said he was looking for a girl named Wendy. The door opened further. The woman who appeared was gray-haired, her face as plain as a dumpling, but her eyes were as brisk as her voice. "Gone; moved out a couple of weeks ago." She nudged the slavering Boston bull terrier back into the sun porch with her foot. "That's her place across the hall there, used to be."

The television had grown louder, aromas from a kettle of steaming vegetables bathed his face, and the pop-eyed bull terrier eluded the land-lady's ankles to stand at Wilson's feet, stiff-legged and harmless, panting in the cool of the hallway. The girl had left ten days earlier, but without a forwarding address. She'd left the mattress behind; the landlady had her room deposit and wouldn't return it until the flat was emptied.

"Living alone? No, there was this fella moved in with her. That's why I told 'em to git, both of 'em. No doubles here. He was trouble too, trouble from the first. Played that stereo turned up loud all the way. Couldn't hardly hear yourself think, it was so bad. You a relative of hers?"

"No, just a friend."

"That girl needs friends. She sure does."

He asked the landlady if he could leave a message for Wendy. She seemed hesitant at first. "Less I see of them, the better."

"I'd appreciate it," Wilson said.

The woman nodded. "I could leave it with her mail, I suppose."

Wilson scrawled out a message in his pocket notebook. "Wendy—Tell Cronin I'm looking for a mechanic to restore a 1971 Alfa Spider. Good pay." He tore it out, folded his business card inside, and handed it to the woman.

"She was driving a new car last time I saw her," the landlady said as she took the message, "but she hasn't paid me her phone bill yet."

"What's her last name?"

"Murdock. I thought you said she was a friend."

"I'd heard she was married."

"Don't have to be nowadays. Come and go like alley cats. She owe you money?"

"No, nothing like that."

"Just asking," she replied with sudden coolness, her curiosity ended. She shut the door.

Though the rain had stopped, the tires hissed along the wet pavement. A cold front was moving through but would be gone by morning, the radio weather bulletin predicted, bringing clear skies for the weekend. Wilson was going to the Shenandoah the following morning, to look at a farm. He started to turn off the radio but refrained as he heard the music, whose blandness dissolved the grime of the morning like a solvent. Carried along by the flow of traffic, he imagined Betsy at that hour, standing in front of her class; his older son, scrubbing for surgery in a Boston hospital; and Paul, the younger, settled at his typewriter over a draft editorial for his Oregon newspaper. He felt for a moment that surety that sometimes comes to husbands and fathers who, however disappointing their own careers, know their efforts weren't entirely wasted. Feeling that eased the shame of thinking how astonished or even disappointed they might have been had they known what he'd done with his morning.

6.

Donlon seemed hypnotized by the woman, hovering over her and sending curious looks down her low-cut silk dress. "I suppose it's the weather that keeps me indoors," she said in her dark, rich voice. She'd once been a handsome woman and the ghost of that beauty was still apparent. Her silver-gray hair was almost white in the lamplight, the silhouette striking, but the dark-brown eyes seemed clouded as they'd looked up at Wilson, obscured by a hint of gray film. He'd thought of cataracts. Seeing her more closely, Wilson was all the more perplexed by Donlon's fascination. Her arthritic fingers were as gray as chalk, her mouth a seam of pale pink, imperfectly painted, the color straying above the upper lip and onto the creased skin.

"That's what is so depressing," she intoned, "not being able to get about because of this dreadful rain."

Her name was Cornelia Bowen and she sat on a cushioned rosewood chair in the second-floor living room belonging to Ed Donlon's law partner, the cocktail party's host. The room was overly warm from the log fire and the crush of late arrivals, come from some nearby diplomatic reception. Through the open door of the terrazzo sun porch behind her, a breath of cooler air stirred from the open window.

Joining them, Wilson had noticed Leyton Fischer on the porch. He was about to move down the steps toward him, curious about Nick Straus's sudden transfer at the Pentagon, but Ed Donlon restrained him, as if what Cornelia Bowen was saying was of tragic importance.

She was describing her fall on the first-floor landing of her Georgetown house six months earlier, when she'd broken her ankle. Her chauffeur and handyman had died the previous spring, collapsed suddenly on the rear patio as he carried a sickly potted plant from the solarium for its rejuvenation by the May sun.

Wilson found it difficult to muster much sympathy, unlike Donlon. "I certainly hope you're not alone now," Ed said, concerned.

"Oh, no, there's Mrs. Childers, my housekeeper. I don't believe you ever met her. She's almost seventy-five now."

"It's the pervasive unremitting vulgarity," a woman's caustic voice intruded from behind Wilson's right shoulder. "You knew it was coming, you could predict it—just commerce and convenience. First the flip-top box, then the pull-tab beer can, next the throwaway razor, now throwaway sex. All-night porno on cable TV . . ."

She must be a Democrat, Wilson thought.

"I do a little needlepoint," Cornelia Bowen was saying, "but only for short periods because of my eyes. . . ."

"So you know what was next," the caustic voice continued relentlessly, "everything quick, cheap, and convenient. I mean, look at this administration. The quick script, the instant fix." Wilson moved his head to identify her, but her back was to him. "Next it'll be the digestible booze bottle and the do-it-yourself funeral. A closet-sized microwave oven in the basement." A squall of cigarette smoke enveloped him as a silvery-blond head leaned into view and a slim hand carried away the cherry table's only ashtray.

"Where'd you read that?"

"Who's got time to read in this town? Where else? Standing in the Safeway line, looking at the *National Enquirer,* like everyone else. Like Reagan, getting his morning brief at the White House."

"I do less reading now," Cornelia Bowen droned on.

"A little white flash of light and *poof!* That's it. You can put hubby number three in the flowerpot with the African violets. . . ."

"A few old friends come by to read to me now and then. It's rather a lost art, isn't it? I felt a little foolish at first, very embarrassed for them, but that's passed now. I don't feel much like an invalid at all and I think my readers enjoy it as much as I do. We look forward to it. Leyton is reading Jane Austen to me—he's just next door. You should come read with us, Edward."

Donlon looked like a flattered choirboy in the sacristy whom the bishop had just deigned to address. "Oh, yes, I think I'd like that," he said quickly.

"We're finishing *Mansfield Park,"* she continued. "I insist Leyton leave it with me so he won't finish it alone during one of his trips. He's made two to Europe with the Secretary since May and one to the Middle East. Leyton's suddenly indispensable, to me and it seems everyone else."

Wilson had never cared much for Leyton Fischer and now, hearing Cornelia Bowen's voice, he found his disapproval touching her as well. She reminded him of an elderly dowager whose recollections had so enthralled his parents when he was growing up and whose grass he'd been condemned to cut one entire summer after her gardener had ruptured himself. Her memory was like Cornelia Bowen's, a scented private garden where she lived alone, her preoccupations never touching the lives of others beyond her high brick walls. Her friends never died. They were just shown out the ornate cut-glass front door by her white-gloved houseman one summer day, the roses in full bloom, and never returned.

"No poetry these days?" Donlon was asking softly, bending his head near.

Wilson wandered away, determined to leave now, with or without Donlon and Mary Sifton, but at that moment more guests were arriving and a handful departing, blocking the landing at the top of the stairs. The host had been ambushed just outside the door, deep in conversation with a departing congressman. A few couples waited near the door to say their farewells, their smiles already prepared.

Wilson moved in the other direction, toward the small bar set up just inside the library doors across the room. The dry heat had grown sticky. The two black waiters behind the bar, forced to the corner by the congestion, were sweating and overworked, like croupiers at a gaming table.

"Those kitschy clothes she wears, for one thing," whispered a woman from behind Wilson as he waited. "A cabinet wife? I mean, where does she think she is? Not Washington. Nibbling quiche and gushing trendy non sequiturs that don't mean boo to anyone?"

Wilson asked for a whiskey.

"Look, sweetheart, her clothes are her own business, O.K.?" grumbled a husband's voice. "Sometimes you don't look so hot yourself."

"Did you ever ask yourself what I spend on clothes?"

He moved on into the library, drawn there by the Civil War maps and prints on the rear wall above the bookcases. A tall, gray-haired man stood there too, his back to the room, a drink in his hand as he studied the titles on the bookshelves, as if waiting to leave, like Wilson. The prints and maps were reproductions and expensively framed. Wilson lost interest and turned back.

Leyton Fischer had joined Cornelia Bowen and Ed Donlon near the entrance to the sun porch.

"Edward was telling us you'd joined the private sector," Leyton Fischer said to him as he strolled up. "I must say that came as a surprise."

Fischer, slight and gray, wore a gray suit, vest, and his customary bow tie. An indistinct gray mustache gave the stamp of inconsequentiality to the small face.

"Something a little different," Wilson said, remembering how carefully one had to handle Leyton, who stored up imaginary grievances like a vain woman.

"Oh, I'm certain of that; the Center is certainly different if it's anything. I remember I once talked to your Dr. Foster. Foster, is that his name?" Fischer frowned, attempting to restore to vagueness a name he could have no earthly reason to remember.

"Foster, that's right," Wilson said. Seeing Leyton Fischer's dreary smile, he felt a certain affection for their poor, maligned Dr. Foster.

"Foster, yes. I once talked to your Dr. Foster, who called to ask if I would appear on a panel the Center was sponsoring."

"Leyton works such terrible hours these days," Cornelia Bowen reminded them in a whisper.

"Rather odd, I thought," Fischer continued prudishly. "Something about behaviorism and foreign policy." He smiled for Cornelia Bowen's benefit. "I couldn't make heads or tails of it. I had to decline, of course—quite preposterous."

Donlon looked on indignantly. Wilson said nothing, his interest in inquiring about Nick Straus's transfer at the Pentagon gone.

"I think I've told you how many trips Leyton has made with the Secretary," added Cornelia Bowen.

Fischer inclined his head near hers as he stood behind her chair. "Are you sure you're comfortable there? It is getting late." The balsam of tenderness was offered in a low, patronizing voice and she yielded to it, like a sleepy child, her hand touching his sleeve.

"I do feel a little tired."

"Shall I get the car?"

Wilson, turning to remind Ed Donlon that he was leaving, was surprised at the look on his face. It was the face of a cuckold, angry and outraged. Only then did Wilson remember who Cornelia Bowen was.

The night was chilly as Mary Sifton, Donlon, and Wilson walked back through the quiet Georgetown streets toward Donlon's house. Mary was still curious about Cornelia Bowen, but Donlon, whose behavior seemed increasingly eccentric, refused to answer. Mary Sifton was slight and dark-haired, in her early forties. She took tiny steps as they walked and Wilson could imagine her handwriting as he slowed to keep stride—tiny, precise, and always legible. *"Chacun à son goût,"* she said wistfully. "I suppose you read poetry to her."

233

Donlon refused to answer.

"I have a feeling you're losing your intellectual verve," she said sadly after a few more steps. Then, to Haven Wilson: "When we first met, Ed seemed to me very intellectual. Now he seems to have lost those interests. Could it be that I was deceived?" Her way of speaking was as precise as her footsteps. Behind the words he heard a shrewd, finite little mind, but too shrewd, too finite. The illogic of emotions would always elude her, as Ed Donlon would soon escape her. She would always be disappointed. "No theater, no concerts, nothing at all these days." She gave a small, pathetic sigh. "I'm not a very political person, Mr. Wilson—"

"It's Haven," Donlon said.

"Haven, then. Please don't walk so fast. I'm not a very political person, Haven. I think Ed is tiring of my world."

Wilson had stopped again, waiting for her. Donlon waited too and gruffly let her take his arm. The old brick sidewalks were uneven and she moved carefully in her high heels. "She was probably very attractive once," she resumed in a tiny voice. They emerged into the brightness of Wisconsin Avenue. A police siren wailed in the distance. "Where did you meet her?" Donlon stubbornly didn't reply, his thoughts his own. "Who was the man with her?"

"A bloody idiot!" he exploded.

Donlon had been thirty at the time, a young Treasury lawyer. She was nearly forty, the wife of a senior Treasury official appointed under the Eisenhower administration. Their affair had lasted a year, Wilson recalled now, but Donlon still talked of her when he and Wilson had shared offices at Justice twenty-five years ago.

They walked the rest of the way in silence. Wilson declined the invitation to join them inside, and found his car nearby.

His office was chilly. The streetlamps bathed the dark front rooms with their frosty light and drew eccentric oblongs on the office walls. Only his desk lamp was lit, mixing splashes of odd color from the small squares of cathedral glass at the top of the bay window. The limbs of the maple trees were limned across the floor. He stood at the desk, his coat still on, looking at the telephone messages left for him. Betsy had called twice; so had Rita Kramer.

He telephoned the hotel suite and it was a long time before a sleepy voice answered. Artie Kramer wasn't there. He'd flown to Los Angeles that afternoon with Chuckie Savant and Franconi, not to return until the following week.

"I dozed off, watching television," Rita said drowsily. "I wanted to tell you they'd gone. What'd you want to talk to him about?"

234

"I wanted to ask about that telex he sent you, telling you to break off the talks about the house. Do you know how he sent it?"

"Telex, but it got all screwed up."

"Whose telex?"

"Through Strykker's office in L.A., I think. Why?"

"Just wondering."

"It's a funny time of night to be wondering." A silence followed. "Another goddamned weekend," she continued sleepily. "I guess you've got yours all planned."

"I was thinking about going out to the country."

"Lucky you. I suppose I'll stay cooped up in this hotel room. Numero seven eight one, I wear it on my back; my nightie too. Ten years to life, that's what the judge gave me." She laughed self-consciously.

"That's no way to spend the weekend."

"Yeah? Any suggestions?" He didn't know what to tell her and stood in awkward silence. She spoke first. "If you get any, give me a call. I'll be here."

"I'll do that," he said.

Betsy was in bed when he reached the house in McLean, but still awake, her voice strange. He turned on the bed lamp and sat down next to her. She turned her head away.

"What is it?" he asked, touching her shoulder. She shook her head without answering. "I know it's something." He thought she'd been crying. She rarely cried, but when she did always concealed it from him. "Come on, tell me."

She didn't answer. On the bedside table under the lamp was a letter from their son Paul in Oregon. He read it as he sat on the bed next to her. Paul had quit his newspaper job and was now playing the banjo in a pickup band he'd been sitting in with on Saturday nights. Like the other band members, he was working in a fruit-packing plant, and he'd moved in with the lead guitar player and his girl friend to save money. He had fifty dollars in his bank account.

"Is this it?" he asked. "Is this what you're upset about?"

She didn't answer, still turned away from him, her face hidden from him in the shadows.

"Betsy? Come on, let's talk about it."

But she still didn't turn and he sat there stroking her arm and shoulder, the house dark and silent below. He didn't know how long he sat there at her side, but gradually the present gave way to the past and the figure lying silently on the bed was Betsy twenty-two years earlier, lying in another darkened bedroom, racked by the first pains of labor, her husband sitting helplessly at her side then too, aware for the second time in his married life of how absolute was the physical distance that separated them. Paul was her last-born, the birth that had given her the most pain. In labor she'd been alone, as she was alone now in the second-floor bedroom. Her body had given up another, leaving hers behind, an agony Wilson hadn't shared, and this was still her legacy, twenty-two years later.

"It wasn't just Paul's letter, was it?" he asked, still touching her forehead, but she was sleeping by then, and watching over her silent figure, he felt the same inconsolable desolation that had come to him so many years ago as he watched her unconscious form being wheeled into the delivery room.

7.

Despite sunny predictions, the November Saturday remained cold and overcast. The cold front that was to be drawn away like a winter eiderdown from the Virginia countryside stalled in place. The weatherman's television maps and satellite imagery, so reassuring the night before, glowing into suburban living rooms like Prospero's magic, had been in substantial error. The President had canceled his weekend at Camp David; a launch at Cape Canaveral had been postponed for two days; but at a village firehouse an hour from Washington toward the Shenandoah, the November rummage sale was being held, rain or shine, to benefit the volunteer fire department. The paint was scaling from the old clapboard dormers; the roof leaked. A cabin on Rag Mountain had burned to the ground in late October when a four-inch pumper hose ruptured.

In a suede jacket and plaid skirt, Betsy Wilson wandered curiously among the outdoor tables set up in front of the firehouse, looking at the old depression glass, the ancient bottles, old cutlery, and brass wall fixtures brought from local attics and basement cupboards for the semiannual sale. She carried a small pumpkin under one arm. From each pocket of her suede jacket stuck an ear of hard yellow corn still in its stiff husk. She'd bought them from the third-grade table at the far end of the display, not because she knew what she was going to do with them but because she'd found the small, shy salesmen there irresistible.

Wilson trailed after her, carrying a jug of hard cider. He watched as she stopped at a table of more expensive merchandise and picked up a silver candle snuffer with a wooden handle. Two gray-haired women in tweed jackets and hunt-country hats were standing at the end of the table, identifying antique silver in their browsing voices. He saw Betsy watching them curiously, studying their coats and their shoes, the antique snuffer forgotten. Turning, she saw him and rolled her eyes hopelessly.

"It's nice," she said as they returned to the station wagon. "A nice town; money too, but nice. Old money, I suppose. Why didn't we bring my car? This car's disgraceful, Haven."

"It's a bad road where we're going."

"How far away is it?"

"Just a couple of miles."

He drove away from the village and they turned off the state road onto a secondary lane that meandered through pastures, rolling fields, and woods. She sat looking out the window silently. He turned into a gravel road and she looked at him suspiciously. The gravel road ended abruptly at an old fence with a rusting *For Sale* sign nailed to the top beam. "Is this it?" she asked.

"Almost." He got out, opened the gate, and then drove through, but fifty yards beyond, the muffler and differential began to ring out against the exposed rockbed and he slowed to a stop. "We won't make it like this. We'll have to walk."

He'd last seen the farmhouse in the spring, when the real estate agent had driven him out in a four-wheel-drive jeep. A tenant farmer had occupied it at the time, but the family was gone now and the road was overgrown.

The wind was fierce on the exposed hillside, bothering Betsy's dark hair. He saw her shiver as she pulled up her collar. "Maybe it's too cold for you?" he called from the other side of the car.

"No, I'm fine." She shivered as she drew on her gloves. "What on earth happened to all that sunshine the weatherman promised?"

"Aborted, like the launch at Cape Canaveral. Maybe Pennsylvania's got it."

"The weathermen are supposed to know."

"He's just an expert. Weather trajectories go crazy like everything else. Maybe this one blew up on the pad, like the Pershing II launch."

She wound a scarf around her head as they walked. "So now the Republicans are responsible for the weather too." She moved carefully down the overgrown road, trying to avoid the tangle of thorn and thistle, dried now, the blooms long scattered. "Is this a real country house we're going to see or is it a Tidewater country house?"

"The real McCoy; no plumbing."

"I should have known," she said with a smile. "Carter country."

They climbed a hill between two apple orchards and emerged at the front of the farm itself, a hundred acres of rolling pasture and cropland fenced in front with locust, black with age. The deserted farmhouse lay in a grove of old maples overlooking a secluded valley. Once a log cabin, it had been added to over the centuries and covered with stucco at the turn of the century. A stone chimney lay at each end of the steep tin roof. The front and rear porches had fallen off. An old tin heating stove, bottomless hulks of gasoline cans, and the headpiece of an iron bed lay rusting in the weeds to the side. A mattress had been left behind near a rear shed where a pickup truck stood, its tires and engine gone. *"Haven,"* Betsy muttered, but he'd stopped under the maple trees, head cocked, eyes not moving from the house. She watched as he turned to look back over the secluded valley and the dark-blue shadow of the mountains along the horizon. "When did you first see it?"

"Last spring," he said. "A farm family was living here, it was raining, and the real estate agent wanted to leave before we got stuck. Then the tenant farmer didn't much want us around, either."

"What else haven't you told me?"

"Nothing I can think of."

He wanted to see the interior, but the doors were locked. He found an old board and prodded the windows until he found a sash he could raise, and they climbed in. The interior was dark with shadow, the smell of the old fireplaces as palpable as smoke. Their breath showed on the raw air. The old pine floors were uneven and had settled with the foundations along the outer walls. Chipmunks and mice had left acorns and persimmon seeds near the kitchen baseboard.

"It would take an awful lot of work," Betsy said, cautiously exploring the rooms. "Do you mind if I tell you something?"

"No, go ahead."

"I don't think you could live here, not someplace this remote."

He didn't answer, kneeling on the hearth as he inspected the chimneys. She watched him silently and then, as if conscious of her words, turned to the window to look out over the side meadow. "That isn't to say it wouldn't be a perfect weekend house. It's a lovely view, isn't it?"

They climbed out the window and she stopped to retie her scarf, still looking back at the house. "I think that's where Paul gets his ideas, more from you than me. As the youngest, I think it was harder for him." She stood in silence, still contemplating the house. "I think that's why he went all the way to Oregon, to do something on his own."

"I think that was part of it."

She turned. "What's down there?" She looked past the old maple tree behind the house, toward the rear meadow. "What's that?"

"An old barn, back in the trees. A pond too."

She wanted to see them. They walked down the slope to the pond, overgrown with willow, silver maple, and wild cherry along its fringes.

Duck down floated on the dark surface, and a few curls from preened tail feathers lay at the water's edge. As they moved around the pond a green heron took flight, pumping its wings lazily as it circled back toward the woods. They continued in silence down the slope along a broken stone fence. The wind had risen, bending the tops of the towering sycamores, as white as bone against the dark, ragged clouds overhead. From deeper in the woods came the creak of the tall timber. She moved against the wind along the stone fence, eyes exploring the hillside and the low-flying clouds.

"Strange," she said as they paused at the edge of the woods on an outcropping of rock. "Strange but lovely."

"What?"

"The weather, this, everything."

"It's the cold front moving through," he said.

"They loved the country so," she said, looking away. "I wish they could be here, both of them. They'd love it, Paul especially—"

"It'd be a place where they could come," he said.

"It could be, couldn't it? That's nice to think about, but what about the weeks in between?" They walked on up the hill. "Being a McLean widow is easier than being a Shenandoah widow."

"I might open a law office nearby."

She seemed to smile. "No, you couldn't. You'd be miserable, the way Nick Straus is. Washington's your life, not rural Virginia."

"Not anymore."

She nodded. "We'll see," she said.

8.

"A friend from the Bureau, an old pal," Buster Foreman confided in a bright whisper over the restaurant table. "I'm hitting fungoes with him Friday afternoon down at his office—bouncing the questions at him, he's poppin' 'em back. Then we move to this Irish bar down the street. He gives me an earful." He looked enormously pleased, Wilson thought, and why not? He was back in his element.

A bright autumn sun painted Pennsylvania Avenue outside and the light-blue haze lying over the streets and sidewalks, crowded with the noon-hour exodus. Except for the chilly wind pushing swift, broken clouds over the rooftops, the day seemed almost springlike. They sat on the balcony of an Italian restaurant. The downstairs was crowded, shrill with lively voices and noisy busboys rattling dish carts. A tableful of World Bank employees in front were celebrating someone's transfer.

"He gives me the name of this old investigator at the Labor Department to fill in a few details," Buster continued. "I go see him this morning. The guy's down there raking leaves, just sitting there in this office, nothing to do, eating his heart out. That's where the investigation started, the special investigation unit at Labor, but the FBI took it over, a jurisdictional dispute."

"We're still talking about Caltronics," Wilson said.

"Still Caltronics. I find out how this Caltronics went big time, a couple of multimillion-dollar contracts for two big insurance companies out West, one in Arizona, the other in Nevada. Caltronics took over the whole operation—financial management software, accounting, claims processing, the whole bag. They set up the systems, designed them, taught them, and walked out—some real big money."

The waitress had returned and stood behind Wilson, who hadn't seen her. Buster ordered for him. "Bring him a tall frosty, like mine; his pacemaker just went on the fritz." She left the menus behind and went away.

"How long ago was that?" Wilson asked.

"Three, four years, maybe," Buster said. "But what happens is no one's satisfied with the systems. They keep redesigning the software, sending people back, all kinds of cost-plus contracts. For Caltronics, the billings are really adding up, maybe triple the original contract. It's real expensive for this one insurance company in Arizona. It's got a liquidity problem, it's being squeezed dry. You beginning to get the picture?"

"Maybe. Go ahead."

"Someone's siphoning money out," Buster said. "So that's the first thing, someone's bleeding this insurance company dry and Caltronics is helping them do it. The second thing is who's behind these insurance companies. A couple of big West Coast unions got behind both of them. They handle their group life insurance, health and welfare premiums, their pension plans, the whole bundle, so now we're talking about even bigger money—a cash reservoir like Hoover Dam. What's that mean? You've got kickbacks and payoffs to handle, the money that gets funneled back to the local business agents and welfare fund trustees. But that's just the small stuff. Sound familiar?"

"I think so," Wilson said. "Caltronics is in on the skim."

"In on the siphoning, in on the skim, and doing a lot of churning of its own. That was the deal when Caltronics got the original contracts. This shyster that started Caltronics was a big accountant for these West Coast unions—"

"Strykker's his name."

"They didn't tell me his name," Buster said. "Just that it was his ties to these unions that got the Labor investigation unit suspicious, that and the cash problems this insurance company was having. They started nosing around."

The waitress returned and Wilson sat in silence until she'd left again.

"So what I'm saying," Buster said, "is that Caltronics was in on a multi-million-dollar siphoning scheme draining assets from a couple of union-backed insurance companies."

"How far did the investigation go?"

"Not very far. They hardly got their nose under the goddamn tent. The FBI stepped in and took over after some Caltronics agent was accused of bribing a government contracting officer. That's when they stomped all over the Labor unit's investigation. Because of this bribery charge, the U.S. Attorney's office got a court-approved wiretap, but what they're really looking for is more stuff on this multimillion-dollar siphoning scheme. After a couple of months, a district judge gets wise. He's looking at the transcripts and he finally figures it out. They're trolling for evidence unrelated to the bribery investigation and he denies the wiretap extension."

"A screw-up," Wilson said.

"A royal bureaucratic fuck-up, take my word. The investigation leaks and now everyone's running for cover—Caltronics, these insurance companies, the West Coast unions behind them. All of them."

"But not Pete Rathbone," Wilson said. "Caltronics has all these problems and Rathbone gets tapped to take over—a little political muscle."

"That's the way it works," Buster said.

"So what's left of the government case?"

Buster laughed. "Who do you think?"

"Fred Merkle?"

"Just Fred Merkle over at Justice, trying to keep his project alive."

"Someone from upstairs puts a little pressure on him, they'll blow him away. No wonder he wouldn't give me anything."

"It's a political wash," Buster said.

"It wouldn't happen that one of these West Coast unions came out for the Republicans last November, would it?"

"Oh, shit, yes," Buster said happily. "What do you think? Private initiative—that's the big ticket these days. What the hell else? That's the dominant social force, isn't that what Bob Combs said? They're gonna sell off the fucking National Weather Service, sell NASA to McDonnell-Douglas, Yosemite to Pacific Cascade." He raised his arm for the waitress and then pushed aside the beer glass with his folded arms as he leaned against the table. "Forget about this Caltronics mess. Let's go talk to your pal Bernie Klempner. He's the bastard I want to nail."

Wilson watched the waitress approaching. "We'll get to Klempner," he said. "It may take a little time, but we'll get there."

9.

Wilson was surprised to see Chuck Larabee that evening among the academics, former government officials, and businessmen attending a national security issues forum held by a Washington public policy association at its building on M Street. Wilson had come to hear two of the speakers, who had been recommended to him for the directorship of the Center. He'd arrived late. During the refreshment break, he'd been intercepted by Larabee, cornered near the high draped windows overlooking the street. A briefcase was in one muscular hand, a canapé in the other.

"Sour grapes, that's all it is," Larabee told him, short-breathed, his voice creaking like an overloaded elevator. "These guys are all on the outs, crying on each other's shoulder."

"What brings you here?"

Larabee's dark jacket was rumpled, cigarette ashes were spilled down the lapels and dark tie, and one hand still clutched the heavy briefcase.

"Minerals. I wanted to hear this one expert, only he doesn't show." Larabee held the briefcase awkwardly under one arm while he consulted his program. "The rest of these guys are just the old Kennedy or Carter crowd; they couldn't knock the skin off a rice pudding. Hey, did you hear about the F-16 sale to Venezuela? Those pals of mine I was telling you about got a piece of it." He stuffed the program into his jacket and brought a cigarette from his shirt pocket, grappling now with the lighter and the heavy briefcase, beads of moisture bright on the tanned forehead. "I told you things would be loosening up, didn't I? Morocco's looking good too, Maverick missiles maybe. C'mon, let's move over there." A few conversational groups had gathered nearby, waiting to be recalled inside, but Larabee led Wilson to the far corner. "Minerals are the stuff these days, lemme tell you," he continued. "That's the guy I came to hear, only they write him off the program."

"Minerals?"

"We're in a minerals war—strategic minerals, strategic reserves. You hear anyone talking about that inside? They're way behind the power curve. We're being targeted—it's a resource war against us and our allies. South Africa, the Philippines, you name it. Cobalt, chromium, manganese, copper. That's why you've got this new stockpile policy—a hundred million in strategic reserves, but that's only half of it. We've got to change the

242

antitrust laws, change the depreciation on stockpiles. We need tax incentives, financial incentives. It won't be long before you get the small investor putting his money into strategic minerals, a whole new growth industry. So I'm looking into it, me and a couple of friends. It's national security too, otherwise they'll have us by the throats. . . ."

"So military hardware isn't your only interest," Wilson said.

"You gotta diversify. I'm spread all over, Wilson; I go with the flow. Maybe things will get pretty rough one place, you move over into another. I'm a market man, Wilson, same as you. You gotta keep yourself recession-proof, not so much tied to these recession cycles we've been going through. When I heard you took this job with this metals tycoon, McVey, that's what I figure. You and me, we think in the same groove. You're making yourself recession-proof. McVey, he's minerals, I hear. Maybe timber, maybe shipping, Nova Scotia coal, but minerals are his big ticket item. . . ."

Across the room, the policy association secretary was summoning the guests for the final hour of the program.

"I talk to a man I know, an investment counselor, big Wall Street connections. Cosmos Club, Metropolitan Club, he's right up there. So after we talk about minerals, I ask myself, Who's handling McVey's interests, who's doing his work up on the Hill?"

Wilson moved forward slowly, following the crowd that was reassembling. Larabee trailed after him with his cardiac rasp:

"Lawyers I can get, Wilson, like CPAs, secretaries, or bookkeepers. They all come cheap these days. Every time the Pentagon knocks out a promotion list and they put a few more bird colonels or four-stripers out to pasture, I get 'em pounding on my door. I get résumés, I get people from the Hill, I get ex-staffers, I get the guys that marked up the bill and know a whole lot more about the loopholes than the fucking congressmen that got their name on it. They all think they got something to sell. Sure they do— for twenty dollars a day. Do you wanna work for twenty dollars a day, Wilson? Fifty? A hundred? That's twenty-five thou a year. I pay my secretaries thirty."

They'd reached the last canapé table.

"What I'm looking for is the big account," he continued. "They don't come easy. Someone who walks in the front door and brings the big bucks with him."

"McVey manages his corporate interests out of New York," Wilson said. "It's not something I know anything about."

Larabee seemed not to have heard. "What if I was to throw a little business into that little hobby shop McVey is bankrolling over there in Foggy Bottom. You do a few studies for me: Latin America; the Middle

East. Security studies. Hey, did I tell you the Arab Emirates package is gonna fly? Hawk missiles, it looks like. Some friends I know got a piece of it. This Awacs sale has busted everything loose. So I give you a little business, research studies, maybe three, four grand worth. What's the chance McVey would move a little corporate business my way? Let's say I was to handle some of his mineral work, you're in for ten percent. That's off the top. I keep it in escrow, and if we go partners, it's more. You gotta think long-term, Wilson, the big score. . . ."

The lecture had begun and the doors were being closed.

"Are you going in?" Wilson asked. Nothing he had said had made the slightest impression upon Larabee.

"No, I gotta run. Think about what I said. We'll talk some more one of these days."

Wilson followed his hurried retreat across the room. He watched him pause, grab a canapé from the table and put it in his pocket, take another, pull his coat and hat from a chair inside the door, and continue on down the staircase, briefcase in hand, hat on the back of his head, coat flying, munching on his early dinner.

You poor bastard, he thought. Still standing in front of the closed door, he discovered that he'd lost all interest in the conference going on inside. He turned away to find his own coat and leave.

Betsy and Haven Wilson were sitting in the rear study after dinner, she with her afghan, he with a few project proposals he'd brought from the Center. At her suggestion, he'd built a fire in the fireplace and now, papers slipped aside, he watched the flames in silence.

"Those are the logs I cut at Ed Donlon's place last spring," he recalled sleepily, breaking the silence. "It's funny how you remember things like that."

"You have a special feeling for that place, don't you?"

"I used to. I suppose I still do. I don't like to think about it. Ed never goes out there anymore."

"What about the old farm we looked at that day?" she asked, putting the afghan aside. "How do you feel about that?"

"It interests me. A lot could be done with it." He reached to his side and turned off the table lamp.

"I was thinking about it today," she said, her hands still idle, her head back against the couch. "If you're really serious, we should talk about it."

"You never showed much interest. I didn't want to push you before, not with everything else."

"Why would I have shown any interest? I always thought of it as a kind of escape for you, talking about moving to the country. Being a Washington widow was bad enough, but being left by myself a hundred miles out in the country would have been worse. Your life was too much centered in Washington. You only talked about moving when you were annoyed or frustrated. Even the boys noticed that."

"The boys did?"

"All the time. It was a sort of joke among us. They knew you'd never leave Washington, not really. You and Nick are the same. You simply can't let go. Ida and I were talking about it today."

He sat watching Betsy's silhouette in dismay. "It wasn't just restlessness—it never was. Is that what they thought?"

"Children see things, much more than you think they do."

The phone rang and he got up slowly. "How do you feel about it now? The idea of a country place? We wouldn't have to give up this house—not right away."

"I was thinking about it today. It intrigues me, what you said that day, having a country place where the family could get together—children, grandchildren, whatever. . . ."

Wilson took the call in the hall, still looking back through the doorway toward Betsy. Impatient to resume their conversation, he was annoyed by the interruption. Someone was calling from a public telephone. He could hear the sounds of traffic in the background.

"Who is this?"

"Oh, shit yes, man, you know me," came the cryptic reply. "Agent Orange, friend. You've been chasing me down, so get this address and get it good. I'll only go around once, man. . . ."

"Come to my office, then—"

"Listen, fucker, I got this big wound between the ears and it's not getting any better. You've been nosing around looking for me and I figure I owe you one, so take down this address and bring me money—you listening?"

Wilson was listening. An address on U.S. Route 1 between Arlington and Crystal City—a bar, a service station on the corner and a phone booth in between. He was to wait there for a call the following night at ten o'clock.

10.

Dr. Foster was drifting haplessly through the exit chute of his congressional testimony, white water now growing more stormy as salvos of derision lifted from both sides of the congressional dais facing him. Intimidated by those booming public voices, he was sweating shamelessly, his collar damp and wilted, his hand shaking so terribly that he hadn't the courage to lift the chrome-plated carafe on the table to his right to refill his empty water glass. His mouth was as dry as cotton. As he was answering the last question, his swollen tongue had stuck to the roof of his mouth like a lump of toffee, and he'd been unable to disengage it to finish the sentence.

"What you're sayin' here, as I understand it," rumbled the Republican from Oklahoma, "is that we ought not be he'ping some of these South American military regimes, as you call 'em, never mind what the Russians and Mr. Castro are doin'. . . ."

He paused to let Foster resume.

"What I wath thaying—" Foster's tongue stuck again and he had no choice but to fill the glass from the carafe, very sloppily too. His trembling hands spilled more water to the table as he drank. A pool of water gathered at the base of the microphone. Conscious suddenly of death by electrocution, he moved his hands back, but that quick end to his humiliation seemed more charitable than the growing fear that he would faint dead away, his gaseous head now emptied of that burden of scholarly freight he'd rehearsed so carefully over the weekend. His mind was filled instead with the hot dry chaff of the family corn crib back in Iowa, to which he used to escape when a hog or a beef was butchered.

Tom Foster's son a history perfessor? Well, I be. I knowed he was cut out to do something had to do with readin' an' writin'. . . .

The chairman's deep voice revived him. "Try moving the microphone a little closer, Dr. Foster. We're almost done now. . . ."

Four congressmen flanked him along the raised bench of the hearing room, which seemed to Foster less a court of chancery than a tribunal of the inquisition. The paneled committee room was horribly bright from the television lights that were just being turned on. The spectator chairs had only been half-occupied until just three minutes earlier, when the next witness had entered, the senior State Department spokesman for Latin America, accompanied by his legal adviser, two deputy assistant secretaries, and an aide carrying a voluminous briefing book. This entourage was followed by a score of journalists, television reporters, interested congressional aides, and foreign diplomats, all avidly awaiting the administration's latest policy utterance on El Salvador and Latin America.

Dr. Foster had heard the bustle, the murmuring voices and the scraping chairs, and knew that what he feared most had come to pass. The klieg lights came on. A moment later, out of the corner of his eye, he caught sight of the overflow of spectators, now spilling along the walls and into the chairs immediately behind him. The committee chairman banged his gavel. In the time it took for the commotion to dim and the room to settle into silence, Foster was sickeningly aware of how enormous his audience had become.

At the end of the second row, Dr. Foster's roommate—a slight wispy research librarian from the National Archives—was overcome by the same sudden vertigo that had stricken Foster. He slipped from his chair and fled up the aisle. With that alacrity for which he was noted, Shy Wooster quickly left the wall near the door to occupy the vacated seat, forcing a matronly reporter from a Midwestern news service who'd moved toward the same seat to retreat to the rear.

As the din subsided, Foster felt the blush rise from his armpits, ascend to his neck and cheeks, and begin to ring in his ears. Naked before the tribunal, he was aware of the enormous hole in the toe of his right sock, the gaping cavity in his right rear molar, and the frayed elastic band of his drooping shorts, pressing against his chubby back. Quite suddenly he saw himself not as a scholar, a psychohistorian, or a Soviet expert at all but as a fraud—a plump, frightened, middle-aged homosexual sitting in his yeasty underwear before this hoary inquisitional court, these black-suited heterosexual parsons from the hinterlands, sitting in sanctimonious judgment over all that gave substance and passion to his life. Could John Donne ever get a sonnet read here? William Byrd perform a motet? Jefferson engage in philosophical discourse, Tillich discuss his tormented sexual life, Niebuhr publish an essay? No, these were the same canting philistines who'd pursued him all his life, who had driven him out of Iowa, out of graduate school, out of government, and out of teaching . . . these same dull, sanctimonious, coarse-faced bigots—

"Dr. Foster, are you gonna answer the question?" the congressman drawled with a trace of impatience.

Foster's mind teetered backward, his damp eyes swooned back in his skull, his shoulders swayed, and he was on the brink of fainting dead away when a sudden angel of deliverance danced across his hot eyelids—a plump, pink-clad coquette in tights, tiptoeing seductively across the stage of the rapt State Department press room; and behind the Spanish fan and false eyelashes he recognized Henry Kissinger as Carmen, doing his Waltz of the Toreadors for a lovesick Washington press corps.

"That's not precisely what I meant," Foster found himself saying, miraculously revived.

"Maybe you could explain it, then."

"What I meant to say was that we can't have it both ways. By 'we' I mean the United States," he added hastily, suppressing the innuendo.

"Both ways? I don't follow you."

You wouldn't, Foster thought stupidly, gazing at the repellent heterosexual face. "What I mean is that we can't continue to claim that our system, our way of life, offers the best hope for others in the world while we continue to support stability over justice and oppression over reform." He was reading again, his face still flushed, but his voice stronger.

"That's what you said in your statement," the congressman interrupted wearily, lifting a copy of Foster's prepared statement from the notes in front of him. "You already said that, but what I want to know is how we do it. How do we handle all of this Communist subversion in Latin America if we don't give them military help?"

"By not aligning ourselves with their oppressors," Foster replied, but the words seemed so trite that he blushed again.

"Give the Russians an inch and they'll take a mile," his interlocutor rumbled on. "We've gotta deal with that. So far you haven't told us how. If you wanna know what the Russians are doing down there in Latin America, you ought to come around to some of our classified briefings, see what we see."

The congressman's reference to details not available to the general public, like any references by a high priesthood to their occult mysteries, whether in the Masonic order, Skull and Bones, or the Vatican's bank accounts, carried a note of moral superiority. Dr. Foster hesitated a moment, unable to think of any reply except the obvious one: *Show me.* "I'm not really sure what the Russians are up to," he began evasively, but then, conscious of his own voice, added hastily, "Behavior often gets terribly muddled. Confused, I mean." But that too wasn't quite right. "Perceptions, I meant to say, not so much behavior."

"You'll have to explain that one to me, Doctor," the congressman declared, grinning as he watched Dr. Foster mop his brow. "I'm just a plain ole country boy."

"I meant to say that we often flaunt an idealistic view of our own actions," Foster answered, aware that he was straying from his script, "but take a much more cynical view of Soviet behavior."

"Can't trust 'em, that's why," the congressman said, recognizing his opening. "You mean to sit there and tell me you don't know that?" He smiled for the benefit of those spectators who'd sighed audibly at the doctor's naiveté.

"I think you've described the very problem I'm trying to get at," Foster said guiltily, departing even further from his text. "That very bias—"

"*Bias?*" The congressman leaned forward. "Bias? What kind of bias?"

"Our own biases, I'm afraid," Foster offered without conviction. This was the section of his presentation that Haven Wilson had deleted at the Center, convinced that the committee would make short work of it. "I mean by that that we use one set of ideals or attitudes to defend our own actions and another set entirely to judge the Russians or for that matter any regime we find objectionable. I'm talking about the double standard."

The hearing room was silent. Troubled that the subcommittee was being led into a cul-de-sac, the chairman leaned back to confer with the counsel. The congressman was still bent forward intently, glowering at Foster.

"I sure wish I knew what you meant by that," he said.

"I mean that we take an idealistic or anthropomorphic view of our own motives," Foster replied, licking his dry lips, "and a much more cynical or ratomorphic view of the Russians. It's almost as if their cerebral cortexes were totally different."

The congressman continued to study Dr. Foster's flushed face as he silently digested this strange scrap of scientific information. Then he seemed to understand. "You saying the Russians act like rats?" he asked with that histrionic acuteness that was the despair of his opponents and the delight of the Oklahoma prairie towns. A murmur of laughter lifted from behind Foster. "He said it, I didn't," the congressman drawled as he leaned back, lifting his huge hands from the dais in helpless innocence. "He said the Russians are ratomorphic, they act like rats." The laughter came again and he leaned forward over his folded arms to exploit his advantage. "Is that what you study over at that research center of yours, running rats around all day to see how they act like Russians?" He lifted Dr. Foster's prepared statement to read aloud the Center's full name. "The Center for Contemporary Studies—is that what you call it?" he asked, having given the title the full benefit of his Oklahoma drawl, the same kind of heavy sarcasm used by Foster's high school history teacher back in Iowa—but first and foremost, the football and basketball coach— to announce to a snickering class the latest title of one of young Foster's history essays.

"I'm afraid you misunderstood me," Foster said weakly.

"Well, maybe you ought to explain it to me, explain it to all of us." Foster cleared his throat and brought the microphone nearer, opened his mouth to begin, but then realized that he hadn't the slightest idea of how to commence. They waited. "Take your time, son," the congressman chided, with a tolerant smile, winking at the audience. "That's a whole lot of learning you're carrying around in your head and it's not all gonna come jumping out on the table at the same time, like a bushel of bullfrogs, if that's what you're scared of." The audience laughed. "We're ready when you are."

"Thank you, Congressman." Foster spoke very slowly, the words found only with great effort. "What I meant to say was that while we credit ourselves with very complex human attributes—love, loyalty, generosity, intelligence, empathy, compassion, and so on—we do less for others. We assign the Soviet Union or the Soviet leadership, for example, a far cruder or primitive character, that of rats or pigeons. Less mammalian than reptilian. As if they didn't have sons or daughters, homes or birthdays, and so forth—" *Birthdays?* he thought too late, lulled asleep by his own sonority. Where in God's name had that come from? He cleared his throat again. "That is the behaviorist view—the 'ratomorphic' view I spoke of. What it means is that in our foreign policy choices, we treat the Russians the same way behaviorist psychologists treat the rats and pigeons in their laboratories. By that, I mean that they are thought to respond to only the most primitive stimuli—"

The laughter had come again. Shy Wooster, seated two rows behind Dr. Foster, immediately took out his pocket notebook.

"Come again?" said the congressman. "You got me a little confused, Doctor. Sounds like you've got a lot of folks confused."

Very loudly, as if to dispel any misunderstanding that might have been caused by his soft, quavering voice, Foster said: "We claim that we act only out of idealistic and humanitarian motives, but not the Russians. We claim we act logically and reasonably at all times, but not the Russians. We believe, in short, that we are guided by lofty principles, but the Russians, base ones, and that as a result they must be disciplined as one disciplines rats and pigeons in a behaviorist laboratory. Pain or pleasure, you see, penalties or rewards." Dr. Foster paused, aware for the first time of the stunning effect his amplified voice had had on the committee members. "This is what I call the 'ratomorphic' view of Soviet character," he said in conclusion, his voice sliding away like a frightened boy's.

In his notebook, Shy Wooster was writing: *There is a scientific basis to Russian cunning and deceit. It has been proven in the scientific laboratory in experiments with rats.*

"That's very interesting," the congressman declared, making a few notes himself, "very interesting. And what are you saying, that it's scientific or not scientific?"

"Pseudoscientific, of course," Foster replied weakly. "It's a very primitive tool for trying to cope with quite complex events, like Afghanistan or Poland. We believe we can control Soviet behavior by quantitative techniques, the way we condition the reflexes of rats and pigeons. It doesn't take mind or idealism, if you will, into account. But it's a primitive, mechanistic view, behaviorism is—a nineteenth-century view, which is now being applied to foreign policy. That's what Dr. Kissinger's version of détente was. And that's why it didn't work." His hand reached for the water glass. His mouth was growing dry again.

"Hold on a minute, Doctor," the congressman broke in. "You're getting me all mixed up. You say détente didn't work or couldn't work? I don't understand what you're saying. Are you for it or agin it?"

"What I'm saying is that Dr. Kissinger and others interpreted détente in a very limited way," Foster said. "They saw it as a kind of behaviorist box within which they could confine the Soviet policy animal and then manipulate him the way the behaviorist manipulates his laboratory creatures."

The dais was silent, like the room behind him. Foster was reluctant to continue, but then the committee chairman nodded to him impatiently. "The underlying assumption behind all this," Foster resumed, "is that Soviet policymakers have an intelligence quotient similar to rats and pigeons and can only be trained like such creatures, conditioned by their own brute, primitive reflex. Appetite, you see; aggression. Unless so contained, the Soviet Union will continue to be aggressors. You can't change them any more than you can teach rats or pigeons to think or tie their shoes; therefore they must be conditioned by the application of penalties and rewards, a kernel of corn or an electric shock. That was our old version of détente—"

"And it won't work?" the congressman asked.

"It's inadequate," Foster offered. "It's too primitive to explain Soviet policy choices. In any case, the U.S. is incapable of playing the role of an omniscient, omnipresent global laboratory scientist, able to keep the world in his behaviorist box. That's quite impossible."

"But we did it," a congressman intruded loudly from the far end of the bench, "we did it. We've done it since '45—kept the Russians right at home, kept them from overrunning Europe, Korea, the Middle East. We did it because we had the military power, because we had the bomb, and that's what it'll take to keep them there. That's what this new defense budget is all about."

"What he's saying," the chairman amplified, "is that we had a policy that worked in Europe. We had the bomb, we got NATO together, and we contained Soviet military power. Using your terminology, you might say we 'conditioned' Moscow to our way of thinking. That's how come Europe is still Europe. You can't tell me the Soviet Union doesn't understand force. Let's just say we helped along in the conditioning process. But we're talking about Latin America and how to handle that subversion down there—"

"I'm afraid I disagree," Dr. Foster called out.

"How's that? Disagree? How can you disagree with that? It was our nuclear superiority that held back the Russians all that time, just as it's holding them back now. How can you say they haven't been conditioned by that?"

"I'm afraid that's the tragedy," Foster replied sorrowfully, "that's the terrible tragedy about all this. We've conditioned ourselves, that's all."

The television lights, which had mercifully dimmed five minutes earlier, came back on. The hush had returned to the restless audience behind him. The chairman called upon Foster to explain.

"No one knows what the map of Europe might have looked like today without NATO or the hydrogen and atomic bomb," Foster said. "Granted. But we did have those bombs, just as today we have these massive nuclear arsenals on both sides. And because we possessed these weapons first and have continued to increase our stockpiles, we've become the prisoners of the assumption that the Soviet Union has been restrained only by our nuclear superiority. We've become the prisoners of the assumption that without our nuclear superiority, the Soviet Union would have been true to its ratomorphic or aggressive nature. But in that way, you see, our own nuclear armaments have become living proof of an unrelenting Soviet hostility. Our own military establishment is day-to-day evidence of the Soviet Union's brutal intent, just like the bars in the lions' cages out at the Washington Zoo. No, I disagree with you, I'm sorry to say, and this is the greatest tragedy of all. All of this shows that we've only conditioned ourselves by these massive nuclear armaments, just as the Russians have conditioned themselves. We've become the pathological prisoners of these stockpiles. We've finally succeeded as a nation in conditioning ourselves to that same primitive, unreflective, ratomorphic psychology we once assigned the Russian leadership. There's no better evidence of it, I regret to say, than those who sit in the White House and the Pentagon . . ."

The chairman had begun to gently tap his gavel, the crowd had begun to stir, but Dr. Foster, a few bare breaths left in his weary lungs, was determined to continue:

". . . at this very minute. Their presence should remind us of the sort of obsessive, primitive, fear-ridden leadership we've created for ourselves after thirty-five years. No, Mr. Chairman, I'm sorry to say we've only conditioned ourselves. . . ."

The banging of the gavel had grown louder, terminating what the chairman now identified as a partisan assault on the present administration and inadmissible under the rules of bipartisanship.

There were no further questions. "Thank you, Dr. Foster," the chairman concluded briskly. "We'd like to thank you for sharing your views with us."

"That was a right interesting presentation you made, Doctor," said an unfamiliar voice as Foster bent at the corridor water fountain to rinse the disagreeable metallic taste from his dry mouth. He felt enervated, weak-kneed, damp, hot, and humiliated, so drained by his inquisition that he had absolutely no recollection of the words he'd uttered during those final minutes. But he also felt relieved and elated, free of a burden that had been haunting him for weeks. The world looked brighter, cleaner, simpler, and less hostile, as it might to a man who had just escaped execution. "Real scientific," the voice continued. "How do you spell that, that 'ratomorphic'?"

Foster told him, still leaking water to his vest and tie. He'd expected his roommate to be waiting for him, but he had vanished. Instead a handful of reporters followed him into the corridor to ask a few questions.

"I expect you must be a student of eugenics too," Shyrock Wooster said, taking a card from his pocket as he returned the small notebook, "you an' that Center over there. Must be doing some right interesting work. We need more scientific studies on what the Russians are up to, a whole lot more. Maybe it's something in the genes that will tell the answer. You do any government work?"

"A few endocrine studies, biopathology," Foster muttered.

"Well, I'll be. Haven't heard much about that." He passed Foster his card and held out his hand. "Nice to meet you, Doctor. Maybe sometime we can get together, swap a few ideas. You ought to get some of these scientific studies of yours published—some magazine where they'll get national attention."

And with that, Shy Wooster turned and went back down the hall to the hearing room. He paused outside the door to make another entry in his notebook and then stepped inside to hear the testimony of the Assistant Secretary for Latin American Affairs.

"No, I'm sorry, Congressman," the Secretary was intoning in his rich, fruity voice. "I'm afraid that's not an expression I'm familiar with."

"'Ratomorphic,'" repeated the congressman in his Oklahoma twang. "You never heard of that? Well, maybe you oughta look it up. Shows you striped-pants diplomats don't know everything."

Dr. Foster found his roommate on the steps outside, pale and anxious, standing to one side, avoiding the few departing spectators. "I was so mortified," he confided, "I just couldn't stand it any longer, not what you were going through."

"It wasn't easy," Foster confessed, annoyed that his nervousness might have been that visible. "But I think I got myself under control." On the whole, he felt quite pleased, pleased enough so that as he went down the steps, his gait grew bolder. A departing reporter recognized him and waved. Foster waved back. As he reached the pavement and turned, waiting for his companion, a young college girl behind him on the steps nodded and smiled. "I liked what you said," she told him. "Really neat."

"Well, thank you," Foster said, pleased.

"Me too," volunteered her companion as they passed. "You really had them shook."

"What'd they say?" his roommate asked as he joined Foster, watching the two girls go up the street.

"Do you have to know everything?" Foster said, looking at the pale, shrinking recluse at his side. He looked so absurd Foster gave a vulgar laugh.

Oh, dear, he thought instantly, hearing that loud, lewd sound. *What have I done?*

11.

The yellow caution lights blinked off and on at the intersections, but the lonely boulevard was as deserted as the nearby freightyards. Only an occasional automobile sped by, trailing the sound of its engine long after it had passed. It was a poor place to have a flat tire, find a cab, or meet someone with a dubious reputation. Cronin's call had come at the telephone booth a little after ten o'clock. Ten minutes later, Wilson parked his car in front of the closed diesel fuel depot. The bar with the yellow neon beer sign in the window was dark, the heavy metal grille locked. No lights showed in the solitary house where the little girl had been pulling the rusty wagon. He crossed the broken asphalt street, head bent against the wind. The chain-link gate was closed but unlocked, the heavy padlock hanging open in its hasp. He entered and closed the gate behind him. The windows of the office were dark. A night-light burned dimly in the reception room beyond the glass door. As he moved, the moon drifted from behind the high broken clouds, its cold pallor touching the windshields of the rental cars. Steam boiled up from the pumping shed of a depot across the railroad tracks.

As he moved into the shadows at the rear of the lot, he identified the silhouette of a car backed up against the door of the maintenance garage. Its rear end was elevated, as if on racing slicks. Approaching, he saw the interior light blink on momentarily, to reveal a figure leaning forward over the wheel. As Wilson bent to look in the passenger window, the light went out and the door was pushed open. He heard the sound of a radio playing softly, a woman singing in a low, strident voice.

"Cronin?" he called.

"Who else? Climb in where it's warm and cozy, just me an' Grace Slick."

"How about a little more light first?"

"What do you think, I got a zapper in here?"

"Turn on the light."

Wilson waited. A moment later the weak passenger light came on. The figure behind the wheel wore a wispy beard and his hair was long over his neck and ears. Wilson couldn't be certain it was the same face he'd seen through the Alfa window that drizzly day on the ramp; the sunglasses had made the big difference. He wore a bulky jacket similar to a GI field jacket and he was holding a can of beer. The light went out. "You got my money?"

"Your check? Not with me, no."

"Don't shit me, man. What the hell am I here for? You owe me three hundred."

"You'll get your money," Wilson said, still holding the door open.

"You know what I went through to get that goddamn check to you? I was sweating blood, man! I got nothing, zilch, not a fucking dime, on account of that three hundred I gave you!"

In the darkness Wilson couldn't see the face, but the voice told him enough. He stayed outside the car.

"I'm flat broke, missing two checks. I got a job waiting out of town, only I gotta get there first! I need that three hundred to get on the road and you tell me you haven't got it!"

"I can have it for you tomorrow, but I want to talk first."

"What about?"

"The accident on the ramp that morning."

"An accident, so what?"

"Why were you out there?"

"What the hell's it to you? I was out driving around. Who the fuck are you—my probation officer, some VA snooper? How'd you find out my name?"

"Why'd you give me the Caltronics card?"

"Because I had to get the shit out of there, what else? I see this card, I use it. So what? What's it matter whose card?" Wilson heard the sound of a beer can rattling to the floor and the sound of another being opened.

"Is this your car?" he asked, straightening to search his coat pockets for his gloves. The car seemed familiar and now he remembered. He'd seen it parked nearby the day he'd visited the lot.

"Some mechanic's. Went up to Philly to pick up a car. Why?"

"How come you're sitting in it?"

"Because he left it here, because I got keys, man. How'd you think I got in the gate? You wanna go sit in the fucking office instead so you can call the cops? What are you asking all these questions for?"

"I told you." He let the door swing back. "You'd better go get yourself a

255

lawyer, a lawyer and a little protection. Some people are going to be looking for you." He stepped back.

"Just hold it!" the young man said. "We're not finished yet! What are you on my ass for?"

"I told you. I want to talk."

"Yeah, talk, just talk. Like always. You think you're gonna rip me off, think I'm a fucking lush sitting here, screwing up my head. Only if the cops show, I've got an ejection seat this time, right out the fucking tube." His hand rested on the dashboard shelf, pointing toward the front gate. The moonlight moving through the windshield splashed it radium blue, like the small hand of a cadaver. It was a hand curiously without strength, Wilson thought, not a mechanic's at all. The face was still hidden in the shadows. "Someone shows, I'm gone, man—right out the fence there."

It seemed an empty boast, like everything else Wilson had heard. "When they want you, they'll find you," he said, pulling on his gloves, "just as I did."

"So what the shit's going on, what's all this garbage you're giving me?"

"That's what I want to talk about. But this isn't the place."

A car passed slowly in front of the gate. He thought it might be Buster Foreman's car, prowling the lonely street in front after he'd failed to reappear, but it was too conspicuous for Buster. The headlights were also too dim, as if the alternator wasn't charging properly. Uneasily, Wilson followed its taillamps up the bumpy street. It turned into a lot and the lights were extinguished.

He turned back.

"Hold it," the young man said. He'd left the car to stand in the moonlight, looking across the engine hood toward Wilson. "How much money you got on you?"

"Eighty, ninety dollars. Why?"

"All I care about is getting on the road. I don't know anything about what you're talking about, I don't know shit. Someone wants to pull me in, O.K.—let 'em. I've been crazy-rated by the VA, man—eighty percent wacko, ask the D.C. cops. What are they gonna do, lock me up again? O.K., let 'em. The VA wants me to turn myself in for sixty days anyway—post-traumatic stress syndrome, you ever heard of it? I don't, so they cut off the disability check. The D.C. cops bust me once and a guy at Caltronics gets someone to bail me out, so I owe him a favor. What the fuck more do you wanna know? We're drinking buddies and I do him some favors. He likes my war stories, like those shrinks over at the VA that wanna turn me into a fucking vegetable. I drink a lot on account of these two heads I'm wearing half the time, a goddamn plate in my skull, and now you're on my ass on account of some goddamn card I pass you out the

256

window. So that's my life story, all I know, so gimme what you've got in your wallet and I'll get the fuck out of here. . . ."

He'd moved toward Wilson as he rambled on, one hand held out, one hand in his pocket, but stopped as Wilson mistrustfully pulled his own gloved hands from his pockets.

"Who at Caltronics?"

They stood in silence, facing each other across the front of the car.

"Go fuck yourself."

Wilson said, "When you're ready to collect your three hundred, give me a call." He backed away and then turned.

"'Oh, shit, daddy, another of them Vietnam weirdos, a VA whiner,'" Cronin mimicked in a thin, nasal voice, his approximation of the twang of middle America. "You think I don't know you, fucker? Who sent you after me?"

"I told you."

"You told me nothing, zilch, just a lot of garbage. You're looking for something, something that smells like big money. Who else is looking? Who else knows you're out here?"

Wilson thought it prudent not to reply, and once more they confronted each other, some twenty feet apart, Wilson the taller, Cronin lean and slight, a veteran from another generation, a little high, suspicious, certainly confused, but also curious, Wilson thought, warned of conspiracies he didn't understand.

"Who were you doing favors for at Caltronics?" he repeated. Cronin didn't reply. Wilson waited, then took a cautious step backward, then another, and finally turned back across the moonlit lot. Cronin followed him at a distance. As Wilson reached the door of his car, he heard the other man call out to him and waited. Cronin locked the gate and crossed the street after him.

"His name was Morris," he said. "I needed the money, same as I do now. I got a job waiting down in Houston, but I've gotta get there first. How much could you let me have, like tonight?" He didn't look at Wilson as he spoke, but was gazing down the darkened street where the car was waiting.

"In cash, what I have with me, a check for the rest," Wilson said. "I'd make it five hundred in all if you tell me everything you know."

He gave Wilson the name of a tavern farther out Route 1 toward Fort Belvoir and told him to wait in the rear parking lot. Then he crossed the street and stood under the streetlight and lifted his hand, like a man signaling for a cab. As Wilson drove away, he saw through the rearview mirror a set of weak headlights move out of the darkness toward the lonely figure under the streetlight.

Wilson turned the corner, headed toward Fort Belvoir. Then he reached under the seat and brought out the car telephone Buster Foreman had installed that afternoon, repeated the new address, and said a car would be following him.

He found the tavern twenty minutes later. The neon sign in front advertised drinks, dinner, and live country music on Saturday nights. A few cars and pickups were parked in the gravel lot in the rear, where Wilson waited. Five minutes later, an old Ford Falcon turned into the drive and he recognized the same faulty headlights he'd seen on the street in front of the car lot. The rocker panels were rusted out, the front fenders were ragged, and it carried Virginia license plates. A dark-haired girl was driving. Cronin sat next to her on the front seat. She didn't leave the car.

"It was this Monday night, something queer happens," Cronin mumbled without enthusiasm, not looking at Wilson but concentrating on the flattened cigarette package he was shredding between his fingers. "Morris catches me in the lobby at Potomac Towers and asks am I gonna be around. I'd just brought this car over from Alexandria and I figure he's got trouble with this Mercedes he's leasing, the one he's always got trouble with. So I tell him I'll be in the office. It's locked up by then, but I open up and wait around. . . ."

They sat in a small, dark booth in the rear. The wall lamp didn't work. The dance floor and the small bandstand were deserted; only a few of the booths that lined the walls were occupied. A stereo system piped country and western music into the room from the bar in front. A small middle-aged waitress in a black nylon dress had brought them beer.

"So all of a sudden he comes busting into the office, really pissed. He asks could he use the phone quick, only he doesn't wait, just grabs it up off the desk and calls someone. I hear him tell whoever he's talking to he's not in his office now, so they can talk. I think maybe it's a woman he's talking to, on account of this secretary he's been dating upstairs at Caltronics. Then he really gets burned and I know it's not a broad, either. I've got a nose for what's not my business, so I go outside to the write-up counter. Then after a while he gets calmed down and he's telling this guy he has to go up to Newark for this funeral tonight so he can't meet him. Then he says maybe at National Airport in half an hour, an hour. Then he gets pissed again—"

"What did he say?"

"What he said before, when they were first talking."

"What were his words?"

Cronin still didn't lift his eyes as he turned the flattened cigarette package in his fingers. "'Double-crosser,' 'double-dealer,' shit like that. 'Fourflusher,' like they'd been double-crossed. I remember because I was think-ing I wouldn't want Morris pissed at me. He gets ugly, real weird sometimes, cold fish eyes. They give a guy chicken skin."

"He was calling the man on the phone a double-crosser?"

"I think they were talking about someone else. But he's pissed at this dude he's talking to. 'You calling me a liar?' he says, like he was supposed to do something and didn't do it. Anyway, it's not my business. After he hangs up he's still hot. He's got this briefcase with him and he tells me he's on his way to catch the shuttle up to New York. He wants me to check out the Mercedes while he's gone. Wet weather comes, he's got problems with the electrical, the solenoid sticks, he can't turn it over. He tells me he's been having problems all day. Then he gets pissed again, like maybe he shouldn't go to New York, this other problem that's come up, some guy trying to put the heat on him, some government guy."

Cronin paused to drink from the beer glass, his eyes turned to the deserted dance floor, where a couple stood alone, as if trying to decide whether or not to dance.

"Did he say what kind of problem?"

"He says maybe a shakedown, only he's not sure. He does a lot of government work, Morris does. We talk about it sometimes. The time we drove up to Atlantic City that weekend, all the way up that Saturday he tells me about these contracting officers he works with, how some of them always got their hand out. Only he tells me this time he doesn't know where this guy is coming from?"

"Sorry?"

"He doesn't know where this guy is coming from," Cronin muttered, still swallowing his words, "this guy that's maybe trying to do a number on him."

"You think that's what the phone conversation was about?"

"Yeah, the way he's acting. He's got a lot of government contracts he's working on around town and he doesn't know how this guy fits in. He's got the name on a piece of paper. He wrote it down while he was talking on the phone and he keeps looking at it, like it doesn't mean shit to him. That pisses him off too. Morris is the kind of guy that's gotta know everything going on, everything—the kind of guy who doesn't want anyone getting behind him. Like this corporal I knew in 'Nam, always the last man. That's how Morris was." He paused, but this time to look at Wilson, as if he might explain it. "I think he must have done a little time. I think he's still got some troubles left over, like maybe someone's still out to nail him."

"You think the government might be still after him?"

"Yeah, like they're gonna bust him again. Is that right, is that why you're on his ass?"

"He might be a federal witness. Did he ever tell you the government was after him?"

Cronin considered the question silently, removing another cigarette. "He was all the time nervous, like he was gonna get busted," he resumed finally, "but he never said anything. Except once, maybe. He was having car trouble and it drove him up the wall, a car undependable like that. I was kidding him, telling him someone making his money shouldn't have any worries. He gets hot, then gives me a lot of shit about how easy I've got it, that when you fuck with some of the guys he knows, you wind up where nobody's listening, in a Hefty bag someplace, in some Jersey scrap iron yard, buried a couple of tons deep in a bale of highway meat. I figure he's trying to tell me how tough he is. So I think maybe he did a little time once. So that night when we're walking out to his car, I tell him maybe he ought to check this guy out if he's so worried about it—"

"The man whose name he wrote down?"

"Yeah," Cronin muttered, looking away. "I tell him about the time up at Flushing when I was working for this car agency and this shithead comes sneaking around, asking questions, checking up on me. I get the manager to give me his name, look him up in the book, and follow him to work one morning. He's a fucking investigator for the VA, snooping around trying to find out whether this physical disability I'm claiming is for real. We have it out right there in the parking lot. He gets a little shook and files a complaint, saying I'm harassing him, but so what? It gets it out in the open. Anyway, I'm telling Morris all this, just shooting the shit the way we always do, just talking. I don't want any of his problems. He's got big money, maybe, but it's not buying him anything. So we look at the car and I tell him I'll pick it up in the morning."

Someone entered from the side door and Cronin silently watched him as he strolled toward the bar in front.

"So that's when he gets the idea. He thinks the story about the VA investigator is pretty funny, turning the tables like that. He hates the fucking government like I do. So what's when he asks me to do him a favor, check this guy out for him the way I did up in Flushing, find out who he's working for, where he reports in the morning, and then let him know when he gets back from this funeral in Newark. I figure he's putting me on, but he pulls out his wallet. 'Five hundred bucks,' he says, just like that. 'I don't wanna have to worry about it all the time I'm up in Newark.' I think he's shitting me and I tell him maybe I can't find out. 'Just tell me you tried,' he says, and he pulls out these hundred-dollar bills from his briefcase and stuffs them in my pocket, like a goddamn handkerchief, the same way he did when we were up in Atlantic City that second time. I didn't wanna go because I'm broke almost, just twenty bucks. We're about ready to walk in the Golden Nugget up there and he asks me how much I've got. I tell him and he stuffs these twenty-dollar bills in my coat pocket. I tell him maybe I'll lose them. 'Just tell me you tried,' he says, just like that night in the parking lot.''

"He took these hundred-dollar bills out of his briefcase?"

"Yeah, just reached in and there they were. He doesn't even open it all the way. It doesn't sound right to me. Five hundred bucks to find out where a guy's working? That's a little screwy, I'm thinking, crazy, like something I'd do. But it worries me a little, all these problems Morris has. I try to give the money back, he won't take it. So I tell him, what if this guy is FBI or something and busts me instead? I was joking but I'm serious too, you know what I mean?"

"What did he say?"

"He just laughs it off. 'Tell 'em to come see me,' he tells me. 'I'll blow the fuckers right out of the water.' What do you think he meant?"

Wilson sat back at last and lifted the glass from the table. "I don't know, not yet. So that's how you happened to be behind me on the ramp that morning. Morris gave you my name."

"Yeah, it was on the slip of paper."

"I fucked it up good," Cronin admitted. "I had the five hundred and I got bombed that night, really stoned. I wake up at five A.M. in this supper club parking lot out in Fairfax, a headful of nothing, like I'd just been medevacked up from Tayinh. I should have turned turtle, but I get on the road and find this place, find the house, and start cruising around, trying to bury this garbage dump I've got in my skull. I come around in front of your place twice, it's raining, and on the third pass some schoolkids are waiting at the end of the road, maybe for a school bus, and they give me this weird look, so I park it this time, up on the hill, and lift the hood, like I've got this ignition problem, and that's where I am when I see this station wagon come out of the drive. I take off."

"Until the beltway ramp."

"You lose me on the beltway but I catch up again, coming off the ramp. Then I get fishtailed by these fucking cops and I'm climbing your bumper. I'd blown it and a couple of cop cars are stopped down there, just waiting to bust me. I can't find my goddamned wallet, I've got a headful of shit, and then you stick this goddamned card through the window—"

"Where was your wallet?"

"I couldn't find it. I thought maybe I'd dropped it back on the hill when I was farting around with the ignition. It's under the seat, I find out later. All I can turn up in my pockets is this goddamn Valium, the front seat smells like a bartender's rag, and these cops are getting nervous. I get the cops up there, they'll bust me. Man, I wanna do the right thing, just get the shit out of there, so I grab up this goddamn card off the dash—"

"A Caltronics card," Wilson said. "Why Caltronics?"

"I cleaned out a car, two of them. Leases they turned in the day before. They left their shit all over and when I delivered this car, I cleaned 'em out, dumped it in the Alfa. A whole box of cards I was gonna turn in, cards they never used. I figure it doesn't matter. Then when I get my head together down the road, this coffee shop, I start getting worried—I'd fucked up and maybe Morris is going to know. I figured if I dropped this three hundred on you, telling you I was leaving town, that'd cool you off, but I was chasing a headful by then. I can't even go in to work."

"You didn't think I was government, then," Wilson said.

"I didn't care, man. Why should I care? You're selling real estate if anyone asks. You're gonna take the money and forget it. I got two hundred out of it. I don't have any problems with the government, only the VA. I didn't want any of Morris's trouble, not with the Hefty bag crowd, not with anyone else—not when they told me he'd blown town with all this money in his briefcase."

"After you were fired for missing three days' work, did the police ever talk to you?" Wilson asked.

"No way," Cronin said softly, shaking his head, "no fucking way. Eighty percent wacko, the VA says. 'A fucking animal runnin' loose, that's what you are, Cronin.'"

"Who told you that? Not the police."

"The screw at this nut ward—oh, yeah. I get into a fight over on Sixteenth Street, this bar over there, and I get the shit pounded out of me—not by the bartender, either; the fucking cops. Then up in New York, the Flushing cops, twice. This last time over on Sixteenth Street, they book me after they find this Valium on me and I don't have the VA prescription. They're going to take me out to St. Elizabeths in the morning. At three in the A.M. they bring this other guy in, this guy the D.C. cops pick up just coming off Memorial Bridge. He's living out of a locker down at Union Station. He can't get his VA records straightened out, like me, so he comes up here from down in West Virginia and flips out. He gets all his shit together and he's gonna bury it this time, dump it in a body bag and bury it, man, every fucking thing they gave him—Purple Heart, Silver Star, all of it—so he takes it out of this locker, dumps it in this waterproof bag, and that's what he does—"

"What?"

"Buries it. He buries it over at Arlington, just inside the stone fence halfway up the hill, he tells me. He's coming back now, just come off the bridge in a pair of GI fatigues and an Army jacket, only he's got this trenching tool stuck in the back of his belt and the D.C. cops stop him. It's two o'clock in the A.M. He's a jogger, he tells them, just jogging, but they flash him over and then see this dirt on his knees and elbows, then they turn him around and spot this blood dripping down his pants from this goddamn trenching tool and one of 'em says, 'What the hell have you been doing, sojur, where you been digging at?' 'My grave, fucker,' he tells them, 'right across the river over on the hill,' and this other cop says, 'Oh, shit, man, another of them Vietnam weirdos, a VA whiner,' and the guy tries to deck him, and the next thing he's lying in the road, bleeding like crazy, and they've got two more cars there, a couple of riot guns, and three or four cops are spread out along the road near the Lincoln Memorial like a goddamned SWAT team, looking for where his buddies are at, only there aren't any buddies, just him. Just him, just me, like I'm sitting here now—"

"When was this?" Wilson asked.

"Last year. So the D.C. cops got us both booked that night and they think they've got a couple of animals just escaped from the zoo. They dump us in this meat wagon the next morning and take us out to the funny farm. Straitjackets, man, like we're gonna trash the place. I'm three weeks out there. The girl I was going with quits on me."

He lit his last cigarette, the package from which it had been drawn in ribbons now, scraps of paper torn in an odd design.

"This guy from West Virginia, from outside Beckley, West Virginia, this big hillbilly that's buried his shit in this body bag over at Arlington . . ." His voice seemed tremulous for a moment, as if he were about to lose it, but the quaver passed. "The last time I see him he's like a vegetable, like a fucking two-hundred-pound turnip. He turned himself in, they were cleaning him up. That's what they wanted me to do, sign myself in. Me, no way. 'You want the fucking cops to do it, Cronin,' this goddamn runt orderly tells me when I'm checking out, 'like an animal, Cronin, because that's what you are.' The shrink is standing there too, so is this nurse. So I tell them, tell all of them, this little sawed-off midget first of all, 'Yeah, man, because I want it that way, just the way I am. I don't want to turn myself in, I don't want little squirts like you in their rubber boots and their rubber aprons hosing out my mind like it was some fucking GI latrine; I wanna remember things just like they are, including assholes like you just the way they are, just the way I am, because that's all I've got.' So that's on my record too, how they had to cut back on the disability. So what do you think I'm gonna do—start looking for the cops to talk to because maybe I'm the last one to see him before he blew town that night with a hundred grand he swiped from Caltronics? No way. I'm just gonna fade away like I

263

did, real easy like. I got no problems, I don't want any. All I wanna know is what's going on, why all this shit about this goddamn card? What the hell's the government after him for, anyway?"

Cronin couldn't remember the names of the people he'd met at the occasional Saturday night party at Morris's garden apartment at Potomac Towers. Some were Caltronics business associates, others local contacts, a few girls he'd met in singles bars. Cronin had a poor memory for names and the hour was late.

"Try thinking about faces, then," Wilson suggested. "Faces, voices, how he handled them. Think of it that way and then think about the call Morris made in the car rental office. Maybe that will tell you something."

"I didn't know any of them," he mumbled.

"How about the way he talked to this man he telephoned? Maybe that'll tell you something."

"Like what?"

"How well he knew him, whether he was a friend or a business partner. Someone close or not so close."

"Like he was a buddy," Cronin said mechanically. "Someone he could walk all over and he wouldn't get pissed."

"A friend, then."

"A friend and maybe not a friend. Hot and cold."

"Mixed feelings," Wilson suggested.

"Yeah, like that," Cronin said carelessly, sitting up again, fighting drowsiness. His concentration was drifting.

"Hot and cold. Someone he could kick around and would come back for more," Wilson continued.

"Yeah, like that."

"Someone he didn't respect, but maybe someone he had to put up with."

Cronin's head had begun to slump again. "Yeah, like he could wipe his feet on him and the jerk would just roll over."

"Who did you meet at his apartment that would meet that description?"

"I dunno," he said wearily. "Some guys from Caltronics, but I don't know their names. When he gave a blast at his apartment, he treated everybody like a buddy, like a good host, but he didn't have any close friends. He made sure everybody was having a good time. I dunno their names."

"Hot and cold, you said. Think of it that way," Wilson proposed. "A Saturday night at Morris's apartment. Someone he can kick around and watch him roll over, then hand him a drink and pat him on the back."

Cronin's eyes swam away.

264

"Strykker," Wilson suggested."

Cronin thought for a moment, but shook his head. "What's his first name?"

"Nat Strykker. Sixty maybe, gray hair."

"Naw, never heard of him. Too old, anyway."

Wilson waited. "Someone he can kick around and then watch roll over." He paused. "Then he picks him up and dusts him off."

Cronin seemed to be remembering something, head turned away, as if listening. "Yeah," he said finally, "there was this one guy. Morris was real tough on him, like he didn't want him hanging around, not with this singles crowd. Like he embarrassed him or something." He paused in recollection, more alert now. "He was that kind of guy, an asshole, a jerk you pitied the way he was."

"You remember his name?"

"No, I only saw him twice, I think it was. I remember this one night he shows up with this twenty-year-old chick who looked like she just stepped off a topless bar down on Fourteenth Street. It was real late, the guy's bombed, and Morris isn't going to let him in. There were just four of us and we're sitting around chewing the fat, me, Morris and these two chicks, listening to some music, and this clown shows up with this hooker. So Morris finally lets him in, this asshole, only he dumps this dumb broad with these two secretaries and me and yanks Morris out to the kitchen to talk. Morris really let him have it that time, right out in front of everyone, and we all felt pretty goddamned stupid, everyone except this clown and this cheap hooker. But Morris finally goes out to the kitchen to listen to this big deal this guy came to tell him about. That was the second time I'd seen him. The first time was this real live party Morris has going and this same clown shows up, not invited. He's alone this time and he's trying to get laid, but none of these girls there even look at him. So he ends up on the couch with me, telling me how he used to work with the SFers in 'Nam, ripping off all these Vietnamese names—Lang Vei and Ap Tan Hoi—how he nearly got his balls taken off by this Bouncing Better over near the Cambodian border. Then Morris tells him he's fulla shit and to stop screwing up his party. Yeah, he was the kind of guy Morris treated hot and cold, a big-deal expert like the guy on the phone. But you had to feel sorry for him, a fifty-year-old dude with this meat wagon face and those tight collars, hustling those twenty-year-old hostesses. . . ."

"You say you don't remember his name," Wilson asked, putting down his glass for the final time. He had had three bottles of beer on an empty stomach. The lights had now blinked off and on three times and he was grateful he wouldn't have to drink another.

"No, shit, I don't remember. I'd forgotten all about him. Ex-Navy, I think. I think that's what he told me. A health nut. He said he worked out every day in this gym in his office building. Said he'd been in Special Forces, detached duty, but he smelled like Saigon."

"How about Larabee?" Wilson suggested. "That ring a bell?"

"No, nothing. I didn't know his last name."

"Chuck, maybe?"

Cronin smiled sleepily, red-eyed. "Oh, yeah," he said softly. "'Chuckwagon Chuck,' that hamburger face he had. That's what Morris called him, a real creep. Maybe it was him. Oh, sure, man. That's maybe who it was."

Wilson was at home, half-asleep in his chair, when Buster Foreman finally called. He'd followed the old Ford Falcon to an all-night pizza parlor on Telegraph Road. They'd left the car in the rear parking lot and the dark-haired girl had gone inside for a few minutes. The young man in the field jacket had waited for her in a new Toyota parked nearby. She'd come out, gotten behind the wheel, and driven out the beltway to a town house complex near Rockville, Maryland. An expensive town house, fairly new, at the end of a cul-de-sac. The Toyota with Maryland plates was parked in the drive.

Part Five

1.

It was after midnight. Cora Pepper lay awake on the bed in the small cottage behind the truck stop, watching the passing lights slide across the low ceiling overhead as the tractor-trailers climbed the grade outside in low gear, bound for North Carolina, or came highballing down the hill, eighteen or twenty-two wheels whining, each to a different chorus, carrying her mind with them as they rolled away. Eyes closed now, she saw the dark hills beyond Knoxville, felt the embrace of the warm cab about her, as comforting as the flannel blankets which covered her, and sleepily followed the headlight beams rolling west along the interstate. Nashville and Memphis would slip by, and then the Mississippi. Ships they were, crossing the continent by night; the dark landscape that engulfed them stretched away like the sea. Dawn would lift like the discovery of landfall. The time Tom Pepper had driven a tractor-trailer from Greenville to Muskogee, Oklahoma, and had taken her with him, she'd gone to sleep on the bunk behind the cab, bathed in greenish-blue light, a sea voyager, a child again, flushed with the excitement of a long-awaited holiday arriving with the morning, and had awakened at dawn among the gray hills of Arkansas. As the miles had sped past that sunny morning, she'd known that this was the kind of life they should have found for themselves while it had still been possible, leaving far behind the ramshackle gas stations and the hole-in-the-wall restaurants that had become their livelihood, their life together.

Her eyes still closed, her mind carried her now beyond Arkansas and Oklahoma to Arizona and California. This was where they should have gone, years earlier, fled in a rig of their own to find some rural community in California or Oregon where they could have begun a truck garden or managed an orange grove, but now the dream dissolved and the sunlight faded. She was once more conscious of her tired body, her aching feet, and the suffocating despondency of her physical and mental exhaustion: *Where would they go now?*

The bed beside her was empty. She opened her eyes to watch again the lights from the trucks sliding across the ceiling. As the high-pitched whine trailed off, she could hear the low sound of the radio in the front room and then, much more sharply, the dry click of bones and her husband's heel and toe taps.

She'd first discovered his eccentric talent years ago when he was living alone in a weed-grown trailer halfway between her lunch counter and Frogtown, but he'd told her to hush up about it. The first time he'd tap-danced for her, they were drinking whiskey alone in his trailer. It was late at night, he had his arm around her, and they were listening to a country music station on the radio. When the disc jockey announced that the next record would be Hank Snow's "Golden Rocket," Tom Pepper had jumped up as if stung by a bee. "You like that record?" he'd asked. "I sure do," she'd told him, and before she knew what was happening, he'd changed his shoes, rolled up his cuffs, and grabbed up a pair of polished spare-rib bones from the shelf behind the radio. The next thing she knew, he was tap-dancing, toes and heels flashing away on the linoleum floor in front of her, dry bones clacking between his fingers at the same time. She'd never seen anything like it. There he was, Tom Pepper, a one-man jamboree, road and minstrel show all rolled into one, dancing away like a madman to Hank Snow's "Golden Rocket."

What'd you think of that?" he'd asked her afterward, red-faced and out of breath, but grinning like a fool.

"I never seen anything like it. I never did. Who learned you all that?"

He'd learned it from a colored man over at the workhouse in Nashville— a check kiter from New Orleans. Tom Pepper was doing ninety days, the colored man six months. Time was heavy on their hands in the evening. "Sixty-five years old, that old man was," Tom Pepper had told her. "Lordy, he could move them feet, faster'n anything I ever saw. His daddy died at a hun'ert an' two, like his daddy before him. You know how come?"

"How come."

"Tap dancing. Keeps you spry, keeps the blood moving, the joints oiled up. Don't give old age a chance to come creeping in. Ain't nowhere for him to go, that's what he told me. You think that's something, wait'll Homer an' Jethro come on. You'll see some sparks a-flying."

"What was you a-doing in the workhouse over in Nashville?" she'd asked suspiciously.

"Ninety days, like I said."

"I'm not talking about that, dummy. How come you was there?"

"Had a fight, busted out a police car winder. Some honky-tonk next

268

door was playing music too loud all night long an' didn't even have no liquor license."

"It's nothing to be proud of," she'd told him. "I don't want to get myself mixed up with any jailbird; any musician, either."

"Hell, I ain't no musician. I ain't no jailbird, neither, not no more. Tap dancing keeps you young, keeps you frisky, draws all the meanness out. . . ."

He'd been right about that. He'd had no more problems with the law. He had no public ambitions; he never danced in front of an audience and had no desire to, although after their marriage and his two bankruptcies, she would sometimes say, "One of these days it'll sure enough come tap-dancing time. You and them skinny legs of yours will be the only thing between us and the poorhouse. And it'll be me a-holding the tin cup. . . ."

She told him the same thing just a week earlier, after the independent gas and diesel fuel distributor had given them notice that he would be reducing his operations and closing down the marginal outlets, like the pumps out front. They'd been expecting the notice for some time. Without the diesel fuel and gasoline, the truck stop would become just another abandoned building at the side of the road, like their other restaurants back in South Carolina and the roadside stand up near Gatlinburg.

She was still awake as the bed groaned, two shoes fell to the floor, and the covers lifted. "Frisky tonight, ain'cha?" Tom Pepper said, trying to tickle her. "All ready to go, ain'cha?"

"Never you mind. Don't be doing that now." She hated being tickled.

"Hot stuff, ain'cha. Gimme some of them covers."

"You go pulling them covers off me, you'll be waking up on the ground outside." She often wondered where he got his energy.

"You'll be waking up with me, then. When anyone puts me in the ground, I'll be taking you with me."

"I'll go too," she said. "You ain't leaving me behind to pay all them bills of yours."

He was still breathing hard, his heart pumping furiously. "Oh, Lordy," he sighed as he settled back. "I'm plumb wore out."

"You'll be having a stroke, you keep up all that foolishness."

"I wasn't doing any foolishness; I got me an idea. Got me an idea an' I was working it out."

"What kind of idea?"

"I knew that'd wake you up. Gotcha in'er'sted, don't I?"

"I heard of some of your ideas," she said without enthusiasm. "It was your ideas got us in all this mess."

"We're gonna put it all behind us. Let loose of that cover. I see you holding on. Gimme some."

"You're gonna jerk it off me."

"No, I ain't. Let loose a little." She relaxed her grip and he sank back again. "Gonna put it all behind us," he vowed, "gonna hit the road. Pack up that truck and hit the road."

"Where to?"

"It was that fella here from Wash'n'ton give me the idea, that fella that was here with Dorsey, remember?"

"The one you wouldn't talk to about Bob Combs, all that meanness he was doing. You oughta be ashamed of yourself."

"Just hold your horses. Just lemme take care of it. So I got me this idea. I gotta whole lot in my head besides just a franchise business, a whole lot in my old filing box too. . . ."

She'd heard him that evening rooting around in the filing cabinet in the office where he kept old records dating back to his Army days, his prison parole after his manslaughter sentence, his years as a car salesman in South Carolina, including his time with Bob Combs.

"So how come you wouldn't talk to this man from Washington?"

"'Cause I'm gonna tell you why. You just listen. Don't go butting in. What we're gonna do is pack up that old van truck and hit the road."

"Where to?" she repeated.

"I'll tell you where to. To someplace where there ain't no hard times, where everyone's got him a gov'ment job, walking around the streets with money to spend. Where they got a whole lot more tourists than that goddamn whiny old bellyaching switchback road out yonder. Listen to it. Goddamn, all night long. . . ."

She heard a truck climbing the grade. "Don't you go talking about that road like that. That road done us a whole lotta good in its time." Her eyes were open and she looked at the ceiling as the lights slid across, down the wall, and then dimmed away, but the singing of the tires still hovered there and her eyes were suddenly warm with tears as she remembered the many years here and the sadness of it all.

"We're gonna leave all this mess behind us soon as we can get packed up. Those pumps close down on Friday night, we'll be closing with them."

She wiped her eyes against the pillow. "You can't just be walking off, leaving all them bills, all those creditors we got."

"Won't be walking off—just a temporary shutdown while we get us

270

some new working capital, get us a new gas and diesel fuel distributor-ship."

"Now I know you're lying," she said.

"I ain't lying!" Tom Pepper cried out in exasperation. He'd been think-ing about the road outside, chained to him all those years, rattling in his sleep, like the leg irons he carried as a penitentiary prisoner working at a granite quarry.

"When you're thinking one thing and telling me another, you're a-lying. You said we was gonna pack up and hit the road, and now you're a-telling me it's just a temporary closedown. Where is it you're wanting to go? Truthful now."

"Somewhere you won't find no hard times like this, where everybody's got him a federal job."

"Must be Kingsport, then," she said with a sigh, "where everyone works for TVA."

Tom Pepper sat bolt upright in bed. "Kingsport! What kinda tomfool dummy would go up to Kingsport to make him some big money! I'm talking big times and you're talking Tennessee dog-scratch! You sure do make me wonder sometimes, Cora, you sure do. I might as well be talking to that mirror on that dresser yonder." He sank back down. "Oh, Lordy me."

"That dresser's paid for. All the ideas you ever get in your head never get paid for. Where is it we're going?" Her eyes were closed. He didn't answer, his back to her, insulted. She waited a few minutes, but he still didn't answer. "Well, that's all right," she said sleepily, rolling to her side. "It must not be very big if you forgot already."

"Wash'n'ton, D.C., that's where we're headed," he declared, turning again to hover over her. "How do you like them apples?"

"Sour and half-baked," she said, the way she always did when the ques-tion came. "You're thinking about Bob Combs and all that trouble he did back in South Carolina; that's what's got you all started up."

"That's only some of it. They got other things up there too, all that gov'ment payroll, all them tourists. We could open up a franchise up there."

She was silent, her eyes still closed. "What kind of a bird is it that don't fly?" she asked finally.

He knew the answer. "What kind do you think?" he said irritably. "The kind you're always asking about, the kind I'm always telling you about. A jailbird."

She waited another minute. "You'd better get them skinny legs of yours a-moving, then," she said sleepily, "dancing up a storm, 'cause with what you're thinking, you're gonna get us both locked up or throwed out in the street."

2.

Ed Donlon and Mary Sifton had been asleep in the bedroom on the second floor of the Georgetown house when he was awakened by the sound of the downstairs door being closed. After a minute he heard Grace Ramsey's light tread on the stairs, heard her passing the half-closed bedroom door and then climbing to the third-floor guest room. The door closed softly and a few minutes later he heard the faint joyful sounds of Mozart.

It was two o'clock in the morning.

He had no idea where she had been. Although he'd adjusted to her mysterious goings and comings, he hadn't reconciled himself to them. She had one or two old friends she occasionally visited until late in the evening—shut-ins, she'd told him—but he wasn't sure who they were or where they lived. She'd gone to the Eastern shore several weeks earlier, the guest of her in-laws, but had returned abruptly early Saturday afternoon, complaining of creaking floors, ugly drafts, and strange water marks on the ceiling above her bed in the old prebellum house.

He foresaw a creeping hypochondria growing toward paralysis, similar to the ailment that had claimed his mother's spinster sister in the old Victorian house in Trenton.

When Mary Sifton was in the house, Grace avoided her and took her meals alone. She ate very little. Her body, once slender and graceful, seemed consumed by some wasting affliction, a dolor as much mental as physical. The brown eyes framed by the pale golden hair were darker than ever, but the face and arms were frail, amphetamine-thin. Her too large dresses and blouses hung on her bony shoulders; her hair had lost its thickness and seemed sparse, even dingy. She began to keep her hair concealed much of the time, even when she was indoors, pushed into an old brown beret. Wearing the beret, her legs encased in thick woolen stockings, like leg warmers, wearing a long skirt, a flowing scarf, cracked leather boots, her lean face almost Tartar-like without make-up, she resembled some fading figure from the stage or the ballet, slightly dotty now as her beauty had withered beyond the glare of the footlights, her face a mask, her thoughts fixed inscrutably upon some mad, manic choreography of her own making.

She sometimes described her outings to Donlon when they had dinner alone, only the newly hired housekeeper in attendance. She visited galleries, attended lectures on every conceivable subject, from El Salvador to Chinese porcelain, went to poetry readings, afternoon chamber music or organ recitals, auctions, performances at the Kennedy Center, or did research on her family genealogy at the Library of Congress.

One afternoon he encountered her by chance among the record shelves at the back of the Book Annex in Georgetown. Her face was turned away and he didn't recognize her. A brown shopping bag was over one arm, a large artist's portfolio under the other. A clerk was watching her curiously and Donlon, too, was attracted by this wild, romantic figure. But then, quite unexpectedly, he was reminded of the old white-haired woman with the grease-stained shopping bag who'd prowled the back alley behind his parochial school in Trenton. Forty years had passed since he'd remembered, but there she was—the derelict with her matted white hair, toothless jaws, and ratty old coat, accompanied by a half-blind brindled bulldog as she picked her way among the refuse cans, Donlon's voice the loudest as they taunted her with a rhyme of his own invention, for which the nun in charge of play period had cuffed his ears:

> Annie Parker! The trashcan queen!
> Bought her face on Haller-ween!

And then Grace Ramsey had turned. Donlon, recognizing the face, fled in confusion.

He'd seen her again without recognizing her as he'd emerged from a tobacco shop on Wisconsin Avenue—a willowy figure sweeping along the sidewalk in front of him. She'd turned into his street and he'd quickened his pace to learn where she lived, only to follow her to his own doorstep.

Roger Buckman, her New York lawyer, had called him three times to ask about her—whom she was seeing, the state of her health, how she was managing her solitude. She'd missed two appointments with a New York surgeon and both were concerned. Her in-laws in Maryland had also telephoned, still perplexed about her sudden departure that Saturday morning. Donlon had tried to reassure all of them, but what could he say?

Cornelia Bowen also pretended concern about Grace, who had accompanied him during his first visit. They'd remained only ten minutes. Grace had announced abruptly that it was time to go, just as he had accepted Cornelia's invitation for a drink. He'd returned alone a week later. Taking leave of Cornelia that night, leaning over her chaise longue, he had given her a fond kiss. Her response had been encouraging enough so that his lips remained in place and his left hand began exploring the scene of the crime twenty-eight years past. The hand moved down her neck and under her dressing gown, curious as to how those contours might have changed after all those decades. They'd changed very little, he discovered, but then the phone had rung, he already had his overcoat on, and so they'd separated. He promised to return. He was still giddy with suspended passion as he reached his front door.

On several occasions he thought Grace Ramsey was on the verge of leaving, although she'd said nothing to him. His clues about her intentions were invariably oblique ones. One evening he heard her talking on the telephone to New York and supposed she'd at last called Roger Buckman. He took the return call himself after Grace had departed for the evening and found himself talking to the manager of a Park Avenue hotel unable to provide her with the numbered suite she'd asked for on the date she'd requested. She had similar conversations with hotel managers in Palm Beach and Nassau. Reviewing his monthly telephone bill, he also discovered that she'd called his wife, Jane, in Connecticut every week and that their talks had been long ones. Her plans became more muddled after she informed him that she had decided to sell the house on the Potomac— sell it at any price. She loathed it and would never set foot in it again. Her principal concern was the volumes from her library. After the transfer company had moved her possessions to a storage vault in Maryland, she spent an afternoon at the warehouse, carefully segregating her books. She returned in a taxi with three heavy cartons of books, which Donlon carried up the stairs to the third floor, not daring to ask her what this latest maneuver meant.

Because of Grace Ramsey, his relations with Mary Sifton had become more difficult. The two women never spoke. Mary Sifton came less frequently. Because he was more and more unwilling to leave the house in Grace's eccentric care—hearth fires left burning, the front door unlocked, the electric range still glowing after an afternoon teakettle had been heated, the tea brewed, and the teapot grown cold—he extended the housekeeper's hours from seven in the morning until seven at night. He now had another feminine presence to contend with. He began missing his gin bottles.

"You're not sleeping with her by any chance?" Mary Sifton asked in annoyance one night on the telephone after he'd told her he wouldn't be accompanying her to a recital at the Library of Congress.

"Don't be ridiculous, for God's sake."

"Then why is she still there?"

"Because it's the only place she has. She always came here when she had a problem."

"She's trying to separate us."

"She isn't. She lives her own life."

"So what's her problem?"

"I don't know but she'll work it out."

"So you just give her free board and room while she does. It's a menagerie over there. Don't you know she's flaky? She could be a pyromaniac, with all those fires she keeps going."

"She doesn't like chilly rooms."

"She's taking advantage of you, Ed. Don't you know that?"

"She's not taking advantage of anyone. She just needs people who care about her the way Jane and I did."

"Jane! Jane's in Connecticut!"

"Maybe so, but in a way she's still here, like Brian. That's what she feels. She's Brian's godmother, I told you that."

"What about her own family?"

"She doesn't have any, just us. How many times do I have to tell you?"

"Even you're beginning to sound a little flaky. Are you drunk?"

So now, convinced that once more Grace had forgotten to turn the night lock on the front door, Donlon slipped from the bed, drew on his flannel bathrobe, and went downstairs. He'd been right. Grace had gone upstairs without even turning the night latch.

"What is it?" Mary Sifton whispered as he padded back to the bed.

"She didn't lock the door."

"That's all?"

"What do you mean, that's all? She didn't lock the door."

"How long have you been up?"

"Just this minute."

She sat up in bed. "Are you sure?" She'd heard the music and was looking overhead. But then the music stopped abruptly and all was silence. "I smell sherry."

"That's gin from last night. Sure I'm sure. What do you think I've been doing?"

"Three guesses."

Upstairs, Grace Ramsey sat in bed, reading Wallace Stevens. The book was one she'd brought from the storage vault that week, an old friend, long sought, long missed, but now returned. It had once stood in the house above the Potomac, a companion from happier times, but now had no other place to claim. It wasn't a book found in airport kiosks, in drugstore racks, or near grocery checkout counters, the merchandise of transit, flight, or forgetfulness. It was an old friend, like Jane Donlon, now in Connecticut, belonging to places of permanence, like this bedroom and this house.

She was conscious of the hour, of the darkness outside, of the two presences downstairs, of other presences here upstairs, even next door, in Brian's old room; and now she felt in communion with them all. Her skin glowed, her mind was luminous, a filament that burned through these enclosing walls as she was absorbed into this old text, expecting the miracle of forgotten incantations, as old as Hecuba, that would restore to her their full power. And so at peace here, vibrant and alive, she found them, and so they did:

> There is nothing until in a single man contained
> Nothing until this named thing nameless is
> And is destroyed. He opens the door of his house
> On flames. The scholar of one candle sees
> An Arctic effulgence flaring on the flame
> Of everything he is. And he feels afraid.

3.

They were celebrating in the hotel suite.

"I figured it would happen," said Artie Kramer. "I'm not a dumdum, but I'm not always wise about how the feds work. I figured it would happen, just like Pete said it would. I feel pretty good about it. Don't you feel good about it, babe?"

"Yeah, I feel real good," Rita said dryly.

"You don't look it. Do you think she looks it, Chuckie?"

"She looks it," Chuckie said, refilling his champagne glass. "How about some more bubbly, Mr. Strykker?"

"Have some more, Nat. Forget about your ulcer. It'll pick you up, that cold you got."

Strykker mutely held out his glass. He sat on the edge of the damask chair, the puff of henna-colored hair electric in the lamplight, his chocolate-colored suit sharply pressed, the cuffs flared over the patent-leather shoes. A moment before, a vial had been plugged into the socket of his left nostril, lifted there by a plump hand, the other hand pressing delicately on his left eardrum, but now the vial was back in his pocket.

"You look sad, Nat," Artie Kramer continued. "I told you it'd work out this way, just like Pete said."

"I'm happy for you, Artie. An assistant secretary—who'd have thought it?"

"I called my old lady down in Miami soon as the White House called. She wanted to know when I was going to be on TV."

"We were all rooting for you, Artie," Edelman said, getting to his feet.

away at the long auburn strands, cropping them silently in a jagged fringe just below her ears.

4.

"You have some new information," Fred Merkle asked dryly from behind his desk, "or is this another fishing expedition?" The gray afternoon light from Constitution Avenue flooded through the window behind Fred's chair, fracturing Haven Wilson's concentration and dissolving Merkle's bony face in a haze of silver grays, like the glare from a sun-glazed pond. Conscious of the annoyance, which gave Wilson a sleepy, puzzled look, Merkle turned to rotate the blinds and turn on his desk lamp.

"Both," Wilson said from the brown leather chair in front of the desk. "A couple of weeks ago, I mentioned a name to you. Artie Kramer, a Caltronics officer. I just heard he's been given a political appointment."

"So I heard. The announcement was made yesterday."

"You're not pleased."

Merkle shrugged indifferently. "Not my bailiwick. Is that what you wanted to talk about?" His face seemed tired.

"I suppose that means the case against Caltronics is now closed."

"You could interpret it that way."

"And if it's closed, maybe you can answer a question that's been bothering me. A loose end that won't go away."

"What's the question?"

"It's about Morris, the Caltronics salesman who managed the Washington office, the guy that disappeared. Was he the bribery suspect?"

Merkle looked away, rolling an old-fashioned barrel pen between his white fingers. "I seem to recall that he was," he said, frowning as if recalling a fragment of ancient history.

"A possible witness too?" Merkle didn't answer, but Wilson hadn't expected him to. "I understand that when he disappeared he had a hundred thousand dollars with him."

Merkle considered the question thoughtfully and finally nodded, still looking away toward the far window. "He made some substantial withdrawals the week before he left. Whether he had the money with him when he disappeared isn't clear."

"Has Caltronics brought charges?"

"They say they intend to. Embezzlement, conversion, I'm not sure. The auditors disagree on how much money's missing, and that seems to be holding up legal action."

"Tell me something about Bernie Klempner," Wilson continued. He watched Merkle turn to him, surprised. "Where does he fit in?"

"I'd rather not get into that, Haven."

"You got us together once. You arranged that meeting outside."

"Call it poor judgment," Merkle acknowledged with a weak smile. "We were getting no place officially. I thought by going out of channels, I could make things happen. They didn't."

"I hear Klempner's got a hunting license. What he bags, you'll look at, and vice versa. An informal arrangement."

Merkle got up from the desk, opened the blinds again, looked down into the street, and then joined Wilson in an adjacent leather chair in front of the desk. "Bernie can sometimes be very useful. He has a special talent for operating in those gray areas—those gray areas where the law leaves off and litigation begins." He smiled suddenly. "That's a sure sign of old age. More and more when I dictate these days, I have a queer feeling that I'm quoting someone. Most often I am. Myself, twenty years ago. The euphemist of the criminal division subculture." He smiled again in self-deprecation.

"You mean Bernie can break the law and you can't."

"That's well put too," he acknowledged. "Cynicism is the cross we all bear these days."

"Has Bernie ever taken a dive?"

Merkle looked sharply at Wilson. "Bernie? Oh, Lord, no. Never."

"You're sure?"

"Absolutely. He's one of the few people I trust without reservation. That's not to say he doesn't always look or act above suspicion, but that's been his advantage. The wrong kind do trust him—always. Why do you ask?"

"Morris disappears with all this money in his briefcase. Klempner has him staked out from next door and doesn't know a thing. That's a little odd, isn't it?"

"Not odd at all. That can be explained."

"So how useful was he on this Caltronics case?"

"Nothing has quite worked out on this Caltronics case," Merkle said, rising restlessly. "But Bernie's no more to blame than anyone else." He moved again to the window.

"So Klempner does have a hunting license."

"Does that look like snow? I haven't put on my snow tires yet. I think it does look like snow. Awfully early, isn't it?" He turned back to his desk, still standing as he sorted through the memos on his blotter. "Caltronics just dried up, Haven. It happens all the time. Investigations go nowhere and you move on to more important things. We could never get the Nixon administration to move on organized crime, remember? Every administration brings in its own priorities. These days it's drugs and they're borrowing from our budget to get it moving. That's something people don't think about. The budget problem."

Wilson stood up. "I understand."

"When you've got a budget crisis, you put your assets to work where you can get the best results—cost efficiency, you see." He lifted a memo from his desk and pondered it with mock seriousness. "The fact is we've got too small a staff and too many investigations, too big a backlog. Supply-side investigations, you might say. The cost-efficient wash."

"You mean you had a little political heat from upstairs," Wilson said. "Do me a favor, Fred."

"I'll do what I can, but don't misunderstand, Haven. We didn't make that Caltronics case. Nothing we could take to a grand jury."

"Do me a favor anyway. Call Klempner and tell him about our talk today. Everything. Even my suspicions about his taking a dive. Tell him that worried you a little—"

"Are you serious?"

"I'm serious. Just do it and then maybe we can roll this thing up the right way. That's what you want, isn't it?"

Chuck Larabee's office was on the third floor of an old building on K Street. The three small rooms behind the pebbled-glass door were dim with the imperfect light leaking in through unwashed windows overlooking the building's center well. The smell of boiled coffee from a morning percolator still stained the air.

Larabee was out and his elderly secretary thought it doubtful that he would return—it was then after five. But Wilson was curious about his office and accepted her invitation to wait in a leather chair just inside Larabee's office door. She was nearly seventy. Her hair was as thin and dry as milkweed, tinted a curious color that might have been a powder-puff peach or tangerine; her face was soft and downy, and she wore nursing home shoes. She had that air of sweet fatuity and senile incompetence that he associated with long-retired government secretaries of a long-vanished era, brought out of a tiny apartment at the far edge of Connecticut Avenue for some small salary to complement a smaller pension.

She had been busy as he arrived, standing at the side of her desk as she painstakingly copied names from an aerospace industry catalogue onto three-by-five cards. She had no idea what purpose it served, except that Mr. Larabee wanted it done, and her uncertainty only increased her ineptitude. She gossiped through the door as she worked, something no efficient secretary could have managed, and she managed very poorly. During the fifteen minutes he was there she managed to complete only three cards. She lost her place in the catalogue, forgot the page number, misplaced her glasses, which she removed every time she pursued a new train of thought, couldn't locate the cards she'd already filled out, and dropped her pen on the floor. When Wilson retrieved it from under the desk, she told him his shoes needed resoling.

She talked to him of the old Agriculture Department, romaine lettuce at the supermarket, pets in apartments, and dark muggers in darker hallways. As he listened, he left the chair to study the plaques, citations, and framed pictures that decorated the walls of Larabee's small office. Painted plaster of paris or wooden ship medallions hung there, the kind passed out by U.S. naval vessels in foreign ports. There were framed CINCPAC citations, letters of appreciation from South Korean officials, a testimonial from a Thai general, warm messages from congressmen and senators he'd escorted through the souvenir shops of Seoul or Hong Kong, a certificate of attendance at a Vandenberg AFB missile launch, and a diploma from the Industrial College of the Armed Forces.

Larabee's deserted desk was stacked high with *Congressional Records* and old *Early Birds*, the Pentagon morning news sheet. Behind the desk was a typing table, and behind that, a small telex.

The other wall was covered with photographs, most of them group photographs, taken at a number of installations abroad or aboard U.S. vessels in foreign waters. Some were signed, many weren't; the majority had been taken by U.S. Navy or government photographers. There was Larabee with various congressmen on the flight decks of U.S. aircraft carriers, with touring senators, on the steps of American embassies, Larabee on the tarmac of foreign airfields in front of Air Force 707s ferrying junketing groups from the Armed Services or Foreign Relations Committee.

"I just don't know if he's coming back or not, Mr. Wilson," the secretary informed him from the door as she pinned on her hat. "He's probably gone to the health club across the street, the way he does." She gave him the name.

"Do you happen to know his telex number?" he asked as he opened the office door.

She didn't know. He seldom used it and kept the key locked up.

But it was the memory of those photographs that Wilson carried with him as he stood outside, looking for a cab. He'd never understood it, even recognized it, until that afternoon as he stood in Chuck Larabee's office. Perhaps this was because he'd been so much a part of it himself. It was all there, a chronicle of these past three decades—of this city that sent its emissaries out year after year, session after session, sent out its mercantilists of arms, aid, goodwill, and evangelism, all fanning out across the globe like circuit riders or drummers, these self-proclaimed experts who were once small-town pharmacists, lawyers, oilmen, staff aides, or astronauts, their briefing books filled with facts, their heads swollen with sanctimonious self-importance, small-town virtue, and courthouse democracy, Chautauqua-circuit busybodies and pettifogs carrying their instruction to Malaysians, Arabs, Turks, Chinese, Koreans, Afghans, blacks, and Indians, and on behalf of whom? For an American people whose deepest instincts were not for politics but the escape from politics.

5.

The headline of the Top Secret DIA daily intelligence summary appearing that morning stunned its readership and shocked the higher echelons of the Pentagon, who thought the innermost mysteries of their sanctum sanctorum secure from the laity. Staff aides and secretaries scurried for cover. The switchboards in the executive offices in the A ring lit up as subordinates called in, seeking guidance. Phones jangled through B, C, and D rings as the news spread. Cries of recrimination vibrated through the closed doors of the highest offices, and for a few hours that morning the building oscillated like some sedate old Italian opera house rung by a cacophonous twelve-tone premiere.

"Well, just how in the goddamned hell did he get there?" cried a deputy secretary to his senior aide after one such meeting. "Whoever's responsible, get him up here!"

"Do you realize what was on the President's desk this morning?" a livid White House counselor asked a senior Defense official at nine-twelve. "Do you have any idea what was waiting on his desk? Now that he's got it in his mind, how do you expect us to get it out? He's got a press conference tomorrow!"

The White House had received twenty copies; so had the National Security Council, State, CIA, a handful of House and Senate committees, OMB, and Treasury.

"Damage control, that's the main thing," counseled a nervous Pentagon press spokesman, perplexed by the tumult about him, but his bafflement was characteristic. He had a smooth voice and a pleasant delivery, but he knew little about arms control issues. Before his appointment he'd been a publicist for a Houston mobile home manufacturer.

On the floor below, Leyton Fischer had taken his copy of the DIA daily intelligence summary from his in box, preparing to cast it aside immediately, as he usually did, when a lurid banner headline, *New York Post* style, caught his eye. He blinked, paused for a minute, moved his eyes to the window, blinked again, and let his eyes creep back to the bold red type. No, it was still there. The headline read:

32,159TH NUCLEAR WARHEAD OPTION TARGETED!
PENTAGON POINTILLISTS PAINT OUT PEVEK!
HERRING CANNERY IS 32,159TH!

The text of the story identified the Soviet target just assigned the U.S. strategic nuclear arsenal by the Strategic Target Planning Staff. Pevek was an isolated Russian community on the Kamchatka peninsula in the Bering Sea. The small herring plant on the Shelekhov Gulf employed thirty-five workers, but because some of the tinned product was supplied to the Soviet Navy, the Strategic Target Planning Staff had assigned the 32,159th nuclear target option to the antiquated Pevek herring works and the nearby Pevek boat repair shed, which employed twelve workers.

The story in the DIA summary lifted the secrecy from a subject only a very few were privy to. The shortage of legitimate military and industrial targets in the Soviet Union when compared with the size of the U.S. strategic nuclear arsenal had long been an embarrassment to those few officials who were aware of the Pentagon's bookkeeping problem. There were simply too few legitimate targets for an arsenal that was multiplying like kudzu grass.

The dilemma had been best expressed a few months earlier by an Air Force general, a member of the Strategic Target Planning Staff whose responsibility was to identify military and industrial targets in the U.S.S.R. and Eastern Europe for U.S. strategic nuclear warheads. His remarks, to Leyton Fischer's astonishment, were inserted at the bottom of the second paragraph.

"Goddammit," he'd told a recently assigned STPS staff member who'd expressed amazement at the imbalance of targets and nuclear warheads. "Do you think any U.S. postmaster in his right mind would open up five hundred more post offices in Arkansas tomorrow just because Congress gave him this big new budget to spend and it was the congressman from Arkansas that did it? Hell, no; he'd turn back the money. But you put a little political heat on him, like the kind of heat we've got, and by God he'd find them right quick—put a post office right up beside every gas pump, cow pasture, and bass pond in Arkansas if he had to. That's all we're doing, in a manner of speaking, with those warheads—just delivering the U.S. mail."

If only a few senior officials were aware of the problem, even fewer were sensitive to it. Like every other national security issue of existential importance—whether the Soviet Union had in fact achieved strategic parity, whether the Soviet SS-18 and SS-19 ICBMs were as accurate as those handful who understood their own logarithmic proof claimed, whether the Soviet civil defense effort was a primitive Muscovy reflex or a sinister Politburo calculation, whether the MX missile was a counterforce weapon or a first-strike killer—the dilemma was hidden behind a veil of secrecy so impenetrable that only a few were aware of it. In addition, the U.S. SIOP, or nuclear targeting plan, was couched in technical jargon so opaque that the physical nature of a given Soviet or East European target was further concealed from recognition. Like obscurantist high priests or existential theologians, the technicians seemed intent upon bamboozling not only others but themselves.

The DIA daily intelligence summary had lifted the cloak of concealment from the sixteen most recently selected targets. The Pevek "Soviet Naval Stores Resupply Facility—SN-16" was in fact the antiquated Pevek herring works, a ramshackle wooden structure with a tin roof, employing thirty-five civilian workers. The other targets recently added to the U.S. SIOP included a milk factory in Uzbekistan, an NCO rest and recuperation center nearby, and two truck deicing sheds in the Siberian Arctic—all of them now fresh new dots on that canvas of the Soviet Union and Eastern Europe reaching from the NATO frontier to the Bering Sea, dotted in with hues of varying megatonnage, like a pointillist's finished painting, and which, one day touched with fire, would strip-mine the Soviet Union from Minsk to Sakhalin.

But that wasn't all Leyton Fischer found. Even more alarming was an article on the second page, announcing the triumph of the new U.S. strategic doctrine implicit in a November National Security Decision Directive signed just recently at the White House. Was the latter aware of its import? The anonymous author seemed to be. DETERRENCE OFFICIALLY BURIED! the banner announced. The article that followed explained the new strategy, based not upon the intellectually bankrupt deterrence deadlock, whose sophistries had long since been exhausted, but on unequivocal U.S. superiority. Once the U.S. nuclear edge was reclaimed, the strategic arsenals that had formerly been the inert guardians of national survival would be converted into instruments of political power—"leverage," in the White House lexicon. The passive U.S. Minuteman missiles—"fixed like some clumsy woolly mammoth in the heroic but futile reactive mode of a bygone ice age"—would be replaced by the MX missile, the centerpiece of the new strategy, a foraging first-strike killer. Soviet adventurism would be a lonely swimmer in the uncertain seas inhabited by this cruising great white shark—predatory, unpredictable, and ruthlessly malevolent, like the D-5 submarine-launched missile soon to follow.

Leyton Fischer read on, hypnotized by the analysis, dumbfounded by the details cribbed from internal DOD memoranda, staff studies, and closely held options papers for the Secretary, which he'd heard rumors of but never examined. The second-page essay made crystal clear what had long been denied by the Pentagon and others in their speeches and congressional testimony: the new strategic game plan was only the old containment policy, now brought up to date on a scale impossible to imagine— the conversion of nuclear and conventional superiority into effective political power, coercive if need be. *Was it true?* It seemed difficult to deny. The language was bizarre.

On the third page was an article describing a series of Soviet missile test failures for the Mod-4 ten-warhead SS-18 and SS-19 ICBMs, supplying details long suppressed by DIA's special-watch group. By then, Leyton Fischer had guessed who was responsible for the articles.

A fourth-page feature was more mundane. Entitled MISSILE MAKERS PENETRATE PENTAGON, it listed the names of senior planners and strategists recruited by the Pentagon from the defense and aerospace industries since the last election, particularly those who'd played the most aggressive role in drawing up the new $1.6 trillion Pentagon budget. Their previous associations were news to no one. What was incredible were the verbatim phone conversations cited in the article, obtained from either FBI phone taps or NSA intercepts, describing their attempts at sabotaging the comprehensive test ban treaty and SALT II. Three conversations described tactics for removing certain individuals from the Geneva test ban talks and the SALT II delegation. In one conversation, a hawkish Senate aide and a senior ACDA official had described leaking sensitive intelligence reports in an attempt to derail the congressional prospects for SALT II, an effort made moot by Afghanistan in any case.

The aide was Les Fine.

In a corner of the back page was a small box, bordered in black, like an obituary, entitled BRIMSTONE CHRISTIANS JOIN BEGIN'S NEW IRGUN IN BURYING ARMS CONTROL. Les Fine was again mentioned as the Likud's agent in Washington strategy sessions.

Leyton Fischer was puzzled. Brimstone Christians he could understand, but he'd never heard the phrase "New Irgun." What did the author mean—that Les Fine was an ideological agent or simply a Zionist fellow traveler of Menachem Begin's fanatical right wing?

Still incredulous, he'd turned back to the front page, when the door opened and Les Fine stood there, holding the DIA summary, barely able to speak, his eyes glowing, like Iago's Moor.

"There's a madman—a madman at work—" His lips were white. He still held out the DIA daily summary in his small white waxen hand. "He has phone taps—intercepts. Blood libel—"

Blood libel? Hardly possible, Fischer thought, convinced he knew who was responsible for the morning edition of the DIA summary.

The man was Nick Straus, and his intentions were not to shock the higher echelons but to educate them. Straus had also known that many of those details would be leaked.

In the DIA daily summary suite, the old civil servant sat propped like a cadaver in front of his staff, minus Nick Straus. On the desk in front of him was a mock-up of the daily intelligence brief as he'd prepared it the previous day. Next to it, its headlines as obscenely lurid as when he'd first seen them that morning, was the tabloid copy as it had been delivered to the basement printing press the evening before. There was no resemblance between the two. There was also no doubt as to who had made the substitution, who had inserted his own copy for theirs, who was responsible for the entire treasonous edition. He was the first man to arrive each morning, the last to depart each night, whispering away down the corridor on his rubber-soled shoes as if no one were there at all. He had remained behind to deliver the DIA copy to the printer the previous night, had remained to edit the galleys, and had even lingered to oversee the first press run.

"Did anyone actually see him preparing the copy?" asked the old chief. On the glass-topped desk in front of him was an apothecary's glazed bottle of colorless liquid, from which he was daubing with a cotton swab the eczematous ooze on the backs of his hands. In the last hour, it had freshened to the brightness of a second-degree burn.

"No, sir."

"Deliver it?"

"No, sir."

Across the way, Nick Straus was returning to his secretary's desk with the morning telegrams from the message center. He'd spent a restless night, dreading the morning confrontation, but now, distracted by the sudden vacuum around him, he felt an easing of his qualms. He hadn't been invited to the meeting taking place in the director's office, but knew its purpose. The phones had been ringing without interruption for two hours, the old man had twice left the office at a trot, summoned on high, and no one had dared look in his direction. The CIA, the State Department, the National Security Council, and a handful of Senate staffers had called to ask for extra copies of the morning edition containing information so sensitively classified that none of them had ever seen it before, but no copies were available. All remaining copies had been confiscated and attempts were under way to reclaim and shred those already distributed. Futile efforts had been made to locate the night-duty supervisor at the basement printing shop, but his shift was over. A D.C. taxi driver in his spare time, he'd already taken to the streets and was en route to Dulles with two fares.

In all this, Nick Straus continued to be ignored. Despite the slamming doors, the jangling phones, the whispered conferences, and the scurrying figures, no one even glanced in his direction. He was mystified. Was it that he was no longer clothed or that he no longer existed? No, he was there, clothed as usual—flesh and spirit both. Was it then that they felt themselves naked? Were they embarrassed for themselves rather than him, or humiliated on his account, sparing him the mortification of acknowledging through eye contact what they knew he felt? Or was it that they pitied him?

Only after silent reflection did he understand what had happened. They were sparing themselves. It was self-discovery they were avoiding in averting their eyes, ignoring him because they had been betrayed and were ashamed, not because their emperors had no clothes but because they all had no clothes, ten thousand Pentagon faithful scurrying about in this frantic state of infantile nudity because for a few precious hours someone had stolen their secrets. But new clothes were on the way, the error would be undone, and by noon they would all be decently clad again.

They were like middle-aged patrons fleeing a raid on a promiscuous massage parlor or a homosexual Turkish bath, he decided. The Pentagon a massage parlor? No, that wasn't it. Yet the thought remained. It was true. The drapes are pulled down, the shades flung up, the windows and doors flung open to passing view, and this is what you discover—intelligent, loyal, decent, middle-aged men doing these wicked, disgraceful, obscene things. They should be ashamed. A farmer in Kansas would be ashamed, a druggist in Oregon, an assemblyman in New York, a cotton broker in Memphis—they would all be ashamed.

In his small cubicle he sadly called Ida and said he would be home early. He told her to go to the hairdresser's and get a nice permanent. They were going out to dinner.

"Sometimes you make my hair curl as it is," she said. "I don't need a permanent. Tell me now."

"I have decided to live a more productive life. Today is the beginning. Man and conscience are joined. Nick is Straus."

He began to clean out his drawers. Thirty minutes later, two Pentagon security officials appeared in the suite. The old civil servant conferred with them in a whisper and then joined Nick Straus alone in his office. As he sat down slowly in the chair opposite Nick's desk, Nick knew the man's accusatory brief was fully prepared: he looked the more guilty.

"I take it you've seen the morning summary," he inquired with bland deception, scratching the backs of his hands. Nick detected the odor of formaldehyde. He knew the subject would be approached in painfully oblique fashion, as with the secretary who'd burned up the automatic coffeemaker, just as he knew the denouement would be tortuously melodramatic for the benefit of those outside. He meant to dry up the old reprobate's fustian juices before they reached operatic pitch.

"Yes, I did," Nick said modestly. "As a matter of fact, I wrote it myself." The old jaw dropped like a cormorant's. "That's right, I wrote it, wrote it all, every word."

The old man sagged forward, but Nick suspected he was gathering himself for another swoop. *"Wrote it all?"* he whispered with staggering slowness.

"Every word. The material upon which it's based is all in the special-watch safe—"

"In the safe?" His breath seemed to have stopped, his metabolism shocked into some ancient, Galápagos-tortoise pace, another time dimension entirely.

"I meant to include among the newest SIOP targets the army button factory on the Dnieper, but I thought I'd made my point—"

"Button factory!" The words left a faint fog of saliva on the air. It was all the old man could do to lift his trembling hand toward Nick Straus. *"You're under arrest,"* he whispered. He tried to arise, seemed about to slip to his knees, but then grasped the doorknob to keep from falling. *"He's under arrest,"* he gasped, riding the swinging door backward, out of the room. *"He's under arrest. . . ."*

Nick was taken by the two agents to an office in Pentagon security. Forms were filled out, his plastic identification badge was taken from him, and he was escorted upstairs to Leyton Fischer's suite, where two senior DIA officers and the DIA deputy counsel were waiting.

After an hour of questioning, Nick was released and asked to return in two days with his attorney.

By then the contents of the DIA morning summary were being hastily reproduced by Xerox machines in intelligence offices all over Washington in advance of the DIA recall. In the Intelligence and Research watch center on the seventh floor at State, the original copies had been confiscated, but too late—Xeroxed duplicates were already circulating in the offices of the Soviet and Eastern European analysts, many of whom had long been suspicious of the Pentagon's nuclear targeting policy. Across the building on another corridor, in policy and plans, State's own think tank, foreign service officers and administration appointees were gathered around the office's single copy, anxiously trying to unravel the Pentagon and White House conceptual puzzle that had left them in the dark for ten months. The same curiosity brought office routine to a temporary halt in a few rooms at the CIA, NSA, and the National Security Council. A little after eleven o'clock, a Top Secret précis of the DIA morning brief was left behind in the White House press room by the acting press spokesman, prepared to deal with any questions that might arise—they would stonewall it, they'd decided—but the memo was quickly recovered. No questions were asked.

At a meeting at the same hour in the Executive Office Building, an NSC staffman was meeting with a congressional legislative assistant. He'd arrived out of breath, five minutes late, just returned from studying a copy of the DIA document.

"Some GS-16 over at DIA popped his fuse this morning," he began by way of apology, "flipped his lid and blew a whole list of nuclear warhead targets. A lot of other sensitive stuff too."

"Who was he?"

"I dunno; some crazy from the DIA daily summary staff—went ape, they say. Paranoid, been under a psychiatrist's care. Used to work at CIA, probably had a few grudges."

"Any possibility of getting a copy?"

"A guy from the *New York Times* asked me the same thing. No, not unless you've got a Top Secret clearance, that or a friend who does. What's on your mind this morning?"

"I was wondering how the El Salvador military package is shaping up. The congressman would like to see something he could support."

"Yeah, well, we cleaned it up a little. The claymore mines are still in, but we've taken out the white phosphorus grenades, a few antipersonnel weapons—the baddies. So I think now it's a package we can all get behind, a real bipartisan Christmas tree, you know what I mean?"

6.

Haven Wilson had drafted a few pages of preliminary recommendations concerning the Center's reorganization, including the names of those scholars or associates who should be replaced. It was this list that gave him the most difficulty. He had reluctantly concluded that Dr. Foster should go, so should Dr. Pauline Rankin, so should Dr. Dobler and his two associates at the thalamus laboratory, so should Dr. Coswell, the disarmament scholar who'd left a briefcase containing sensitive documents on the

Metro. Included among them was the only draft of the sole study he'd written in eleven months.

Wilson had reviewed his recommendations with Ed Donlon one afternoon during lunch and Donlon, over a third martini, had agreed. He told Wilson that the Center's collection of scholars reminded him of a House of David baseball team he'd seen play at Princeton during his senior year, all bearded, like Hebrew prophets—"a collection of foul balls, freaks, and fungoes," Donlon had told him, "not good enough for the minors and not ready to get a shave and go to work someplace, like the rest of us, so that's all they were, a traveling circus, like the Center over there."

Donlon had spent the remainder of lunch trying to recall the names of the Princeton baseball team that year, who the captain was, who were the football lettermen on that team, who'd scored the winning touchdown in the Yale Bowl that November at New Haven, and whether he was now a Chicago insurance executive or a Red Bank lawyer. Donlon told him the names of the Princeton single-wing backfield that year with mystical reverence, leaning drunkenly over the table, eyes lit by the mythical recollections of those burnished, innocent autumn afternoons.

Wilson left the luncheon more concerned about Ed Donlon and his midday drinking habits than about the future of the Center.

He also discussed his initial recommendations with Angus McVey, who'd begun to appear more regularly at the Center now that Dr. Foster had moved back to his old office. Wilson didn't give McVey his draft, but instead talked in a general way about his findings and mentioned a few names. McVey seemed uneasy. Although it was a foregone conclusion that Dr. Foster was not the man for the directorship, he thought that Foster had made a place for himself. His testimony before the House subcommittee had attracted a good deal of notice, not only in the Washington press and the wire services, but in a flood of requests for copies of his testimony and dozens of invitations from various organizations around the country, inviting him to lecture. A handful of congressmen had been impressed and a New York Democrat had introduced his statements into the *Congressional Record* with the observation that Dr. Foster's characterization of U.S. attitudes toward the Soviet Union as "ratomorphic" would become part of the currency of "nuclearspeak."

The fact that Dr. Foster's comments on behaviorism and foreign policy had attracted so much notice owed much to their apparent novelty, but some credit was also given to two stories that appeared coincidentally in the *Washington Post* on the day following his testimony.

One described the misfortune of a nuclear missile mechanic at Grand Forks Air Force Base in North Dakota. Enrolled in a Minuteman missile class, he'd been shocked to discover that U.S. nuclear targeting policy included a first-strike option. According to Jack Anderson, the Air Force instructor had told his class that turning the missile ignition key should become a "Pavlovian reflex," and those so trained "should salivate at the very thought of such an opportunity." By the end of the second week of instruction, the Air Force was aware of the young man's reservations about the first-strike option. Asked by an instructor whether he had any reservations about turning the missile ignition switch—the Pavlovian reflex—the young mechanic admitted he did. He was immediately dismissed from the class, sent to a psychiatrist, and assigned other duties, principally at the base golf course, retrieving from the high grass errant golf balls, dispatched there by off-duty Air Force officers whose enthusiasm overpowered their aim, like those who'd targeted the Pevek herring factory.

In the *Post* headlines the same day appeared the following announcement:

HAIG SAYS U.S. PUT LIBYAN LEADER QADDAFI "BACK IN HIS BOX"

Rereading the quotations from his testimony in the *Washington Post*, Dr. Foster was amazed at his remarks. In retrospect, he had little recollection of what he had said or how he had said it: only the primal drive for self-expression was recalled. He remembered more vividly his profound physical discomfort—his dry mouth, his drooping shorts, and his flushed, burning face—yet there it was:

> We've become the pathological prisoners of these stockpiles. We've finally succeeded as a nation in conditioning ourselves to that same primitive, unreflective, ratomorphic psychology we once assigned the Soviet leadership.

How was it possible? He had said that? A man was able to speak the truth once or twice in his lifetime, and he supposed, almost sadly, that his time had come. The fact that the media, too, seemed to vibrate mysteriously with these same hidden truths about the national psyche seemed to confirm it. Reading the stories about the Minuteman missile mechanic at Grand Forks Air Force Base and the return of the Libyan leader to his behaviorist box by the global psychologist Dr. Haig, Foster decided that these emanations weren't so coincidental after all, but were ghostly percolations from some deep underground source. He was, he decided, much more Jungian than Freudian in his psychohistorical research.

But neither psychological pioneer told him which persona to choose in facing his future—a loud, bold, occasionally vulgar public voice, like that he'd heard on the steps of the Rayburn Building, or a faint, dim, shrinking private one? As guest lecturer and opinionmaker, he would have to choose.

Angus McVey had been equally elusive about Pauline Rankin's future. The fact that the Lenin letters were forgeries didn't bother him in the slightest. "Oh, yes," he told Wilson. "I was very suspicious of the Lenin letters at first and was even warned against them by a few scholars, but even so, they intrigued me. The fact that they might be forgeries seems beside the point. It's not so much what was intended but what was created, isn't it? They exist, don't they? I mean, someone created them. The universe itself might have been created in such a way, mightn't it?—a poor joke, you see—but so long ago that we're now spared from thinking about it. Other interpretations have come along since, in any case. At this point, the question of their authenticity is beside the point—like Pauline's relationship to these letters. I don't suppose it matters to me in the slightest that they're forgeries. Do you see?"

Wilson didn't see—he'd never before heard McVey speak in quite this way—but he conceded the point, aware for the first time that Angus McVey's version of the Center differed fundamentally from his own.

"Besides," McVey had added wearily, "I rather prefer those patchily educated in some ways, indifferent to the daily headlines. Where else could they go?"

Pauline Rankin's reaction was much more dramatic. Wilson had shown her the analysis by the Soviet specialist at the Library of Congress and they'd talked about it. He suggested that since the Lenin letters were probably forgeries she might take a fresh look at her project—Feminism as the Font of Bolshevism—and recast it in another form. Dr. Foster, for example, had recommended that rather than a historical work, funded by the Center, she think in terms of something more liberal, say a project financed by the National Endowment for the Arts.

She'd lost her temper.

"For what? A ballet, something in blank verse! What are you talking about?" Tears of indignation shone in her usually calm eyes. "Why do you believe these so-called Soviet experts? Do you know who they are? They're all Poles, Middle Europeans, Russian émigrés, Slavic chauvinists! Of course they'd claim the letters are forged—what would you expect them to say! It's a closed male society, like the Center!"

She'd gone out, slamming the door.

Billy O'Toole was another Center employee Wilson had worried about, although his work was with the ground crew. After Pauline Rankin's arrival, he seemed to spend a great deal of time in and around her office— painting, waxing, washing windows, sweeping, running errands for her. But Billy, as if forewarned, had disappeared a few weeks later, after handing in his resignation.

A few weeks after that, the receptionist at the front desk had reported seeing him in a supermarket out on Connecticut Avenue near Pauline Rankin's apartment, pushing a shopping cart through the aisles. He seemed quite preoccupied with his new domestic tasks, buying groceries for two from a penciled list, wearing a white houseman's jacket.

7.

A light snow had begun falling that Friday afternoon, swept from the roadbeds by the passing cars like white dust. A faint accumulation was visible on the sidewalks and the circular drive as Wilson and Buster Foreman entered Potomac Towers.

"What the hell is it with you, Wilson?" Klempner asked softly, rising from behind his metal desk, where he'd been waiting since three. He'd been to see Fred Merkle that morning and had twice called Wilson, who had been meeting with Nick Straus and unable to see him. "Why all this poking around? You on some kind of crusade because some shithead lawyer from Utah got your job over at Justice? What are you trying to prove? What the hell's going on?"

Wilson introduced Buster Foreman. The strawberry blonde who'd shown them in went out, got her coat and purse, and left by the front door.

"What did Merkle tell you?" Wilson asked. An electric heater was plugged in on the floor near the desk. The large room beyond was gray with afternoon shadow.

"He said you were asking about Morris, asking about me. He said maybe I'd better talk to you, that you were onto something."

Wilson sat looking at the calendar that hung on the wall behind a file cabinet. Two FBI achievement awards were framed nearby. "You were in the FBI Atlanta field office, I remember."

"Yeah, twice. So what?"

"You ever get up to South Carolina?"

"A couple of times. Why?"

"You knew the Combs crowd back in those days—Combs, Shy Wooster?" Wilson was still studying the calendar.

"I heard about them, everyone did. How come you're asking?"

"Did you ever run into someone named Smooter Davis? A black man, used to hang around Bob Combs's car lot."

Wilson could hear the traffic passing on the boulevard below, a door slamming someplace, then the steady creak of Bernie Klempner's leather-upholstered chair as he sat slowly forward. "What the shit is it with you two?" he asked softly. "What the hell are you after? Smooter Davis? What the hell you come in here talking about Smooter Davis for?"

"You knew him?"

"Yeah, I knew him. So what? What are you asking?"

"If you knew Smooter Davis," Buster said.

"Yeah, I knew him, I told you. He worked for me in South Carolina—under cover. An informant. What the hell business is it of yours?"

"What happened to him?"

"Nothing happened, nothing except he blew it. They scared him off. I got him a job in Tucson, working for the office out there. What's this all about?"

"Where is he now?"

"How the hell do I know? Last time I heard, he had this big beer distributorship in Oakland, a couple of bars. Doing real well. Why?"

"You ever hear him talk about a Birdie Jackson down in South Carolina?" Buster asked.

"Birdie Jackson? No." Klempner glanced at Buster suspiciously, then back at Wilson. "Why? Should I?"

"A black lady, had a little house next to the Combs lot. It burned down."

"So why are you asking me?"

"She thought Combs and Shy Wooster burned it," Buster said. "She said Smooter Davis saw them do it."

"What are you two up to, anyway?" Klempner demanded. "You get Fred Merkle all hot and bothered about this eighty thousand Morris disappeared with, like he's beginning to think maybe I got a cut of it, and then you show up here asking me about Smooter Davis. I got a reputation to protect, a business. What the hell are you trying to do—make me look bad?"

"We're interested in Bob Combs," Buster said. "We heard you used to keep tabs on Combs when you were with the FBI."

"Sure I did. I kept tabs on a lot of people."

"Smooter Davis was your informant—"

"I told you that—"

"Only he sees Combs and Wooster burn down this house in South Carolina back in '59 and you don't remember anything about it. That figures. Combs is your client now."

"Are you crazy!" Klempner cried. "In South Carolina back in '59! People telling us we're going to have to get the national guard out, get troops in the streets to handle South Carolina, Georgia, Alabama, and Mississippi, and you're asking me if I know anything about some colored woman's house that got burned down! Where have you been for the last thirty years!"

"With Bob Combs and Shy Wooster lighting the torch and your informant standing there watching them—"

"So what!" Klempner stood up, almost turning over his chair, one arm pointing off angrily in what Wilson assumed to be the direction of South Carolina. "You've got all this trouble, all these redneck troublemakers, the Klan even, you've got interstate traffic in guns and dynamite, dozens of informants out, and you want me to roll up a whole informant network to nail two shysters for burning down a colored woman's house! What's wrong with you, Foreman? That's not even a goddamn federal case you're talking about, even if I knew anything about it!"

"So Smooter Davis never told you about it."

"Not that I remember, no. And if he had, what did you want me to do about it? Go talk to the county sheriff! If the local cops up there had been willing to talk to us, Smooter Davis wouldn't have been there in the first place. For God's sake give me a little credit. You guys have your head up your ass." He sat back down, still glaring at Buster Foreman.

"So you never got anything on Combs?" Wilson asked.

"Combs? Shit, no. Some of that bunch over at the used-car lot, yeah. Two indictments, I think. But what we were after was the bigger picture, the Klan's organization, how all these groups tied together. Conspiracy. For when the lid blew off. . . ."

"What about Wooster?" Foreman asked.

"Shy Wooster? Shy Wooster's just a dimple on Bob Combs's ruby-red ass. Nothing to him. How'd you get hold of all this?"

"Buster did some checking," Wilson said.

"Maybe you could put us in touch with Smooter Davis," Buster suggested.

Klempner looked from Foreman back to Wilson. "Sure I could get in touch with him. He'd laugh you guys right out the fucking door."

"How reliable was he?" Wilson asked.

"Not bad at first. Real good. Then he fell apart. He hated those bastards down there. He couldn't handle it the last six months. It was eating him up. If he wasn't on the sauce, he was in the sack with someone. When he was on the sauce, he used to tell us the Rotary and Lions clubs up there were organizing a militia, had an armory out in the woods, trained every Tuesday night. Crazy stuff. He called me back in the late sixties, when we had the riots up here, when they were burning up Fourteenth Street. He saw it on TV, was even watching it out in Oakland when he called. 'Hey, baby. Burn, baby—burn.' That's all he said. Yeah, I can put you in touch with him. He'd chew you two honkies up like peanut brittle."

296

Wilson sat in silence for a minute, looking again at the FBI certificates. "We were going to suggest a deal," he said finally. "A trade-off. Something helpful to both of us."

"What kind of deal?"

"You tell us what you've got on Combs, we tell you what we know about Caltronics, how maybe you can dish them, these hustlers you don't like. Maybe get Fred Merkle to reopen the case."

But Klempner had shifted forward indignantly. "You bastards were gonna squeeze me!"

Buster Foreman looked at Wilson, who couldn't think of anything to say. "I suppose," he conceded at last.

"You've got some goddamn nerve, Wilson. Some goddamn nerve, that's all I can say. A guy with your reputation. That really burns me. That really burns the shit out of me, Wilson, trying to squeeze me. Getting Fred Merkle a little sweaty under the collar about me taking a dive and then coming around here to cut a deal. I ought to throw you out of my fucking office."

"I suppose so," Wilson said. "High road, low road, like you said."

"I'm really disappointed."

Buster Foreman, who'd been leaning back in his chair, balanced on two legs, brought it emphatically to the floor. "Yeah. Now that we understand each other, let's cut out the horseshit."

"What horseshit?" Klempner said. "I still ought to throw you guys outta here."

"Chuck Larabee," Wilson replied. Klempner turned in surprise. "You know him, don't you? I'll tell you about a funny conversation I had with him a month or so back, when he was fishing for information about what I was doing those days; then you tell me what you know. How about it?"

"It better be good," Klempner said grudgingly.

"You're right. Larabee's a small-time hustler, not too bright," Klempner began, finally satisfied. "Ex-Navy, like you said. A couple of years ago he comes to see me after I open the office upstairs. He's got a shopping list, surveillance gear he's trying to buy, claims he's doing the security work for a couple of California firms. He says he's got some close ties to some Navy lab people at China Lake out in California, the Navy testing center. He wants to get his hands on some underwater detection systems, protecting some kind of salvage operation off San Diego. He wants some other stuff too—radio-controlled fuses, low-light TV monitoring gear, some other systems he says they're developing out at China Lake. He claims this salvage operation is real sensitive, hush-hush cargo. He's gotta protect the operation. It sounds fishy, so we run a tracer on him and find out he's got some ties to an outfit that's peddling stuff on the embargo list to the Middle East and Latin America. We figure the end-user certificates will be phony, like the export licenses, and we can get an indictment. So I set it all up, working with Justice and Treasury, but he never shows his face again. Not until a few months ago."

"You think he was warned off?" Wilson said.

"I think so," Klempner said. "Maybe someone told him I still had some buddies over at Justice, at the Bureau. But I don't follow up. I hear his name around town, a small-time blowhard always trying to cut a big deal but's never made it. Then early this year, who should come walking in my office upstairs but Chuck Larabee. It's the same old shit—hush-hush, real sensitive, big security problem, real big contract, eighty grand up front, only he can't handle it alone. . . ."

The phone rang and Klempner switched the automatic answering lever and sat back.

"He says he's into security assistance programs now, everything opening up—Middle East, Latin America—all this military crud he's got a piece of. He asks me how business is and I tell him it's crummy, just me in the office and a couple of guys in the field, everybody cutting back. I had to lay off four of my old staff. So he says maybe he could move this big security contract my way. He's not set up to handle it. He says he can put me in touch with this California firm, a big computer software outfit that's getting bigger all the time. Big government contracts, some hot new algorithms they've designed for the Triton submarine fire-control systems. But they've gotten too big too fast. They're looking for a security consultant. All he wants from me is ten grand if I sign the contract, a finder's fee."

"Oh, shit, yes," Buster said.

"Typical," Wilson muttered.

"Yeah, typical. I can't believe this guy, not when he tells me how he's heard I've got some real close ties with the government still and this would help me land the contract. So I tell him O.K., business is bad, sure I'll talk to them. I'll talk to anyone. I can hardly pay the rent on this big office I've got upstairs. So he says he'll set it up."

"So you go see your friends down the street," Wilson said.

"I end up with Fred Merkle and he tells me about this Caltronics firm, how they've got big problems with the U.S. Attorney's office in L.A., with the Labor Department, with the FBI. He gives me the brief, Merkle-style. But they haven't made the cases yet. They're still working on them, but it looks like a dead end."

Larabee had set up the meeting with the Caltronics agent in from California to locate an office. He and Klempner met at the Hyatt Regency for lunch. Larabee was also supposed to be there, but didn't show up. The

Caltronics representative was a young man named Morris—cocky, aggressive, and something of a smart-ass, according to Klempner, who'd spent most of the two hours listening to Morris describe his sales exploits, how many government contracts he'd landed for Caltronics since he'd joined the firm. "The guy bugged me, for some reason," Klempner said. "Too flashy, too much talk—a goddamned latrine lawyer. He told me how much money he'd made the last ten years since he got back from Vietnam, every year his commissions bigger. He sold insurance for a while, then took a year off to study computer science, but even then made more money on the side than he'd made the year before. He was a manipulator, the kind who thinks he can hustle anyone, including me while he's sitting there drinking Cold Duck, giving me all this shit. Maybe it was all that money he made, I don't know, but he pissed me off. . . ."

They'd ended up back at Potomac Towers, where Morris had looked at a suite of offices available on the fourth floor. He'd looked at Klempner's office on the floor above.

"We're standing up there in my office," Klempner said, "in my goddamn office, and this Morris kid, twenty-four hours in Washington, tells me I'm getting ripped off on the rent I'm paying. Then he takes me downstairs, down to this manager's office, the same cheapskate I've been knocking heads with for five years, hustles this dude for that suite next door at a knockdown price, negotiates a contract on these two rooms if I want it, we sign and walk out. I've never seen anything like it. When this Morris tells me he's going to be a millionaire by the time he's thirty-three, I believe him. . . ."

"A real hustler, then," Wilson said.

"Hustler! This guy Morris could sell warts at a beauty contest. You can't believe the kind of nerve that kid has."

"So it was his idea you move next door?"

"Not his idea, it just happened. I mean, he just wanted to show me he could do it. Afterwards, he said it would help swing the contract with Caltronics if I was interested, but that was just talk. That kid could make you believe anything. That's why I was surprised when I found out that Morris was the Caltronics agent suspected of bribing that GSA contracting officer."

"People like that have to succeed," Wilson offered. "They can't fail, ever. Go ahead."

The Caltronics office opened a few months later, with Morris in charge. Klempner did a few small jobs for them as the office was being set up, on a straight fee basis, and Morris told him that the Caltronics lawyers in Los Angeles were drawing up a longer-term contract. "A couple of times we talked about the long-term contract. He asked me about a price, what I got when I was handling those pharmaceutical companies, and said I should go for something bigger. He says this is going to be a special contract. Real special. A complete study of Caltronics' security situation—that's what he called it, 'security situation'—all of it wrapped up in this big report I was to do for them. Then one day at lunch, he tells me what he's got in mind. Eighty thousand up front when I file an outline and fifty to follow when the final report is in. Can you believe that shit?"

"I think so," Wilson said. "What kind of report?"

"What else?" Klempner asked.

Morris wanted to buy the status of the government's case against Caltronics—wiretaps, FBI logs, summaries, anything in the dossier. He thought Klempner could get it for him.

"He tells me it'll take a week to get the money together, the eighty grand, only he's not saying how he's going to make delivery. He's slick, cagey, real sharp, not a guy who's gonna make a mistake. All he tells me is that I'm to get this outline together and have it ready in five days. I'll get a call on the fifth day, maybe late, maybe seven o'clock, and he'll tell me where to drop the outline and where I can pick up the briefcase."

"He trusts you by then?" Wilson said.

"I'm his buddy. Hell, yes, he trusts me."

"Does he ask you whether anyone in Washington is working the case?" Wilson continued.

"Yeah. I tell him me. Just me and a bookkeeper down at the Justice Department, that's all. The U.S. Attorney's office out in L.A. may have a few people nosing around, but they're on a cold trail."

"When he makes his pitch, did he say why he picked you, why Signet?"

"He said he heard Signet was an FBI front and civil service salaries are lousy. Yeah, I know, that sounds stupid, but not when this kid Morris is talking." Klempner got up from behind the desk. Wilson got up too and they moved through the door into the outer office, where Klempner turned on the coffee machine. "I think it was Larabee that fingered me for Morris."

"He didn't say why he wanted the Justice Department investigation, did he?"

"No, he just said he wanted the whole bag, not just the Justice Department case, not just the bribery case—I mean all of it, everything the Labor investigation unit had turned up, these two insurance companies, this skim that was going on. You figure what he wanted it for."

"So what happened?"

Klempner shrugged. "I never got the telephone call. I was waiting here, right over there at the bench, rebuilding an old telephone tap. I waited until nine, I think it was. I never got the call. I figured Morris must have gotten cold feet or couldn't get the money together. The next thing I heard, he'd disappeared with the eighty thousand. The lawyers next door were claiming a hundred, that he'd cleaned out the local Caltronics accounts. They were claiming embezzlement, conversion, I heard, but they don't file charges."

Wilson paused at the workbench, piled with electronic equipment, pressure sensors, and an exotic-looking device for reading an electric typewriter's impulses. He turned to the telex machine, turned it on, heard the circuits come alive, and then turned it off again.

"What about the Caltronics teletype?" he asked. "Were you reading that too?"

"Yeah, but they didn't use it much." Klempner turned the dial of a cabinet safe and pulled open a lower drawer. He removed a sheaf of telex messages from a binder.

"Do you remember a telex to Rita Kramer from the West Coast, from her husband, Artie, warning her that I was a fed?"

Klempner didn't remember. "The first time your name came up was when you walked through the back door over there."

The snow was still coming down in the dimming light beyond the window, a furious whiteness battling the air. Wilson could sense his breath on the air, as if he were just entering a dark, cold house. "When was the eighty thousand to be delivered?" he asked. "On a Monday night?"

Klempner turned. "Yeah. Why?"

"You say you don't know how or where the money was to be delivered, whether Morris was to deliver it himself or use a bagman?"

"He didn't say. How come?"

"I think he had a bagman in mind. Morris to pick up your outline, someone else to deliver the briefcase." He stood looking toward the window and then turned. "A Marx Brothers movie, like you said once. It was a heist—a two-way heist. Pete Rathbone was going to heist the Justice Department cases against Caltronics through the front door, using Artie Kramer to do it, perfectly legal all the way, in broad daylight, while Strykker was trying to burgle the safe, find out just how much they had on him. He was nervous. Maybe he didn't trust Rathbone. Maybe Morris just sold him a bill of goods. Morris is slick, all right, a very convincing talker."

"You know Morris?" Klempner asked.

"The night Morris was to make the delivery, he got a telephone call downstairs," Wilson said without answering the question. "Someone warned him off. Whoever it was told him the feds were just waiting to break the case wide open, that you were lying when you told him you could handle it." He looked at the telex. "He even told him I was a fed, maybe trying to entrap Artie Kramer the way you were trying to entrap

Morris. So he told him to hold up, not do anything until they could check it out some more, find out what we were up to. Lie low, just like Pete Rathbone told Artie Kramer. They were falling all over themselves. They still are."

"Who called him?"

"I'm not sure," Wilson said. "Probably Larabee knows. I think he lets Strykker use his telex. That's probably where the message was sent telling Rita Kramer I worked for the Justice Department."

In Klempner's office, Wilson called Fred Merkle at home.

"Bernie Klempner and I want to talk to you, Fred. Could we get together at eight?" He listened and turned toward Klempner. "Tomorrow may be too late," he said. "Tonight, O.K.? A U.S. marshal and a warrant.

"Do you think you could get Chuck Larabee to meet us at Fred Merkle's office? Eight o'clock?" he asked Klempner after he hung up. "If you could, we could wrap this up tonight. I've got to go out to St. Elizabeths to check on something."

8.

The exercise rooms of the men's health club on the sixth floor of the K Street office building were deserted that snowy Friday evening except for the weight and body-bag room. Chuck Larabee had been working out alone when Klempner surprised him.

"Dog food," Klempner said, pumping the leather medicine bag so violently against Larabee's midsection that he went down again, his flushed face drenched with sweat, his lip cut, his gray sweatshirt soaked. "You don't wanna go talk to Merkle, we'll try dog food for a change. What do you figure people spend a year—ten, fifteen million? Come on, Larabee, tell me about dog chow. How much?"

He lifted Larabee by a limp arm, eased him back against the padded wall, and bent to retrieve one of the leather gloves that had fallen from Larabee's dangling hand. "Come on, Chuck babe, try again. We go three rounds this time, you do the talking. I'll only use my left, O.K.?"

Larabee, seeing his opportunity as Klempner pulled on the body-bag glove, swung groggily with his right hand but missed. Klempner, in coat and tie, did a small shuffle as he moved in. "Left hand up, right. That's it, except higher. Now you're getting it. Coming at you now, Chuck. Ready? That's it, keep the left up there." He dropped his own left and feinted with his right. Larabee took the feint, moved his hands, and Klempner smashed him sideways along the padded wall. Larabee reeled drunkenly along the wall, stumbled, and collapsed to his knees.

"What are you trying to tell me—you don't know dog chow, is that it? What about something you know about? Something easy—like Morris. You don't wanna talk to Merkle about Morris? Shit, you're a tough customer, Chuck. You're really making it tough on me. How about kid prostitutes—that your category? What about runaway kid prostitutes in the U.S.—a hundred, two hundred thou? Come on, Chuckie. . . ."

"Keep away from me," Larabee muttered, drooling blood from his cut lip as he leaned exhausted against the padded wall.

"What do you say—a hundred thou?" Klempner continued softly. "Don't be wrong, Chuck, I wanna keep you in one piece for Merkle. What do you think—got any ideas?" He picked Larabee up and draped him across the leather vaulting horse, walked around to the other side, and lifted Larabee's chin with his ungloved hand. "Got an answer yet, Chuck? No? It's the old gong show for you." He knocked him off the vaulting horse. "Six hundred thousand kid prostitutes in the U.S.—runaways. Read about it in the barbershop magazine. Doesn't that turn your stomach, Chuck? I mean, even a shit like you's gotta have feelings. How about video games? You like Atari, Chuck. You play a little Atari over in that Crystal City pad of yours? Come on, man, there's gotta be something you know about. You don't know about Morris and that scam of his, we'll play video games, right?"

"Leave me alone, you crazy . . ."

"Crazy what? Get it out, Chuck. Crazy what?" He dragged Larabee across the room and lifted him up against the body bag. "Hold on right there, just stand up, Chuck, like someone was taking your picture. That's it. So how much are these video games gonna gross this year—two million, three million?" Larabee held to the swaying bag. "Come on, Chuck, give it some heavy thought. How much?" Larabee didn't answer. Klempner hit the bag softly once, then a second time, then battered it away from Larabee's embrace. Larabee stood there, exposed, and Klempner slammed him in the stomach.

"Hey, Chuck," he said softly, bending over him again, "you were standing in the nitro zone, pal. Six billion, Chuck, that's the gross—bigger than the movies. Was that what you were thinking? You gotta get it out, man, like what happened that night Morris disappeared. No use keeping it all in. Six billion, Chuck. That's a whole lotta money for electric Ping-Pong, isn't it? A whole lotta money for a bunch of cheesy functional illiterates the schools are turning out just so they can hang around the fucking arcades all day. They won't turn out any better than me and you did, Chuck—me a sadist, you a goddamn pimp. What do you figure for a country that lets half a million kid prostitutes walk the streets up in New York and then spends a couple of billion dollars a year on dog chow and electric Ping-Pong? How does a shithead like you figure it, a fucking meatball in a classy gym like this that when a guy comes at him can't think whether to hold up his dukes or his pants. You're in a bad way, Chuck. So tell me about that Caltronics scam. Who was it warned Morris off that night? I've got a reputation to protect, asshole. Some of those guys down there at Justice think maybe I got a piece of that money. . . ."

Klempner rolled him over, flipped his arm behind his back, and locking his knee against Larabee's midsection, brought the arm up. "Come on, Larabee. I'm gonna break your fucking arm, you don't bend—"

But Larabee cried out and Klempner relented. He stood up and crossed the room to unlock the door. He stooped at the water fountain in the hall outside, red-faced. A small Filipino in white ducks, white sneakers, and white shirt padded up the corridor from the locker room with a few towels over his arm. He stopped to look in the door.

"You looking for something?" Klempner asked.

"Mr. Larabee."

Klempner moved back to the door. "He's been sparring, shadow boxing a couple of rounds."

"I have to close up."

"I'll tell him, he's all punched out."

Klempner went back into the room and shut the door. "Come on, Larabee, let's go. Where's your self-respect, lying there like a goddamn douche bag." He straddled him and lifted him by his waist, pumping air back into his lungs. "You were an old Navy man—right, Chuck? How about Vietnam? I heard you were in Vietnam. What'd you do—run the Saigon commissary?" Larabee's mouth opened, he stirred crablike on the floor, and Klempner dragged him back against the padded wall. "What about combat stats over there in Vietnam, Chuck? You know anything about that?" He gently slapped his face and Larabee slowly opened his eyes. The knock came at the door. "Think about how many GIs got their wounds in combat, Chuck."

The Filipino gym attendant stood at the door, wearing an overcoat and holding a gym bag. He said he had to leave.

"Tell you what I'll do," Klempner proposed, taking out his wallet. He removed five dollars. "It's Chuck's birthday. He says take your kids to the flicks. He'll lock the door after him."

"Tell him to turn the key twice."

"Got you—twice. Twice, you hear that, Chuck?" He shut the door.

Larabee had slumped silently to his side, head against the mat as he gazed at the stooping Klempner with glazed, distant eyes.

"You're gonna get a cardiac," Klempner said even more softly. "You're gonna get a fucking cardiac right here and on Monday morning that's the way they're gonna find you, just slumped over like that. Your lips are turning blue already; that's a bad sign. I mean, a guy boozes too much, smokes too much, grunts around in the sack too much with these hookers, and then comes over here to work it all out, and it just breaks him all up inside. You're feeling that now, aren't you? Feeling it all inside, like the old ticker's about to peel its skin. Your knees are dancing, like your chest. Feel your chest, Chuckie. Go ahead, feel it—what they call a fibrillation. That's tough shit, Chuckie babe, because we've still got five rounds to go. . . ."

He jerked Larabee to his feet, slung one arm over his shoulder, and carried him across the room to drape him over the leather vaulting bar. Larabee grunted unintelligibly, his eyes rolled back in his skull, and he slid back to the floor mat, where he lay on his back, eyes open, blinking at the wire-caged lights overhead.

"You wanna tell me about it now, Larabee?" Klempner whispered, bending near. "Tell me what you're gonna say when we go down and talk to Fred Merkle. I'm not gonna ask you again. . . ."

Larabee seemed to respond, holding his chest, his eyes half-open.

"Was it you called Morris that Monday night, told him to lie low?"

He was slow in answering and Klempner grabbed his arm.

His eyes closed again. It was a long time before he answered, as if he were carefully hoarding his breath in lungs that wouldn't survive the night.

"Strykker," he said weakly. "I didn't know anything, but it had to be Strykker."

He was still wobbly when Klempner led him into the Justice Department suite where Fred Merkle and Wilson were waiting. His feet shuffled, like an old man's. He didn't seem to know where he was as he collapsed down in a chair, but Klempner said he was ready to make a statement. Fred Merkle took one look at his face and decided not to wait. On the basis of what Haven Wilson had already told him, he'd decided to move immediately, before it was too late.

The short, dark day was over. It was a quiet suburban night in a quiet suburban neighborhood. The snow flurries were still intermittent, barely discernible in the pools of white light atop the rustic lampposts of the Rockville subdivision. A faint frosting of snow lay over the streets and lawns, over the parked cars and the rail fences. Living room windows were lit, soft rectangles of orange and yellow blooming softly out from behind the white-shrouded shrubbery.

In the first sedan, a federal marshal and a Justice Department investigator sat in the front seat. Wilson sat alone in back. Klempner followed in his own car.

A new Toyota was parked in the drive of the last town house, not used since the snow began to fall. A television set was turned on in the living room. Wilson rang the door chimes and the U.S. marshal moved to one side of the porch, Klempner to the other. A thin, dark-haired woman in jeans opened the inner door.

"I'm from up the street," Wilson said, taking off his hat. "I wonder if I could talk to your husband."

"What about?"

"The Optimist Club raffle; I mentioned it to him the other day."

She stood watching him uncertainly, drying her hands on the towel. "I'll get him."

He appeared a few minutes later, beard and hair even longer now, sleepy-eyed, in stocking feet, wearing a flannel shirt. Only after he turned on the porch light did he recognize Wilson and then stood looking at him suspiciously. "What the shit do you want?"

"To talk for a few minutes?"

"Nothing to talk about. I told you all I know."

"It'll just take a minute."

He hesitated, looked back in the hall, and then pushed open the metal storm door. "Listen, hey—" Then he saw Klempner's huge figure standing to one side. "Fuck you, man." He slammed the door shut.

"Take the back," the marshal called, and Klempner bolted from the porch and around the side. The marshal pushed in through the front door, Wilson at his heels. They went down the hall, down the steps, and into the bright kitchen. The sliding door that led to the terrace was open. The dark-haired girl was backed up against the refrigerator. "U.S. marshal. Does he have a weapon?"

"He doesn't even have his shoes on."

"It's all right," Wilson told her. "Nothing's going to happen to him. The marshal's got a warrant."

Footprints led across the terrace and disappeared into the small, dark yard. Klempner stood at the side gate. "Not this way," he said. The girl turned on the patio lights and followed them out. "Let me talk to him," she said.

"Go ahead."

"Come on, Gary! Don't be stupid, it's a U.S. marshal."

They waited, looking out into the darkness. "Is there a way out?" the marshal asked.

"Just the high fence. Come on, Gary, don't be dumb. They want to talk, that's all!"

Again they waited.

"Come on, Morris—use your head!" the marshal called.

"Listen to him, Gary!"

After a moment they heard his voice. "I wanna lawyer." It was muffled and weak.

"He's in the toolshed," she said. She brought a flashlight from the kitchen and handed it to the marshal. "Just ask him nice. He's all talk. He wouldn't hurt a fly."

She watched as they went back toward the portable toolshed built up against the high paling fence. The marshal flashed the light against the closed wooden door. "Come on out, Morris," the marshal said easily. "We'd like to talk to you."

Silence. Then, "Get that Klempner hoodlum away from me."

"He's not going to bother you. I asked him to come along. You're in U.S. custody."

They waited. A few minutes passed and then the door opened slowly. Morris came out, his hands locked behind his head. He blinked painfully in the powerful beam of the flashlight. The marshal lowered the light and Morris marched back across the snowy yard in his stocking feet, his hands still behind his head, elbows out in some heroic parody of a Hollywood war movie.

"You can drop them now, Morris," the marshal told him as they reached the terrace steps.

Morris turned to look at Wilson, like an actor who'd just given a cunning performance. "Like the tiger cage at Lang Vei, right, Wilson? Man, I really had you fuckers going, didn't I? You really gobbled that shit up."

"It was stupid, the whole masquerade."

"How'd you know?"

"Little things. Your hands, for one. You talk too much, for another. The St. Elizabeths incident never happened."

"Shit, man, what'd you want me to do? I was home free until you come nosing around. I had to lose you quick."

"Where's Cronin?"

"He freaked out. The same day he crashed you on the beltway. Wendy and me took him up to that VA hospital in New York." Klempner came up the steps behind him and Morris said, "Hey, you got a cigarette, Klempner? I'm still your main man, right? Federal witness program?" But Klempner made an abrupt move toward him and Morris bolted through the door. "Hey, listen, no rough stuff. I'm gonna make you guys look real good, what I got on that schlemiel Strykker and his Caltronics scam. . . ."

In a locked closet upstairs they found a briefcase with thirty-eight thousand dollars. There were bankbooks for three local accounts and statements from two banks in the Bahamas, with over two hundred thousand dollars on deposit.

While Wendy put some clothes in the washer for Morris to take with him, they sat in the breakfast nook, listening to Morris's story. He was very much a man of roles—quick, cunning, and convincingly plausible, a man who could persuade others as brazenly as he could deceive himself that he was always precisely who he claimed to be.

Strykker was behind the scheme to buy the government's case. Worried about what the U.S. Attorney had uncovered of his personal financial dealings, he'd turned to Larabee, who'd identified Bernie Klempner as an old FBI agent with close ties to the Justice Department, who might be willing to help. Morris had been brought from the West Coast as the middleman. But the more Strykker learned of Klempner, the less he liked it. He began to get cold feet, not entirely convinced that Klempner wasn't part of an FBI sting. When Artie Kramer sent a telex from the West Coast warning that Wilson was a federal agent, that was all he needed. He called Morris that Monday night and told him not to deliver the money. Klempner was working for the FBI.

"That was the double cross I told you about," Morris reminded Wilson.

"Who was to be the bagman for the eighty thousand? Cronin?"

"Yeah, Cronin. We had it all set up. Then Strykker calls me and the only thing I can drag out of him is your name. He tells me the feds are everywhere, but all I can get out of him is your name and how he's got this bleeding ulcer thinking about it. So Cronin and me decide to check you out, but Cronin gets high that morning and screws up. He clobbers you with his Alfa and then he blows sky high—the shakes, man, the dry heaves, the whole snake pit. When we take the Alfa back to the lot that night, he rams the gate and crashes a tow truck. Then he takes a fucking tire iron out and finishes the Alfa off. He's wacko by then and I've gotta take care of my buddy, so Wendy and me take him up to New York, up to that VA hospital that knows his case—"

"The two-hundred-pound turnip," Wilson said.

"Yeah. Maybe. Then I get back to town, I find out the office is closing down, eighty grand's missing, and someone's fingering me. I get hold of Strykker. He tells me to lie low, keep the money for a while, things are working out another way. Me, I don't mind. I kind of like the life style—"

"You mean you were squeezing Strykker," Klempner broke in, leaning over the table. "Squeezing him on account of what you had on him, what you had on Caltronics. Then when it all blows over, you come crawling back out of the woodwork and squeeze him some more, a lifetime annuity for you and your girl friend."

Morris was pulling on a Shetland sweater Wendy had just brought him. "I was waiting for the right moment," he said. "Waiting to come talk to you guys, cut a deal, like we're doing now. Isn't that right, Wendy?"

"Leave me out of it," she said.

"Why'd you finger Larabee that night we talked?" Wilson asked. "How come Larabee?"

"I dunno. I was tired, carrying a headful. I just wanted to get the hell outta there."

"Strykker said he wouldn't give Gary any more money," Wendy volunteered from the ironing board.

"Hey, what'd you say that for?" he protested.

"You were putting the heat on Strykker, weren't you?" Wilson continued. "Working an extortion scam of your own."

"You guys got it all wrong. I was waiting to cut a deal—"

"Listen, you little bastard," Klempner said aggressively, leaning across the table to seize Morris's wrist. "You don't know who the hell you are—you never did. Just any fucking shoe fits, you wear it, the way you always have."

"Hands off the threads, turkey," Morris said, pulling his arm free. "That's federal merchandise you're dicking with—right, marshal? He's pissed because he didn't get his eighty grand. I'll put that in my statement too."

"I expect you would," the marshal said.

By the time they reached Fred Merkle's office, Morris had dropped his accusations against Klempner. To Merkle, Morris was simply what he claimed to be, a frightened, ingratiating federal witness.

9.

The snow still sifted down lightly as Nick Straus arrived at the Pentagon that morning. The parking lot in front of the mall entrance was only randomly occupied. The gauze of gray gave the Washington skyline across the Potomac a secretive, medieval look.

The five men met in the office of Leyton Fischer, who had failed to appear. Nick was without counsel. He was wearing a coat and tie, his brown oxfords freshly shined. His wife had chosen the tie, her favorite, a rep tie with blue and yellow stripes. This was to be the end of it, she'd told him, his conscience declared after all this time. She'd understood after they'd talked for three hours the previous evening, unraveling his geopolitical detective story. Would they understand? He now had his doubts. His hands were cold.

A senior DIA brigadier general sat nearby, tall, sandy-haired, and in uniform. He wore a single decoration—the combat infantryman's badge over his breast pocket. The Pentagon lawyer who was to be the interrogator sat to his left. He was balding and deep-voiced, his suit rumpled, his trouser cuffs stuffed in arctics. A briefcase stood on the rug at his feet and a notepad rested on the arm of the leather chair. General Gawpin had appeared, dressed in Saturday mufti, a blue sports jacket and dark slacks. Portly and jowlish, he seemed the middle-aged caricature of the young lieutenant who'd been one of the first Americans across the Rhine at Remagen so many years ago. He'd won the Silver Star as a T-26 Pershing tank commander with the 14th Tank Battalion. Les Fine sat alone to the rear. Nick Straus felt a twinge of remorse as he recognized the slight shrunken figure, seated apart from the others, his dark eyes burning with anger.

In response to the lawyer's questions, Nick explained that the materials he'd published in the DIA daily summary had been drawn from the documents available in Colonel Collins's safe at the DIA special watch. The interpretations had been his. He wasn't certain why the phone taps and FBI logs were there, but he had his suspicions. In the spring of 1971 and again in 1974 and 1975, a series of leaks had occurred during the SALT negotiations which had threatened to compromise the talks. The Pentagon, which had opposed the U.S. negotiating position, was the prime suspect. The FBI had been called in to investigate but hadn't identified those responsible. General Gawpin had been on the Pentagon's SALT advisory staff at the time and was one of those suspected of the leaks. "Perhaps General Gawpin knows why the special watch received transcripts from the FBI investigation," Nick suggested. "I've no idea how they got there."

General Gawpin chewed his cigar, winked at the brigadier, and said nothing.

Nick told them that his purpose in publishing his special issue of the DIA daily summary was to expose to executive view some of the more terrifying secrets of the Pentagon's strategy. One was the hallucinated SIOP targeting plan. Another was Pentagon hypocrisy in claiming it was interested in arms control. The intent was as he described it: to convert nuclear superiority into political power, coercive if need be—a strategy which stood nuclear orthodoxy on its head. The Pentagon claim that the new strategy was intended to give the U.S. the capacity to resist Soviet nuclear blackmail was a hoax. It was the Pentagon itself that was planning nuclear intimidation in preparing for a protracted nuclear war. . . .

"These are his interpretations." General Gawpin broke in irritably.

"I've been following these issues for over twenty years," Nick said. "You can't hide the intent from me."

"You'd say you've had more experience than General Gawpin?" the lawyer asked. "Than Mr. Fine?"

A geopolitical detective story, Nick had told Ida, but she had a talent for riddles. He wasn't sure of the lawyer. "Each understands these matters in his own way," he said. The snow fought the wind at the window and he watched it silently for a minute. "I know what General Gawpin's position has been over the years," he began again. "His position hasn't changed. He has never accepted the idea of nuclear parity with Moscow. He never will. Mr. Fine's situation is different. He once supported détente. This was when he worked on SALT I with Kissinger at the National Security Council." He avoided Les Fine's eyes as he spoke but felt the flush rise on his cheeks, acknowledging Fine's presence. "He lobbied for SALT I on the Hill. A moral necessity in a nuclear age, that's what he used to say. Those were Kissinger's words, by the way. Mr. Fine believed at the time that the two superpowers had no choice but to find some kind of stability, some kind of equilibrium. The possibility of nuclear devastation made it a moral necessity. That's what détente was at the time."

Gawpin removed his cigar. "Which the Sovs violated. Détente was their Trojan horse." Nick gazed at him thoughtfully, conscious of the broken veins on his cheeks and nose.

The lawyer said, "You say Mr. Fine believed in détente and now he doesn't. Is that why you attacked him in the DIA daily summary?"

"I didn't attack him."

"You claimed he'd been in contact with a foreign embassy, the Israeli embassy."

"The phone taps and the FBI logs speak for themselves."

"You think he gave information to the Israelis, classified information?"

"Possibly, but so have I," Nick said. "When I was at the Agency, I often met with Israeli diplomats and analysts. We exchanged ideas. I found it helpful."

Surprised, the lawyer consulted his notebook. The room was silent. In the outer office, a phone was ringing. The snow still pelted down.

"What is this New Irgun you mentioned?" the brigadier asked hoarsely. "What kind of conspiracy?"

The intrusion of that rough, military voice seemed to Nick to give a crude new dimension to the room. "It's a catchword, not a conspiracy," he said warily. "I saw it scrawled on a poster in the DIA special watch."

"What'd it mean to you?"

"A propagandist. A right-wing propagandist. In Mr. Fine's case, someone who borrows the tactics of Begin's old Irgun Zvai Leumi to terrorize his congressional and public constituency, not with grenades and machine guns, but with the prospect of Soviet nuclear blackmail."

The brigadier smiled in surprise, looking at Gawpin. "What do you think of that?"

Nick was annoyed. "Of course he's a propagandist. Don't be fooled. These are tactics, nothing more. Like the old popular front."

"To do what?" asked the lawyer.

"Armies need a band to march by," Nick said. "Men like Fine and General Gawpin supply the tune. In Fine's case, to maintain the anti-Communist crusade, to keep in step this militarized diplomacy against Soviet imperialism." He glanced at Fine. "The old defensive mentality, the Haganah mentality, isn't enough. New strategies are needed, new tactics. Like the Pentagon's strategic alliance with Israel and Egypt in the Middle East. What would Ben-Gurion have said to that? But that's revisionism too, Begin style. The old moral commitment now recast in military terms. Realpolitik. What Kissinger taught in 1973."

The lawyer was confused. "I'm sorry," he complained, "but I don't follow this."

General Gawpin's chair creaked under him as he shifted forward. "Don't worry about it," he muttered. "What is it's bothering you?" he asked Nick. "You don't approve of this military alliance in the Middle East? What would you suggest, Doctor?"

"The Pentagon once supported Iran in the same way," Nick said. "Are you asking me to put Israel and the Shah's Iran in the same category? With Mobutu? With Somoza? A military alliance, nothing more?"

"That wasn't my question," Gawpin said.

"It was for me. Israel is a moral cause or it is nothing. I may disagree on strategy, on tactics, but not that. For you here in the Pentagon it doesn't matter. Israel is, just now, a guarantor of your military and strategic interests in the Persian Gulf, just as the Shah once was. But for men like Les Fine to join you I think a tragedy. Tragically wrong, like my brother-in-law. He joined the popular front too, the right-wing popular front, like Mr. Fine did just after the 1973 Yom Kippur War. He brought the cold war out of the closet too and has been beating the drum ever since, like Mr. Fine, not because he believes it but because he thinks it the only solution to Israel's isolation." He sat back slowly, regretting his outburst. "I didn't mean to compare Mr. Fine with my brother-in-law," he apologized. "He's an emotional man. Mr. Fine isn't."

312

"What did the Yom Kippur War have to do with all this?" the lawyer asked General Gawpin in bewilderment.

"Why don't we let Dr. Straus tell us," Gawpin declared.

Poor, gullible man, Nick thought, looking at the lawyer's guileless face, as virginal as that continental democracy that had once declared its independence from the sinister intrigues of European cabinet diplomacy, only to fall victim to those geopolitical gurus who now practiced in Washington what they could no longer practice in Vienna and Berlin.

"For many Americans," Nick said, "the 1973 Yom Kippur War began to make clear what the ultimate consequences of détente might be. Détente and Vietnam, which supplied the final evidence. Détente was, for them, the diplomacy of U.S. weakness, not strength. Kissinger's manipulative diplomacy was no substitute for U.S. military power, détente's moral cause no substitute for other causes. For some, Kissinger's and Nixon's deception during the Yom Kippur War suggested that it was only a matter of time before Israel's interests would be sacrificed."

"I would call that a highly subjective interpretation," General Gawpin broke in.

"So it is," Nick agreed sadly, "but the diplomatic record speaks for itself. Golda Meir expressed it best. The Arabs now had oil, and in such a world Israel's cause could no longer be a just one. But she wasn't talking just of the Arab oil embargo. She was talking of the world she'd seen emerge since 1967, the world of geopolitical and strategic advantage, the world of power without principle. The same world the Pentagon was considering when it stalled on the military resupply to Israel during the first week of the war because of its fears of Arab reaction. The same world Nixon was thinking of when he sent his secret letter to Brezhnev on October 20, proposing that the U.S. and the Soviet Union seize the opportunity to impose a comprehensive peace in the Middle East. Brezhnev had made a similar suggestion at San Clemente the previous June, but it had been rejected. Nixon was weaker now, weakened by the problem with the tapes. A desperate man, hearing rumors of impeachment, hoping to salvage his presidency." He looked at the lawyer. "The day of the massacre, the 'Saturday Night Massacre.' Probably you remember?" He saw nothing in the man's eyes. "In Moscow the following day," he resumed, "Kissinger agreed to the cease-fire without consulting the Israelis, despite his assurances Israel would have time to consolidate its military gains. Mrs. Meir felt betrayed. She suspected Nixon and Kissinger had concluded a secret agreement to reimpose the 1967 borders." He shrugged, depressed by the recollection. "What could she think? Israel would once more be asked to pay the price of an Arab military defeat. All she'd asked for was justice, for

313

Israel's right to exist. With the Arab oil weapon, the Europeans could no longer be counted upon, not the Japanese, not the third world. Now Kissinger's expedient realpolitik seemed an unreliable arbiter of what served Israel's interests. The tide was running out—"

"Brezhnev threatened to intervene in the Middle East," Gawpin intruded boisterously, shoulders thrust forward. "Threatened to send Russian soldiers to Egypt. We went to the brink over that and the Sovs backed down."

Nick nodded in recollection. "I remember, yes. On October 24, Brezhnev sent a letter to Nixon asking that the U.S. join in sending Russian and American troops to Egypt under U.N. auspices to enforce the cease-fire. It was Kissinger who described the letter as an ultimatum."

"I don't remember that," Gawpin said.

"The letter arrived shortly after Kissinger had a shouting match with the Israeli ambassador in Washington. He told him the U.S. would never go to war because of Israeli violations of the cease-fire. A blustering match, I should say."

"I don't remember that, either," Gawpin grumbled.

"Nixon was sleeping when Kissinger chaired the meeting in the White House situation room to consider the U.S. response. He wasn't wakened. More of Kissinger's bluster, this time leaked to the press."

"I don't see your point," the brigadier said.

"My point is that this incident wasn't another Cuban missile crisis," Nick said, "despite the mythology that's grown up around it."

"I suppose we have to take your word for that," the lawyer declared.

"It doesn't matter. The diplomatic record speaks for itself. How others interpret it is something different, and that's what interests me. For many people, the experience of the Yom Kippur War and the withdrawal from Vietnam raised doubts not only about détente but about the credibility of any U.S. military commitment abroad."

"Obviously," Gawpin pointed out, extinguishing his cigar in the metal urn in front of his chair. "What the hell'd you expect?" He glanced at his wristwatch.

"For them," Nick concluded, "détente meant that the U.S. would ultimately be confined to the Western Hemisphere. That's where détente would end. No longer would the American public, exhausted by Vietnam, support the projection of U.S. power overseas. For people with global causes, it wasn't enough, just as a nuclear deterrent that was purely defensive in nature, protecting the continental U.S., wasn't enough. Not for people like the general here, not like Les Fine. Both are evangelists, each for his own reasons."

"By 'global causes,' he's talking about U.S. vital interests," Gawpin said, winking again at the brigadier.

The lawyer, restlessly consulting his own watch, nodded in mute agreement.

"And that's what's behind this rhetorical terrorism, all this demonology about what Moscow intends," Nick continued. He no longer had their attention. Even Les Fine was pulling his coat from the adjacent table, preparing to leave. "These are the slogans of the popular front," he continued hopelessly, "that's all. Just like the thirties, the forties. The tragic thing is, this hysteria is so falsifying the historical record that we no longer seem to understand the world we live in."

The lawyer was closing his notebook as Nick droned on. Les Fine had risen to silently cross the room. As the door shut firmly behind him, Nick felt like a man being abandoned in an empty room with only his own voice to console him. It was Les Fine he'd been appealing to all that time, and now he had nothing more to say.

"We appreciate your directness," the lawyer declared as he returned his pen to his coat pocket. "It's been useful."

"Very helpful," Gawpin agreed, rising stiffly.

The brigadier stood up and manfully offered Nick his hand. "I like a man who sticks to what he believes, right or wrong," he said, looking Nick straight in the eye. His grip was like iron.

If the brigadier, the lawyer, and General Gawpin admired candor, Nick thought, shaking hands all around, it was only because nothing he had said had made the slightest impression on any of them. He was just a weepy-eyed, slightly dotty humanitarian, agonizing over genocidal questions the past had since disposed of, locked behind history's closed door.

Nick found Les Fine standing on the top step of the mall entrance, waiting for his car, eyes lifted out over the snowy parking lot. Nick stopped as he pulled on his gloves, trying to think of something to say. Fine turned finally, glanced at him, and looked away. In that instant of recognition, the dark eyes that had so often troubled him these recent weeks, filled with the anger and humiliation of decades of helplessness, seemed remarkably calm.

"You're badly deceived," Fine said, looking away. "I had nothing to do with your removal from these various posts. You torment yourself."

"That's possible," Nick muttered in embarrassment.

"These obsessions you spoke of are yours, not mine. You have a persecution complex."

"My brother-in-law tells me the same thing."

Fine turned to look at him disapprovingly. "Who is this scapegoat brother-in-law you keep mentioning?"

"He is me, under the skin, just as you are me, under the skin," Nick said, but the humorless, reproving face disappointed him. "He is a lawyer in Chicago," he continued sadly, regretting his whimsy. "An important lawyer with Washington connections. You talked to him once."

"I did?"

"When you were lobbying for SALT I. You met with a group from Chicago, some very important fund-raisers. This was during the Yom Kippur War in October 1973. You tried to get them to oppose the Jackson Amendment to help speed up the weapons transfers the Pentagon was stalling on."

"Was I successful?"

"No, I'm sorry to say."

Fine seemed to smile. "Good. It was blood blackmail. A shrewd man, your brother-in-law. You should listen to him these days." The car arrived and Fine went down the steps.

"Shrewd, maybe," Nick called after him indignantly, "but even he wouldn't believe all these lies you're telling."

But Les Fine only waved without turning.

10.

Rita and Artie Kramer had planned on driving to Annapolis that Saturday morning for the weekend, but he'd been called away late in the morning by Nat Strykker. Reluctant to go out because Artie might return, she waited alone in the suite, a restless, angry prisoner in quarters she'd grown to despise. The afternoon dragged on. She watched the snow flurries dim into invisibility and the streetlamps come on, ragged moons of milkweed through the cluttered air. The rooms were silent—no radio, no television, nothing at all.

You selfish bastard, she raged, a little after five o'clock, as the darkness was almost complete beyond the windows. Her bag was packed and waiting near the bedroom door.

She'd gone into the kitchenette to refill her glass when she heard the door open, and she quickly returned to the front room. Kramer came in, his face gray with fatigue, his tie loosened, his coat hanging open. Chuckie Savant was at his heels.

"Where the hell have you been?" she demanded.

"I'll be the laughingstock," he mumbled. "The whole town. You, me, all of us." He dropped his coat and hat on the chair and staggered across the rug to collapse on the couch. "That's the last straw, I'm telling you—never again. Get me something cold to drink."

"Get it yourself," she said coolly. "Where's he been, Chuckie?"

"With Nat Strykker and his lawyers. Nat's in real trouble. The government got his money back."

"What money?"

"The money Morris got to try to buy the government case. Now Morris is in protective custody and he's squealing his head off."

"About what?" she asked.

"About a lot of things. Don't take it so hard, Artie," he said to Kramer. "It's got nothing to do with you."

"Nothing to do with me!" Artie cried. "It's my company you're talking about! A criminal indictment! That's ten to twelve years they're gonna hang on Strykker."

"Don't kid, Artie," Rita said. "I'm not in the mood."

"Who's kidding? Get me something to drink."

"What's he talking about, Chuckie?"

"Bribery," Artie said. "Bribery and corruption, maybe labor racketeering. Churning some accounts. Overbillings on government contracts, maybe five, six million worth. That's what I'm talking about."

"When did you find this out?"

"Today with Strykker's lawyer, they were sweating it out of him," Chuckie said, still standing with Rita near the couch where Artie had sprawled. "He was in real deep, Nat was. Didn't know which way to go, what the government was going to hit him with. That's why him and Morris tried to buy the government case—"

"He shoulda let Rathbone handle it," Artie said. "Pete Rathbone was gonna take care of all that trouble. He would have taken care of everything. . . ."

"You knew about this?" Rita asked, surprised.

"I knew Strykker had some kinda big trouble, I didn't know what."

"The lawyers said these overbillings would just be a civil suit," Chuckie Savant offered. "Something they could work out a settlement on, an out-of-court settlement—"

"Shut up! I don't wanna hear. I've got a migraine. Oh, man, have I ever got a migraine." He shut his eyes, leaning back against the couch.

"Did you hear all this?" Rita asked Chuckie.

"Not all of it. Nat's taking it real bad, all broken up."

"He should be."

"It's crazy what they done!" Artie shouted, opening his eyes.

"Just take it easy," Rita said calmly. "I'll fix you something."

317

"On account of this, the goddamn government is whipping up a curse on all of us!"

"Shhhh. Talk to him, Chuckie," she urged, turning toward the kitchen.

"Listen," Chuckie began softly, "listen, Artie—"

"Shut up! I'll have the goddamn IRS in my pajamas for the next ten years. You too!" he called after Rita. "Every time you open up a closet out in L.A., ten guys fall out! I come here because I'm patriotic. I didn't come here to have these dumdums do a number on me!" He looked back at Chuckie Savant. "Call the house in L.A., go ahead, call 'em. Ask the housekeeper who's been hanging around, has she seen anyone suspicious. Go on."

He collapsed back against the couch and shut his eyes. Rita returned with a drink and put it in his hand. "It's going to be all right," she said. "whatever Strykker did, it didn't have anything to do with you. So just take it easy."

His head was still back. He said, "It's a sad day for Uncle Sam when Artie Kramer has to go back to L.A. with his tail between his legs."

"Go back to L.A.? How come?"

"You don't understand because you don't know what it was about. Pete Rathbone told Strykker to take it easy and he got nervous. If I'd known all he'd been doing, I'd be nervous too." He lifted his head to look at her, as if he'd just remembered something reassuring. "One thing I'll say about L.A. At least you know what kind of schlemiels you're working with."

"So why do you have to go back to L.A.?"

"Don't be stupid. How's it gonna look, the White House makes the announcement about the political appointment, this big stockholder in Caltronics, Artie Kramer, and right there next to it is Strykker's picture, the Caltronics biggie, and how he and his company are getting indicted on criminal charges back on the West Coast. I didn't come here to be any embarrassment. That's what the lawyer said too."

Chuckie Savant came back. "The only one she's seen is the Gonzales lawn crew that came yesterday."

Kramer sat up alertly. "How many was there?"

"She didn't say. Probably two, like usual."

"Three," Artie said quickly. "And I'll bet he wasn't no Mex, either. Call her back."

"So it's all decided about going back?" Rita asked.

"I'll tell the White House on Monday," Artie said, watching Chuckie Savant return to the bedroom.

"I don't understand why Strykker and this other man tried to buy the government case," she said after a minute. "I mean, what good would that have done? If they had something on him, they still would have come after him, wouldn't they?"

"Don't be stupid," Artie said. "He wanted to find out what they had on him, get his lawyers wise, maybe fix the books. Use your head."

"I am using my head, and it sounds stupid to me."

"Yeah? Why'd the Russians steal the atomic bomb? You think that was stupid? Same thing with Nat Strykker. So when the USG dropped it on him, he'd know what it was. What's so goddamned funny. I'm dying inside and you're laughing. What'd she say, Chuckie—two or three?"

11.

Ed Donlon and Mary Sifton had had an argument earlier that week.

"Not only is our affair over, but I'm afraid I don't even like you very much," she had told him over lunch on Wednesday, conscious of the attention he'd been giving the young waitress. "You have no idea what modernity is all about. You also drink too much. Do you have any idea how much you drink? If you did, you wouldn't sit there ogling that girl that way—not at one o'clock in the afternoon."

"Sure I know what modernity is about," Ed said. "It's sitting through an idiot play, like the one you've got tickets for tonight, or reading some idiot book, like the one you gave me last week, and at the end the writer telling you that you're an idiot for paying any attention to him, that the human race is an idiot, that history is a sinkhole full of idiots, only he's not because he's literate enough to rise above it. That's modernity. . . ."

"You're an incurable romantic. That's why you drink so much."

She'd gone to the theater alone. He hadn't seen her since. His nights were again his own.

On this snowy Washington evening, past and present were inextricably mixed as he fixed his third martini and carried it upstairs with him. He showered and dressed, aware that the house was empty, the room above dark. He had no idea where Grace Ramsey had gone. He'd heard her talking on the phone that afternoon, inquiring about airline schedules.

Downstairs again, he emptied the martini shaker—more there than he had realized—wrapped himself in scarf and overcoat, and stepped out the front door to a lost world miraculously restored. White sculptures lay along the fence palings and tree limbs, wrapped the streets and sidewalks, and recovered long-forgotten memories.

Donlon at nineteen, waiting under the clock at the Biltmore in New

York on a snowy Thanksgiving night for an aspiring ballet dancer who never appears. He goes to a Jean-Louis Barrault movie in the Village instead and picks up an art student in a nearby bar. On a studio couch covered with cat hairs, they make love until four in the morning, when her roommate returns and interrupts to ask if he has any cigarettes. He returns to Princeton on the Sunday afternoon train, flannel suit covered with cat hairs, awed by the power of feminine abstraction.

Donlon at eighteen, a snowy December night in Louisville, attending his cousin's debut at the Spinsters Cotillion at the Pendennis Club. Donlon driving his uncle's vintage Packard through Cherokee Park, the road ahead of him a seamless white, Jack Frost in the trees, an all-night disc jockey from Chicago playing fairyland music. His toes are warm, he is slightly inebriated, and he is punished by a pair of very painful gonads. Next to him on the plush seat is a complaisant young woman from Darien, Connecticut, two years older, come to attend her college classmate's debut. Her cheeks are plump and wind-chapped from a recent skiing weekend, she has barrel thighs, small shoulders, and a pug nose. She and Donlon have been necking continuously in the lounge chair of the sun porch since three o'clock. He's unbuttoned her brassiere and plumbed the small cold breasts with one hand while the other has skirmished her pubic mound but gone no further. They're surrounded by prone couples. An inquiring adult occasionally turns on the overhead light. Dawn will soon show its crapulous Peeping Tom head through the frosty windows.

They take a drive and the cold air revives them. She begins to recite what she remembers of Dylan Thomas's "A Child's Christmas in Wales" as Donlon turns into Cherokee Park toward a dimly remembered trysting place near a fountain. But snow is heavy on the hills and roads, thickening on the windshield, and his cautious speed and the privacy of their grotto tempt his partner to throw caution to the winds. She tosses her cigarette out the window and with one hand seizes his waistband while the other unzips his fly. Seduction, Donlon thought, paraphrasing Degas, required the cunning of a crime, but as he turns into the curve a cold hand is groping boldly in his underpants, Jack Frost is nipping at his testicles, and Christmas rockets are bursting across the windshield. His feet rattle on brake and accelerator, the car toboggans into the curve, twists sideways across the icy road, bongs a stone bridge, and careens into a snowy bog.

Her head has struck the windshield. She's lying against the door. "For God's sake," she weeps. "I mean, how cherry can you get?"

Scrambling out of the car, Donlon finds himself standing on its side. A car with chains passes, crammed with high school rowdies. "Hey, buddy, your fly's open! Next time try taking your pants off first!"

Donlon redivivus now, marching through the Georgetown streets toward Cornelia Bowen's house, his face stung Princeton orange by the chafing flurries, on his way to an affair twenty years suspended. These aren't this year's streets, not the present snow he feels. Past and present are mixed, holiday cotillions and dawn breakfasts, the bloom of a fifth of gin on his cheeks.

Walking into his past, he crossed Wisconsin Avenue, hardly aware of the traffic creeping past. Cornelia Bowen was forty when they'd first met, Donlon ten years younger. She was the wife of a senior Treasury official and Washington held little interest for her. Her children were away in boarding school; theater, music, and art had been her diversions in New York, but politics dominated the table talk at her Georgetown dinner parties. One evening she'd discovered a young man whose memory for Yeats was greater than her own. In the spring they began meeting discreetly at the Corcoran Gallery on Sunday afternoon, her husband's day for golf at Burning Tree. Donlon had an apartment nearby.

He moved through the sifting snow, turned a corner, and found the house up the narrow street near the middle of the block. Her house. Or was it? A woman answered his ring, leaning on a cane, white-haired, her hair in disarray.

Standing on the stoop, he awkwardly searched his memory for the name of Cornelia's housekeeper. "Sorry," he apologized. "Mrs. Bowen told me your name, but I've forgotten. She's in, isn't she?"

A difficult moment followed.

"You caught me by surprise; I said eight," she replied, opening the door. "Don't just stand there. Have you been drinking?"

Vulgar familiarity for a housekeeper. Why was his gin bottle her business? Whose grandmother was she, anyway? Not his, thank God. Affronted, he went in silently, hat in hand. The door shut. Two minutes later he was back on the street, shaken. A lewd mistake, but not his.

He moved on, up the street, following the lights, marching now toward the clock at the Biltmore, where he would wait for an aspiring ballet dancer who would never appear.

The Italian restaurant high on Wisconsin Avenue stopped serving at ten, but the snowy streets had reduced the evening trade and emptied the two dining rooms by nine-thirty. Donlon sat alone at a rear table, carrying on an imaginary dialogue with the hostess. She was seated at an adjacent table, trying to ignore him as she reviewed the evening's receipts. He was finishing a bottle of red wine.

"Let me offer you some," he said, lifting the bottle again.

321

"No, thanks," she repeated for the third time. She didn't lift her head.

Thoughtful for a moment, aware of the superb acoustics of the empty room, he cleared his throat. "'Too long a sacrifice,'" he announced with a certain wilted Irish charm, "'can make a stone of the heart.'"

"You can say that again," she mumbled, adding up a bill.

He waited, hurt and disappointed. She said no more. "Sorry to keep you waiting like this. Maybe someone's expecting you."

"Not tonight. The snow's keeping everyone home, which is where I should be."

Her hair was reddish black, her bright mouth was as small as a parakeet's, but she had a stunning torso. Under the white blouse she wore a black brassiere. A deep shadowy canyon lay under the V of her blouse, ready for siege.

"I live nearby," he said, encouraged.

She ignored him, shuffling the receipts together.

"We could have a drink first."

"I'll bet," she said. "Angelo doesn't like that much."

"Like what?"

"Walking out the front door with the customers."

"Well, I think Angelo's right. Good old Angelo."

"A matter of self-respect, Sicilian pride."

"Good old Sicilian pride." He raised his glass. "'I leave both faith and pride, to young upstanding men, climbing the mountainside.'"

"You can say that again."

He watched her with glazed disapproval, arm still lifted. Then he put the glass down. "Never water the Beefeaters," he said dully.

She lifted her tired eyes. "What are you—a college professor or something?" She got up heavily, pushing up from the table. Her hips were wide and lumpy. "You ought to find a cab and go home. Twenty minutes from now you'll be stranded. That's why we're sending everyone in the kitchen home."

"Why don't I do that," Donlon agreed, hearing an invitation to a tryst.

The cashier locked the door behind him and he waited at the curb beyond the mounds of snow churned up by the passing cars. The restaurant's lights went down and the waitresses and busboys began to leave. She wasn't among them. He flagged down a cab, but the driver wouldn't wait. He waited alone. Ten minutes later a small Volkswagen left the side parking lot and stopped nearby. "No taxi! Stranded!" he called out, scrambling over the mound of snow.

She cranked down her window with professional patience, her voice weary but wise. "We got a rule inside—don't insult the customers. It's late and I'm tired and I don't wanna insult you anyway. You're a nice man and maybe you're a college professor. My old man may not have any college degree, but he'd break you in two. You understand what I'm saying?"

She drove off.

He began walking, struggling down the treacherous pavement, but only as he moved into Georgetown was he aware of how complete was its transformation. It was an Alpine Village. A cross-country skier slid by; two more followed. Cars were stalled here and there along Wisconsin, some abandoned. Beer steins were brought from bars by those recruited inside to help the disabled. Couples walked in the street, holding hands. His throat grown dry, he joyfully joined a group of revelers helping push a stalled van out of a drift and then down the hill. He followed them into a disco bar—crowded, noisy, full of wassailers, like himself—followed them into the smell of hops, damp wool, cedar chips, and Saturday night intoxication.

To a young waitress at the serving space next to his stool, bright-eyed and red-cheeked, flushed by the conviviality of this snowy Washington night, he said, "'We feed the heart on phantasies.'" She pretended she heard, smiled, took her tray, and hurried away. Donlon took the smile as an invitation to the dance.

He ordered a double martini, but it was poorly mixed. When he complained in his friendly, old-chap, tally-ho style, reminding the young bartender of the perils of cheap gin and cheaper vermouth, the young man said, "Look, it's a busy night, friend. If you don't like it, take your business down the street."

"In dulci jubilo," Donlon said.

He'd been here before. He remembered those young faces in the far corner—the ski sweaters, the two young men in tails. Weren't they from the Pendennis Ballroom in Louisville, friends of his cousin Hillary? He recognized a table of drinkers from Stowe, Vermont, and that holiday when he and George Ramsey had competed for a week in sleeping their way through the Sarah Lawrence Alpine Club. "Nice to see you again," he murmured affectionately to two young women in nylon parkas, just entering. So they were all here, these old friends from Princeton, New York, Trenton, Louisville, and Stowe, come to attend winter's debut at Georgetown's festive après-ski.

He asked for another double martini. His bladder painful, he moved to the men's room at the rear as his drink was being mixed. In the washroom mirror he discovered a poor dim dishonored replica of his own face, as muddy as those pathetic oil portraits Jane once painted of him, her family, and her friends—this before her Corcoran instructor advised her to transfer her talent to clay and stone, where her crimes against humanity went undetected. The face troubled him. Returning to the front bar, his nostrils reeking of mothballs, his right leg wet, he found someone had taken his stool. He didn't protest. As he reached forward to take his glass, a young woman turned suddenly:

"Would you stop breathing on me, for Christ's sake!"

Obviously a mistake. He opened his mouth, but no words came. He'd forgotten her name. "Sorry," he managed finally.

She turned back to the bar and he watched in fascination as a long arm reached behind a tweed-clad back from a stool away. Sly fingers that weren't his teased the soft hairs at the base of the young woman's neck.

She turned immediately. "I'm warning you!"

He smiled, finding the face crudely familiar. "Tally-ho," he remembered. "'Rody, blow the horn.' Nancy, isn't it?"

"No, it's not Nancy and someone's gonna blow your horn if you don't keep your goddamn hands to yourself."

"Come on, leave her alone, will you?" her companion asked.

"Charley, would you get this guy off my back and find him a table somewhere."

"Come on, mister, I told you," said the bartender. "Take your business down the street."

"Is this not a public house?" he asked, eyes drawn to some ribald face, satyr or goat, he wasn't sure, cropping glass bottles along the mirrored shelf behind the bar. His hat was on crooked, his tie caught on one shoulder, like an epaulet.

"I mean, look at the poor guy, would you?" someone pleaded.

The bartender gently obliged, removed the glass from his hand, and guided him out the door. He made no protest. He couldn't focus his eyes. With careful dignity, he fell across the bank of snow at the curb and into the street. He hadn't seen it and now that he did, sat atop it, blissfully breathing in the cold, dark air. He stood up at last, eyes stung bright by the cold. He found the middle distance—a familiar sign down the hill—and made for it. The world had come back into focus—joyous world, magnificent world. He was amazed. Skiers slid by gracefully, couples walked hand in hand, a snowball sped over his head and vanished into the night, like a meteorite.

At the entrance to his street, a small car without chains or snow tires was stuck in a drift at the curb. Four hefty female college students were straining against the rear end, trying to push it free into the downhill lane. Gallantly he moved to their assistance. In the darkness there was confusion for a moment as the driver and one of the pushers changed places. In the melee he found his hands pressing heroically against two soft plush fenders in ski pants, his right thumb dangerously near that crevasse—

"Hey!"

324

The car was mercifully free. So was he. His street was dark, the snow drifting down.

Old lecher with a love on every wind.

He moved with dignity, erect and graceful. Disasters had been avoided, humiliations adroitly sidestepped. He had a precise notion of who and where he was, himself, Edward Donlon, this vast hovering presence extending over Alpine Washington from Bethesda to Alexandria, seeing all, forgiving all. Crossing an icy patch near his front gate, he lost his balance momentarily but didn't fall. Perilously close, though. No one had seen— only Bishop Berkeley and himself.

At the top of his porch steps, he said adieu to the evening, his consort, bowing, then leaning forward to blow his breath back into the air. Still leaning forward, he slowly drank it in again, as if drawing this entire intoxicating evening into his lungs for safekeeping until tomorrow evening at seven, when, from this same porch, he would blow it out and resume his pilgrimage. The effort left him dizzy.

He struggled on the porch to find his door key. The key was inserted but the door swung open, unlocked, and he moved into the familiar warmth of his front hall. A pair of matched leather bags stood alongside the staircase.

Grace Ramsey's?

The lights in the front room were on. So was the lamp in the small hall between the dining and living rooms. He heard an oddly familiar voice, a woman talking—not the housekeeper's Maryland nasality, not Grace Ramsey's secretive murmur, but a sharp, incisive voice. He moved on, through the living room.

"I think he just walked in—wait a minute. Ed? Ed, is that you?"

He stood looking into the small lamplit hall where Jane stood, telephone in hand. She looked very tall, very elongated, somehow thinner. Her hair was cut short. She wore a gray tweed suit and the hall reeked of strong cigarette smoke.

"Yes, it's Ed. He looks snockered. Are you snockered, Ed? I'm talking to Greta in Old Lyme."

She held out the phone, but he didn't know what to say. He felt like Tom Thumb, fallen into the milkmaid's churn.

"Yes, I'm afraid he's sloshed, too shocked to say a word. The weather's absolutely atrocious, as I said. I was delayed out of New York for four hours and we flew into Baltimore, of all places. I despise flying anyway and my angst level was absolutely poisonous. I couldn't cope. Fortunately my seat companion helped—a doctor, totally nonthreatening. I could let myself go without feeling victimized. . . ."

What barbaric intruder was this?

". . . no psychic massacres yet. Yes, he just walked in and we haven't talked. He certainly looks nonvindictive, but you can't tell what kind of wormwood his thyroid is secreting. . . ."

He listened woodenly, without the strength to remove his coat. She watched him as she talked on. "Yes, Grace met me at Baltimore—she hired a car. She's been *so* supportive in all this. . . ."

She was whispering now, her back to him. Wizened and old, he'd shriveled like a sea orchid, brought up from the depths. He was still standing there when she hung up. She took off his hat, then helped with his coat, stripping it from the back, the sleeves turned inside out and pulled off from the rear, like a straitjacket. She led him across the room and up the steps.

Who was this person?

At the landing, catching the warm wind of some gentle fragrance, he clumsily tried to embrace it, but a firm knee backed him away.

"Don't be archaic; this is strictly a cooperative household. Grace has been warning me for weeks you were tottering on the brink, but I had no idea it had gone this far. Your breath is absolutely atrocious."

He leaned backward, looking up, but reeled, losing his balance. Jane held him under the arms. Still he looked up. *Grace Ramsey, a spy in his house?*

It was true. She was there, standing at the banister on the third floor, looking down, hovering over the stairwell like the Queen of the Night, come to safely return this house, this home, this family, to her fairyland cuckoo kingdom.

"Yoo hoo." He waved feebly, moving his fingers.

She helped him up and led him into the second-floor bedroom, where she helped him undress. He ignored the pajamas she'd found for him and crawled into bed in his undershorts. "I'm going to stay and help you, but you've got to cooperate," she said. She paused at the door. "Do you want me to leave the light on?" He didn't answer and she went out, shutting the door behind her.

He'd heard their whispers and recognized their conspiracies since he'd learned to walk, wakened to their morning intrigues and fallen asleep to their nightly plots—he the only son in a Victorian house where every room was filled with the echo of feminine strategies. A cook in the kitchen, a laundress in the basement, two spinster aunts on the third floor, a grandmother in her front suite, four sisters with bedrooms side by side on the second floor. They planned the luncheon menu over breakfast, the dinner menu over lunch, his tea dance partners, social responsibilities, barber, and yard chores over dinner, when his father's place was often empty. His father preferred to work late in his downtown law office by then, near a private club, and spent the passive weekends of his middle age locked away in his downstairs study rereading Prescott, Thoreau, and P. G. Wodehouse, or listening to his Bix Beiderbecke record collection or the afternoon Phillies games to escape that shrill incessant attention of a nine-woman household.

Young Donlon had been their prisoner instead—seventeen bloody years of it until he'd escaped to Princeton, where he'd disguised his rebellion by conquest and seduction. But after each possession, each solitary victory, one more remained. Yet he'd fooled no one. They had suckled him, coddled him, bathed him, clothed him, tutored him, taught him, fed him, fondled him, fucked him, and now they would claim him. He was theirs once again, as he had been all the time. A woman upstairs, a woman downstairs, a woman with his gin bottle—he was a prisoner of the sisterhood.

Now he heard luggage bumping up the stairs, whispers, sly laughter. Then low voices and the clink of glasses. The ceiling was dark. What strange constellations were wheeling overhead? He strained to listen. A creak of bedsprings? He sat up immediately. Still more? Now a bed banging. He flung the covers aside and leaped out. Two's company, three's a carousel.

Wait for me!

"Don't be baroque." Jane reacted angrily, escorting him back down the stairs from Brian's old room, where he'd discovered them making up the bed she intended to occupy for the time being.

A prisoner again in his own bed, he'd expected her to lock the door behind her this time. She didn't.

He was disappointed.

12.

Nick Straus had gone to see Leyton Fischer that snowy evening to apologize. It was a sad house. A faint musty odor hovered on the air—old furniture, old rugs, old brass, old memories—a melancholy interment watched over by this waspish caretaker with his sprained right foot in a ski sock. He'd slipped on the icy curb outside that morning and painfully twisted his ankle. The rooms of the first floor were unused, the furniture protected by white dust covers. Fischer led him to the large study at the back of the house. The bay window looked out over a dark rear garden. Bookshelves lined the walls, a small mound of coal glowed cherry red in the fireplace beyond the brass fender.

"I came to apologize," Nick told him. "I'm sorry to have involved you in this and I came to apologize."

"You needn't. I understand—certainly I understand. The time had come, I suppose." Fischer's gray hair was damply combed and he wore a dark blazer and an ascot.

"I simply wanted to bring a few absurd facts to official attention."

"Of course; don't apologize. Would you like a cocktail, maybe some sherry?" Decanters of sherry and port sat on the nearby table, both less than a quarter full. A small puddle of wine lay next to a nearby glass with a drop of liquid in the bottom.

Nick declined.

Fischer didn't repeat the offer. He refilled his glass with a trembling hand. More drops leaked to the table. "I probably should have left years ago—after '62. The truth is it's been terribly lonely since Celia died."

He sat down in the leather chair nearby, opposite Nick. They sat in silence for a minute. "The truth is it won't matter what you did. The people you intended it for are incapable of dealing with these problems, intellectually incapable. In the end this nation will get exactly what it deserves."

Nick watched him drink and then put the glass aside.

"The moral equivalent of an enlightened foreign policy would be a Beethoven string quartet, I suppose. I once put it to them in those terms."

"To them?"

"In 1962, during the Cuban crisis, when I was working in the basement of the White House, the NSC. We were trying to orchestrate—that was the word we were using"—he smiled wanly—"'orchestrate' our response to Khrushchev's missiles in Cuba: Navy, Air Force, Army, the remnants of the Cuban brigades, British, French, NATO, and so forth. This is what I told them. I said it required a sensitivity, moral as well as intellectual, that was quite beyond these crude instruments available to us. I said this at a meeting in the White House situation room. A subcabinet official lifted his finger and pointed at me. 'From now on, you're for it, and I don't want to hear another word.' He didn't. After the crisis, I was sent over to State. I've kept my silence ever since."

"I didn't know that," Nick said. "I'm sorry. I should have."

"There's no reason you should have known," Fischer said, with a trace of annoyance. "Please don't be pious, Nick. The course we're setting for ourselves will end in disaster. There are people other than yourself who know this. I've known it for twenty years."

A rosebush tapped against the bay window at Leyton Fischer's back, moving with the blowing snow. A gardenia in final bloom with drops of water on its petals floated curiously in a silver bowl on the table in front of the window, like some offering to someone departed. Nick heard the wind trapped in the courtyard.

". . . bankruptcy or catastrophe, that's where it will lead. The treasury exhausted, the economy broken, that's where they're taking us. Withdrawal will follow, total withdrawal to these shores; it's inevitable. We'll be out of Europe in four years."

"I'm surprised to hear you say that."

"It's the stupidity you despise—the dullness, the mediocrity, the arrogance." He looked away suddenly. "That's the rage that grows. That's what you feel. Someone once said of Carlyle that his rage was such that only the end of the world would consume it. That's what one feels. If it were to happen, I would have absolutely no regrets, none whatsoever."

"There are things that might be done," Nick suggested.

"What? Nothing. It's too late. We can no more change the situation than we can change medieval Europe." He got to his feet, hobbled about a table, and stood at the bookcase on the far side of the fire. "Our knowledge of medieval Europe will tell you." The book for which he was searching was too high to reach. "It's based upon chronicles written by churchmen," he continued, limping back to his chair, "by ecclesiastical sycophants whose belief influenced every fact they collected and every Latin sentence they wrote." He refilled his sherry glass. "Now, of course, the view of medieval Europe as devoutly religious is indestructible, not because it's true but because the documents by which we know it were written by those who believed it, who wanted others to believe it, and who were incapable of believing anything else. The same can now be said of the modern world about us—Soviet, Chinese, third world. We in Washington study a popular text written by barbarians. . . ."

It was the malice Nick found so ugly, the venom of all of those years. "I didn't know you felt that so strongly," he said after a minute.

"Why should you be surprised? You think as I do. Why do you suppose I kept telling DIA that you were their man when they were looking for an absolutely reliable Soviet analyst?"

"I've often wondered."

"I knew your views were mine—a kind of double, able to do things I couldn't. That in a moment of utter madness, your judgment could be relied on."

"I'm sorry then, Leyton."

Fischer still watched him disapprovingly. "You've always faced the same problems as I, the same prejudices. For others, my private and personal views have always been a problem. You learn to hide them. What choice did I have?"

"I understand that now."

"I was a conscientious objector in '41. My parents were Quakers. You didn't know that, did you?"

"No, I didn't."

"Being Jewish, I suppose you've faced it all your life," Fischer continued, and Nick Straus could think of nothing helpful to say. "I mean in the sense that your very existence is a problem, as it were," he resumed randomly. "For others and for yourself. But wherein yours was inherited, mine was acquired," he added, and then sipped from the glass. "You have no idea of the anguish in accepting such a burden. On the other hand, one should never look on suffering itself as proof of moral superiority. I dislike that kind of smugness," he said. "Intensely. If that were the case, the barrios of Latin America would be full of saints, wouldn't they?"

In that veiled look and that fatuous question, Nick Straus perceived the ugly truth about Leyton Fischer. He despised him, but he felt no anger, only pity. *As in fact they are,* he thought in reply. "I didn't realize you were Catholic," he said.

"Yes, shortly before Celia—"

He couldn't bring himself to say it.

"Yes, I understand. But in these times, I sometimes think everyone's existence is problematical."

"I was thinking more of uniqueness," Fischer said dryly.

Nick Straus heard a breath from a tomb, the chilling exhalation of a mind that had long ceased to exist, unique the way an extinct nebula might have once been unique, now only a cold white fog on a dark photographic plate.

He crept down the narrow street in the light snow, invisible in the darkness yet touching his face and powdering his woolly shoulders. Because of the treacherous streets and the abandoned cars, he'd left his automobile across the river in Rosslyn. It was almost seven. As he began crossing the bridge, he heard the sound of a plane descending through the darkness overhead, but could see nothing, not even its navigation lights.

He hesitated. Was this to be the night an inbound jet lost its navigation beam and smashed into Key Bridge, a flaming Ferris wheel, Nick Straus the only pedestrian casualty? The conversation in Leyton Fischer's rear study was so bizarre that it might have been a warning. He continued on. The river flowed under him, dark and invisible. As he approached the center, a sanding truck churned slowly by, following a snowplow, and the walkway vibrated oddly under his feet. The wind had died down, but his steps grew more cautious.

How could it be that those so capable, so intelligent, so decent, so alive to feelings in their friends and families, in a scrap of bureaucratic prose, a few bars of music, or lines of sentimental verse they treasured, could be so indifferent to the pain and degradation of so much of the life that shared this planet? How could it be? How could they commit themselves to barbaric strategies that promised so much more? How could it be that they could so hypocritically treasure their own personal anguish, like Leyton Fischer, as if it were some exquisite proof of their moral superiority, like a Renaissance masterpiece hung in the privacy of their study and only to be enjoyed there? Was moral sensitivity a private art gallery only the rich could afford, a novel by Proust only the intellectual could understand?

He looked back over the city as his steps slowed. The evidence was everywhere. One had only to look to see, to read to understand. *Where is it all going, this madness? Where is it taking us?* The offices were empty now, like the corridors, the committee rooms, the secret caucus chambers. The rituals were suspended—the bustle, the ceremony, the self-important routines, the thousand daily decisions that sustain each day anew and end it as they ended the last, no nearer, no farther, the promise always the same.

His footsteps had slowed to a stop. A second plane lumbered overhead; the wind was in his ears. Snowflakes dissolved against his cold cheeks.

Now he didn't move. I'm not asking for miracles, he heard himself saying. I'm not asking that you reveal your mysteries so even the blind can see. I'm not asking for divine messengers or television miracles, some mysterious spacecraft descending on this city so that we can all recover our sense of the miraculous. I'm not asking for these things. All I'm asking is for some small sign that all this matters to you.

He had stopped at the center of the bridge. The wind was still in his ears. The snow flurries had diminished, but he didn't notice. The cold was cruel, but still he waited. A moment passed, then another, but he continued to wait, looking back over the city.

Nothing. He heard nothing, only the wind. He moved away, ashamed, no longer sure whether the wetness in his eyes was from the wind, the snow, or something else; but then the reply came.

Consider the imagination as it must be, it said.

He stopped, head lifted, frozen in place, waiting.

Consider the imagination as it must be, it continued, *not unique in one man but alive everywhere, unique in all—friends and enemies, those who suffer, those who don't. Consider the imagination as it can only be in all its immensity, here and everywhere. Consider that and now tell me what miracle you want performed.*

But he had nothing more to ask. The curtain of snow had lifted, the lights had everywhere brightened, as if from the descent of some radiant galactic vessel, and its miracle was there, spread out before him in the winter night.

Part Six

1.

Shy Wooster believed there were two Americas—the public America and the private America. The events of public America were everywhere on conspicuous display—on television and radio, in films, newspapers, magazines, books, the *Congressional Record,* in the speeches of its European critics, and the comic book imaginations of its fanatical enemies, like Fidel Castro and the Ayatollah Khomeini. The private America was everywhere hidden—in small towns, in factories and office buildings, on farms, in the hollows of Appalachia, the scrub country of South Carolina, or the rubble of the South Bronx—in short, in all those places where the burden of intolerable lives wasn't numbered by the Iranian hostage clock once kept by American television newscasters.

He believed, moreover, that there was little relationship between the two. This was his despair. He knew that whatever public America's occasional triumphs—as in electing one of their own, a movie actor, as President—the balance would ultimately return to private America.

The public America, like the television commercials that simulated it, was one of surfaces—garish colors, predatory purposes, contrived emotions, vulgar self-confession, climactic moments, and theatrical success. The private America, he knew from his own youth in rural South Carolina, was one of habit, routine, work, self-absorption, and solitude. To vindicate its existence, public America spent much of its time snooping about trying to determine what private America was thinking.

But even then—in the public opinion poll, the statistical survey, or the marketing study—private America remained elusive. When a private American greets a political pollster on his doorstep, he immediately lifts his voice into a quasi-public register, the answer supplied by the question.

"It's like looking through a keyhole at another eyeball peeking back," he'd often declared when public opinion sampling was undertaken by one of Bob Combs's foundations. He put no faith in them.

The public opinion pollster would tell you that Americans had opinions about Poland, El Salvador, South Africa, and every other country recently in the headlines, but Shy Wooster wouldn't.

"Live and let live, that's what they think, and anyone who comes up with a different answer is lying to you," he would insist. "You get the draft going again to send American soldiers to El Salvador or Saudi Arabia and you'll find out right quick what they think of both of them places. Not worth one American life, that's what. Live and let live. The same reason everybody down in South Carolina got so riled up when all those out-of-staters come down to South Carolina back in the fifties. We weren't minding their bus'ness, how come they all come down there mindin' ours? I tell you why. It was our self-respect they was stompin' on. . . ."

Security, privacy, self-respect.

In his political notebook, Shy Wooster had once written a few lines that, in his opinion, defined the character of this private America the opinion-tasters and poll-takers were all the time trying to seduce out from behind the screen door. The vainglorious bunting the politicians draped themselves in and the lofty abstractions invoked by the intellectuals—words like "freedom," "democracy," and "human" or "civil rights"—meant no more than a Sunday school anthem to private America. It was as experience, not abstraction, that their values were defined, and what they expected of their political institutions was simple and direct.

> Most Americans keep a Bible in their homes but they don't go running to look up chapter and verse every time they think a neighbor is sinning against them.
>
> Not many Americans keep the Constitution or the Bill of Rights handy to check up on what Washington's doing but they don't have to. They know sure enough what they want, just three things: security, privacy, and self-respect. When someone in Washington goes to messing up and they're getting a little less of any of these three, they'll know right away and then they'll get mad.

Politicians, bureaucrats, jurists, and social engineers who tampered with American institutions in such a way that any of the three were in jeopardy did so at their own peril. Government intervention in private life, as in the case of forced busing, violated two of these canons: privacy and self-respect; gun control violated all three. Welfare and free food stamps violated the workingman's self-respect: he worked for the bread on his table, why not everyone else? The Vietnam yippies had also violated his self-respect, just as the Iranian mobs had violated the nation's, for which Carter had paid the price.

And so it went in Shy Wooster's estimation—over two hundred years of national experience embodied in just three simple words. Private America wasn't interested in what it might be but in what it was, despite the clamor of those who insisted they be something else. Hardly enough to create an imperium or to lead a global crusade; not enough even to send a few battalions to El Salvador.

But enough so that when Shy Wooster saw the letter to Senator Bob Combs from the Mount Zion Reformed Baptist Church announcing its congregation's forthcoming visit to Washington by chartered bus, he was troubled: his security, his privacy, his self-respect. Included among the visitors' names was that of a Miss Bertha Jackson.

2.

On her last day in Washington, Rita Kramer appeared in Haven Wilson's office, already in transit, her hair shorter, her luggage ready to be packed. Last week's snow still lay in a gray batting along the curbs and walks. A winter dimness was in the streets and a surflike dolor in the dark sky rolling endlessly over the rooftops like the scud of the Atlantic east of Chincoteague or Hatteras, but the temperature was mild, a feathery autumn dampness in the air. Artie Kramer and the others had returned to Los Angeles. She was flying to New Jersey to spend some time with her relatives before she returned to California.

"Do you want to tell me voluntarily or do I have to drag it out of you?" she said as she sat down. "It was a joke right from the beginning, but I kept a straight face; so did you. So what did Peter Rathbone have up his sleeve, sending Artie here? Maybe Iran made a lot of us patriots all of a sudden, but that doesn't mean we're all going to be Secretary of Defense. So what was it all about?"

A new administration, he told her—new people, new priorities, and new opportunities. Rathbone had served in the White House once under Nixon and knew how it worked. When he was offered the presidency of Caltronics and an attractive stock option late the previous year, he also intended to resolve two embarrassing cases, one a bribery investigation and the other fraudulent practices involving two large insurance companies, perhaps labor racketeering. Both investigations were incomplete.

When Rathbone learned that Artie Kramer was eager for a government job, he encouraged him. If Rathbone had used direct political pressure to get both investigations closed down, he would have failed. The White House would have reacted and so would the Justice Department. He'd approached the problem more obliquely—a low-risk gamble, using Artie Kramer as his stalking horse.

"Washington is a big place," Wilson told her, "and on any given day there's an awful lot going on. When you try to interfere too directly, you send up red flags and people react. That's not what Rathbone was after. Sending your husband here was very low-key, I suppose you'd say. He was just one name among many."

"Go for it, little man," she broke in indignantly, "and if you fall on your face, no skin off my nose."

"To know what Rathbone was after," he continued, "you have to know how a name check works, what they call an indices check. When you have a political appointee, the FBI and Justice run an indices check. They tap into these computerized indexes that tell them what they have on an individual, positive or negative. Here it gets a little complicated."

"Go ahead."

"When you have a court-authorized wiretap, like the one that the U.S. Attorney in L.A. got on Caltronics, every name you pick up has to be logged. On a big case, that can mean twenty or thirty thousand references. So that's what happened: they ran an indices check on your husband and they tapped into these two investigations, both incomplete. That was the second step."

"What was the first?"

"Sending Artie to Washington. So now, two steps and the White House knows about these two investigations. They're brought to official attention over there. Rathbone hasn't done a thing—hasn't lifted the phone, hasn't called anyone asking for a political favor, hasn't used any muscle at all— just sent your husband to Washington and let the machinery grind away."

She was confused. "So they say no dice?"

"No, the investigations aren't finished. Your husband isn't a principal but he's tied to Caltronics, a vice-president. The White House would look a little silly if it ignored the Justice Department indices check, made the political appointment, and two weeks later the U.S. Attorney brings criminal charges against Caltronics. So the White House doesn't know what to do. It's a hot potato. Maybe they ask Justice to give them more information. Justice can't give them more; they don't have it. So no one does anything. The machinery has broken down. But now Rathbone has his opportunity. The political pressure starts—a few letters from congressmen Artie had helped, letters from a few campaign types out in California, all asking the same question: What happened to Artie Kramer's political appointment? They don't ask about Caltronics, just your husband. Here's a big Republican fund-raiser, our friend, the White House's friend, his name has been sitting there for months. What's happening? Do something. Just make a decision one way or another."

"It's the squeaky wheel that gets greased," Rita said. "Artie was just Rathbone's squeaky wheel. . . ."

"Pretty much. So that's it. The White House decides to do something. They don't want to offend their political supporters, but they also don't want to get the Justice Department bureaucracy or the U.S. Attorney's office on their backs." She'd been drawn to the edge of the leather chair, sitting forward, the fur coat shed behind her, her elbows on her knees. "Are you sure this interests you?"

"It does, absolutely."

"No one told you?"

"Who, for Christ's sake? Go on, tell me."

"So it's decision time. It's a small problem, nothing that needs top-level attention. Some small White House gofer will do. He's told to come up with a solution. And here you have to take something else into account—the Washington multiplier effect."

"The what?"

"You know what it is—you see it all the time. Multiplier effect . . . money or status index . . . the flunky syndrome."

"Make it simple."

"The next time you're in a crowded restaurant, give your waiter ten dollars and tell him you want two aspirin. For as long as it takes to get the two aspirin, he'll be deaf to everyone else. It works in this town every day. When a senator's secretary makes travel reservations, a late flight to Dallas that's already overbooked, she'll come up with the tickets. When some White House flunky calls up a federal agency and asks for a staff study, maybe some paper someone has casually mentioned in a meeting that might be useful, it's got to be handed over by the close of business. That's the multiplier effect, the flunky syndrome. The flunky always wears the big man's shoes. If he's a White House flunky, he rules by right of the President of the United States. So when he goes over to the Justice Department to resolve a problem involving two ongoing investigations, people are going to bend over backwards to try to find a solution."

"I think I'm beginning to get it."

"That's the third step. Maybe this Justice Department official he talks to is a political appointee himself. If he isn't, the White House gofer will find one who is, someone who's sympathetic. So our senior bureaucrat over at Justice asks the people downstairs to show him the two cases that are causing this minor problem. He gets a staff counsel to look at them. He gets someone else to review them. They think alike, these three, problem-solvers. On any issue in which the interests of the given agency aren't overriding, then the White House interest will prevail. In this case, the investigations are incomplete, nothing has happened in eight to ten months, and the government still can't make the cases. So the solution is obvious. Justice is wasting its time. The downstairs civil servants are told to suspend the investigations, put their assets to better use, and get on with something productive. Stop spinning your wheels, get yourself in gear, go for something that will pay off, not those old hangovers from a former administration. So they close the investigations. The White House problem is solved."

"And that's all there is to it?"

"Until someone comes walking in the door with new evidence, something they're not going out to look for. It's a political decision, but that's not the way it looks on the books—a bureaucratic decision too. It's a political wash. The past is scrubbed clean. Caltronics can forget about its old problems. Perfectly legal, no laws broken, just the usual partisan politics, grinding away. . . ."

"And that's what Rathbone was after until Strykker screwed it up."

"Strykker does things the old-fashioned way. Crude, no finesse. He was out of his class, like you said. He was probably confused about what Rathbone intended. He doesn't know this city."

"He was dead set against Artie coming." She sat back at last, crossing her legs. "It's goddamn depressing."

Wilson shrugged, amused. "Hoffa said the same thing when the Kennedys were elected."

"And you're hooked on it."

"Washington? I don't know." He looked out the bay window. "My friends are here."

He walked back with her toward the hotel, by way of the Potomac. The gulls were flying and the wind from the river smelled of the sea.

"Poor Artie," she said, her hands deep in her pockets as she looked out across the tide. "It all seems so simple for him."

"For a lot of us."

"Not you." She glanced at him, cheeks drawn in, her gaze as fragile as porcelain. She seemed about to say something, but then turned away and they started back. "You think you'll ever break away?" she asked finally.

"Maybe. I've been thinking about opening a rural law practice, like the one my father had."

"Where?"

"Out in Virginia someplace, small-town Virginia."

"You couldn't live out there any more than I could." She stopped to watch him, smiling. "Stop kidding yourself. It's just a middle-aged pipe dream, like me living in that Grace Ramsey house. Nice but no dice. We're not the type, you and me. Some dreamers we are."

"Maybe." They walked on.

"What would your wife say about it?"

"She wouldn't be enthusiastic, not yet. Maybe in time."

"She's just being realistic. Artie wouldn't go for my life style either, not what I really want. What's her name?"

"Betsy."

She'd stopped again. "Betsy," she repeated. "I'll bet I know what she's like. You don't talk about her much, do you?"

"No, I suppose not."

"'Still waters run deep,' that's what my grandmother used to say. It was so trite it drove me batty. Now I think she's right. It's that way with you and Betsy, is it? I kinda figured it was—especially that weekend you didn't call, that Saturday you said you might. Maybe you've forgotten."

"No, I remember."

They walked on in silence. "So do I," she said finally.

They stopped in front of the glass doors to her hotel.

"I guess this is it," he said. He was no longer conscious of the rough cheeks, the careful make-up, or the dancer in Baltimore she'd once reminded him of.

"I guess so."

"I enjoyed it," he said. "Maybe that sounds a little trite too, but it's true. I'll miss seeing you."

"Maybe I'll remember that when I'm down and out." She watched a taxi that was just arriving. "I hate goodbyes, I always have. They're like funerals. I'd rather break out the champagne."

"Then we won't say goodbye."

"Maybe one day we can celebrate, just the two of us. I think they owe us one." She looked away again. "Anyway, if you ever get to California, think about giving me a call."

"I'll do that." He moved aside awkwardly to let someone pass.

"We could break out a bottle at the beach house," she said, smiling. "Just the two of us. By the time you got back here, it'd all be ancient history."

"If I get out that way, I'll call you."

"Sure," she said. "You're a goddamned liar, honey, but thanks anyway. You don't go back, never—not even a look. Like me with Artie, you have to be that way, too dependable. What'd it ever get us? You think I don't know you by now? If I didn't, things might have been a little different for both of us. . . ."

"If you ever get too confused about what's going on in Washington, give me a call."

"I will. Thanks for everything, sweetie."

She kissed him quickly on the cheek, and turned away through the glass doors, leaving only that unmistakable fragrance behind.

It followed him back to the Center, and as he lifted his head at the front gate, it was still there. It was, at that moment, as if something had been taken from him, something found as well, and he stood holding the gate open, looking back down the street.

"Sorry . . ."

A deliveryman from a local parcel service confronted him awkwardly, unable to enter. He moved aside, then remembered his four o'clock appointment and followed the man up the walk.

3.

Birdie Jackson arrived in Washington in mid-January.

By then, a great deal had happened at the Center and elsewhere, although the quality of public life in Washington remained much the same.

A small theater group was holding tryouts for a play called *Inessa,* by a former political scientist and Soviet scholar named Pauline Rankin, now turned playwright. She was a tweedy type, a chain smoker, and she supervised the tryouts herself, aided by her friend and factotum, William O'Toole, who was possessed of remarkable powers in his own right, including an astonishing memory. The bond between them was difficult to define, but genuine. On several occasions, when searching for a word or an expression not immediately on the tip of her tongue, she would turn to him and he would supply it, as he had supplied, several months earlier, the name of the town and the lake where she had spent her summers as a child, too small to know the names of either, but terrorized for years afterward by that infinite body of water stretching away from the foot of the cliffs. Whether she thought he had psychic powers or had suffered his youth as she had suffered hers and thus could speak from a common memory wasn't clear. What was clear, however, was that their lives had somehow merged.

Pauline Rankin wasn't the only associate at the Center to step out on her own. Dr. Foster had also become a public personality of sorts, familiar on the lecture circuit, on panel discussions, and on an occasional late night TV talk show. By then he'd discovered his public voice, which proved to be similar to the one Haven Wilson had encountered on his first trip to the Center—elusive, sly, shifting constantly in and out of false registers, of somewhat ambiguous gender. It was a voice perfect for television talk programs. He wrote several articles on behaviorism and foreign policy, but "ratomorphic" was now so widely used by the nuclear freeze advocates and the unilateral disarmers that its authorship was forgotten. "If it had been a mouthwash, I'd have made a million dollars," he said, smiling sadly over sherry at a League of Women Voters reception in Bethesda following yet another lecture. A TV host on a late night program discovered by accident Foster's gift for unmasking the historical pretender in contemporary public figures—Alexander Haig as St. Ignatius de Loyola, Brzezinski as Count Casimir Pulaski, Senator Jesse Helms as Cromwell, and George Will as Tom Sawyer's bookish cousin, Sidney, the immaculate boy in the front row who could always define the long words in the geography book the dissolute boys in the back row couldn't even pronounce.

The success led to a contract with a New York publisher for a book to be called *Impersonations,* which would describe the extent to which public life was dominated by masquerades of one kind or another—movie actors as presidents, senators as generals, generals as statesmen, Wall Street bankers rolling over Arab petrodollars as third world humanitarians, neurotic poets and essayists of exquisite sensitivity as the urchin street conscience of the Latin American barrios, Marxist-Leninist despots as libertarians, and a pluralist nation of private pursuits impersonating a crusading, evangelical world power.

Would anything ever again be what it seemed? Dr. Foster would ask at the end of these televised performances, smiling wistfully. But nothing had ever been what it seemed—not Greece to the Romans, not Rome to eighteenth-century England, not England to the colonies, not the colonies to the Indians, not the Indians to Rousseau, Jean Jacques or Henri. So Dr. Foster was saying nothing new, but TV hosts are impresarios of the moment, not the past. Aware they had a popular commodity on their hands, they sighed in puzzled respect and tried to look profound.

Even Angus McVey was persuaded, against his will, to make a public appearance, in the documentary film Jennifer's friend was making on Washington policy centers and think tanks. Nick Straus had become director of the Center by then and Angus McVey had reclaimed the old office once held for him. In that room lined by some of his favorite books brought from Boxhill Farm—Tacitus, Locke, Macaulay, Burckhardt, and Jefferson—fixed in the glare of the strobe lights, and confronted by a single cameraman and a single director, his granddaughter looking on, he had rendered unto Caesar what was Caesar's, in a thin, quavering voice:

"I should think it's perfectly obvious. During the past thirty years, we've seen the Holocaust, a world war, the hydrogen bomb, a man on the moon, the assassination of one President and the resignation in disgrace of another, a futile, monstrous war in Southeast Asia undertaken by the most decent country in the world with the most rational of justifications. We've seen millions die of starvation while our own granaries were filled to overflowing, small genocidal racial wars of unparalleled brutality occur throughout the third world while the U.N. Secretariat in New York employs ten thousand civil servants to denigrate the West, all this and then you ask me why I'm pessimistic about the probability of nuclear devastation—"

"*Cut!* Let's back up again. There's a shadow there."

"Yeah, I see it," said the cameraman.

"There's a shadow on your face, Granddad," Jennifer apologized.

"Let's take it again," called the young director. "From where he said it was perfectly obvious. O.K., let's take it from there. Ready? Let's go—roll it."

Angus McVey had no script. He looked at them in astonishment. The moment was gone, swept past, and he with it. Repeat it? What sort of debased specie was this? Words repeated, coarsened and worn until they lost all identifiable moral content? Couldn't they understand what those words had cost him? Twenty, thirty years of his own life. Were they to be repeated like parts in a television commercial? No, of course they didn't understand. And recognizing too late the truth of this latest medium, he unfastened the microphone with trembling fingers. Then he rose with silent dignity, straightened his jacket, and vanished through the door, like some lonely centennial comet, his rendezvous with this modern generation of celluloid illusions and contrived spontaneity now kept but concluded, *sub specie temporis.*

He continued his solitary trek through space, moving painfully on his stiff joints. He would send for his car, but got no farther than the half-closed door of Nick Straus's office. He hesitated, knocked at the casing, and then peeked in. Nick was sitting in front of the gas fire, a manuscript on his lap. He put it aside and invited Angus in, grateful for the opportunity to resume that dialogue they'd been carrying on these past weeks, *sub specie aeternitatis.*

Nick Straus had met twice with the staff of the Senate Foreign Relations Committee, which had begun preparing for spring hearings on arms control, the most extensive in years. A copy of his DIA daily summary had been bootlegged to a staff member, who'd circulated it to a handful of senators as suspicious as Nick Straus about the administration's intentions regarding arms talks with Moscow. Several were even more vehement than Nick in maintaining that the Pentagon's insistence on acquiring a first-strike weapon under a smoke screen of phony arms control was dangerously undermining deterrence and greatly increasing the probability of catastrophe. He'd met privately with two senators and they'd talked for almost three hours. He was told his revelations had been useful for those already dubious of the administration's intentions.

He was asked to prepare for the Senate committee three papers for the May hearings, whose purpose would be to draft a resolution to be sent to the Senate, expressing both Senate and public concern about the urgency of arms control talks with the Soviet Union and greater flexibility by the administration.

It was during these conversations that he was asked to join the Foreign Relations Committee staff. He declined, regretfully, explaining that he'd just accepted the directorship of the Center.

With the preparation of the three papers, Nick Straus began the reorientation of the Center, which had too long been administered for the benefit of its own technicians. It was to be a kind of public forum, an ombudsman, intended to clarify the crucial issues of the day. Public issues were too often obscured by executive secrecy, privilege, and cant. The government erred in claiming that the issues were so complex that only the experts could determine the relevancy of a given policy. It was the government itself, Nick insisted, that was the poorest guide possible through the secretive, relativistic maze of fact, conjecture, and fallacy that lay behind a given policy choice, like the MX missile. The public may not have been experts in these technical details, but neither were they intimidated by them. On the larger issues, they knew whether a given policy was wrong or right, and this was their strength. The Center would help make that strength public.

Angus McVey gave him his enthusiastic support. So did Haven Wilson, who'd made his final recommendations and retired from involvement with the Center. Putting aside for the time being his plans for opening a law practice in rural Virginia near the old farm he and Betsy had bought, he joined a small Washington law firm. He was now a commuter again, with a large, airy office overlooking K Street, his own private parking space, and a dozen associates, many of them former government lawyers.

It was in the third week at his law office that he read one morning of a decision by a Tennessee federal district court that brought to mind Birdie Jackson and prompted telephone calls to Foreman and Bernie Klempner. The three of them met for lunch several days later. They talked for two hours and Klempner promised to consult his records. The information Klempner discovered there and a subsequent visit to the Justice Department's civil rights division were what convinced Haven Wilson that he should talk to Birdie Jackson when she visited Washington.

Birdie Jackson had had recent chest pains and was under medication when she'd visited Washington. Her doctor had advised against the trip but she'd come anyway, arrived by overnight bus with members of two Baptist church congregations from South Carolina. Buster Foreman met her the evening of the first day in the lounge of the Beltway Motor Lodge, where she was staying. She was relieved to learn that Smooter Davis was safe and sound in Oakland, California, but was puzzled that she hadn't heard from him during all those years. Buster didn't tell her that Davis had refused to return Haven Wilson's telephone calls or acknowledge receipt of his registered letter.

She told Buster that she'd received a letter and a mysterious package from Cora Pepper, sent to her in care of the Mount Zion Church. It had been mailed from Newport News, Virginia. She and Tom Pepper were on their way to Washington, but their truck had broken down outside Newport News. Cora was working in a motel, Tom Pepper as a short-order cook. The package she'd sent contained a wad of yellowing newspaper clippings with marginal comments by Tom Pepper, auto delivery receipts from Georgia, Alabama, and Mississippi used-car retailers, carbon copies of typewritten notices of meetings at Bob Combs's hunting camp, and two faded Polaroid photographs taken during one of those meetings. In one, Buster could make out the porcine face of Shy Wooster, standing next to a beer-bellied man wearing a barbecue apron, holding a barbecue fork in one hand and an automatic shotgun in the other. He was identified by the handwriting on the back as a Klan official from Foley, Alabama.

Cora had explained in the accompanying letter that she'd collected the papers from Tom Pepper's old bankruptcy files—they had been given up not willingly but grudgingly: her husband had planned to use them to interest Bob Combs and Shy Wooster in investing in his fast-food franchise. The memorabilia concerned those years Tom Pepper had worked at the Combs car emporium in South Carolina, when he had been privy to the conspiratorial goings and comings of those difficult times.

Haven Wilson looked at the envelope's contents after Buster Foreman brought them to him the same night. The meaning wasn't entirely clear for each document, but the pattern was. The dates were what interested him most.

Wilson met with Birdie Jackson in his K Street office the following morning. She was smaller and more frail than he'd expected. Her voice was weak and slightly hoarse. As Buster helped her from the portable wheelchair to the leather armchair, Wilson had misgivings about subjecting her to a long and arduous public trial.

She listened silently as he described her case against those who'd burned her house and those who, knowingly or unknowingly, had aided and abetted them. He told her what Bernie Klempner had confirmed a week earlier—that he'd been warned by Smooter Davis that a few Klan sympathizers from the next-door car lot had been planning arson the week her cottage had burned. The target had been the Mount Zion Church, which had recently sponsored a private excursion to join an NAACP sit-in in Selma, Alabama. The warning had been passed to the FBI in Washington, to the civil rights division at Justice, to the FBI field offices in South Carolina, and to local law officials. None had acted on the information. Her case would be difficult, but he thought he had enough evidence to prove a violation of federal law and a conspiracy to deprive her of her rights for reasons of race. The suit would be brought against the U.S. government.

She was surprised and disappointed. "The gov'ment, the U.S. gov'ment?" she asked weakly. "Wash'n'ton?"

"It's the government's responsibility," he said. "The government knew about a conspiracy next door and did nothing."

"It wasn't Washington. It was Mr. Bob Combs and Mr. Shyrock Wooster. They done it."

"This would come out in the suit," Buster said. "Combs and Wooster both."

"Then it's them two I'll take to court," she insisted.

Wilson explained why that would be impossible. Both men would be protected under the law. The essential issue was the failure of the U.S. government to protect her rights when it had knowledge that a conspiracy was taking place.

She sat gazing at him in disappointment.

"Remember when Smooter Davis once told you that Bob Combs's day in court was coming?" Buster Foreman said quietly. "Combs, Wooster, all of them? This would be that day."

"The U.S. government?" she asked plaintively. "It's the government that's given me what I got. How'm I gonna walk up to the courthouse and ask the judge to put the U.S. government in jail? How'm I gonna do that? Lordy, I don't want to spend the rest of my days fighting the U.S. government. I couldn't never rest, couldn't sleep at night. Someone always slippin' 'round my house. My daddy'd turn over in his grave. 'What you done, chile,' he'd say. It'd be me lockin' myself up—not Mr. Shyrock Wooster; not Bob Combs, either. It's between me and them, and goin' to the courthouse against the U.S. government won't make it right."

They couldn't convince her. The most she would promise was to think about it, to talk to her minister at the Mount Zion Church, and to a deacon, as old as she, whose judgment she trusted.

Only as she was leaving did she seem to remember something and turn back from her wheelchair to look at Haven Wilson.

"I don't know you," she said, "but I want you to promise me something. Don't go talking about this, don't go sending me letters, something my cousin could read, don't go putting ideas into her head. Don't you go making bad worse with that girl. I don't want no one knowing about this, not till I think about it."

Haven Wilson wasn't sure what she meant, but Buster seemed to understand. "He won't say a word, I promise," Buster assured her.

It was a sunny but chilly day. Buster and his wife took her to lunch and afterward drove her up Pennsylvania Avenue to the Senate office building for the visiting group's meeting with Senator Bob Combs—a ten-minute photo session followed by a ten-minute speech by the senator on the state of the Union.

Buster and Birdie waited at the top of the steps for the Mount Zion delegation, whose bus hadn't appeared. She preferred to rest outside in the weak winter sun, sitting in her wheelchair, silently following the faces of those climbing the steps, curious as to who they were and what their business was.

"He really thinks I can do that?" she asked Buster, "Take the government to court?"

"He sure does."

"It's a whole lotta business I don't know nothing about," she admitted. "All these folks here."

Buster's wife circled the block a third time and drove on, searching for a parking place. The two were still waiting when a pair of men left a cab at the curb and came up the steps.

Buster recognized Shy Wooster a minute before she did. With him was one of Combs's staff aides, arriving for the three o'clock meeting.

Wooster paused at the top of the steps, handkerchief at his mouth to wipe away the last traces of a long prime-ribs-and-Burgundy lunch. He glanced at Buster and then at the small figure in the wheelchair, who sat watching him silently. Something in her regard troubled him and he looked back as he held the door open for his companion. He may have remembered then, meeting her calm, unflinching eyes, because he nodded affably, but she didn't return the nod, and his gaze shrank away, retreating from further contact as he looked out over the street and the few irregular clouds marching above the rooftops, perplexed, as if he'd lost something there. Then he turned and went inside. Unchallenged now, her eyes moved on—beyond the door, Buster Foreman, the figures on the steps, and the busy street, moved out beyond the sun-splashed buildings and the surrounding streets and river, the sloping hills and the towns and cities beyond, as if in sovereign possession of them all, no longer conscious of her small black hands, the handkerchief she clutched, the awkward wheelchair that had become a cruel appendage to her tired body, the youth and middle age that had vanished, the children that had never come.

But the moment passed and she felt the pain return. Her head inclined forward and her hand moved to her heart. Powerless to do otherwise, she had lived so long with her faith that her body seemed a prison to her.

"Are you sure you're all right?" Buster asked.

She nodded, wiping her eyes. "I was thinking of my daddy," she whispered, turning her head away from two security guards on the steps. Frightened and alone, she had fled backward for an instant, yielding the present to the past, like Ed Donlon under the clock at the Biltmore, young Lieutenant Gawpin crossing the Remagen bridge in his new Pershing, or even Bob Combs and Shy Wooster, bringing their pastoral boyhood in South Carolina to a waiting nation. "I was thinking how he used to take me an' Mama fishing with my cousins down on the Savannah River," she said, watching the irregular clouds march over the rooftops.

The bus arrived. The visiting delegation from Mount Zion was dignified and elderly, all dressed in Sunday finery, the women wearing corsages. Two of the men wore American Legion hats.

"Looks like they're coming to a funeral, don't it?" Birdie said as they mounted the steps. "Mercy, lookit that."

They were met at the door by one of Bob Combs's staff aides and led down the long intimidating corridor to a formal reception room where Bob Combs was waiting, standing just inside the door. Shyrock Wooster was at his side, plucking at his French cuffs, elbows held out like a tin soldier's as he introduced each of the guests to the senator, so expertly reading out their names from the forgotten nameplates on their coats that it seemed to the embarrassed visitors he'd known them all his life.

Birdie Jackson was the last to enter, her wheelchair still pushed by Buster Foreman. A photographer was taking pictures as the guests passed through the receiving line, and Buster's concentration was momentarily shattered by the glare of a flashbulb as he eased Birdie Jackson across the threshold.

"Well, I declare," he heard Shy Wooster say. "Lookit who it is, come all the way from Frogtown. I expect you don't remember me, do you, Miz Birdie?"

"'Deed I do," he heard her say, surprised at the strength that had seeped back into her voice, which rang as clear as a bell. But even that didn't prepare him for the transformation brought by the flesh-and-blood presence of Bob Combs and Shy Wooster after all those years.

"Well, what do you think of that, Senator? I didn't think you'd remember, Miz Birdie, I sure didn't."

"How'm I ever gonna forget? It was you an' Bob Combs burned down my house. If I'd been home that Sunday evenin', you an' them yellow shoes'd never got past my screen door."

There was a moment of utter silence as her accusing voice traveled the length of the room.

"*A-men,*" a soft voice called out far to the rear.

Buster Foreman would remember Bob Combs's shocked pink face, searching the dark countenances gathered behind him, Shy Wooster's efforts to move the South Carolina journalists and the photographer back from the wheelchair, and then the flare of another flashbulb that sent magnesium ghosts dancing through his head.

"Just home folks here today, boys," Wooster drawled. "You press stringers come to the wrong place. A little misunderstanding, that's all. Give the little old lady a little breathing room—"

"Misunderstandin'? What you talkin 'bout?"

"When'd it happen, Miz Jackson?"

"Ain't no misunderstandin' about it. It was a blowtorch offa Mr. Bob Combs's garage bench that fired up my kitchen wall that Sunday night, an' it was Mr. Shyrock Wooster a-holdin' it, same as he was holdin' that bag of skunk medicine when it blowed up in Mr. Tyrone Collier's Cadillac automobile."

"*Praise the Lord.*"

"When was this, Miz Jackson?"

"Y'all move on out now, just home folks here today, no press allowed—"

"When was your house burned down?"

Buster Foreman still had a grip on Birdie Jackson's wheelchair, standing just inside the door, and it was Buster who decided that the time had come for Birdie to make her departure.

"There was a lotta folks knew about it. Cora Pepper was one. Smooter Davis another. It just may be that we'd ask the federal judge down there in the U.S. courthouse to prove it."

"Is that why you're in Washington, Miz Jackson?"

"Time to go," Buster whispered over her shoulder, and with that, he moved the wheelchair back out the door and down the long corridor, the two South Carolina newspaper stringers still in pursuit.

"Mercy, I didn't mean to say all that," Birdie said from the back seat as Mrs. Foreman drove away. "I just don't know what took holt of me."

"I think I do," Buster said.

"How long did Mr. Wilson say it'd take to get him a case together?"

"Three or four months?"

She gave a deep sigh and sat back again. "You tell him I'll just have to go ahead an' do it, then. I wouldn't want all those folks back there thinking I was saying what I didn't believe." She looked out the window. "I sure do hope I git my strength back."

4.

Arriving those Saturday mornings at the remote Virginia farmhouse, the station wagon loaded with tools, bags of mortar, and groceries for another weekend of brush clearing and renovation, Betsy and Haven Wilson were greeted sometimes by deer browsing in the front meadow, by an occasional chimney swift or titmouse trapped in the downstairs rooms, by signs that raccoons or possums had come to scavenge. The foxes had been there too, resentfully prowling the evidence of their husbandry from the previous weekend. Their spoor wasn't indiscriminate, like that of the chipmunks or the field mice or the blacksnakes that lived in the old stone foundation or the nearby maple trees, but was deposited accusingly on the ashes of the previous Saturday and Sunday campfire, on a heap of plaster rubble torn from the kitchen walls, or brush cleared from the rear slope.

As they lay exhausted and stiff on their mattress in one of the empty upstairs bedrooms, they heard the raucous high-pitched barks from deep in the rear woods, but misinterpreted them. Betsy thought they were screech owls. But one moonlit night in February they were awakened after midnight by the familiar cry just outside the window, and through the pane discovered the fox standing in the moonlight near the dying embers of the fire they'd built that evening, as visible in the frosty light as the deer that morning in the front meadow.

Betsy had hired an architect and they worked from his plans. A local brick mason relined the old chimneys, a rural plasterer restored the deteriorating walls. Restoration was Betsy's object, not rebuilding. She stripped the hide of old paint from the pine woodwork by hand. When friends from McLean dropped by one Sunday afternoon and suggested the addition of a rear redwood deck, she looked at Haven in silent astonishment, as if her intentions were so clear by now that only the willfully blind could misunderstand. She resisted weekend visitors because they intruded upon their privacy and complicated their work schedule, as they also disturbed her concentration. She dressed as she pleased when the two of them were alone—tennis shoes, loose shirts, paint-splattered jeans or denim skirts—bathed in a washtub in the kitchen at night, only the moon watching, and then would race upstairs, flushed and still damp, her flesh tingling, to take refuge under the covers with him in the cold room. In the morning he would go downstairs while she waited for him to bring her clothes. The energies each found in the other during those solitary weekends seemed to astonish both of them.

"I was embarrassed, standing in front of my class this morning," she told him one Monday evening during dinner, after a Friday and Saturday night at the farm. "I think I was blushing."

He'd known what she meant; it was no less mysterious to him. He'd resisted casual or curious visitors for the same reasons.

The two bathrooms had been completed and the house was more habitable the bright Sunday afternoon Ed Donlon visited them after his lunch with Angus McVey. He was alone in his BMW. In tweed jacket and crushed Irish hat, he seemed proud of his sobriety. He gave the house his approval. Betsy's dishevelment seemed to intrigue him—her dark hair tied up in a bandanna, the loose, paint-speckled T-shirt, and the ripped tennis shoes. He announced he'd taken up bird-watching. He rose quite early these mornings, but bird-watching was more than just an urban indulgence while waiting for the coffee to boil; Jane needed her rest, you see. He was back to a two-woman household again. Grace Ramsey had departed once more. The Aegean, he thought, but couldn't be sure. Jane's studio was now on the third floor and her statuary in the back garden. He chased starlings, nesting chickadees, titmice, juncos, even a grosbeak, from the crypts and hollows of her mounted pieces. On Saturday mornings, he occasionally took his binoculars along the C&O canal.

He talked as he followed them about the rear meadow, where they were staking out a vegetable garden, avoiding the patches of mud, the sere stalks of last autumn's burrs, and the string lines. Like the gold-and-purple finches in the nearby woods, drab in their winter colors, some brightness, too, had fled from Ed Donlon's eyes. He left promptly at four. Dinner on the dot these days, artists need discipline, a continuing TV series on Sunday night public television he'd grown fond of—all these explanations offered with the authority of an asylum parolee who assures others he rules the ward with an iron hand.

In April, Ida and Nick Straus joined them for their first weekend visit. Betsy was worried that the Strauses would either be inconvenienced by the disarray or feel like intruders during a long working weekend. She'd planned to put her first plants in. The weather conspired against her. The day was cloudy and dark, rain intermittent, the wind cold. The spring sunshine that had been promised went elsewhere, flooding the offshore

Atlantic, where acres of vacation light poured down on blue combers, mackerel, and yellowfin, while the weekend homesteaders of the Shenandoah shivered under gray scud and a blustery wind. Ida brought a few plants for the garden, potted at home in McLean, but the weather kept them indoors. Returned the night before from a two-day national security seminar at Cambridge, Nick Straus seemed discouraged. Confusion everywhere, he told them—confusion on the right, confusion on the left. The final morning of the conference, one group had circulated fliers inviting the participants to a Saturday antinuclear demonstration at New London, Connecticut, where a newly outfitted nuclear sub was to sail, bound for an Arctic patrol. It carried World War II's firepower in its hull, the flier declared, but the crew was born circa 1950 and didn't recall those details, which had been programmed instead in its computerized fire-control systems. Few of the officers had ever seen the aurora borealis, either, but a Navy artist's facsimile was painted on the ward room door. The final afternoon of the conference had deteriorated into a shouting match between the extreme right and the extreme left.

The shuttle from Boston to New York, New York to Washington, had been late, La Guardia and National airports both shrouded by rain. His seat companion out of New York, a strange-looking U.N. official, had refused to give up his queer, bulky briefcase to the hostess for storage in the overhead compartment.

"Nick," Ida protested.

He smiled, looking to Betsy for support. She didn't like flying any more than he did. "You have to be careful who your seat companions are on the planet these days," he said.

He relaxed as the afternoon passed. They inspected the garden and the rear meadow during a break in the drizzle, frightening two ducks from the pond. Under the raw, cold sky, surrounded by wet meadows and dripping woods, the old house seemed even more remote. Nick prowled the rooms with Betsy, trying to decipher its history. At dinner, he teased her about her politics. He told her he'd recently discovered a former X-rated movie house near Dupont Circle where old newsreels were shown to middle-aged audiences like them, seeking escape from the present on rainy afternoons. *Pathé News* and *March of Time* film clips take them backward to the childhood verities of black and white, where their dreams began. Today might be a sleepy Sunday afternoon in December 1941, Pearl Harbor a tranquil lagoon where the China Clipper lands en route to Shanghai, carrying Humphrey Bogart and Peter Lorre in wrinkled tropical suits. Tomorrow, Washington contracts as the B&O evacuates Coxey's Army of civil servants to the hinterlands to rusticate in rural cabins. The banks reopen. Millions of small depositors return with their savings to reinvest entrepreneurial initiative. Roosevelt abdicates and the face of our grand-father, who owned the corner pharmacy with its white marble soda fountain and its five-cent ice cream, withdraws in horse-drawn carriage down Pennsylvania Avenue to the White House.

"Sound familiar?" he asked, smiling again.

"Almost," she said.

They talked until midnight and slept late the following morning. The peas didn't get planted, the cabbage plants weren't put out. After lunch they walked in the woods, searching for the first dogwood blossoms. Re-turning slowly through the back pasture near the creek, they found a small orange intruder, brought down by random winds and deflected cold fronts, caught in the lower branches of a young persimmon tree. Haven Wilson thought it was a hunter's cap, Nick Straus a meteorological device. It was neither. It was a schoolboy's balloon, trailing a length of cotton cord to which was attached a small crude card, sealed in plastic. They read it together, standing on the stone outcropping. The fifth-grade printing on the card read:

> My name is Mark Parsons. I am doing a science experiment.
> Please send me the following information:
> 1. Where did you find the balloon?
> 2. When did you find the balloon?
> 3. Who are you?
>
> *Fifth Grade, Taylor Elementary School   Roaring Springs, Pa.*

In certain parts of America, fifth-grade science was another kind of innocence, Betsy reminded them. Nick, accustomed to the deciphering of other trajectories these days, was still looking at the card, moved. So was Ida.

"We'll have to answer it," Nick insisted, lifting his eyes.

"Please do," Betsy said, as if not surprised it had been there at all.

"If I didn't know you better, I'd say that came out of your own seventh-grade science class," Haven said after the Strauses had driven away, the balloon on Ida's lap.

She laughed and they walked back toward the house. The light was fading, but she didn't want to leave, not yet. They still had a few minutes left to them, time enough to count the ducks coming in to the rear pond.

ABOUT THE AUTHOR

W. T. TYLER, whose real name is S. J. Hamrick, served for more than twenty years in the U.S. Foreign Service in many overseas posts, including Europe, the Middle East, and Africa, and also on several assignments in Washington. He is the author of three previous highly acclaimed novels—*The Man Who Lost the War, The Ants of God,* and *Rogue's March*—and lives and writes in Virginia.